AND BABY MAKES THREE
is the incredibly popular miniseries by SHERRYL WOODS
that has won the hearts of readers everywhere.

It all began with the Adams family of Texas...
A Christmas Blessing, SE #1001 (Luke & Jessie's story)
Natural Born Daddy, SE #1007 (Jordan & Kelly's story)
The Cowboy and His Baby,
SE #1009 (Cody & Melissa's story)
The Rancher and His Unexpected Daughter,
SE #1016 (Harlan & Janet's story)

Then came
AND BABY MAKES THREE: THE NEXT GENERATION:
The Littlest Angel, SE #1142 (Angela & Clint's story)
Natural Born Trouble, SE #1156 (Dani & Duke's story)
Unexpected Mommy, SE #1171 (Jenny & Chance's story)
The Cowgirl & the Unexpected Wedding,
SE #1208 (Lizzy & Hank's story)
Natural Born Lawman, SE #1216 (Justin & Patsy's story)
The Cowboy and His Wayward Bride,
SE #1234 (Harlan Patrick & Laurie's story)
The Unclaimed Baby,
Single Title (Sharon Lynn & Cord's story)
Suddenly, Annie's Father, SE #1268 (Slade & Val's Story)

Now the family's grown to include
**AND BABY MAKES THREE:
THE DELACOURTS OF TEXAS:**
The Cowboy and the New Year's Baby,
SE #1291 (Trish & Hardy's story)
Dylan and the Baby Doctor,
SE #1309 (Dylan & Kelsey's story)
The Pint-Sized Secret, SE #1333 (Jeb & Brianna's story)
Marrying a Delacourt, SE #1352 (Michael & Grace's story)
The Delacourt Scandal, SE #1363 (Tyler & Maddie's story)

SHERRYL WOODS

AND BABY MAKES THREE:
SECOND TRIMESTER

Published by Silhouette Books
America's Publisher of Contemporary Romance

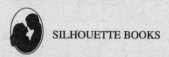 SILHOUETTE BOOKS

ISBN 0-373-20183-4

by Request

AND BABY MAKES THREE: SECOND TRIMESTER

Copyright © 2001 by Harlequin Books S.A.

The publisher acknowledges the copyright holder of the individual works as follows:

THE RANCHER AND HIS UNEXPECTED DAUGHTER
Copyright © 1996 by Sherryl Woods

THE LITTLEST ANGEL
Copyright © 1997 by Sherryl Woods

NATURAL BORN TROUBLE
Copyright © 1998 by Sherryl Woods

Visit Silhouette at www.eHarlequin.com

Printed in U.S.A.

CONTENTS

Dear Friends,

From the moment I introduced Harlan Adams in *A Christmas Blessing,* I fell in love with this wise, indomitable, funny, meddling father. Unfortunately, he had a wife, the mother of all those wonderful Adams men. Because fiction is the one place where you can kill inconvenient people without getting arrested for it, Harlan's wife died tragically in a riding accident. And two books later, Harlan was introduced to strong-willed attorney Janet Runningbear, thanks to *her* incorrigible fourteen-year-old daughter. *The Rancher and His Unexpected Daughter* got off to a rip-roaring start, and one of the most beloved characters in this series got to have his own love story.

Once Harlan became a force to be reckoned with, there was no way I could let this series go, and so in *The Littlest Angel* I moved on to the next generation of Adamses, beginning with Angela. And in *Natural Born Trouble* you'll get a chance to spend time with Dani, the animal-loving stepdaughter who proved to Jordan Adams that he was fatherhood material.

I hope you enjoy getting to know more of the Adams clan. After so many books, they feel like family—a big, rambunctious crowd that it's always fun to come home to.

All the best,

Sheryl Woods

THE RANCHER AND
HIS UNEXPECTED DAUGHTER

AND BABY
MAKES THREE

Chapter One

Harlan Adams walked out of Rosa's Mexican Café after eating his fill of her spicy brand of Tex-Mex food just in time to see his pickup barrel down the center of Main Street at fifty miles an hour. In the sleepy Texas town of Los Piños, both the theft and the speed were uncommon occurrences.

"Ain't that your truck?" Mule Masters asked, staring after the vehicle that was zigzagging all over the road, endangering parked cars and pedestrians alike.

"Sure as hell is," Harlan said, indignation making his insides churn worse than Rosa's hot sauce.

"That's what you get for leaving your keys in plain sight. I've been telling you for months now that times have changed. The world's full of thieves and murderers," Mule said ominously. "They were bound to get to Los Piños sooner or later."

Given the time it was wasting, Harlan found the familiar lecture extremely irritating. "Where's your car?" he snapped.

Mule blinked at the sharp tone. "Across the street, right where it always is."

Harlan was already striding across the two-lane road before the words were completely out of his friend's mouth. "Come on, old man."

Mule appeared vaguely startled by the command. "Come on where?"

"To catch the damned thing, that's where," he replied with a certain amount of eagerness. The thought of a good ruckus held an amazing appeal.

"Sheriff's close by," Mule objected without picking up speed.

Harlan lost patience with the procrastinating that had earned Mule his nickname. "Just give me your keys," he instructed. He didn't take any chances on Mule's compliance. He reached out and snatched them from his friend's hand.

Before the old man could even start grumbling, Harlan was across the street and starting the engine of a battered old sedan. That car had seen a hundred thousand hard miles or more back and forth across the state of Texas, thanks to Mule's knack for tinkering with an engine.

Harlan pulled out onto Main Street, gunned the engine a couple of times, then shifted gears with pure pleasure. The smooth glide from standing stock-still to sixty in the blink of an eye was enough to make a man weep.

In less than a minute his truck was in sight again

on the outskirts of town and he was gaining on it. He was tempted to whoop with joy at the sheer exhilaration of the impromptu race, but he had to keep every bit of his energy focused on his pursuit of that runaway truck.

The chase lasted just long enough to stir his ire, but not nearly long enough to be downright interesting. Not a mile out of town, where the two-lane road curved like a well-rounded lady's hips, he caught up with the truck just in time to see it miss the turn and swerve straight toward a big, old, cottonwood tree. His heart climbed straight into his throat and stayed there as he watched the drama unfold.

He veered from the highway onto the shoulder and slammed on his own brakes just as the truck collided with the tree. It hit with a resounding *thwack* that crumpled the front fender on the passenger side, sent his blood pressure soaring, and elicited a string of profanity from inside the truck that blistered his ears.

"What the devil?" he muttered as he scrambled from the borrowed car and ran toward the truck. Obviously the thief couldn't be badly injured if he had that much energy left for cursing.

To his astonishment, when he flung open the driver's door, a slender young girl practically tumbled out into his arms. He righted her, keeping a firm clamp on her wrist in case the little thief decided to flee.

She couldn't be a day over thirteen, he decided, gazing into scared brown eyes. Admittedly, though, she had a vocabulary that a much older dock worker would envy. She also had a belligerent tilt to her cute little chin and a sullen expression that dared him to yell at her.

Taken aback by her apparent age, Harlan bit back the shouted lecture he'd planned and settled for a less confrontative approach. He could hardly wait to hear why this child had stolen his pickup.

"You okay?" he inquired quietly. Other than a bump on her forehead, he couldn't see any other signs of injury.

She wriggled in a game effort to free herself from his grip. He grinned at the wasted attempt. He'd wrestled cows ten times her weight or more. This little slip of a thing didn't stand a chance of getting away until he was good and ready to let her go. He didn't plan on that happening anytime soon. Not until he had the answers he wanted, anyway.

"Must be just fine, if you can struggle like that," he concluded out loud. "Any particular reason you decided to steal my truck?"

"I was tired of walking," she shot back.

"Did you ever consider a bike?"

"Not fast enough," she muttered, her gaze defiantly clashing with his.

"You had someplace to get to in a hurry?"

She shrugged.

Harlan had to fight to hide a grin. He'd always been a big admirer of audacity, though he preferred it to be a little better directed. "What's your name?"

She frowned and for the first time began to look faintly uneasy. "Who wants to know?"

"I'm Harlan Adams. I own White Pines. That's a ranch just outside of town." If she was local, that would be plenty of explanation to intimidate her. If she wasn't, he could elaborate until he had her quivering with fear in her dusty sneakers for pulling a stunt like the one that had ended with his pickup wrapped around a tree.

"Big deal," she retorted, then let loose a string of expletives.

She either wasn't local or it was going to take a lot more to impress her with the stupidity of what she'd done. "You have a foul mouth, you know that?" he observed.

"So?"

"I'll just bet you don't talk that way around your mama."

The mention of her mother stirred an expression of pure alarm on her delicate features. Harlan sensed that he'd hit the nail on the head. This ragamuffin kid with the sleek black hair cut as short as a boy's, with the high cheekbones and tanned complexion, might not be afraid of him, but she was scared to death of her mother. He considered it a hopeful sign. He was very big on respect for parental authority, not that he'd noticed his grown-up sons paying the concept much mind lately.

"You're not going to tell her, are you?" she asked, clearly trying to keep the worry out of her voice and failing miserably. For the first time since she'd climbed out of his truck, she sounded her age.

"Now why would I want to keep quiet about the fact that you stole my truck and slammed it into a tree?"

A resurgence of belligerence glinted in her eyes.

"Because she'll sue you for pain and suffering. I'm almost positive I've got a whiplash injury," she said, rubbing at her neck convincingly. "Probably back problems that'll last the rest of my life, too."

Harlan chuckled. "Imagine that. All those problems and you expect to blame them on the man whose truck you stole and smashed up. You and your mother have a little scam going? You wreck cars and she sues for damages?"

At the criticism of her mother's ethics, her defiance wavered just a little. "My mom's a lawyer," she admitted eventually. "She sues lots of people." Her eyes glittered with triumphant sparks as she added, "She wins, too."

An image suddenly came to him, an image of the new lawyer he'd read about just last week in the local paper. The article had been accompanied by a picture of an incredibly lovely woman, her long black hair flowing down her back, her features and her name strongly suggesting her Comanche heritage. Janet Something-or-other. Runningbear, maybe. Yep, that was it. Janet Runningbear.

He surveyed the girl standing in front of him and thought he detected a resemblance. There was no mistaking the Native American genes in her proud bearing, her features or her coloring, though he had a hunch they'd been mellowed by a couple of generations of interracial marriage.

"Your mom's the new lawyer in town, then," he said. "Janet Runningbear."

She seemed startled that he'd guessed, but she hid

it quickly behind another of those belligerent looks she'd obviously worked hard to perfect. ''So?''

''So, I think you and I need to go have a little chat with your mama,'' he said, putting a hand on the middle of her back and giving her a gentle but unrelenting little push in the direction of Mule's car. Her chin rose another notch, but her shoulders slumped and she didn't resist. In fact, there was an air of weary resignation about her that tugged at his heart.

As he drove back into town he couldn't help wondering just how much trouble Janet Runningbear's daughter managed to get herself into on a regular basis and why she felt the need to do it. After raising four sons of his own, he knew a whole lot about teenage rebellion and the testing of parental authority. He'd always thought—mistakenly apparently—that girls might have been easier. Not that he would have traded a single one of his boys to find out firsthand. He'd planned on keeping an eye on his female grandbabies to test his theory.

He glanced over at the slight figure next to him and caught the downward turn of her mouth and the protective clasping of her arms across her chest. Stubbornness radiated from every pore. The prospect of meeting the woman who had raised such a little hel lion intrigued him.

It was the first time since a riding accident had taken his beloved Mary away from him the year before that he'd found much of anything fascinating. He realized as the blood zinged through his veins for the first time in months just how boring and predictable he'd allowed his life to become.

He'd left the running of the ranch mostly in Cody's hands, just as his youngest son had been itching for him to do for some time. Harlan spent his days riding over his land or stopping off in town to have lunch and play a few hands of poker with Mule or some other friend. His evenings dragged out endlessly unless one or the other of his sons stopped by for a visit and brought his grandbabies along.

For a rancher who'd crammed each day to its limits all his life, he'd been telling himself that the tedium was a welcome relief. He'd been convinced of it, too, until the instant when he'd seen his truck barreling down Main Street.

Something about the quick, hot surge of blood in his veins told him those soothing, dull days were over. Glancing down at the ruffian by his side, he could already anticipate the upcoming encounter with any woman bold and brash enough to keep her in hand. He suddenly sensed that he was just about to start living again.

Janet Runningbear gazed out of the window of her small law office on Main Street and saw her daughter being ushered down the sidewalk by a man she recognized at once as Harlan Adams, owner of White Pines and one of the most successful ranchers for several hundred miles in any direction. Judging from the stern expression on his face and Jenny's dragging footsteps, her daughter had once more gotten herself into a mess of trouble.

She studied the man approaching with a mixture of trepidation, anger, and an odd, tingly hint of anticipation. Ever since her move to Los Piños, the closest town to where her ancestors had once lived, she'd been hearing about Harlan Adams, the man whose own ancestors had been at least in part responsible for pushing the Comanches out of Texas and onto an Oklahoma reservation.

The claiming of Comanche lands might have taken place a hundred years or more ago, but Janet clung to the resentment that had been passed down to her by her great-grandfather. Lone Wolf had lived to be ninety-seven and his father had been forced from the nomadic life of a hunter to the confined space of a reservation.

Even though she knew it was ridiculous to blame Harlan Adams for deeds that had been committed long before his birth or her own, she was prepared to dislike him just on principle. What she hadn't been prepared for was the prompt and very feminine response to a man who practically oozed sex appeal from every masculine pore.

He was cowboy through and through, from the Stetson hat that rode atop his thick, sun-streaked hair to the tips of his dusty boots. His weathered face hinted at his age, which she knew to be somewhere in his fifties, but nothing about his easy stride or his broad shoulders added to that impression. He had the bearing of a much younger man.

In fact, Harlan Adams strolled down the sidewalk, her daughter in tow, with the confidence of a man who was comfortable with himself and with the power his wealth had earned him. To dampen any spark of fascination he might arouse, Janet quickly assured herself it was more than confidence she saw. It was arrogance, a trait she despised. Since there was no mistaking his destination, she braced herself for his arrival.

A few minutes later, with the pair of them seated across from her, she listened with a sense of growing horror as Harlan Adams described the theft of his truck and the subsequent accident, which had clearly done more damage to the truck than it had to Jenny. Her daughter didn't even seem flustered.

"He shouldn't have left the damned keys inside," Jenny muttered.

"Watch your tongue, young lady," Janet warned.

A heartfelt apology rose to Janet's lips but before she could begin to form the words, she caught a surprising glint of amusement in Harlan's startlingly blue eyes. She'd been anticipating the same mischievous dark brown eyes each of his sons reportedly had, according to the fond reminiscences of the local ladies. They must have inherited those from their mother, she decided. Harlan's were the bright blue of a summer sky just rinsed by rain.

"Jenny, perhaps you should wait in the other room, while Mr. Adams and I discuss this," she said, sensing that the twinkle in those eyes might mean an inclination toward leniency that wasn't altogether deserved.

The last of her daughter's defiance slid away. "Am I going to jail?" she asked in a voice that shook even though she was clearly trying desperately to sound brave.

"That remains to be seen," Janet told her without

so much as a hint that she thought jail was the last thing on this particular victim's mind.

"Are you going to be my lawyer?"

Janet hid her face so that Jenny wouldn't see her own smile. "If you need one," she promised solemnly, doubting that it was going to come to that.

Sure enough, the second Jenny was out of the room, Harlan Adams chuckled. "Damn, but she's a pistol. She's got the makings of one heck of a young woman."

"If she doesn't self-destruct first," Janet muttered wearily. "I'm not sure I understand why you find all of this so amusing."

He grinned at her and her heart did an unexpected little flip. There was something so unexpectedly boyish about that lazy, lopsided smile. At the same time, the experience and wisdom that shone in his eyes was comforting. Something told her at once that this was a man a woman could always count on for straight talk and moral support. A little of that misguided resentment she'd been stoking slipped away.

"Remind me to tell you about the time one of my boys rustled a bunch of my cattle to start his own herd," Harlan Adams said, still chuckling over the memory. "He was seven at the time. Try taking your daughter's mischief and multiply it four times over and you'll have some idea why I can't work up too much of a sweat over one stolen truck."

"She could have been killed," Janet said grimly, realizing as she spoke that she was shaking at the very thought of what could have happened to Jenny.

"But she wasn't," Harlan reminded her in a soothing tone that suggested he knew exactly the sort of belated reaction she was having.

"Then there's the matter of your truck. I'm just getting my practice off the ground here, but I can make arrangements to pay you back over time, if that's okay."

He waved off the offer. "Insurance will take care of it."

"But it's my responsibility," she insisted.

"The danged truck's not important," he countered emphatically. "The real question now is how to make sure that gal of yours doesn't go trying some fool thing like that again."

His unexpected kindness brought the salty sting of tears to her eyes. Janet rubbed at them impatiently. She never cried. Never. In fact, she considered it a point of honor that she was always strong and in control.

Suddenly, for some reason she couldn't fathom, she was not only crying, but actually considering spilling her guts to a total stranger. Harlan Adams was practically the first person in town to be civilized to her, much less kind. Truth be told, the move to Texas was not turning out anything at all the way she'd imagined it would.

"I'm sorry," she apologized. "I don't know what's wrong with me or with Jenny. I never cry. And she used to be such a good girl."

Harlan's expression remained solemn and thoughtful. "You know," he said, "I used to teach my sons that tears made a man seem weak. The past year or so, I've had a change of heart. I think it takes someone pretty strong to acknowledge when they're feeling vulnerable and then deal straight-out with the pain they're going through.''

Janet guessed right off that it was his wife's death that had brought him to a change of heart. The word on Mary Adams was mixed, according to the gossip that folks had been eager to share. Some thought she'd been an elegant, refined lady. Others thought she was a cold, uppity witch. One thing no one disputed, however, was that Harlan Adams had adored her and that she had doted on him.

Janet had wondered more than once what it would be like to love anyone with such passion. Her own marriage had been lukewarm at best and certainly not up to the kind of tests it had been put through. She'd been relieved to call it quits, eager to move far from New York and its memories to the land Lone Wolf had described with such bittersweet poignancy. She had legally taken the name he'd dubbed her with as soon as she'd settled in town. A new name, a fresh start for her and Jenny.

She glanced up and realized that Harlan's warm gaze was fixed on her. He was regarding her with more of that compassion that made her want to weep.

''Why don't you tell me what's been going on with that girl of yours?'' he offered. ''Maybe we can figure this thing out together.''

Surprised at the relief she felt at having someone with whom to share her concerns, Janet tried to describe what the past few weeks had been like. ''I thought coming here was going to make such a difference for Jenny,'' she said. ''Instead, she's behaving as if I've punished her by moving from New York to Texas.''

''Quite a change for a young girl,'' Harlan observed. ''She's at an age when leaving all her friends behind must seem like the end of the world. Hell, she's at an age when *everything* seems like the end of the world. Besides that, it's summertime. All the kids her age around here are caught up with their own vacation activities. Lots of 'em have to work their family's ranch. Must seem like she'll never have a friend of her own again.''

Janet didn't like having a total stranger tell her something she should have figured out for herself. She'd been so anxious to get to Texas after the divorce, so determined to get on with her life and to get Jenny settled in a safer environment than the city streets of Manhattan that she hadn't given much thought to how lonely the summer might be for her daughter. She'd been thinking of the move as an adventure and had assumed Jenny was doing the same.

Now it appeared that the kind of energy that might have resulted in little more than mischief back in New York was taking a dangerous turn. She cringed as she pictured that truck slamming into a tree with her daughter behind the wheel. If her ex-husband heard about that, he'd wash his hands of Jenny once and for all. Barry Randall had little enough room in his life for his daughter now. If she became a liability to his image, he'd forget she existed.

''I have an idea,'' the man seated across from her said. ''I don't intend to press charges for this, but we don't want her getting the idea that she can get away with stealing a car and taking it joyriding.''

Janet was so worried by the prospects for Jenny getting herself into serious trouble before school started in the fall that she was willing to listen to anything, even if it was being offered by the exact kind of man she'd learned to distrust—a rich and powerful white man. A Texan, to boot. A sworn enemy of her ancestors.

"What?" she asked warily.

"I'll give her a job out at White Pines. She can earn enough to pay off the cost of the truck's repairs. That'll keep her busy, teach her to take responsibility for her actions, and wear her out at the same time.''

"I said I'd pay,'' Janet reminded him.

"It's not the same. It was her mistake.''

Just one of many lately, Janet thought with a sigh. Perhaps if Jenny hadn't shoplifted a whole handful of cosmetics from the drugstore the week before, perhaps if she hadn't upended a table in Rosa's Café breaking every dish on it, Janet might have resisted a suggestion that would have kept her in contact with this man who made her pulse skip. The kindness in his voice, the humor in his eyes, were every bit as dangerous to her in her beleaguered state of mind as Jenny's exploits were to her future. At the rate she'd been going since they got to Texas, she'd either end up in jail or dead.

"Do I have any choice?" she asked, all but resigned to accepting the deal he was offering.

He shrugged. "Not really. I could sue you, I suppose, but that gal of yours says you're the best lawyer around. You might win, and then where would I be?''

Janet laughed at the outrageous comment. A man who could keep his sense of humor in a circumstance like this was rare. She just might be forced to reevaluate Harlan Adams. And he might be just the kind of good influence her daughter needed. There was no question Jenny needed a stern hand and perhaps a stronger father figure than her own daddy had ever provided.

''Are you really sure you want to deal with a rebellious teenage girl for the rest of the summer?'' she asked, but there was no denying the hopeful note in her voice as she envisioned an improvement in Jenny's reckless behavior.

''I'll take my chances,'' he said solemnly, his gaze fixed on her.

Janet trembled at the speculative gleam she saw in his eyes. She hadn't had this kind of immediate, purely sexual reaction to a man in a very long time. She'd actually convinced herself she was capable of controlling such things. Now not only was Jenny out of control, it appeared her hormones were, as well. It was a dismaying turn of events.

It also served as a warning that she'd better be on her guard around Harlan Adams. It wouldn't do to spend much time around him with her defenses down. He was the kind of man who'd claim what he wanted, just as his ancestors had. Whether it was land or a woman probably wouldn't matter much.

She adopted her most businesslike demeanor, the one she reserved for clients and the courtroom.

"What time do you want her at White Pines?" she inquired briskly, prepared to temporarily sacrifice her emotional peace of mind for her daughter's sake.

"Dawn will do," he said as he rose and headed for the door.

He must have heard her faint gasp of dismay because he turned back and winked. "I'll have the coffee ready when you get there."

Janet sighed as he walked away. *Dawn!* If he expected her to be coherent at that hour, he'd better have gallons of it and it had best be strong and black.

Chapter Two

"I've taken on another hand for the summer," Harlan mentioned to Cody when he stopped by just before dinner later that night.

His son sat up a little straighter in the leather chair in which he'd sprawled out of habit as soon as he'd walked through the door. Instantly Harlan could see Cody's jaw setting stubbornly as he prepared to argue against his father's unilateral decision. Harlan decided he'd best cut him off at the pass.

"Don't go getting your drawers in a knot," he advised him. "I'm not usurping your authority. This was just something that came up."

"Came up how?" Cody asked, suspicion written all over his face. "There's no budget for another hand. You told me that yourself when we talked about it just last week."

"It came up right after my truck was stolen and smashed up," Harlan explained. "Let's just say that no money will be changing hands. The thief will be working off the repair bill."

Cody's jaw dropped. "You hired the thief who stole your car? Haven't you ever heard of jail time? If any of us had stolen a car and gone joyriding, you'd have helped the sheriff turn the lock on the cell."

"It didn't seem like the thing to do with a thirteen-year-old girl," Harlan said mildly. "Seemed to me this was a better way to teach her a lesson."

Cody fell silent, clearly chewing over the concept of a teenage girl as his newest ranch hand. "What the hell am I supposed to have her doing?" he asked finally.

"You're not her boss," Harlan said, amused by the relief that instantly spread across Cody's face. "I am. I just wanted you to know she'd be around. Her name's Jenny Runningbear."

"Runningbear? Is her mother...?"

"The new lawyer in town," Harlan supplied, watching as curiosity rose in Cody's eyes.

"Did you meet her?" Cody asked.

"I did." He decided then and there that he'd better be stingy with information about that meeting. His son had the look of a man about to make a romantic mountain out of a platonic molehill.

"And?"

"And, what?"

"What did you think of her?"

"She seemed nice," Harlan offered blandly, even as he conjured up some fairly steamy images of the raven-haired beauty who'd struck him as a fascinating blend of strength and vulnerability. *Nice* was far too tame a description for that delicate, exotic face, those long, long legs, and eyes so dark a man could lose himself in them.

"Really?" Cody said, skepticism written all over his face. "Nice?"

Harlan didn't like the way Cody was studying him. "That's what I said, isn't it?" he replied irritably.

"Just seemed sort of namby-pamby to me," Cody retorted. "I might have described her as hot. I believe Jordan said something similar after he spotted her."

Harlan bit back a sharp rebuke. His gaze narrowed. "Exactly how well do you and your brother know the woman?"

"Not well enough to say more than hello when we pass on the street. Never even been introduced. Of course, if we both weren't happily married, we'd probably be brawling over first dibs on meeting her."

"See that you remember that you are married," he advised his son.

"Interesting," Cody observed, his eyes suddenly sparkling with pure mischief.

"What's interesting?"

"The way you're getting all protective about the mother of a teenage car thief. What time are they getting here in the morning?"

"That's nothing you need to concern yourself about." He stood, glanced at his watch pointedly as he anticipated his housekeeper's imminent announcement that dinner was on the table. "I'd invite you to dinner, but I told Maritza I'd be eating alone. It's time you got home to your wife and those grandbabies of mine anyway."

Cody didn't budge. "They're eating in town with her folks tonight, so I'm all yours. I told Maritza I'd be staying. I thought maybe we could wrangle a little over buying that acreage out to the east, but I'd rather talk more about your impressions of Janet Runningbear."

"Forget it," Harlan warned. "Besides, since when does my housekeeper take orders from you?"

Cody grinned. "Ever since I was old enough to talk. I inherited your charm. It pays off in the most amazing ways. Maritza even fixed all my favorites. She said she'd missed me something fierce. I'm the one with the cast-iron stomach."

Harlan sighed as he thought of the hot peppers that comment implied. Between lunch at Rosa's and that darned accident, his own stomach could have used a bowl of nice bland oatmeal. It appeared he was out of luck.

"Well, come on, then. The sooner we eat, the sooner I can get you out of here and get some peace and quiet."

"You really interested in peace and quiet, Daddy? Or do you just want to make sure you get some beauty sleep before you see Janet Runningbear in the morning?" Cody taunted.

"Don't go getting too big for your britches, son," Harlan warned. "You're not so old that I can't send you packing without your supper. Push me hard enough, I might just send you packing, period."

"But you won't," Cody retorted confidently.

"Oh? Why is that?"

"Because so far only you and I know about this new fascination of yours. Send me home and I'll have the whole, long evening to fill up. I might decide to use that time by calling Luke and Jordan. They like to be up-to-date on everything that goes on around White Pines. They'll be flat-out delighted to discover that you're no longer bored."

Harlan could just imagine the hornet's nest that would stir up. He'd have all three sons hovering over him, making rude remarks, discussing his relationship with a woman he'd barely spent a half hour with up to now. They'd consider taunting him their duty, just as he'd considered it his to meddle in their lives.

"That's blackmail," he accused.

Cody's grin was unrepentant. "Sure is. It's going to make life around here downright interesting, isn't it?"

Harlan sighed. It was indeed.

"I don't see why I have to work for him," Jenny declared for the hundredth time since learning of the agreement her mother had made with Harlan Adams. "Aren't there child labor laws or something?"

"There are also laws against car theft," Janet stated flatly. "You didn't seem overly concerned about those."

A yawn took a little of the edge off of her words. No one in his right mind actually got up at daybreak. She was certain of it. Even though she'd forced herself to get to bed two hours earlier than usual the night before, she'd wanted to hurl the alarm clock out the window when it had gone off forty-five minutes ago.

She'd dressed in a sleepy fog. With any luck, everything at least matched. As for her driving, she would probably be considered a menace if anyone checked on how many of her brain cells were actually functioning. The lure of a huge pot of caffeinated coffee was all that had gotten her out the door.

At the moment she could cheerfully have murdered Jenny for getting them into this predicament. The very thought of doing this day after day all summer long had her gnashing her teeth. She was in no mood for any more of her daughter's backtalk.

"Why couldn't you just pay him?" Jenny muttered. "There's money in my account from Dad."

"It's for college," Janet reminded her. "Besides, I offered to pay Mr. Adams. He refused."

"Jeez, did he see you coming! I'm free labor, Mom. He'll probably have me scrubbing down the barn floor or something. I'll probably end up with arthritis from kneeling in all that cold, filthy water."

"Serves you right," Janet said.

At the lack of either sympathy or any hint of a reprieve, Jenny retreated into sullen silence. That gave Janet time to work on her own composure.

To her astonishment, Harlan Adams had slipped into her dreams last night. She'd awakened feeling restless and edgy and unfulfilled in a way that didn't bear too close a scrutiny. It was a state she figured she'd better get over before her arrival at White Pines. He had struck her as the kind of man who would seize on any hint of weakness and capitalize on it.

The sun was just peeking over the horizon in a blaze of brilliant orange when she arrived at the gate to the ranch. She turned onto the property with something akin to awe spreading through her as she studied the raw beauty of the land around her. This was the land Lone Wolf had described, lush and barren in turns, stretched out as far as the eye could see, uninterrupted by the kind of development she'd come to take for granted in New York.

"This is it?" Jenny asked, a heavy measure of disdain in her voice. "There's nothing here."

Janet hid a smile. No Bloomingdale's. No high rises. No restaurants or music stores. It was little wonder her daughter sounded so appalled.

She, to the contrary, was filled at last with that incredible sense of coming home that she'd wanted so badly to feel when she'd moved to Los Piños. She considered for a moment whether Lone Wolf's father might have hunted on this very land. It pleased her somehow to think that he might have.

"That's why they call it the wide open spaces," she told her daughter. "Remember all the stories I told you about Lone Wolf?"

"Yeah, but I don't get it," Jenny declared flatly. "Maybe I could just get a job in the drugstore or something and pay Mr. Adams back that way."

"No," Janet said softly, listening to the early morning sounds of birds singing, insects humming and somewhere in the distance a tractor rumbling. Did he grow his own grain? Or maybe have a nice vegetable garden? On some level, she thought she'd been waiting all her life for a moment just like this.

"I think this will be perfect for you," she added as hope flowered inside her for the first time in years.

Jenny rolled her eyes. "If he makes me go near a horse or a cow, I'm out of here," she warned.

Janet grinned. "This is a cattle ranch. I think you can pretty much count on horses and cows."

"Mo-om!" she wailed. Her gaze narrowed. "I'll run away. I'll steal a car and drive all the way home to New York."

"And then what?" Janet inquired mildly. Jenny knew as well as she did that there was no room for her in her father's life. Even though at the moment his selfishness suited her purposes, she hated Barry Randall for making his disinterest so abundantly clear to his daughter.

Jenny turned a tearful gaze on her that almost broke Janet's heart.

"I don't have a choice, do I?" she asked.

"Afraid not, love. Besides, I think you'll enjoy this once you've gotten used to it. Think of all the stories you'll have to write to your friends back in New York. How many of them have ever seen a genuine cowboy, much less worked on a ranch?"

"How many of them even wanted to?" Jenny shot back.

"You remember what I always told my clients when they landed in jail?" Janet asked.

Jenny shot her a tolerant look and sighed heavily. "I remember. It's up to me whether I make my time here hard or easy."

"Exactly."

A sudden gleam lit her eyes. "I suppose it's also

up to me whether it's hard or easy for Mr. Adams, too, huh?''

Janet didn't much like the sound of that. "Jenny," she warned. "If you don't behave, you'll be in debt to this man until you're old enough for college.''

"I'll be good, Mom. Cross my heart.''

Janet nodded, accepting the promise, but the glint in her daughter's eyes when she made that solemn vow was worrisome. The words had come a little too quickly, a little too easily. Worse, she recognized that glint all too well. It made her wonder if Harlan Adams just might have bitten off more than he could handle.

One look at him a few minutes later and her doubts vanished. This was a man competent to deal with anything at all. When he rounded the corner of the house in his snug, worn jeans, his blue chambray shirt, his dusty boots and that Stetson hat, he almost stole her breath away.

If she was ever of a mind to let another man into her life, she wanted one who exuded exactly this combination of strength, sex appeal and humor. His eyes were practically dancing with laughter as he approached. And the appreciative head-to-toe look he gave her could have melted steel. Her knees didn't stand a chance. They turned weak as a new colt's.

"Too early for you?" he inquired, his gaze drifting over her once more in the kind of lazy inspection that left goose bumps in its wake.

"No, indeed," she denied brightly. "Why would you think that?''

"No special reason. It's just that you struck me as

a woman who'd never leave the house with quite so many buttons undone.''

A horrified glance at her blouse confirmed the teasing comment. She'd missed more buttons than she'd secured, which meant there was an inordinate amount of cleavage revealed. She vowed to strangle her daughter at the very first opportunity for not warning her. At least the damned blouse did match her slacks, she thought as she fumbled with the buttons with fingers that shook.

"Jeez, Mom," Jenny protested. "Let me."

Janet thought she heard Harlan mutter something that sounded suspiciously like, "Or me," but she couldn't be absolutely sure. When she looked in his direction, his gaze was fixed innocently enough on the sky.

"Come on inside," he invited a moment later. "I promised you coffee. I think Maritza has breakfast ready by now, too."

"Who's Maritza?" Jenny asked.

Her tone suggested a level of distrust that had Janet shooting a warning look in her direction. Harlan, however, appeared oblivious to Jenny's suspicions.

"My housekeeper," he explained. "She's been with the family for years. If you're interested in learning a little Tex-Mex cooking while you're here, she'll be glad to teach you. She's related to Rosa, who owns the Mexican Café in town."

"I hate Tex-Mex," Jenny declared.

"You do not," Janet said, giving Harlan an apologetic smile. "She's a little contrary at this hour."

"Seemed to be that way at midday, too," he stated

pointedly. "Not to worry. It would be an understatement to say that I've had a lot of experience with contrariness."

He led the way through the magnificent foyer and into a formal dining room that was practically the size of Janet's entire house. Her eyes widened. "Good heavens, do you actually eat in here by yourself?"

He seemed startled by the question. "Of course. Why?"

"It's just that it's so…" She fumbled for the right word.

"Big," Jenny contributed.

"Lonely," Janet said, then regretted it at once. The man didn't need to be reminded that he was a widower and that his sons were no longer living under his roof. He was probably aware of those sad facts every single day of his life.

He didn't seem to take offense, however. He just shrugged. "I'm used to it."

He gestured toward a buffet laden with more cereals, jams, muffins, toast and fruits than Janet had ever seen outside a grocery store.

"Help yourself," he said. "If you'd rather have eggs and bacon, Maritza will fix them for you. She doesn't allow me near the stuff."

"How come?" Jenny asked.

"Cholesterol, fat." He grimaced. "They've taken all the fun out of eating. Next thing you know they'll be feeding us a bunch of pills three times a day and we won't be needing food at all."

"There are egg substitutes," Janet commented.

"Yellow mush," he contradicted.

"And turkey bacon."

He shuddered. "Not a chance."

Janet chuckled at his reaction. "I'm not going to convince you, am I?"

"Depends on how good you are at sweet talk, darlin'."

Her startled gaze flew to his. Those blue eyes were innocent as a baby's. Even so, she knew in her gut, where butterflies were ricocheting wildly, that he had just tossed down a gauntlet of sorts. He was daring her to turn this so-called arrangement they had made for Jenny's punishment into something personal. The temperature in the room rose significantly.

Nothing would happen between them. Janet was adamant about that. She was in Texas to tap into her Native American roots, not to get involved with another white man. She'd tried that once and it had failed, just as her mother's marriage to a white man had ended in disaster exactly as Lone Wolf had apparently predicted when her mother had fled the reservation.

She drew herself up and leveled a look at him that she normally reserved for difficult witnesses in court. "That, *darlin'*, is something you're not likely to find out," she retorted.

Jenny's eyes widened as she listened to the exchange. Janet was very aware of the precise instant when a speculative gleam lit her daughter's intelligent brown eyes. Dear heaven, that was the last thing she needed. Jenny was like a puppy with a sock when she got a notion into her head. If she sensed there were sparks between her mother and Harlan Adams, she'd do everything in her power to see that they flared into a blaze. She'd do it not because she particularly wanted someone to replace her father, but just to see if she could pull it off.

To put a prompt end to any such speculation, Janet forced a perfectly blank expression onto her face as she turned her attention to the man seated opposite her.

"Exactly what will Jenny be doing today?"

"I thought maybe I'd teach her to ride," Harlan replied just as blandly, apparently willing to let that sudden flare of heat between them die down for the moment. "Unless she already knows how."

"Oh, no," Jenny protested.

Janet jumped in to prevent the tantrum she suspected was only seconds away. "She doesn't, but riding doesn't sound much like punishment or work to me."

"She has to be able to get around, if she's going to be much use on a ranch this size," he countered. "I can't go putting her behind the wheel of a truck again, now can I?"

He glanced at his watch, then at Jenny. "You ready?"

Jenny's chin rose stubbornly. "Not if you were paying me a hundred bucks an hour," she declared.

Janet thought she detected a spark of amusement in his eyes, but his expression remained perfectly neutral.

"You scared of horses?" he inquired.

Janet watched her daughter, sensing her dilemma. Jenny would rather eat dirt than admit to fear of any sort. At the same time, she had a genuine distrust of horses, based totally on unfamiliarity, not on any dire experience she'd ever had.

"I'm not afraid of anything," Jenny informed Harlan stiffly. "Horses are dirty and smelly and big. I don't choose to be around them."

Harlan chuckled at the haughty dismissal. "I can't do much about their size, but I can flat-out guarantee they won't be dirty or smelly by the time you're finished grooming them."

Jenny turned a beseeching look in Janet's direction. "Mom!"

"He's the boss," Janet reminded her.

"I don't see you getting anywhere near a smelly old horse," Jenny complained.

"You'd be welcome, if you'd care to join us," Harlan said a little too cheerfully.

"Perhaps another time. I have to get to work."

"Why?" Jenny asked. "You don't have any clients."

Janet winced. The remark was true enough, but she didn't want Harlan Adams knowing too much about her law practice, if that's what handling one speeding violation could be called.

"Business slow?" he asked, leveling a penetrating look straight at her.

She shrugged. "You know how it is. I'm new to town."

He looked as if he might be inclined to comment on that, but instead he let it pass. She was grateful to him for not trying to make excuses for neighbors who were slow to trust under the best of conditions. Their biases made them particularly distrustful of a woman lawyer, who was part Comanche, to boot, and openly proud of it.

"What time should I pick Jenny up?" she asked.

"Suppertime's good enough. You finish up at work any earlier, come on out," he said. "We'll go on that ride. I never get tired of looking at the beauty of this land."

Janet found herself smiling at the simplicity of the admission. She could understand his appreciation of his surroundings. Perhaps even more than he could ever guess.

"Maybe I'll take you up on that one of these days," she agreed. She stood and brushed a kiss across her daughter's forehead. "Have a good time, sweetie."

"Is that another one of those things you tell all your clients who end up in prison?" Jenny inquired, her expression sour.

"You're not in prison," Janet observed, avoiding Harlan's gaze. She had a feeling he was close to laughing and exchanging a look with her would guarantee it. Jenny would resent being laughed at more than anything.

"Seems that way to me," Jenny said.

"Remind me to show you what a real prison looks like one of these days," Janet countered. "You'll be grateful to Mr. Adams for not sending you to one."

Janet decided that was as good an exit line as she was likely to make. She was halfway to the front door when she realized that Harlan had followed her. He put his hand on her shoulder and squeezed lightly.

''She'll be okay,'' he promised.

Janet grinned at his solemn expression. ''I know,'' she agreed. ''But will you?''

Chapter Three

When Janet's car had disappeared from sight, Harlan turned and walked slowly back inside. For the first time he was forced to admit that his decision to haul Jenny Runningbear's butt out to White Pines to work off her debt wasn't entirely altruistic. He'd wanted to guarantee himself the chance to spend more time with her mother.

But now, with Janet on her way back to town and her taunt about his ability to manage Jenny ringing in his ears, he wondered precisely what he'd gotten himself into.

Raising four stubborn sons, when he'd had authority and respect on his side, had been tricky enough. He had neither of those things going for him now. If anything, Jenny resented him and she had no qualms at all about letting him know it.

He sighed as he stood in the doorway to the dining room and studied Jenny's sullen expression. If ever a teen had needed a stern hand, this one did. Whether she knew it or not, she was just aching for someone besides her mama to set some rules and make her stick to them.

It was a job her father should have been handling, but he'd clearly abandoned it. It was little wonder the girl was misbehaving, he thought with a deep sense of pity. Typically in the aftermath of divorce, she was crying out for attention. Maybe she'd even hoped if she were difficult enough, she'd be sent back to her father for disciplining.

It took some determination, but Harlan finally shoved aside his inclination to feel sorry for her. It wouldn't help. He figured whatever happened in the next few minutes would set the tone for the rest of the days Jenny spent at White Pines.

"Thought you'd be outside by now, ready to get to work," he announced. "I won't tolerate slackers working for me."

Her gaze shot to his. "What does this crummy job pay anyway? Minimum wage, I'll bet."

"It pays for a smashed up pickup, period. Think of it as a lump sum payment."

"I'll want to see the repair bill," she informed him. "If the figures for my pay, based on the minimum hourly wage, are higher, I'll expect the rest in cash."

Harlan wanted very badly to chuckle, but he choked back his laughter. This pint-size Donald Trump wannabe had audacity to spare. "Fair enough," he conceded.

"And I'm not getting on a horse," she reminded him belligerently.

"That's something we can discuss," he agreed. "Meantime, let's get out to the barn and groom them. They've been fed this morning, but tomorrow I'll expect you to do that, too."

She stood slowly, reluctance written all over her face. Harlan deliberately turned his back on her and headed out through the kitchen, winking at Maritza as he passed. He didn't pause to introduce them. He had a feeling Jenny would seize on any delay and drag it out as long as she possibly could. She might even inquire about those Tex-Mex recipes she claimed not to like, if it would keep her out of the barn a little longer.

With her soft heart, Maritza would insist on keeping Jenny in the kitchen so she could teach her a few of her favorite dishes and coddle her while she was at it. That would be the end of any disciplining he planned. Until he'd laid some ground rules and Jenny was following them, he figured he couldn't afford to ease up on her a bit. Her very first day on the job was hardly the time to be cutting her any slack.

"Was that your housekeeper?" Jenny asked, scuffing her sneakers in the dust as she poked along behind him.

"Yes."

"How come you didn't introduce us?"

"No time for that now," he said briskly. "You have a job to do. You'll meet Maritza at lunch. She'll be bringing it out to us."

"We're going to eat in the barn?"

Harlan hid a grin at her horrified tone. "No, I expect we'll be out checking fences by then."

She scowled at him. "I thought you were rich. Don't you have anybody else working this place? I can't do everything, you know. I'm just a kid."

"Trust me, you won't even be scratching the surface. And yes, there are other people working the ranch. Quite a few people, in fact. They report to my son. They're off with the cattle or working the fields where we have grain growing." He shot her a sly look. "You had any experience driving a tractor?"

"The sum total of my entire driving experience was in your truck yesterday," she admitted, then shrugged. "You want to trust me with a tractor after that, it's your problem."

He grinned. "You have a point. We'll stick to horses for the time being."

He led her into the barn, which stabled half a dozen horses he kept purely for pleasure riding. Jenny eyed them all warily from the doorway.

"Come on, gal, get in here," he ordered. "Let me introduce you."

"Isn't it kind of sick to be introducing me to a bunch of horses, when you didn't even let me say hello to the housekeeper?"

"You'll get to know Maritza soon enough. As for these horses, from now on they're going to be your responsibility. I want you getting off on the right foot with them." He pulled cubes of sugar from his pocket. "You can start off by offering them these. That'll get you in their good graces quick enough. Let's start over here with Misty. She's a sweetie."

Jenny accepted the sugar cubes but she stopped well shy of Misty's stall. "Why is she bobbing her head up and down like that?"

"She wants some of that sugar."

Jenny held out all of it. "Here. She can have it."

"Not like that," he corrected, "unless you want her to nip off a few fingers at the same time."

He showed her how to hold out her hand, palm flat, the sugar cube in the middle. Misty took the sugar eagerly. He grinned as Jenny's wary expression eased. "Was that so bad?"

"I guess not," she said, though she still didn't sound entirely convinced.

For the next two hours he taught her to groom the horses, watching with satisfaction as she began first to mutter at them when they didn't stand still for her, then started coaxing and finally praising them as she worked. He'd never known a kid yet who could spend much time around horses and not learn to love them. Jenny's resistance was weakening even faster than he'd hoped.

When he was satisfied that her fear had waned, he walked over to her with bit and saddle. "How about that ride now? Seems to me like Misty's getting mighty restless and you two seem to have struck up a rapport."

Jenny regarded the black horse with the white blaze warily. The gentle mare wasn't huge, but Harlan supposed she was big enough to intimidate anyone saddling up for the first time.

"I don't know," Jenny said.

"Let's saddle her up in the paddock and you can climb aboard for a test run. How about that?"

"You're not going to be happy until I fall off one of these creatures and break my neck, are you?" she accused.

"I'm not going to be happy until you try riding one," he countered. "I'd just as soon you didn't fall off and break anything, though I can pretty much guarantee that you'll get thrown sooner or later."

"Oh, jeez," she moaned. "My mom really will sue you if that happens. We'll ask millions and millions for pain and suffering. We'll take this whole big ranch away from you and you'll end up homeless and destitute." The prospect seemed to cheer her.

"I'll take my chances," Harlan said with a grin. "Come on, kid. Watch what I'm doing here. If you don't cinch this saddle just right, you'll be on your butt on the ground faster than either of us would like."

Jenny grudgingly joined him in the paddock. With trepidation clear in every halting move she made, she finally allowed him to boost her into the saddle on Misty's back.

"I don't know about this," she muttered, shooting him an accusing look. "What happens now?"

"I'll lead you around the paddock until you get used to it. Don't worry about Misty. She's placid as can be. She's not going to throw you, unless you rile her."

"Is there anything in particular that riles her?" Jenny inquired, looking down at him anxiously. "I'd hate to do something like that by mistake."

"You won't," he promised.

It only took two turns around the paddock before Jenny's complexion began to lose its pallor. Satisfied by the color in her cheeks that she was growing more confident by the second, Harlan handed her the reins.

Panic flared in her eyes for an instant. "But how do I drive her?"

"You don't *drive* a horse," he corrected. He offered a few simple instructions, then stood by while Jenny tested them. Misty responded to the most subtle movement of the reins or the gentlest touch of Jenny's heels against her sides.

"Everything okay?" he called out as she rode slowly around the paddock.

Jenny turned a beaming smile on him. "I'm riding, aren't I? I'm really riding!"

"I wouldn't let you enter the Kentucky Derby just yet, but yes, indeed, you are really riding."

"Oh, wow!" she said.

Harlan chuckled as she seemed to catch herself and fall silent the instant the words were out of her mouth. Clearly she feared that too much enthusiasm would indicate a softening in her attitude toward this so-called prison sentence she felt had been imposed on her.

"I'm ready to get down now," she said, her tone bland again.

Harlan patiently showed her how to dismount. "I think you're going to be a natural," he said.

She shrugged with studied indifference. "It's no big deal. I'd like to go inside now. Too much sun will give me skin cancer."

He hid another grin. "Run on over to the kitchen. Maritza will give you some suntan lotion. She might even have some of those cookies she was getting ready to bake out of the oven by now."

"Jeez, milk and cookies, how quaint," she grumbled, but she took off toward the house just the same.

"Be back here in fifteen minutes," he shouted after her.

"Slave driver," she muttered.

Harlan shook his head. If she thought that now, he wondered what she'd have to say when she saw the fence he intended for her to learn how to mend.

Janet wasn't sure what to expect when she drove back out to White Pines late that afternoon. She supposed it wouldn't have surprised her all that much to find the ranch in ashes and Jenny standing triumphantly in the circular driveway.

Instead she found her daughter sound asleep in a rocker on the front porch. Harlan was placidly rocking right beside her, sipping on a tall glass of iced tea. He stood when Janet got out of the car and sauntered down to meet her. Her stomach did a little flip-flop as he neared.

To cover the tingly way he managed to make her feel without half trying, Janet nodded toward her daughter. "Looks like you wore her out, after all."

"It took some doing. She's a tough little cookie."

"At least she thinks she is," Janet agreed. She allowed herself a leisurely survey of the man standing in front of her. "You don't appear to be any the worse for wear. You must be a tough cookie, too."

"So they say."

He tucked a hand under her elbow and steered her toward the porch and poured her a glass of tea. Jenny never even blinked at her arrival.

"Business any better today?" Harlan asked only after he was apparently satisfied that her tea was fixed up the way she wanted it.

Rather than answering, Janet took a slow, refreshing sip of the cool drink. It felt heavenly after the hot, dusty drive. Her car's air-conditioning had quit that morning on her way back to town and she hadn't yet figured out where to go to have it fixed. The sole mechanic in Los Piños, a man with the unlikely name of Mule Masters, was apparently on vacation. Had been for months, according to Mabel Hastings over at the drugstore.

"My, but this tastes good," she said, sighing with pure pleasure. "It's hotter than blazes today. I thought I'd swelter before I got back out here."

"What's wrong with your car? No air-conditioning?"

"It quit on me this morning."

"I'll have Cody take a look at it when he comes in," he offered. "He's a whiz with stuff like that."

"That's too much trouble," she protested automatically. For a change, though, she did it without much energy. It seemed foolish to put up too much of a fuss just to declare her independence. That was a habit she'd gotten into around her ex-husband. Weighing her independence against air-conditioning in this heat, there was no real contest. Air-conditioning would win every time.

"Nonsense," Harlan said, dismissing her objections anyway. "It'll give Cody a chance to snoop. He's dying to get a closer look at you, so he can tell his brothers that I've gone and lost my marbles."

Startled, she simply stared at him. "Why would he think a thing like that?"

His gaze drifted over her slowly and with unmistakable intent. "Because I'm just crazy enough to think about courting a woman like you."

Janet swallowed hard at the blunt response. She could feel his eyes burning into her as he waited patiently for a reaction.

"Harlan, I don't want you to get the wrong idea here," she said eventually.

It was a namby-pamby response if ever she'd heard one, but she'd never been very good at fending off the few men bold enough to ignore all the warning signals she tried to send out. She'd ended up married to Barry Randall because he'd been persistent and attentive...until the challenge wore off.

With that lesson behind her, she should be shooting down a man like Harlan Adams with both barrels. Suggesting he might be getting the wrong idea hardly constituted a whimper of protest.

He reached over and patted her hand consolingly, then winked. "Darlin', there is absolutely nothing wrong with the ideas I have. You'll have to trust me on that."

That, of course, was the problem. She didn't trust him or, for that matter, herself. She had a feeling a man with Harlan's confidence and determination could derail her plans for her life in the blink of an eye. She couldn't allow that to happen for a second time.

"You running scared?" he inquired, his lips twitching with amusement.

"Scared? Not me."

His grin broadened. "You sound like Jenny now. I didn't much believe her, either."

"Harlan—"

"Maybe we'd better get this conversation back on safer ground for the moment," he suggested. "Wouldn't want you getting too jittery to drive home tonight. Now, tell me about your day. You never said how business was."

Janet's head was reeling from the quick change of topic and the innuendos Harlan tossed around like confetti. With some effort, she forced her mind off of his provocative teasing and onto that safer ground he'd offered.

"I had a call from somebody interested in having me draw up a will," she told him. "They decided I was too expensive."

"Are you?"

"If I lowered my rates much more, I'd be doing the work for free, which is apparently what they hoped for. The man seemed to assume that since I'm Native American, I handle pro bono work only and he might as well get in on the 'gravy train,' as he put it."

Harlan's gaze sharpened. "You get much of that?" he asked.

He said it with a fierce undertone that suggested he didn't much like what he was hearing. Janet shivered at the thought of what Harlan Adams might do to protect and defend those he cared about.

"Some," she admitted. "I haven't been around long enough to get much."

"Maybe it's time I steered a little business your way."

She suspected that was an understated way of saying he'd butt a few heads together if he had to. She understood enough about small towns to know that a sign of approval from a man like Harlan would guarantee more clients coming her way. As much as the idea appealed to her, she felt she had to turn it down. Barry had always held it over her head that her career had taken off in New York because of his contacts, not the reputation she had struggled to build all on her own.

"No," she insisted with what she considered to be sufficient force to make her point even to a man as stubborn as Harlan appeared to be. "I need to make it on my own. That's the only way people will have any respect for me. It's the only way I'll have any respect for myself."

"Noble sentiments, but it won't put food on the table."

"Jenny and I won't starve. I did quite well in New York. My savings will carry us for a long time."

"If your practice was thriving there, why'd you come here?" Harlan asked.

"Good question," Jenny chimed in in a sleepy, disgruntled tone.

"You know the answer to that," she told her daughter quietly.

"But I don't," Harlan said. "If it's none of my business, just tell me so."

"Would that stop you from poking and prodding until you get an answer?"

"Probably not," he conceded. "But I can be a patient man, when I have to be."

Janet doubted that. It was easier just to come clean with the truth, or part of it at least. "My divorce wasn't pleasant. New York's getting more and more difficult to live in every day. I wanted a simpler way of life."

She shot a look at Jenny, daring her to contradict the reply she'd given. Her daughter just rolled her eyes. Harlan appeared willing to accept the response at face value.

"Makes sense," he said, studying her with that penetrating look that made it appear he could see straight through her. "As far as it goes." He grinned. "But, like I said, I can wait for the rest."

Before she could think of a thing to say to that, a tall, lanky cowboy strolled up. He looked exactly like Harlan must have twenty or so years before, including that flash of humor that sparkled in his eyes as he surveyed the gathering on the porch.

"Looks right cozy," he commented, his amused gaze fixed on his father. "Anything going on here I should know about?"

"Watch your mouth," Harlan ordered. "Janet and Jenny, this tactless scoundrel is my youngest, Cody. Son, this is Janet Runningbear and her daughter Jenny."

Cody winked at Jenny, who was regarding him

with blatant fascination. "Don't tell Daddy, but just so you know, I'm the brains behind White Pines."

"If that were true, you'd have better control over your manners," Harlan retorted.

Janet chuckled listening to the two of them. Talk about a chip off the old block. There wasn't a doubt in her mind that any trait Cody possessed, he had learned it at his father's knee. That included everything from charm to arrogance. Still, she couldn't help responding to that infectious grin and the teasing glint in his eyes as he squared off against Harlan. The squabbles around here must have been doozies.

"Why don't you make yourself useful?" Harlan suggested. "Janet says the air conditioner in her car has gone on the blink. Do you have time to take a look at it?"

"Sure thing," Cody said readily. "Let me get a beer and I'll get right on it."

"I could get the beer," Jenny piped up eagerly.

Cody tipped his hat. "Thanks."

Janet speared her daughter with a warning look, then said to Cody, "If one single ounce of that beer is missing when it gets to you, I'd like to know about it."

"Yes, ma'am," Cody said, winking at Jenny, who blushed furiously.

When they were gone, Janet turned to Harlan. "If he were giving the orders, I suspect Jenny would be docile as a lamb the rest of the summer."

"But he's not," Harlan said tersely. "I am."

"Jealous of the impact your son has on the Runningbear women?" she inquired lightly, just to see if the remark would inspire the kind of reaction she suspected it would.

Harlan's expression did, indeed, turn very grim. "He's married."

She grinned. "I know. Heck, everyone in town heard about his courting of Melissa Horton. It was still fresh on their minds when I moved here. But last I heard, looking's never been against the law. I ought to know. I read those big, thick volumes of statutes cover-to-cover in school."

He scowled. "You deliberately trying to rile me?"

"I didn't know I could," she declared innocently.

"Well, now you know," he asserted.

Janet couldn't help feeling a certain sense of feminine satisfaction over the revelation. But hard on the heels of that reaction came the alarm bells. It was entirely possibly that she was enjoying taunting Harlan Adams just a little too much. She had a hunch it was a very dangerous game to play. He struck her as the kind of man who played his games for keeps.

Chapter Four

Harlan hadn't liked the gut-deep jealousy that had slammed through him when he'd seen the amused, conspiratorial look Janet and Cody had exchanged. Her comment that checking a man out wasn't any sort of legal sin had grated on his nerves just as badly.

Even though he'd guessed that the woman was deliberately baiting him, his blood had simmered and his temper had bordered on exploding. It was an interesting turn of events. He hadn't expected to react so strongly to a woman ever again.

Oh, he'd been attracted to Janet Runningbear the moment he'd set eyes on her. He'd been convinced, though, that he'd deliberately set out to settle her into a corner of his life just to relieve the boredom with an occasional feisty exchange. She was doing that, all right, and more. In spades.

She was stirring up emotions he'd thought had died the day he'd buried his wife just over a year ago. He wasn't so sure he wanted that kind of turmoil.

Unfortunately, he was equally uncertain whether he had any choice in the matter. It had been his observation that when a man was hit by a bolt of lightning—literally or in the lovestruck sense of the phrase—there was no point in trying to get out of the way after the fact.

Given all that, he was almost relieved when Cody announced that the car's air conditioner was working. Janet declined a halfhearted invitation to stay for supper, insisting that she and Jenny had to get home. Harlan waved them off with no more than a distracted reminder to be there at dawn again.

"Well, well, well," Cody muttered beside him.

Harlan frowned at his son's knowing expression. "What's that supposed to mean?"

"Just that it's downright interesting to watch a woman twist you this way and that without even trying."

"I don't know what you're talking about."

Cody grinned. "Then you're in an even more pitiful state of denial than I imagined. Want me to call in Jordan and Luke? Among us we probably have enough experience with women to give you any advice you need. Goodness knows we denied our feelings long enough to drive just about everyone around us to distraction. No sense in you doing the same thing, when we can save you all that time."

"Go away."

"Not till I'm through watching the entertainment,"

Cody shot back as he sauntered over to his pickup. "'Night, Daddy. Sweet dreams."

Sweet? Harlan could think of a dozen or more words to describe the kind of dreams Janet Runningbear inspired and "sweet" would be very low on the list. Provocative. Seductive. Steamy. Erotic. He had to go inside the air-conditioned house just to cool off from the images.

He consoled himself with the possibility that their first two meetings might have been aberrations. Boredom could play funny tricks on a man. The first thing that came along to relieve it might get exaggerated in importance.

Yes, indeed, that had to be it, he decided as he settled into a chair in his office with a book he'd been wanting to read for some time. A good, page-turning thriller was exactly what he needed tonight. That ought to get his juices flowing better than a leggy, sassy woman.

But the words swam in front of his eyes. His thoughts kept drifting to the enigmatic woman who presented such a placid, reserved facade. He'd enjoyed sparking confusion in those dark, mysterious eyes. He'd relished making a little color climb into her cheeks. Janet Runningbear wasn't nearly as serene around him as she wanted desperately for him to believe.

He also had the feeling, virtually confirmed by her earlier, that there were secrets to be discovered, hidden reasons behind her decision to relocate to Texas.

As a kid he'd been fascinated by stories of buried treasure. He'd spent endless hours searching for arrowheads left behind by Native Americans who'd roamed over the very land on which White Pines had been built. Somewhere in the house, probably in Cody's old room, there was a cigar box filled with such treasures.

If Janet Runningbear had secrets, he would discover them eventually. He'd make a point of it.

And then what? He wasn't the kind of man who courted a woman just for sport. He never had been. He'd tried to instill the same set of values in his sons, tried to teach them never to play games with women who didn't fully understand the rules.

Everything about Janet that he'd seen so far shouted that she was a woman deserving of respect, a single parent struggling to put a new life together for herself and her daughter. If he was only looking for diversion, would it be fair to accomplish it at the expense of a woman like that? It was the one question for which he had an unequivocal answer: no!

So, he resolved, he would tame his natural impatience and take his time with her, measuring his feelings as well as hers. It was the only just way to go.

But even as he reached that carefully thought-out decision, the part of him that leapt to impetuous, self-confident conclusions told him he was just delaying the inevitable. He'd made up his mind the minute he'd walked into her office that he wanted her and nothing—not his common sense, not her resistance— was going to stand in his way for long.

"Where the devil have you been?" Mule asked in his raspy, cranky voice when Harlan finally got back

into town on Saturday after four whole days of trying
to keep Jenny Runningbear in line. "Ain't seen you
since that gal stole your truck."

Mule's expression turned sly. "Word around town
is that you've got her working out at White Pines."

Harlan tilted his chair back on two legs and sipped
on the icy mug of beer Rosa had set in front of him
the minute he sat down. "Is that what you're doing
with your time these days, sitting around gossiping
like an old woman?" he asked Mule.

"It's about all there is to do since you dropped out
of our regular poker game to play nursemaid to that
brat."

Harlan accepted the criticism without comment.
Mule grumbled about everything from the weather to
politics. His tart remarks about Harlan's perceived de-
fection were pretty much in character and harmless.

Mule's watery hazel eyes narrowed. "I don't hear
you arguing none."

"What would be the point? You think you know
everything there is to know about the situation."

"Meaning, you think I don't, I suppose. Okay, so
fill me in. Why'd you hire her?"

"Because she owes me a lot of money for repairs
to my pickup," he said simply. "You ought to know.
I had it towed to your garage."

"Ain't had time to take a look at it," Mule said.

"When are you planning to end this so-called vacation of yours?"

"Who says I am? I'm getting so I enjoy having
nothing to do. Maybe I'll just retire for good."

Harlan nodded. "You're old enough, that's for sure. What are you now, eighty?"

Mule regarded him with obvious indignation. "Sixty-seven, which you know danged well."

"Of course," he said. "Must be that boredom ages a person, lets his mind go weak."

"There ain't a thing wrong with my mind."

"Then I'd think you'd be itching to tackle a job like that truck of mine."

"I'll get to it one of these days," Mule said. "When I'm of a mind to."

"If you don't plan on going back to work, maybe you ought to sell the garage. The town needs a good mechanic. Cody had to fix Janet Runningbear's air-conditioning the other night, because you're on this so-called extended vacation of yours."

"Bet he ruined it," Mule commented with derision. "Air-conditioning's tricky."

"It's been working ever since," Harlan said, deliberately setting out to goad the old coot into going back to the job he'd loved. "You know Cody has a way with mechanical things. He's probably better than you ever were and he's not even in the business. Maybe I'll have my truck towed out to White Pines and have him take a look at it."

Mule set his beer down with a thump. "I told you I'd get to it."

"When?"

Mule sighed. "First thing on Monday."

"Fair enough."

"Just don't start bugging me about when it'll be done. Decent work takes time and concentration."

Which meant it might take months before he saw that pickup again, Harlan decided. Still, he couldn't regret his decision to have the truck taken to Mule's garage, rather than someplace bigger or fancier in another town.

His friend had closed up shop almost three months ago for no reason Harlan had been able to discern. He'd been on this strike of sorts ever since. He wasn't likely to be happy again until he had his head poked under the hood of a car.

"Don't look now, but that brat is heading this way," Mule announced. "With her mama. Whoo-ee, she sure is a looker, isn't she?"

Harlan tried not to gape as Janet came into Rosa's wearing a vibrant red sundress that bared tanned shoulders and swung loosely around shapely calves. Her straight, shiny hair hung halfway down her back like a shimmering waterfall of black silk. He stood automatically at the sight of her.

"You again?" Jenny greeted him irritably. "This is my day off. I thought I'd get a break. Shouldn't you be mucking out stalls or something? I hope you're not planning to leave 'em untouched all weekend and expect me to clean up the mess on Monday."

He grinned. "It's nice to see you, too," he commented, and winked at her mother. "Even nicer to see you. Care to join us?"

Janet glanced at her daughter's sour expression, then back at him. "I'm not sure that's such a good idea. The company might ruin your appetite."

"I'll take my chances," Harlan said. "By the way, this is Mule Masters."

"The vacationing mechanic," Janet said, smiling at him.

"Not anymore," Mule grumbled, ignoring the hand she held out. Apparently he had more resistance than Harlan did to Janet's dazzling smile.

"He'll be back on the job on Monday," Harlan explained. "Hopefully his manners will improve by then, as well."

"When a car's as old as mine, it pays to know a good mechanic and I hear you're the best around," she said.

Harlan was impressed that she apparently had not taken offense at Mule's deliberate slight. Maybe she'd been able to judge for herself that it wasn't personal. Mule was just a cantankerous old man. Could be, too, that she'd just weighed his manners against her need for a decent mechanic and decided to ignore his grumpiness.

At her praise for his skill, Mule shot Harlan a triumphant look. "Cody couldn't be that danged good, after all, if she's still on the lookout for somebody who knows his business."

"Cody was just doing me a favor," she acknowledged.

"You get what you pay for," Mule noted in a dire tone as Janet and Jenny sat down in the chairs Harlan pulled out for them.

"As you can see, Jenny's not the only one at the table with an attitude," Harlan commented. "I've been putting up with Mule for years, partly because he keeps my cars running, but mostly because he loses regularly at poker."

"I can play poker," Jenny chimed in. "You guys play for money?"

"Is there any other way to play?" Mule retorted. "Don't play with girls, though."

"Why not?" Jenny demanded. "That sounds like a sexist policy to me. Either open your game to girls or I'll have Mama see that it's closed down."

Mule stared at her in open-mouthed astonishment. Harlan chuckled at the reaction. Jenny had been throwing him off stride the same way all week long.

"Don't play with girls," Mule repeated irritably.

Jenny pulled ten dollars out of her pocket and slapped it on the table. "My money's good."

Janet sighed. "Jenny, that's your allowance for the entire week. If you lose it playing poker, you're out of luck."

Jenny's chin rose a notch. "I don't intend to lose," she declared, leveling a challenging look straight at Mule. "You scared to play me?"

"Dang, but you've got a mouth on you," Mule commented. He glanced at Harlan. "Think we should bring her down a peg or two?"

"No," Harlan said succinctly, his gaze fixed on Janet as he tried to gauge her reaction. "She's already in debt up to her eyeballs."

"That's okay," Janet said. "If she wants to risk her allowance, it's up to her. Of course, I'm going to hate like crazy having to defend all three of you, if you get caught gambling illegally."

"Won't happen," Mule informed her. "Sheriff eats over at DiPasquali's every day. He's sweet on the daughter. Can't budge him out of there for anything less than murder.''

Jenny grinned. ''All right. Where are the cards?''

Harlan sighed and resigned himself to teaching Janet's rebellious daughter yet another lesson. He glanced into Janet's surprisingly amused eyes. ''You in?'' he asked her as Mule shuffled the worn deck he'd pulled from his pocket.

''No, I think I'll just sit here and enjoy the competition. I try real hard not to deliberately break the law, even when there's not much chance of getting caught.''

''And here I had you pegged for a risk-taker,'' Harlan taunted.

Color flooded her cheeks. ''Depends on the risk and the odds,'' she snapped right back. ''Some are worth taking. Some aren't.''

He winked at her. ''I'll bet it's going to be downright fascinating figuring out which are which.''

She swallowed hard and turned away. ''Rosa,'' she called. ''A beer, please.''

That choked voice had Harlan smiling. ''Throat dry?'' he inquired.

''Parched,'' she admitted, meeting his gaze evenly. She ran her tongue over her lips. ''Absolutely parched.''

Maybe the gesture was innocent. Maybe not. Harlan doubted he'd ever know for sure. One thing was certain, she could best him at his own game anytime. The sight of that pink tongue delicately sliding over those lush red lips turned his blood hotter than asphalt on a Texas summer afternoon.

It also rattled his concentration so bad that he lost the first hand of poker to Jenny. So did Mule, which suggested that the thirteen-year-old just might know a little more about the game and gambling than he'd suspected.

He glanced up from his second hand to find Janet's gaze fixed on him. She leaned forward, which caused her sundress to dip a provocative inch or so, revealing just enough cleavage to make his own throat go dry.

"Mind if I take a look?" she inquired, placing her hand over his and turning his cards in her direction.

Harlan sucked in a breath as every muscle in his body tightened at that innocent, cool touch. He glanced into her eyes and changed his mind. There was nothing innocent about that touch. She knew exactly what she was doing. He pulled his cards out of her grasp.

"Trying to rattle me, darlin'?" he asked, amused by the blatant tactic.

Her eyes widened. "Why would I do that?"

"Maybe to protect Jenny's allowance," he suggested.

She grinned and shrugged, clearly not the least bit guilty at having been caught. "Hey, us gals have to stick together."

Mule stood, his whole demeanor radiating indignation. "A man would get shot for cheatin' at cards."

Harlan shook his head at his friend's idea of saloon-style justice. "Sit down, old man. I believe Ms. Runningbear will behave from now on out." He met her gaze. "Isn't that right?"

"I'll be innocent as a lamb," she promised.

"Hands on the table. Eyes straight ahead. Lips locked."

"I can hardly wait to see how long that lasts," Harlan commented.

To her credit, she did exactly as she'd sworn she would. Unfortunately for him, she hadn't mentioned a thing about any part of anatomy below her finger-tips. Just as he was about to bet, he felt a knee nudge his...and stay there. The heat that rose through him this time could have roasted marshmallows. Turned them to ashes, in fact.

He found that he enjoyed the sensation a little too much to tattle on her. He folded and left Jenny and Mule to battle for the pot. Mule took it with a full house to Jenny's two pairs. To his everlasting regret, Janet's knee retreated to a safe distance. It was by far the most intriguing poker game he'd ever played in. So far, it had cost him five bucks.

He considered the money an investment in his future with Janet. He was learning more about her with every hand of cards they played. He doubted she knew how much she was revealing about herself. Maybe she was a risk-taker. Maybe she wasn't. But she was definitely someone who liked to win.

She was also protective as a mother bear with a cub, where Jenny was concerned. And she had an absolutely fascinating, wild flirtatious streak. Just wondering how far she'd take it made his pulse scramble in a way that was downright disconcerting.

"I really think you ought to ante up," he told her as Jenny shuffled the cards for the third hand. He glanced at her daughter. "Deal your mother in this round."

Janet's expression turned faintly uneasy. "Really, I don't think…"

"Humor me," he taunted. "I'll spot you the fifty cents for the pot." He tossed two quarters into the middle of the table.

Jenny paused, waiting for her mother's decision before dealing out the hand.

"Okay," Janet said eventually. "But I haven't had as much practice as Jenny."

Jenny's mouth gaped. "Mom!"

"Quiet, dear. Deal the cards."

Harlan chuckled at the exchange. He had the distinct impression now that everything Jenny knew about poker, she had learned from her mother. It was just one more facet to Janet Runningbear to intrigue him. Apparently she was a bit of a gambler, after all.

She scanned her cards with a practiced eye, tossed two back onto the table and waited for Jenny to replace them. Harlan drew three and wound up with two pairs, but most of his attention was on the woman seated next to him. Her face was an absolutely expressionless mask, a genuine poker face.

Mule bet fifty cents. Harlan met his bet. He wouldn't have dropped out of this hand if they'd been playing for a hundred times that amount.

"That's fifty cents to you, darlin'."

She nodded, not even glancing his way. "Your fifty and fifty more."

Jenny looked from her mother to Harlan and back again. "I'll fold," she said.

"I'm out," Mule concurred, tossing his cards onto the table in apparent disgust.

Janet turned an expectant look on Harlan that had his breath catching in his throat.

"Are you in?" she inquired in a lazy, seductive tone that had him conjuring up images that could have melted concrete.

"You'd better believe it, darlin'. Your fifty and I'll raise you a buck."

"My, my, you are confident," she said, turning to wink at Jenny. "Shall I stay, do you think?"

Jenny grinned. "You can't quit now, Mom. He'll think you're chicken."

"True. We can't have that, can we?" She reached over and plucked five dollars from Jenny's pile of winnings. "I'll repay you in a minute."

Harlan studied her expression before matching the bet. He couldn't tell a thing about whether or not she was bluffing. He dropped his money on the table. "Call."

She placed her first card on the table, an ace of clubs. Her second card was a seven of clubs. Her third, a five of clubs. The fourth was a two of clubs. "Now what do you suppose I have here?" she inquired, lifting her gaze to clash with his.

"Either another club or more audacity than anyone else in Texas," Harlan quipped.

She winked. "Want to go double or nothing on this last card?"

"That ain't the rules," Mule complained.

"Some rules are made to be broken," Harlan said,

his gaze never leaving Janet's. "Not double or nothing. How about loser cooks dinner for the winner?"

The flash of uncertainty in her eyes told him she'd just realized that she'd overplayed her hand. Still, she didn't back down.

"You sure that's what you want? You could just quit now," she said, clearly determined to brazen it out.

"Not on your life. Get that card on the table."

She sighed, an expression of resignation on her face as she dropped an ace of hearts on top of the other cards.

Harlan chuckled. "Darlin', you would have made an outstanding stripper," he teased. "You know a heck of a lot about drawing out the suspense."

"But you can beat a pair of aces, can't you?"

He showed her his two pairs, fours and eights. "Sure can. So, when's dinner?" he inquired as he gathered up the pot.

Jenny chuckled. "You still think you won, don't you? Wait till you try Mom's cooking!"

"Jenny," Janet protested. "How's tomorrow? I'm sure I can grill a hamburger or something that will be edible."

"That'll be a first," her daughter retorted. She glanced at Harlan. "You might want to bring along a roll of antacids. Mom's still trying to figure out how to cope with life without takeout."

"I'm sure anything your mother cooks will be just fine," Harlan said staunchly. "I'll be there about six."

Mule cackled. "Think I'll let the rescue squad know to be standing by just in case."

They could all joke all they wanted, Harlan thought as he tilted his chair onto its back legs and studied the trio. Even if Janet's food tasted like cinders, he had definitely come out of this a winner.

Chapter Five

The kitchen was in shambles. Janet stood amid the collection of messy bowls, streaks of chocolate cake batter and spatters of frosting and despaired of ever getting a meal on the table by six o'clock.

"Why did you let me do that?" she asked Jenny, who was standing in the doorway gloating. "Why on earth did you let me make a bet like that?"

"You sounded like you were on a roll, Mom. How was I supposed to know you just had a piddly pair of aces?"

"Because you know what a competitor I am. I always get caught up in the moment, start bluffing and get carried away. You were doubling your allowance playing poker with me when you were eight for that very reason."

"I know," Jenny said, grinning. "If you'd gotten

any more carried away yesterday, the man would be moving in with us.''

"Hardly,'' Janet denied.

"Mom, it's true. He leveled those baby blues of his on you and you perked up as if he'd showered you with diamonds.''

Janet winced at the accuracy of the accusation. She had enjoyed the challenge and the blatant masculine approval she'd been able to stir with a little teasing. Harlan Adams was the kind of man who could make any woman lose sight of her independent streak.

"All women are a little susceptible to flattery and the attention of an attractive man,'' she said to defend herself. "It's not something to be taken seriously.''

"You've got my jailer coming to dinner in twenty minutes and you think that's not serious,'' Jenny retorted.

"Would you stop calling him that?'' she implored. "Mr. Adams did you a favor, young lady. And the truth is, you're having fun at White Pines, aren't you?''

"Oh, sure, I just love spending my summer vacation breaking my back mucking out that stinky old barn.''

"You should have thought of that before you stole his truck,'' she admonished for what must have been the hundredth time.

"How was I supposed to know that pickup belonged to a man who'd never heard of child labor laws? You probably ought to investigate him or something. He probably has little kids all over that ranch of his, working their butts off." She shot a sly look at Janet. "Little Native American kids, Mom."

Janet chuckled at the blatant attempt to try to push her buttons. "Forget it, Jenny. You can't rile me up that way. There is absolutely no evidence that anything like that is going on at White Pines."

"Isn't that why we're here, though? Aren't you supposed to be righting old wrongs, looking out for the descendents of the Comanches who rightfully belong on that land that Mr. Adams's ancestors stole? Jeez, Mom, we're in town for less than a month and you're practically in bed with the enemy."

"I am not in bed with anybody," Janet said. "Stop with that kind of talk and set the table."

"Okay, but I say you're selling out."

"And I say you have a smart mouth. I'd better not hear any of that kind of talk while Mr. Adams is here."

Jenny nodded, her expression knowing. "I get it. You don't want to tip him off too soon that his days on that land are numbered, right? You'll finish your research, then *bam,* file the papers and boot him off. That's good. I like it. Boy, will he be surprised when he finds out I belong at White Pines more than he does. Maybe I'll even make *him* clean the barn."

Janet was beginning to regret ever having told Jenny how the land that Lone Wolf's father had cherished had been taken over by white ranchers, while the Comanches were forced into smaller and smaller areas and eventually out of Texas altogether.

"Sweetie, there is no evidence that White Pines itself belonged to Lone Wolf's father," she explained.

"True, he roamed all over west Texas and the Comanches believed that the land of the Comancheria was theirs, but it's not as if it was ever deeded to them and recorded as theirs."

"But that's just a technicality, right?" Jenny argued. "You're going to prove that possession was nine-tenths of the law stuff and that the government never had any right to force them out, right?"

Janet had to admit it was a dream she had had, a fantasy inspired by listening to Lone Wolf spin his sad tales. She had vowed at his grave, when she was younger than Jenny was now, that she would try to rectify what had happened to their ancestors.

When her marriage had failed, she'd been drawn to Texas at least in part to see if there was any way at all to fulfill that old promise. Now, while it seemed likely there was much she could do to assist the scattered Native Americans still living in Texas, reality suggested there was little chance she could return their old lands to them. While principle dictated the claims of the tribe were valid, individually their legal rights were murky at best.

"Jenny, you know that's what I want to do, but it's complicated. I can't just waltz into the courthouse and file a few briefs and expect a hundred years of wrongs to be righted. The system doesn't work that way."

"The system stinks," Jenny retorted, thumping the plates onto the table. "And just remember, Mom, Mr. Adams is part of that system."

Janet sighed. It wasn't something she was likely to forget. If the twinkle in his eyes or the fire stirred by a casual touch distracted her, she had only to gaze around at his land to remember what had brought her to Texas.

Every acre of raw beauty reminded her of Lone Wolf's broken father, forced to live as a farmer in an unfamiliar state when tradition and instinct made him a hunter.

In the abstract, it had been easy to hate the Texans who had made that happen. Now, faced with a man like Harlan Adams, who had shown her nothing but kindness, compassion and a hint of desire, it was awfully hard to think of him—or even his faceless ancestors—as the enemy.

So, what did she consider him to be? she wondered as she checked the cake she had baking. Her mother, a full-blooded Comanche, had barely survived a disastrous marriage to a white man. Janet was only half Comanche and her own marriage to a white man had been only minimally better. She'd convinced herself that returning to Texas to learn more about her Comanche heritage was the secret to happiness.

Was Jenny right? Was she selling out already by allowing Harlan Adams to assume such a significant role in their lives? It was not as if she'd had much choice, she consoled herself. Jenny had gotten their lives entwined from the moment she'd impulsively stolen that truck of his.

As for the way she responded to Harlan's warm glances, that was just hormones talking. Her good sense could overrule that anytime she chose—or so she prayed.

She reached into the oven to remove the cake. The

pot holder slipped. Her thumb landed squarely on the pan.

"Damn," she muttered as the round pan clattered to the floor. A crack the size of the Grand Canyon appeared down the middle of the cake. Jenny appeared just in time to stare in dismay at the mess.

"Jeez, Mom, that cake was about the only thing this meal had going for it."

"Don't remind me," she muttered, sucking on her injured thumb. "I'll fill it in with frosting, so it'll look okay. We'll cut pieces from the outside edges. Harlan will never know."

"I don't know. I think after he gets a taste of that limp spaghetti and the wilted salad, he'll be expecting it."

Janet scowled at her daughter. "You're no help. A little encouragement would be welcomed about now."

"You need more than encouragement to bail you out," Jenny declared derisively. "How about a quick trip to DiPasquali's? I could be back before he gets here. He'll never know you didn't prepare every bite yourself."

Janet was sorely tempted to do just that. For some reason that probably didn't bear too close a scrutiny, she really had wanted this meal to go well. She surveyed the mess in the kitchen, then glanced at the clock. He was due in five minutes.

"There's no time," she said, resigned to serving a meal barely fit for human consumption.

"You call. I'll run," Jenny repeated. "If he's here

when I get back, I'll slip in through the kitchen. Just keep him out of here.''

Janet reached for her purse and pulled out a twenty. ''Go,'' she said. A survey of the disaster she'd made of the kitchen had her adding, ''And don't worry about coming in through the kitchen. I wouldn't let Harlan in here if it were burning down and he were the volunteer fireman.''

When Jenny was gone and she'd placed the desperation call to Gina DiPasquali, she left the kitchen and closed the door behind her. If there'd been a lock, she would have turned the key.

At least the dining room looked presentable. Jenny had even picked flowers for the center of the table and had put out the good china and silver. For all of her grumbling about Harlan Adams, it appeared she wanted to impress him, as well. Janet was more pleased about that than she cared to admit.

She was just checking her makeup in the hall mirror when the doorbell rang. Precisely at six o'clock, she noted, checking her watch. She wondered if that was an indication of polite promptness or, perhaps, just a little eagerness. Her heart thumped unsteadily at the possibility that it might be the latter.

When she opened the door, she could barely glimpse Harlan through the huge bouquet of flowers in his arms.

''Did you buy out the florist's entire stock?'' she asked, taking them from him.

He shrugged, looking faintly embarrassed. ''It was late Saturday. She said it would all spoil by Monday anyway, so she gave me a deal,'' he said, confirming what she'd meant as a facetious comment.

"I see."

"I brought wine and candy, too. I wasn't sure which you'd prefer."

"The flowers would have been plenty," she assured him, wondering how the devil she was going to keep him out of the kitchen if she took them in there to put them in vases.

He grinned. "A little over the top, huh?"

"But sweet," she assured him.

"It's been a long time since I've gone calling on a lady."

She could tell. He looked about as at ease as a man making his first trip to a lingerie department. Not even his starched white shirt, expensive black trousers and snakeskin boots could combat the impression made by his anxious expression.

"You seem to forget that this isn't exactly a date," she said to reassure him. "You won dinner fair and square on a bet."

She waved him toward a chair. "Have a seat and I'll get these in water. What can I bring you to drink when I come back? Wine? A beer? Iced tea?"

"Iced tea sounds good. Why don't we sit on the porch? It's a nice night. Or is dinner just about ready?"

"No, dinner will be a while," she said in what had to be the understatement of the decade. However, sitting on the porch was out of the question. He was bound to spot Jenny returning from DiPasquali's. She grasped desperately for an alternative.

"Actually, I hate to do this to you, but my bathroom faucet has been leaking." Even though the tactic grated, she used her most helpless expression on him. "I don't know the first thing about changing a washer. Could you take a look at it?"

He latched onto the request as if she'd thrown him a lifeline. "Just show me the way."

She led him down the narrow hallway to the old-fashioned bathroom, which, thankfully, Jenny had straightened up after her shower. "I bought washers and there are some tools there," she said, pointing.

"I'll have this fixed in no time," he promised, already loosening his collar and rolling up his sleeves. "By the way, it's nice to walk into a house and smell dinner cooking. There's nothing like the scent of chocolate to make a man's mouth water." He glanced at her and winked. "Unless it's that sexy perfume you're wearing."

"I'm not sure it's perfume you're smelling," she said. "It's probably all these flowers."

He shook his head. "They were in the car with me all the way into town. That's not it. I'd say you're wearing something light with just a hint of spice. It's the kind of thing that could drive a man wild."

Janet could feel herself blushing. "Thanks. If you'll excuse me, I'll get these into water."

In the kitchen she put the flowers down on the only clear surface, the top of the stove, and drew in a deep breath. She hadn't realized what a sucker she was for charm. Maybe it was just the sweetly tentative way in which it was delivered.

She didn't doubt for an instant that Harlan Adams

had always been a flirt, but she was also very aware that he was out of practice delivering compliments with all sorts of subtle innuendo behind them. Teasing a woman just to make her feel good was one thing. It was another to be experimenting with dating after so many years of marriage. It made what they were doing here tonight seem riskier and more significant for both of them.

She sighed and forced her attention to the flowers. It took three large vases to handle all of them. She scattered the arrangements around the living room, poured Harlan's iced tea, then traipsed back to the bathroom where she'd left him.

"I brought your tea," she said, keeping one ear attuned to any sounds from the kitchen that might indicate that Jenny had returned. "How's it going?"

"The washer's replaced," he said, his voice muffled. He had his head poked into the vanity under the sink. "Thought I'd check to make sure all the joints were sealed under here while I was at it."

He slid out and grinned at her. "No leaks under there."

She took one look at the streaks of grime on his face and shirt and winced. "Harlan, you're a mess. I'm sorry. I should never have asked you to do this for me, especially when you were all dressed up."

"Stop fussing. A little dirt never hurt anybody. I'll wash up."

"But your shirt…" she protested.

"It's not a problem," he insisted. He shot her a wicked grin. "Unless, of course, you object to a man coming to the dinner table looking like this. I could strip down and let you wash the shirt here and now."

He seemed a little too eager for her to grab at that solution. "Never mind," she assured him. "I'm the one responsible. I can hardly complain, can I?"

Just then she heard the kitchen door slam. She plastered what she hoped was an innocent expression on her face. "Oh, good, that must be Jenny. She's been out for a bit. Now that she's back, I'll get dinner on the table. Go on out to the porch after you've washed up, why don't you? Relax for a minute. I'll call you when everything's on the table."

"I could help," he offered.

"No, indeed. You've done more than enough. Besides, you won the bet. I can't have you helping."

She took off, trying to ignore the fact that there was something a little too knowing about his expression. He couldn't possibly have guessed what she'd done, could he? No, of course not. As long he remained far away from that kitchen, there was no way he could figure out that she hadn't prepared every dish herself.

Jenny was pulling aluminum pans of food out of paper bags when Janet got back to the kitchen.

"Gina said to warm the lasagna again for a few minutes before you serve it. I've already turned the oven on low. The salad's in that package. She put the dressing on the side, so you could toss it in your bowl." She reached into another bag and pulled out a loaf of Italian bread wrapped in foil. "Garlic bread. It goes in the oven, too."

Janet rolled her eyes at Jenny's instructions. "I could have figured that much out for myself."

"Who would guess?" Jenny quipped. "So how'd you keep Mr. Adams out of here?"

"I had him fixing the leak in the bathroom."

Jenny grinned. "Good for you. It's about time he sees what it's like to work for free."

"I don't think he thought of it quite that way. He was doing me a favor." She pointed to the bowl of frosting. "The cake should be cool enough by now. You ice it while I toss the salad."

Twenty minutes later they were seated in the dining room. Janet's heart was in her throat as Harlan took his first bite of salad. Would he be able to tell she hadn't prepared it? It was only lettuce, tomatoes and a few radishes. Surely he wouldn't suspect that even that much had been beyond her skill.

"Delicious," he said. "Jenny, I think you sold your mother short when you said she couldn't cook."

Janet shot a warning look at her daughter. Jenny shrugged.

"It's pretty hard to ruin a bunch of lettuce and some tomatoes," she retorted, avoiding Janet's gaze.

The lasagna was an equally big hit. "Can't think when I've had any better," Harlan enthused. "It's every bit as good as Gina DiPasquali's."

Janet groaned and covered her face. There wasn't a doubt in her mind that the jig was up. "You know, don't you?"

"Know what?" Harlan replied, trying to sound innocent and failing miserably.

"That Jenny picked up the salad, bread and lasagna from DiPasquali's."

He winked at Jenny. "Did she now?"

"How did you know?" Janet demanded.

"Saw her running in the front door of the restaurant as I drove through town," he finally admitted as Jenny chuckled.

Janet glared at the pair of them. "And you let me wriggle on the hook like a big old fish. Did you enjoy watching me squirm trying to keep you away from the front of the house till she got back?"

He nodded. "Sure did." He reached across the table and patted her hand consolingly. "That's okay, darlin'. I appreciate you going to all that trouble to impress me."

Janet moaned. "I did not do it to impress you," she declared adamantly.

"She did it to keep you from getting food poisoning," Jenny chimed in. "You should see—"

"That's enough, Jenny," Janet said sharply. She was determined to get through the rest of the evening with some dignity intact. If she wasn't careful, Jenny would be offering Harlan a tour of the kitchen.

"That chocolate cake sure does smell good," he said. "I know Gina didn't stop by and bake that."

"It's got a great big crack right down the middle," Jenny revealed. "I had to patch it together with icing."

Janet scowled at her. "Thank you for sharing that," she grumbled.

Harlan winked at her this time. "Don't fret, darlin'. With chocolate cake, it's taste, not looks, that count."

''I wouldn't hold your breath on that score, either,'' Jenny warned. ''She probably left out something important.''

If she could have, Janet would have sent Jenny to her room on the spot before she made any more embarrassing revelations. Unfortunately, she could see the injustice of such an act. She was just going to have to survive this debacle and hope that Harlan wasn't one to gossip. Fortunately, she was in town to practice law, not to do catering.

As it turned out, the cake was not only edible, but actually pretty good. At least Harlan ate two slices of it, his amused gaze fixed on her the whole time. He seemed especially fond of the inch-thick icing in the middle.

The minute dinner was over he shooed Jenny off by declaring that he would help clean up. Jenny didn't have to be asked twice. She was gone before Janet could protest.

''You cannot walk into that kitchen,'' she said adamantly, though short of stretching out her arms and trying to bar the doorway, she didn't know what she could do to stop him.

He ignored her, picked up an armload of dishes and headed across the dining room. ''The sooner we get things squared away in there, the sooner you and I can sit on that front porch and enjoy the breeze.''

To his credit, he didn't even blink as he walked into the midst of the mess she'd created trying to make dinner. Maybe he'd served time on KP in the military at some point, she decided as she watched the ease with which he set things right.

"Come here," he commanded when he'd washed the last dish and wiped down the countertops.

"I don't think so," she said, holding up the last plate she was drying as if to ward him off.

He grinned, shrugged and came to her. Before she realized his intentions, he slid his arms around her waist and held her in a loose embrace. "Thank you," he said softly, his breath fanning intimately across her cheek.

"For what?" she asked shakily. Her breath snagged in her throat as she met his gaze.

"For going to so much trouble."

"I told you—"

He reached up and brushed a strand of hair away from her eyes. "I know what you told me, but the fact is you could have served me whatever that was you cooked in the first place and tried to scare me off for good. Instead, you went to a lot of trouble that wasn't necessary. I don't scare that easily."

She sighed. "That's what I'm afraid of."

He studied her intently. The spark of mischief in his eyes raised goose bumps.

"You gonna fall apart if I kiss you?" he inquired.

An unwilling smile tugged at her lips. "I might."

He nodded. "I think I'll risk it anyway," he said softly.

He lowered his head until his lips were a tantalizing hairbreadth above hers. She trembled as she waited for him to close that infinitesimal distance. When, at last, their mouths met, she could have sworn fireworks exploded. She'd been expecting a kiss that was gentle and tentative. Instead, he plundered, claiming her mouth as surely as his ancestors had claimed Comanche land.

After the first startled instant, when she couldn't have moved if her life depended on it, Janet slid her hands from his shoulders into his thick hair, holding him, encouraging him to continue the assault that had her senses vibrantly, thrillingly alive for perhaps the first time ever. Nothing she had shared with her ex-husband compared to the consuming, white-hot fire raging through her just from Harlan Adams's incomparable kiss.

She willed it to go on forever, imagining all of the wicked places it could take her. But just as she was indulging in sensations so sweet her heart ached for them to continue, she heard a startled gasp behind her.

"Mom, how could you?" Jenny protested with all of the hurt and confusion a thirteen-year-old could experience.

The kitchen door rattled on its hinges as Jenny left far more noisily than she had entered.

"I'll go after her," Harlan offered, but Janet stilled him.

"No, it's up to me. You'd better leave, though. She won't want to see you again tonight and this could take a while."

He nodded, reluctance clearly written all over his face. "If you're sure."

"I am. I'll handle it."

"You'll be at White Pines in the morning, then?"

"That might be difficult," Janet said. "She might not want to be there after this."

''A deal's a deal,'' he reminded her, his expression intractable.

She saw then, what she should have recognized before. Harlan Adams had a will of iron when it came to the things he wanted. What worried her was that she'd just had unmistakable evidence that what he wanted was her.

Chapter Six

Harlan was up before dawn the morning following his dinner with Janet and Jenny. By six he was pacing the front porch from end to end, wondering if they would show up and if they did, what kind of reception he might get.

He'd cursed himself a dozen different ways on the drive home the night before. As much as he'd been aching to kiss Janet, he never should have taken a chance on doing it where Jenny could walk in on them. Even a fool would have been smarter than that.

Now, not only had he put his relationship with the intriguing Janet Runningbear at risk, but it seemed likely he'd spoiled the fragile rapport he'd been building with her daughter.

When he finally heard the sound of an engine in the distance, his spirits soared, then crashed just as quickly when he saw that it was Cody's red pickup barreling down the lane.

Just what he needed. He doubted there was a chance in hell he could keep his perceptive son from guessing what was on his mind. And if Cody picked up on his mood, he'd be offering unsolicited advice to the lovelorn and enjoying every minute of it.

"Aren't you supposed to be up north today, checking those fence lines?" Harlan grumbled as Cody approached. "You're getting a mighty late start."

Cody eyed him warily. "You roll out on the wrong side of the bed, Daddy?"

"No, it's just that we could lose a lot of the herd if that fence doesn't get taken care of. I shouldn't have to be telling you a thing like that."

"I'm aware of what's at stake," Cody retorted as carefully as if he'd unwittingly walked into a mine field. "Which is why I sent Mac and Luis up there first thing yesterday morning. I didn't want to wait for today."

"Oh," Harlan said, and fell silent. It took everything in him, but he kept his gaze averted from the lane.

"How's Melissa?" he asked eventually since his son didn't seem inclined to venture any further conversation. He couldn't say he blamed him, given the reception he'd gotten so far.

"Fine."

"And Sharon Lynn and the baby?"

"Fine. Just about the same as when you saw them in church yesterday morning."

Harlan shrugged. ''Never can tell with kids, though.''

''True,'' Cody said, then suddenly chuckled.

Harlan scowled at him. ''What's so blasted amusing?''

''You,'' Cody said. ''What's the matter? Haven't they shown up yet?''

''Who?''

''The tax collectors,'' Cody retorted with heavy sarcasm. He shook his head. ''You are so pitiful. I'm talking about Janet and Jenny, of course.''

''No, they're not here yet.''

Eyes sparkling with pure mischief, Cody added, ''Heard you had quite a poker game with them on Saturday.''

So the cat was out of the bag, Harlan thought, stifling a desire to groan. ''I suppose Mule couldn't wait to report every detail,'' he said sourly, resigning himself to as much taunting as Cody cared to mete out.

''Actually, I heard about it from Maritza, who heard it from her cousin Rosa, who witnessed it all right there in her very own café.'' He grinned. ''And just so you know, Luke's housekeeper also got the word from cousin Rosa, which means your oldest son knows every detail by now, too. He couldn't wait to check out the story with me.''

''Damn, I knew it was a mistake helping that whole darn family to settle in Los Piños,'' he muttered, regretting the day he'd first hired Consuela, who was now working for Luke, and subsequently her cousin Maritza, his present housekeeper. He'd even cosigned the loan for Rosa's damned café. So much for loyalty.

They apparently hadn't been able to wait to blab his business all over hell and gone. "Don't they have anything better to do than gossip?"

"Guess not," Cody said. "Especially not when the news is so fascinating. So, how was dinner with the loser?"

With the grapevine already abuzz anyway, Harlan didn't bother trying to contain a grin at the memory of the meal that Jenny had snuck in from Di-Pasquali's.

"Fascinating," he attested.

"So why the worried look when I drove up?"

He weighed telling his son the truth or at least part of it. Maybe if he swore him to secrecy with a promise of eternal damnation if he broke his vow, he could chance it. If he didn't talk about what had happened, he'd go plumb stir-crazy.

"This doesn't get repeated, okay? Luke already knows too much. I don't want him and Jordan hovering around here, trying to decide if I'm losing my mind."

"It may not be Luke and Jordan you need to worry about," Cody drawled. "If Jessie and Kelly get wind of it, they'll get matchmaking fever the likes of which west Texas has never seen."

"All the more reason for you to keep your trap shut," Harlan said, shuddering at the prospect of all that meddling. "Can you do it?"

Eyes dancing with renewed mischief, Cody solemnly crossed his heart. "Not a word. I swear it. What happened last night?"

"No guffawing, okay?"

"I wouldn't dream of it."

Harlan was doubtful about that, but he decided to chance it. "Okay, let's just say the evening ended on a more awkward note than I might have preferred."

Cody's mouth gaped. "You made a pass at her?"

He made it sound like Harlan was sixteen and had been trying to get into the drawers of the preacher's daughter. "It wasn't a pass, dammit. It was a kiss."

"Well, I'll be damned. I bet Luke you wouldn't have the guts to try that for at least another month."

Harlan groaned. "I knew this was a mistake. I knew it." He scowled fiercely. "You blab one word of this and I'll hang your hide from the oak tree out back just to set an example for your brothers."

Unfortunately, Cody didn't exactly seem to be intimidated. He chuckled even as he said, "Not a word. I already promised. Besides, do you think I want Luke to know I lost the bet? So what was so awkward?"

"Jenny walked in."

"Uh-oh."

"Uh-oh is right. She wasn't happy."

"She's a kid. She'll get over it. Surely her mom has been on dates before."

"Maybe. Maybe not. But it took me most of last week to get a civil tongue in that girl's head. Now I've gone and lost whatever ground I gained."

"What was Janet's reaction to all this?"

"Naturally she was upset."

"With you or Jenny?"

"I'm the supposedly responsible adult. I'm the one who caused the problem."

SHERRYL WOODS   95

"Not if she kissed you back," Cody corrected. "Did she?"

Harlan couldn't help smiling at the memory. "She did, indeed."

"Then you'll find a way to work it out," Cody predicted, apparently satisfied that he'd completed his role as counselor. "I'm going inside for breakfast. All this advice has left me famished."

"You're always famished," Harlan observed. "Doesn't Melissa ever feed you?"

"Sure, but that was two hours ago," he said as he opened the front door. Just as he was about to step inside, he looked back. "Hey, Daddy?"

Harlan's gaze was already riveted on the lane again. "Hmm?"

"Remember what you used to tell us when we were dating?"

His head snapped around. "What?"

"It's not polite to kiss and tell," Cody taunted.

If he'd had something available, he would have thrown it at him. "Then see that you don't repeat my mistake," he warned emphatically. "There will be hell to pay for both of us, if you do."

By eight o'clock Harlan had just about accepted the fact that Janet and Jenny wouldn't be coming. He decided to let it pass for today, but if they didn't show up tomorrow, he vowed to have a little chat with Jenny about paying off debts and living up to obligations. If he was more concerned about his own selfish interests, well, that was something she wouldn't have to know.

He was in the barn saddling up his favorite stallion

when he glanced up to see Jenny standing hesitantly in the doorway. Surprise kept him speechless, even as relief spread through him. When he could keep his tone matter-of-fact, he said, "A little late, aren't you?"

"Mother dropped me off on the highway. I had to walk the rest of the way up the lane."

"I see. Whose idea was that?"

Jenny's chin rose a belligerent notch. "Mine."

He would have guessed as much. It was probably her way of keeping him and her mother apart. The fire in her eyes dared him to make anything of it. He clamped a lid on his desire to challenge her. At least she was here. He considered that a good sign.

"The lane's pretty long," he offered blandly. "Must be close to two miles. You thirsty?"

"A little," she admitted, scuffing her sneaker in the dirt and avoiding his gaze.

"Then, run on in the house and have Maritza give you something cool to drink."

She didn't dash off as he'd anticipated she would.

"Are you going riding?" she asked.

He nodded. "I was about to."

"Can I come?"

"Of course."

"You'll wait?"

"I'll wait," he agreed, trying to remain as nonchalant as she was when he was filled with questions about what had happened after he'd left last night. Her odd mood wasn't telling him much, but at least she didn't appear to be holding that kiss against him. She simply appeared determined to stave off a repeat.

"I'll hurry," she promised, and took off.

He stared after her, confusion teeming inside. Would he ever figure out the workings of that girl's mind?

Jenny was polite, but quiet for the rest of the day. She did everything he asked of her, if not eagerly, at least without complaint. By the end of the day he was longing for a little of the more familiar sass.

"Is your mama picking you up at the house or are you meeting her out by the highway?" he inquired eventually.

"At the highway," she said, shooting a belligerent look at him that confirmed his earlier opinion that this was her way of keeping him and Janet separated.

"You'd better get going then. It'll take you a while to get out there. The humidity's up. Maybe you'd better borrow a baseball cap and get a thermos of water to take along," he said, deliberately emphasizing that the walk would seem even hotter and longer than it had in the cooler morning air.

He let that sink in for a minute, then added casually, "Or I could drive you out."

He could tell from her expression that she was struggling with the offer, weighing the advantages of the quick, cool ride with the disadvantages of having him possibly bump into her mother.

"I suppose that would be okay," she conceded grudgingly. "I don't want to get heatstroke."

"Good thinking," he said. He glanced at his watch. "Should we leave now? It's almost five."

She nodded and followed him to his car, a luxury model he kept in the garage. Her mouth dropped open when she saw it. "How come you drove that pickup, when you had this?"

"It was more practical. I'm always hauling stuff for the ranch."

"Oh." She touched the leather interior almost reverently. "I like this. It's really soft. I'm going to have a car just like this someday."

"I'll bet you will," he agreed. "Are you planning to earn it or steal it?"

"Hey, that's not fair," she protested, frowning. "I'm really not a thief."

"You couldn't prove that by me."

She grimaced. "It's not like I have a criminal record or something. What happened was just like an impulse or something. The truck was there. I could see the keys inside. I took it. I figured it served you right for leaving the keys inside."

He nodded, hiding a grin. It was a bad habit he and all of his sons had. Half of Los Piños was aware of their reckless pattern. This was the first time, though, that anyone had taken advantage of them.

"I suppose it did," he admitted.

She shot a look at him. "Does that mean I'm off the hook?"

"Not on your life. Even if I'd gone off and left it sitting wide open with the engine running, it wouldn't give you the right to take what's not yours."

"Oh." She looked more resigned that surprised.

At the end of the lane she started to climb out of the car. "It's awful hot out there," Harlan observed. "Not much shade, either. Why don't I wait? You can sit in the air-conditioning."

She promptly shook her head. "I'll be okay. Mom ought to be here any minute."

"What if she got held up?"

"By what? A traffic jam?" she asked sarcastically.

"Maybe a client," Harlan said.

"Yeah, right."

"You never know."

"Oh, for Pete's sake, if you want to wait, wait." She closed the door, settled back in the seat and folded her arms around her middle, her gaze directed out the passenger window toward town.

"You want to talk about it?" he asked eventually.

"About what?"

"What you saw last night?"

"No," she said succinctly.

Harlan weighed everything he knew about raising kids and decided once more to let it pass for now. Let Janet hash it out with her first. If they couldn't settle it, then he'd step in and try to clarify what that kiss had been about...assuming he had it figured out by then.

"There she is," Jenny announced, flinging open the car door. "See you."

Her quick flight precluded any opportunity for him to exchange so much as a word with Janet. He rolled down his window and managed a wave that was returned halfheartedly before the car backed onto the highway and disappeared from view as quickly as it had come.

He chafed at letting a thirteen-year-old interfere in his life. He figured Janet ought to be mad as hell about it, too, but she seemed to have accepted Jenny's right to stand squarely between her and him.

For the rest of the week he only managed to eke out bits and pieces of information about Janet from her sullen, tight-lipped daughter. He couldn't seem to break the pattern that had been established on Monday. Janet never came any closer than the end of the lane. Her aloof behavior left him rattled and irritable.

He couldn't recall the last time he'd been so fascinated by a woman. It must have been when he'd first met Mary, though. Not once in all the years since then had he ever strayed in thought or deed.

Mary had been a good wife, devoted to a fault. Sometimes he'd almost regretted the way she'd doted on him to the exclusion of their sons. He'd never doubted her love for Luke, Erik, Jordan and Cody, but she'd focused all of her attention on him. He'd felt cherished and, in return, he had made her the center of his life, as well.

Ever since her death, there had been this huge, empty space inside him. And, despite the attempts of his sons to fill the endless hours of the day, he'd been lonely. He hadn't really recognized that until he'd suddenly felt so alive the minute he'd walked into Janet Runningbear's office after that heart-in-his-throat spectacle of her daughter crashing his pickup into a tree. He wasn't going to give up the feeling she stirred in him without a fight.

By Friday he was at his wit's end. He figured the only way to get back on speaking terms with Janet was to get her clear up to the house. And the only way to do that was to see to it Jenny wasn't waiting at the end of that lane for her.

On Friday morning he enlisted Cody's help. "How about taking Jenny with you this afternoon? It's about time she got a real look at. the workings of this place."

If Cody guessed his father's intentions, he didn't let on. "I won't be back until dark," he warned.

"That's okay."

"Won't Janet be expecting to pick her up at five as usual?"

"I'll keep Janet entertained."

Cody grinned. "If you say so. I'll come back for Jenny at lunchtime."

"Thanks, son."

"Don't mention it."

Jenny rode off with Cody just after noon, looking as besotted as if she'd just been granted a date with her favorite movie star. Harlan spent the next few hours catching up on paperwork in his office, then dressed for his meeting with Janet as eagerly as if they were going out on a date. His sons would have laughed their fool heads off if they'd seen him debating what to wear, only to end up in a pin-striped dress shirt with the sleeves rolled up, jeans and his best boots. A pile of discards worse than any Mary had ever left strewn around covered the king-size bed.

Promptly at five he took a pitcher of iced tea, two tall glasses, a bowl of Maritza's *pico de gallo* and some tortilla chips onto the porch. Leaning back in a rocker, his boots propped on the porch railing, he settled back to wait. He wondered how long it would be before Janet guessed that he wasn't bringing Jenny to the end of the lane and resigned herself to driving to the house to pick her up. He figured fifteen minutes.

He was off by five. At ten minutes past five she came flying up the lane, sending up a cloud of dust. She leapt out of the car, her expression half frantic.

"Where's Jenny? Has something happened to her?"

"She's fine," he soothed. "She's off helping Cody this afternoon. She won't be back for a while yet. Come on up and join me."

Janet regarded the tea and tortilla chips suspiciously. "What's all that?"

"Just a little something to tide us over while we wait. Figured you might be thirsty and hungry this time of day."

"Exactly when are you expecting them back?"

"Seven or so."

She stared at him incredulously. "Seven? Why didn't you tell me?"

"I just did," he said, holding out the glass of tea.

Janet ignored it. Hands on hips, she stared him down, practically quivering with indignation. "What kind of game are you playing, Harlan Adams?"

"I could ask you the same question. You've spent the past five days avoiding me. Whose idea was that? Yours or Jenny's?"

She sighed and sank down onto the top step. She finally accepted the glass of tea and took a long swallow. "A little of both, I suppose."

"Shouldn't you have told me?" he said, mimicking her tone.

"I just did," she said, and chuckled. "I'm sorry."

"No need to be sorry. For a pair of grown-ups we are pretty pathetic, aren't we? Seems to me we should be past resorting to games or letting a teenager rule the way we live our lives."

"We should be," Janet concurred. "It's my fault. I should have insisted on bringing Jenny all the way to the house on Monday, but she was still so upset I gave in and dropped her at the end of the lane. After that, it became a pattern, I suppose. I couldn't seem to break it."

"Don't go taking all the blame. I'm the one who put you in an awkward position in the first place." He looked her over, admiring the creamy silk blouse she wore with a pair of tan linen slacks and a few pieces of expensive gold jewelry. She was all class, there was no mistake about that. "You haven't dated much since the divorce, have you?"

"Not at all."

"So Jenny's still very protective. Is she hoping you'll get back together with her father?"

"No, she knows better than that. He doesn't have time for either one of us anymore. I think that's really the problem. She needs all of my attention right now."

Her expression turned speculative. "It may be that she needs all of yours, too. You're providing a father figure for her. Maybe she's not ready to share you."

"But what do you need?" he inquired softly. "Do you need a man in your life?"

She shook her head. "It's not in my plans right now."

He thought of his sons and how hard they'd fought falling in love. In the end, when the right woman came along they hadn't had a choice, any more than he had when he and Mary had met.

"I wasn't aware you could plan for a thing like that," he said.

"You can certainly avoid putting yourself at risk," she countered.

"Is that what you've been doing since you got to Texas, avoiding risks?"

She nodded.

"Must have been a lousy plan, since we met anyway," he observed, grinning. "Or do you suppose fate just had something else in mind?"

"I don't know what to think," she admitted, then gazed at him imploringly. "Harlan, this can't go any further than it already has."

The wistfulness in her voice contradicted the statement and gave him hope. "I think we both know that's not so," he said. "But I'm willing to slow down and take things nice and easy, if that'll give you some peace of mind."

"Why is it that peace of mind is the last thing I feel around you?" she asked plaintively.

He winked at her. "Darlin', I think that's exactly what we're going to find out. Now, why don't you and Jenny stick around for dinner? Let's see if we can't get things on an even keel again."

Janet protested, but she didn't put much *oomph* in it. After seeing her resort to takeout the Sunday before, he could see why. Any meal she didn't have to prepare herself must have seemed like a godsend. Just like any meal he didn't have to eat alone these days was a genuine pleasure for him.

If he had his way about it, there were going to be a whole lot more evenings starting off just like this one.

Chapter Seven

Janet couldn't quite decide whether or not to be irritated at Harlan's high-handedness in sending Jenny
off to work with Cody. She knew he had done it just
so he could end the stalemate she had started following that devastating kiss.

Jenny's shocked reaction had been partly responsible for her retreat, of course. But it was her own
response that had truly shaken her. She wasn't sure
she was ready to deal with a man as strong-willed
and compelling as Harlan Adams, a man who made
her heart pound and her blood sizzle with lust and
temper in equal measure. She resented the fact that
he had forced her into confronting the issue by facing
him again.

Still, once dinner was on the table, her exasperation
dwindled at an astonishing rate. Apparently she could

be bought for a decent meal she didn't have to cook herself. Tender chicken-fried steak, mashed potatoes and gravy, a salad, vegetables—it was heaven.

Jenny wasn't nearly so easily won over. She sat at the dining room table in stubborn silence, glaring from Janet to Harlan and back again. Apparently she had belatedly guessed that the price of her afternoon with Cody was this unwanted reunion. By the end of the meal Janet's nerves were raw from the tension in the room.

"I think we should go," she said the minute they'd finished dessert. The housekeeper had served a chocolate silk pie that had almost inspired Janet to ask for the recipe until she'd reminded herself what a disaster she'd make of it. "I know eating and running is impolite, but we have things we should be doing."

Harlan regarded her with undisguised amusement. "Such as?"

"Homework," she retorted automatically. "Jenny's doing some make-up assignments so she'll be ready to take advanced English in the fall. She fell behind at the end of the term at home."

"Mom, it's Friday night," Jenny protested, then clamped her mouth shut the instant it apparently dawned on her that speaking out might mean staying at White Pines longer.

Janet hid a smile. "I suppose we could stay a little longer," she said, her expression innocent.

Alarm flared in Jenny's eyes. "No, you're right," Jenny contradicted hurriedly. "I should get my homework done. I have a big project due next week. It'll probably take me hours and hours, maybe the whole weekend. I won't get any sleep at all.''

"Sounds like a tough assignment," Harlan agreed. "What is it?"

Jenny looked trapped. "A paper," she finally blurted in a way that said she was ad-libbing as she went along. "On Edgar Allan Poe."

Harlan leaned back. "Ah, yes, Poe. Now there was a writer. Pretty scary stuff, it seemed to me when I read him."

"You read Poe?" Jenny asked in an insulting tone of disbelief that suggested she was surprised to discover that Harlan read at all.

"Poetry, short stories, just about all of it, I suppose," he said, clearly unoffended. "Of course, by today's standards, I suppose he seems pretty tame. Not nearly as graphic as some writers. It always seemed to me there was something to be said for leaving things to the reader's imagination, the way Poe did."

Jenny's expression brightened. "That's what I thought," she said eagerly, then caught herself. "Never mind. You probably don't care about what I think."

Janet's breath caught in her throat as she waited for Harlan's reply. Her ex-husband had never been interested in hearing his daughter's thoughts on much of anything. For the most part, Barry had believed children should be seen and not heard, unless showing Jenny off had had some professional benefit. He'd enjoyed being perceived as an up-and-coming lawyer and proud family man. When Jenny's grades had slipped in direct proportion to the amount of arguing going on at home, he'd lost what little interest he'd ever had in her school days.

For a time, Janet had been fooled by her ex's superficial evidence of concern and pride. Now that she'd observed Harlan Adams for a couple of weeks, especially when Cody was around to banter with him, she had seen what a genuine family was all about. What she and Barry and Jenny had shared had been a mockery of the real thing, more feigned than substantive.

She watched now as Harlan fixed an attentive look on Jenny. That was the gaze Barry had never quite mastered, an expression of real interest. Seeing it warmed Janet through and through and further endangered her already shaky determination to keep Harlan at a distance.

"Of course I'm interested in your opinion," he assured Jenny. "And if you're going to be in an advanced class, you must be pretty smart."

"My teacher in New York said my short stories and essays are really good," Jenny admitted, pride shining in her eyes. "She said I could probably be a writer someday, if I want to be."

"And do you want to be?" Harlan asked.

Jenny nodded, her expression suddenly shy as she revealed a dream that Janet knew she'd shared with almost no one. It was a tribute to the fragile trust flowering between Jenny and Harlan that she was telling him.

Once again, Janet couldn't help thinking that the theft and subsequent accident that had brought Harlan

Adams into their lives was turning out far better than she'd had any right to expect, especially for Jenny. It made her more determined than ever not to do anything to shake the trust the two of them were establishing, even if it cost her a chance with Harlan for herself.

"I'm going to write about Native Americans," Jenny said. "I want to tell all the stories that Lone Wolf told Mom."

"And who was Lone Wolf?"

"He was my great-great-grandfather. He died way before I was born."

Harlan glanced at Janet. "But you spent time with him?"

"Just one summer," she admitted sorrowfully. "My father didn't want me spending time with my Comanche relatives. He said I'd grow up wild and out of control. One year, though, my mother insisted. She sent me to stay with Lone Wolf on the reservation in Oklahoma. It was the best summer of my life."

"Which almost explains why you ended up in Texas when your marriage ended," Harlan said. "Why here and not Oklahoma?"

Janet flushed guiltily and avoided Jenny's knowing gaze. "Because he talked about Texas a lot and the days when our ancestors lived here," she said, leaving it at that.

Harlan didn't appear convinced. "Something tells me there's a lot more to it," he said.

"Not really," she denied. "I'm just following a little girl's dream."

He shrugged, finally accepting her at her word. "Then we'll leave it at that for now," he said.

There was no mistaking the implication that he wouldn't leave the topic alone for long. Janet wondered how well her resolve would stand up to any real grilling by this man with the coaxing eyes and persuasive charm.

And more and more she was wondering whether she'd be able to go on battling the warm feelings he was stirring in her, the kind of feelings she'd vowed never to allow to deceive her again.

Harlan Adams struck her as a complicated man of many passions. She could only guess how well she would fare if she became one of them. For her own sake, as well as Jenny's, she hoped the moment of truth would be a long time coming.

"Maybe you should think about spending the weekend here," Harlan suggested just then, startling her. Her panic must have shown because he quickly added, "I've got a whole library filled with works by Poe. Jenny could do all the research she wants right here."

As generous and innocent-sounding as the offer was, Janet was shaking her head before the words were out of his mouth. "No, really, it's impossible. We're not prepared for an overnight stay."

His gaze settled on her in a provocative way that made her pulse race. "The closet's always filled with extra toothbrushes, if that's what has you worried," he said.

Janet felt her cheeks flame. He knew precisely what had her worried, and it definitely wasn't toothbrushes or the lack of them. "Thanks for the offer, but no," she said firmly.

"Come on back in the morning then," he said.

In giving in more gracefully than she'd expected, he almost left her feeling disappointed. Obviously she needed to work a little on her backbone. It was apparently as limp as an overcooked strand of spaghetti.

"Jenny can do her research and you and I could go riding," he prodded when she remained silent. "You still haven't seen all of White Pines."

Janet felt Jenny's wary gaze on her, but she avoided meeting her daughter's eyes. There were a lot of reasons to accept Harlan's offer, beginning with the chance it would give her to explore the very land that her ancestors had once hunted on. Jenny couldn't fault her for that.

There was also one very big reason to turn him down: he made her stomach do the most amazing flip-flops every single time he looked at her. If he could manage that after a few relatively brief encounters, what kind of havoc could he wreak during a whole day's outing? In private? Without Jenny's watchful gaze on them every minute?

Would there be more of those bone-melting kisses like the one that had thrown her so off stride on Sunday night? Without a doubt. The heated promise was in Harlan's gaze every time he looked at her. Temptation heated her blood. Longing made her heart thump unsteadily. And the combination had her saying yes before she could stop herself.

Once the single affirmative word was out of her mouth, Janet wasn't sure which of the three of them was most stunned. A pleased smile hovered on Harlan's lips. Jenny retreated into sullen silence. And Janet considered whether a steel rod implant was necessary to stiffen her spine to the degree it needed.

"Shall we get an early start?" Harlan inquired. "Or are you one of those people who likes to laze in bed on the weekends?"

There was just enough seductive innuendo in the question to make her voice unsteady when she vowed that she could be there at any hour he liked.

He grinned. "Brave words," he taunted. "I'll give you a break just this once, though. You get here by ten. I'll have Maritza pack us a picnic to take along."

"For three," Jenny said, scowling at her mother. "I want to come, too."

"Thought you had a big paper to do," Harlan said, but his eyes were glinting with amusement at Jenny's obvious ploy to play chaperone once again.

"I'll need a break," she said. "Otherwise, my brain will probably bust."

"Then by all means, you'll come, too," he replied. "Can't have a tragedy like that on my head."

If he was disappointed, he didn't let it show. Clearly, he understood how important it was for Jenny to feel she wouldn't be intruding.

For that, Janet decided, he would always have her gratitude. And, if he kept up the sweet gestures and the blatant provocation, he might very well wind up with her heart after all. Only time would tell just how terrible or incredible that fate might be.

Janet Runningbear was skittish as a brand-new colt, Harlan decided midway through their ride on Saturday. He'd never met a woman so determined to avoid being alone with a man.

Of course, Jenny was playing right into her mother's hands by acting like the overprotective adult, rather than the other way around. He might have found it amusing and rather gratifying, if it hadn't been so blasted frustrating.

He wanted to get to know this woman, but whenever he steered the conversation in a personal direction, she scooted it onto some other topic faster than a tornado could rip apart a house. He supposed for the first time in his life he was going to have to learn to be patient. His usual habit of making quick decisions and acting on them wasn't going to work with Janet. If he pushed too hard, he knew right now he'd scare her out of his life entirely.

He kept a close eye on her as they rode. She handled herself well in the saddle. Clearly, this wasn't her first ride on horseback. She didn't bat an eye when he picked up the pace. In fact, she shot him a daring look, dug in her heels and sent the mare he'd chosen for her into a flat-out gallop.

Laughing, Harlan didn't even try to keep up. He was enjoying the view from behind too much. She was leaning low over the horse's back. Her long black hair was caught up in a single, severe braid, but tendrils had escaped to curl defiantly along the back of her elegant, exposed neck. A longing to press a hot, lingering kiss to that bare skin washed through him with the ferocity of a summer storm, stunning him with its intensity.

She slowed after a bit, letting him and Jenny catch up.

"Where'd you learn to ride like that?" he asked. "Not in Central Park, I'll bet."

"Jeez, Mom, you never said you'd been on a horse before," Jenny said, looking a little awestruck.

"I learned in Oklahoma that summer. It all came back to me. I remembered how it felt to have the wind in my face. It's exhilarating."

"It shows," Harlan said quietly, his gaze locked with hers. "You've got some color in your cheeks for a change and your eyes are sparkling."

Jenny shot him a suspicious frown, as if not quite certain whether he was making another pass at her mother right under her eyes.

"It's the God's truth," Harlan insisted with a touch of defiance. "Jenny, take a good look at your mom. Have you ever seen her look so happy?"

Apparently by drawing Jenny into the appraisal of Janet's appearance, he managed to allay her fears. She studied her mother, then nodded. "You do look spectacular, Mom. You should do this more."

"Anytime," Harlan said quickly, capitalizing on the small, inadvertent opening. "No need even to call first. If I'm not around, just leave me a note in the barn or let Maritza know you're taking one of the horses out."

"Thank you," she said, rubbing the mare's neck. "I may take you up on the offer. This has been incredible."

Harlan locked gazes with her once more, refusing

to break eye contact as he said, "And it's just the beginning."

Janet swallowed hard under his intense scrutiny. He enjoyed the knowledge that she was responding to him despite whatever reservations she might have. He was finally reassured that this attraction he'd been feeling from the beginning was returned, albeit with great reluctance.

"Come on, you two. I know the perfect spot for our picnic. It's about a mile ahead."

They ambled along at a comfortable pace for the next few minutes, picking their way through a denser stand of trees until they emerged on the shaded bank of a creek. It was too late in the season for the blue-bonnets that usually dotted the area, but it was a tranquil, lovely setting just the same. Harlan had always enjoyed coming here when he needed to ponder some puzzle in his life. The serenity seemed to clear his head.

It was also a romantic spot for a picnic. He and Mary had stolen away here a time or two before she'd decided picnics were for youngsters and they needed more sedate and elegant entertainment. He'd always regretted that they no longer shared this spot and the simplicity of the hours they had once spent here.

He kept a close eye on Janet to gauge her reaction. A soft smile lit her face as she took in her surroundings. She sighed then with what looked to be sheer pleasure.

"Lone Wolf used to tell me about incredibly beautiful places just like this," she murmured, lifting her eyes to meet his again. "I dreamed of finding one. Thank you for bringing us here."

As if she sensed that the undercurrents between her mother and Harlan were getting too provocative and too intense, Jenny cut in. "I don't see what's so special. It's just a dumb old creek. I saw the Atlantic Ocean a couple of times when Mom and Dad actually stopped working long enough to take me. Now that's impressive," she said, shooting a defiant look in his direction.

He grinned at her, refusing to take offense. "It is something, isn't it? But appreciating the magnificence of one doesn't mean you can't recognize the beauty of the other. That would be like saying if you like Monet, you can't like Grandma Moses. Or if you enjoy Bach, it's not possible to appreciate the Beatles."

He pointedly fixed his gaze on Janet when he added, "Seems to me the more experiences you open your heart to, the richer your life will be."

Color rose in her cheeks as his implication sank in. Satisfied that she'd gotten his message, he nodded and busied himself with taking the picnic from the packs Maritza had prepared. He handed Janet a red-checked tablecloth.

"You pick the spot for that," he suggested, then watched as she headed unerringly for his favorite place beneath an old cottonwood. It was the exact spot where he often sat, his back braced against the trunk of the tree as he waited for the sun to set and his tangled thoughts to unravel. He'd come a lot after Mary's death, hoping for understanding and acceptance of the tragedy that had taken her.

Today, for the first time, with Janet and Jenny by his side, he thought maybe he'd found the reason for God's choice. One door in his life had closed and another had opened. He couldn't help wondering with a sense of tremendous anticipation what awaited him on this new adventure.

"You suddenly seem very far away," Janet said quietly as she came to stand beside him.

Harlan noticed that Jenny had already stripped off her shoes and socks and was wading in the creek. For the moment he and Janet had a bit of privacy. He lifted his hand to her cheek in a light caress.

"No more," he murmured. "Now I'm right here, with you."

Worry darkened her eyes at once. "Harlan—"

He touched a finger to her lips. "Shh. For once, don't argue. Let's just see where this takes us. No promises. No commitments. No guarantees. Just be open to the possibilities. Can you do that?"

He felt her tremble beneath his touch, felt her skin heat and saw the glitter of excitement in her eyes. A sigh hovered on her lips before she finally nodded.

"I can try," she agreed, looking anything but certain even as she spoke.

"That's all anyone can ask." He glanced toward the bank of the creek and saw that Jenny was still in view, even though she had her back to them for the moment.

He dropped his voice even lower. "I want very much to kiss you." He allowed the thought to linger between them, allowed the color to climb in her cheeks and the anticipation to shine in her eyes before adding, "But I won't. Not with Jenny so close by again."

It might have been his imagination or wishful thinking, but he thought he detected disappointment shadowing the depths of her eyes even as she murmured her thanks.

He grinned. "That doesn't mean I can't tell you what I think kissing you would be like. Your mouth is soft as a rose petal, Janet Runningbear, and your breath is just as sweet. I love the way your eyes darken when my mouth is this close to yours," he said, leaning down to within a hairbreadth of her lips, then retreating almost at once. This time he heard the shock of her indrawn breath and knew, absolutely knew, that what he saw in her eyes was disappointment.

He ran his thumb along her lower lip. "There will be other times," he assured her. "Private times."

He released her then, amused that she stood as if his hands were still on her, quiet and shaken. He hoped his own emotions weren't half so apparent. One thing for sure, he wasn't half as frightened of what the future might hold as she appeared to be. For the first time since they'd met, she seemed truly vulnerable.

For the life of him, he couldn't decide if that was good or bad. Until he could figure it out, he settled for taming the electricity arcing through the air so they could get through the rest of the day without giving Jenny something more to fret about.

He winked at her. "Come on, woman. Why are you standing there? We've got fried chicken and potato salad and coleslaw to serve up. You must be starving after that ride.''

She visibly shook off the uncertainties that had held her still. ''You're right. I am famished.'' She scanned the creek bank until she found Jenny, then called her, just a hint of desperation in her voice. ''Come on, sweetie. Lunch is ready.''

Harlan settled himself in his favorite position against the tree and listened to Janet and Jenny chatter through lunch. If there was a nervous edge to the conversation, he chalked it up to the electricity that his best effort had failed to diffuse. For better or worse, the attraction humming between Janet and him was powerful stuff. It needed only a chance look, a casual touch, to set it off.

''Is the creek deep enough to swim in?'' Jenny asked after they'd eaten. ''I wore my suit under my jeans.''

''How'd you know about the creek and guess we'd be coming here?'' Harlan asked, more amused than ever by her earlier grudging comparison of the creek to the ocean.

''Cody showed me,'' she said, shrugging, her expression all innocence. ''He said it was your favorite place. When you invited Mom to go riding, I knew you'd end up here.''

That explained the swimsuit and her earlier derisive reaction. The creek had probably looked much more interesting when she'd been here with Cody, Harlan decided. It also explained her determination to come along today. She hadn't wanted her mother alone with him in such a romantic setting.

"Can I go in the water, Mom?"

"Not right after lunch," Janet said at once.

"She'll be fine," Harlan said. "The creek's only waist high at its deepest."

Janet still seemed uneasy—about the swim or being left alone with him, it was hard to tell—but she gave permission.

"You could go in, too," Harlan said when Jenny had run off.

"I didn't wear my suit," she said.

"That's not a problem. Strip down over behind those trees. I won't peek. Cross my heart."

"Yeah, right," she said, amusement making her eyes sparkle.

Harlan's pulse bucked like a bronco. She looked ten years younger all of a sudden. That was the way of flirting, he decided. It lifted spirits and drained away problems, at least for a moment in time. It brought back that starry-eyed anticipation that regrettably seemed to fade once youth had passed by.

"If it's all the same to you, I'll stay right here, where it's safe," she said.

"Darlin', if you think it's safe here with me, your judgment has more problems than that old car of yours."

To his surprise, she grinned. "But you're an honorable man and you've already promised that absolutely nothing will happen as long as Jenny is around."

"That promise didn't allow for the temptation factor. You keep taunting me and I can't be responsible for my actions."

"Then by all means, let's change the subject. Tell me about White Pines."

He leaned back against the tree and linked his hands behind his head just to keep himself from reaching for her.

"It's been in my family since the time of the Civil War," he said, thinking back to all the history that Mary had loved so deeply. She'd been far more fascinated by the Adams legacy than he had been. He'd just loved the land and ranching. It was as deeply ingrained in his blood as whatever DNA there was to identify him.

"That's how it got its name," he continued. "My ancestors moved here from the South and called it White Pines, just like the plantation that had been burned to the ground by Yankee soldiers. Texas seemed like a land of opportunity back then, I suppose. They came here with very little, but with grit and determination the next generations added to that beginning until it became what you see today. The Mexican settlers in the area named the town Los Piños after the ranch, which provided work for so many of the families."

At some point as he talked, a change came over Janet's face. Suddenly she was more aloof than ever and a kind of seething resentment burned in her eyes.

"Is something wrong?" he asked, thoroughly bemused by the change in her.

"Not really," she said, and stood, brushing off her jeans.

The innocent gesture drew attention to her shapely rear end and had Harlan's blood sizzling like an adolescent boy's. But he was too puzzled by the abrupt change in her demeanor to enjoy his reaction for very long.

"Janet?"

"We'd better be getting back."

"You'll stay for supper," he said, making it more a matter-of-fact statement than a question.

She hesitated for just an instant, clearly wrestling with indecision, her expression uncertain, then shook her head. "No. That wouldn't be a good idea."

"Why?"

"It just wouldn't, that's all. We've taken up too much of your time as it is."

Harlan frowned. "What the devil is that supposed to mean?"

"Forget it," she muttered. With that, she bolted in the direction of where Jenny was swimming in the creek. "Jenny, come on now, sweetie. It's time to go."

Janet's strange mood lasted all the way back to the house. For the life of him, Harlan couldn't figure out what had gone wrong. One thing was certain, though. Janet was far more of a mystery than the woman who'd been his mate for more than thirty-five years.

She was strong, as Mary had been. But she was also fiercely independent, burned by what he could only guess had been a lousy childhood and an even lousier marriage. There were apparently other dark secrets he hadn't even begun to discover.

Whatever those secrets might be, he had the feeling her heart had turned to ice in the process. Knowing that might have discouraged some men, but not him. He had a hunch that melting it was going to be downright interesting.

Chapter Eight

No amount of persuading had been able to convince Janet and Jenny to stay for supper on Saturday or to return on Sunday. Harlan decided he must be losing his touch. He thought he'd tried some very inventive arguments, along with a little subtle flirting and a few dares. There had been a brief spark in Janet's eyes at one point, but she'd still managed to decline the invitation, albeit with a satisfyingly obvious hint of regret in her voice.

Watching them leave, he resigned himself to waiting impatiently for Monday morning when Janet would return to drop off Jenny. Maybe then Jenny would be able to shed some light on her mother's abrupt shift in mood.

In the meantime, the hours stretched out ahead of him, promising nothing but tedium. Now that he was starting to feel alive again, he was even less tolerant of the prospect than he had once been.

Short of booting Cody out of his position as ranch manager, he wasn't sure what to do about it. Los Piños was too small a town to need an influential citizen meddling in its affairs. State or national politics had never intrigued him. In fact, the only things that had ever mattered to him were his family and the ranch.

After church on Sunday, he spent most of the remainder of the morning wandering through all the empty rooms at White Pines, trying to remember the days when his sons had made the kind of racket that drove Mary nuts, trying to imagine the big old house echoing with laughter once again.

Jenny's presence lately had given him a delightful hint of what it might be like, at least when she let down her guard long enough to act like a regular thirteen-year-old. Occasionally she and some of Maritza's younger relations would whoop it up in the kitchen, usually when she counted on him being out of earshot. The joyous sound, when he happened to catch it, brightened his day.

Now, though, he tried to picture the generations before him, who had built the ranch into a thriving enterprise. He knew almost nothing about those early days beyond the scant information he'd shared with Janet. Mary had always been exasperated with him for caring so little about the past. He'd been more concerned with the future, with making White Pines into a legacy for his sons and their children.

Ironically, only Cody had really cared about his heritage. Ranching was in his blood, just as it had been in Harlan's. Luke had loved ranching well enough, but he'd had a milewide independent streak that pushed him into starting up his own place, not just as proof that he could succeed at it, but to best his father. Cody had the same goal, it seemed to him. He was just more willing to fight Harlan one-on-one, on his home turf. He seemed to thrive on the war of wills.

Jordan and Erik hadn't been interested in White Pines or ranching at all. In fact, it had been attempts to force Erik into a life that was never right for him that had ultimately led to his death. Riding a tractor one day at Luke's, he'd gotten careless. The tractor had rolled over on him and killed him, leaving Jessie a widow and expecting his child.

Ultimately, Luke had claimed both mother and child, a beautiful Christmas baby named Angela. As happy as they were, Harlan wondered sometimes if they'd ever forget the cost at which that happiness had come.

With Jordan in the oil business and living at the ranch that had belonged to his wife Kelly's family, now only Cody and Melissa and their kids remained at White Pines. Even they, however, lived in their own home, rather than in one of the suites that had been created to house new generations at a time when Harlan had imagined spending his golden years surrounded by family. They were close by, but not nearly close enough to keep him from rattling around in these lonely old rooms.

Only a few hours after his uncommon bout of self-pity, Harlan cursed himself for regretting the lack of company. It just proved that a man should be careful what he wished for.

Cody and Melissa arrived on his doorstep first with their kids, Sharon Lynn and Harlan Patrick. He could tell right off this was no drop-by visit for a quick hello. They seemed ready to settle down for a bit. They'd brought along enough paraphernalia for the kids to entertain them until nightfall.

Luke and Jessie were hard on their heels with precious, sweet-faced Angela. Jordan and Kelly turned up within minutes after that with Dani and Justin James. It was a conspiracy, no doubt about that. He didn't believe for a second they'd all shown up just to get a decent meal from Maritza.

Apparently his housekeeper had known they were coming, though. He noticed that she'd set places for every traitorous one of them at his table.

"So, Daddy, anything interesting going on around here?" Luke inquired after Maritza had served a prime rib big enough to feed an expected crowd, but far too big to pass off as something she'd prepared just for one. Not even his impudent housekeeper was brazen enough to suggest she was having to stretch the lavish spread of food to accommodate unexpected guests.

"Other than the lot of you showing up to beg a meal?" he retorted. "Not a thing."

"Have you met the new lawyer in town?" Jordan inquired with a perfectly straight face. "What's her name? Janet Runningbear? I've spotted her a couple of times myself. She's gorgeous. You thought so, too, didn't you, Cody?"

Harlan scowled at Cody and Melissa, who were looking about as innocent as a couple of tattletales could. If he'd had any doubts about his youngest son having the biggest mouth in the family, his proof was sitting around his dining room table right now.

It was obvious Luke and Jessie and Jordan and Kelly knew every last detail of his fledgling fascination with Janet Runningbear. They'd probably been told the second Cody had finished listening to all of his confessions about that night in Janet's kitchen. That poker game at Rosa's hadn't helped. What Cody hadn't blabbed himself, Rosa had.

"We've met," he admitted tersely, trying hard to avoid making the kind of revelations that would invite more taunting.

Cody chuckled, then covered his face with a napkin to hide his smile.

"Damn your hide, boy," Harlan said to his youngest. "You got any control whatsoever over that mouth of yours?"

"I can't imagine what you mean," Cody declared, feigning a hurt expression that was about as believable as the ones he'd worn on his chocolate-streaked face when he'd sworn he'd never been near the cookie jar.

"If anyone's to blame, it's you," Cody added, trying to pass on the guilt. "You're the one who made a spectacle of yourself at Rosa's. It was the hottest story on the Los Piños grapevine for a solid week. Mule filled in any gap Rosa left in the story. Seemed to enjoy it, too. All I did was confirm a few facts, when asked directly."

"It was a poker game, not a spectacle," Harlan retorted defensively. "Playing cards wasn't a crime last time I checked."

"From what I heard, poker wasn't exactly the only game being played that afternoon," Jordan chimed in with a wicked grin.

Harlan resigned himself to sitting back and taking whatever they were of a mind to dish out. To his surprise, though, he found an unexpected ally in Jessie. She reached over and patted his hand.

"I think all of you should leave your father alone," she protested to the others, a twinkle in her blue eyes. "He obviously doesn't require your meddling in order to have a social life."

All three of his sons hooted. "Meddling?" Luke said to his wife. "You call this meddling? This is child's play compared to what he put all of us through. You and me included, in case you've forgotten."

"I still think you should leave him alone," Jessie repeated firmly.

"Thank you," Harlan said. "But I think you're wasting your breath with this band of hooligans."

"I still have a little influence with one of them," she said, shooting a pointed look at Luke, who was seated on her other side.

"Right," Jordan said. "And I suppose those bags you toted upstairs a little while ago don't indicate that you and Lucas intend to stay right here until morning, just so you can catch a glimpse of Janet Runningbear and her daughter. I'd be happy to describe her, if you'd like to turn right around and go back home.

Tall, slender, mid-thirties, long black hair. Is that what you were wondering about?''

"It's a start," Luke confirmed.

This was definitely a turn of events Harlan hadn't counted on. Janet was skittish enough around him without having to face his whole darn family. He scowled at Luke. "You're staying?"

"Just till dawn," he said with a grin. "I'd hate to make that long drive back tonight. I might fall asleep at the wheel. Besides, you don't get to see nearly enough of Angela. She misses her granddaddy. Isn't that right, sweet pea?"

The toddler dutifully scrambled off her chair and ran around to be picked up so she could deliver sticky kisses to Harlan's face. "Miss you, grandda," she asserted enthusiastically.

"Did you coach her to do that, just so I wouldn't toss you out on your ear?" Harlan grumbled.

Jordan glanced across the table at his wife. "Maybe we should stick around, too. What do you think?"

"I think Luke is perfectly capable of tormenting your father without any help from you," Kelly retorted.

"Thank you," Harlan said to her.

"But I want to stay," Dani protested. The seven-year-old's expression turned wily. "I can help baby sit Angela. Aunt Jessie says I'm really, really good."

"Oh, for goodness' sake, the whole darn lot of you might as well move back in," Harlan declared.

"Don't tempt us, Daddy," Luke advised. "We just might do it, at least until we see where things between you and Janet Runningbear are heading. By the way, have you been locking up all the cars now that her daughter's around here all the time?''

Harlan groaned. He'd always wanted a tight-knit family. He'd always done his darnedest to make his sons feel welcome at White Pines, even after they'd gone on to lives of their own. It appeared he was going to live to regret not booting them all into another state. For the second time in a little more than an hour, he reminded himself to be very, very careful what he wished for in the future.

Janet took one look at the assembled members of Harlan Adams's family as she drove up to the house on Monday and very nearly turned tail and ran. She didn't have a doubt in the world that she and Jenny were the main attraction that had drawn them onto the porch at daybreak. All of the family, she guessed from the size of the gathering, right down to the youngest grandchild. Even her intrepid daughter seemed a little awed by all the attention riveted on them.

"Who are all those people and why are they staring at us?" Jenny asked, regarding the bunch of them warily.

"Now you know how Custer must have felt when he made his last stand," Janet said dryly, then added, "My guess is they're all here to try to figure out if we have designs on their father."

"You mean like wanting to marry him or something?" Jenny asked, astonishment written all over her face.

"That would be my guess," Janet confirmed.

Jenny's mouth gaped. "You don't, do you?"

"I don't," Janet said emphatically.

She wished she could speak with as much certainty about Harlan's intentions. He was the first man in aeons who wasn't the least bit put off by her prickly, independent nature. Even after she'd turned moody on him on Saturday, he'd remained flirtatious and placid.

In fact, if anything, the glint in his eyes burned even brighter in the face of her contrariness. He wanted her and that, in his opinion, was that. He clearly thought it was just a matter of time until he got his way.

Apparently his sons thought as much, too, or they wouldn't be here this morning trying to check out the woman who'd caught their father's eye.

"Go on and hop out," she advised Jenny.

"You're going to leave me here alone with *them?*" her daughter protested, clearly aghast at the prospect. "I don't think so."

"Jenny, I'm sure they're all very nice people."

"Then why are you running away?"

"Because they obviously have an agenda I don't want to deal with," she said.

She cast a quick look to see if she could turn her car around in this unoccupied corner of the driveway or if she was going to be forced to circle all the way around in front of the house, in front of all those fascinated, prying eyes.

Jenny folded her arms over her chest and lifted her chin. Defiance radiated from every pore. "I am not getting out of this car without you."

"Sweetie, please," she implored.

"No way."

"You'll embarrass Harlan."

"And your taking off won't?" Jenny flung back. "Get real, Mom. They're here to check you out even more than me. Maybe you should prepare a little speech denying any interest in Mr. Adams. Maybe then they'd go away."

Janet sighed and threw the car into park and shut off the engine. "Traitor," she muttered at her daughter.

"Don't blame me. Blame Mr. Adams."

Janet glanced in Harlan's direction. He looked every bit as miserable as she felt. "I seriously doubt that this was his idea of a good time," she observed.

"Then he should have kicked them out," Jenny retorted. "If he can't control his own kids, how come you think he's such a good influence on me?"

"It's hardly the same," Janet replied.

"I don't see why. If I'm going to turn out all nosy like them, I'd think you'd want to get me away from here as fast as you could."

Before Janet could come up with an adequate answer for that, Harlan was opening her door.

"I'm sorry," he said in a hushed tone. "I didn't know they were coming yesterday and I sure as hell didn't know they were staying. I couldn't shake 'em out of here to save my soul. I thought about starving them out, but my housekeeper would have fed them behind my back, I'm sure."

His genuine discomfort relieved some of her own

tension. "Jenny thinks you have a serious inability to control your own kids."

He grinned. "I couldn't have said it better myself. I'm still not sure where I went wrong." He held out his hand to her. "Come on. We might as well get this over with. Give it five minutes and you can swear you have a major client coming and that you have to get to town."

She suddenly found his desire to be rid of her in such a hurry a little insulting. "Are you afraid to let them spend too much time with me?" she asked irritably.

His mouth gaped. "With you? Are you crazy? I'm scared silly you'll take one look at the lot of them and never show your face around here again."

She grinned at his adamant tone. "I'm made of tougher stuff than that," she declared. "So is Jenny." She leaned back in. "Out, young lady."

Jenny rolled her eyes. "Oh, all right. But I'm not playing cute for anybody, okay?"

"There was little doubt of that," Janet said dryly, exchanging a pointed look with Harlan, who looked as if he wanted very badly to burst out laughing.

As they approached the porch, three young women came down the steps to meet them.

"Hi, I'm Jessie," the first one said. "We're sorry about all of this, but there's no controlling these guys when they get together to harass their father. We couldn't have gotten them out of here last night if we'd set off a canister of pepper spray in the house. Believe me, I thought about it. So did Kelly and Melissa."

"I even had one in my purse," Kelly said. "I bought it when I lived in Houston. Never had a need for it there, thank goodness, but I thought it might come in handy here last night."

"Too many babies, though," Melissa added. "I'm talking about the ones in cribs, not the ones we're married to. You'd think they hadn't learned to share, the way they've been carrying on about meeting the woman who's stealing their daddy's affection."

Janet warmed to the trio of smiling women immediately. They clearly understood what it meant to hook up with an Adams man. "Believe me, I am not out to steal their daddy's affection or anything else, for that matter."

"It's not entirely up to you," Jessie declared with the kind of clear-thinking logic that cut straight to the heart of Janet's dilemma. "Our husbands may be the stubbornnest set of men in Texas. Not a one of them knows how to take no for an answer. Who do you guess they learned that from?"

"Hey," Harlan protested. "Watch your tongue."

"It's true, Harlan, and you know it," Kelly and Melissa chimed in, laughing at his disgruntled expression.

Janet considered the teasing comments to be very discouraging news. Apparently Harlan detected her discomfort, because he slipped her arm through his.

"Come on," he said. "We might as well get the rest of this over with. Ladies, go tell your husbands to be on their best behavior."

"Don't expect us to accomplish what you couldn't," Kelly teased.

Jenny rolled her eyes. "I told you, Mom."

Harlan glanced at her. "What did you tell your mother?"

"That you must not be half so tough as you try to pretend, if your sons walk all over you."

The sons in question hooted at that.

"Guess she has you pegged, doesn't she, Daddy?" Cody taunted.

"If her mama's half as smart, you're in for it," Jordan agreed, grinning at Janet as he shook her hand.

Luke crowded in next, a sympathetic glimmer in his eyes. "Don't let all the fuss scare you to death. We're not half as intimidating as we sound."

"A bunch of soft touches?" Janet asked doubtfully.

He nodded. "And Daddy's the easiest of all."

"You start giving away all my secrets and that prize bull of mine you want to breed next year won't get anywhere near those cows of yours," Harlan warned.

Luke held up his hands and backed off. "Not another word," he vowed.

The teasing went on for another ten minutes, though, as the three oldest grandchildren raced around the yard. Jenny seemed thoroughly bemused by all the commotion. It made Janet wonder whether she'd been so wrong to insist to Barry that she wanted no more children. Left unspoken had been the fact that she didn't want them with him. Within months of Jenny's birth, she had already sensed that their marriage wasn't going to last the distance. It had taken her more than twelve years to finally cut the ties.

When Melissa shoved a baby into her arms, so she could chase after her daughter who was vanishing around the side of the house, Janet felt a stirring of maternal instinct that was so overwhelming it brought tears to her eyes. She quickly handed the baby over to Jessie, who was standing nearby.

"I have to get to work," she announced to no one in particular.

Harlan was at her side in a heartbeat. "We'll talk later," he said as he walked with her to her car. "I'll come up with some way to apologize for all this."

"It's not like you threw me into a den of starving wolves," she reminded him. "It wasn't that bad. They're nice people, all of them. And they clearly love you and worry about you."

He grinned at that. "Do I look like a man who needs people fussing over him?"

She couldn't help smiling at that. "I doubt they see you the same way I do," she said.

"Oh, really," he said, sounding absolutely fascinated all of a sudden. "And how do you see me?"

"Never mind. Your ego's big enough as it is," she said, and closed the car door in his face.

"We'll finish this discussion tonight," he shouted as she drove away.

The challenge in his voice and the gleam in his eyes stayed with her the rest of the day. At least a dozen times, as she talked with the few potential clients who called, an image of Harlan's face popped into her head. His strength and compassion, along with that taunting, unmistakable desire, kept her from regretting the day she'd moved to Texas.

Too many of the calls were from people only interested in hiring her if she'd work free, or from people with ugly accusations to make about her being an uppity Indian. She found the atmosphere of bias and distrust both discouraging and infuriating.

By the time she returned to White Pines to pick up Jenny, she had a thundering headache and a chip on her shoulder the size of a longhorn. The sight of Harlan waiting on the porch for her, a pitcher of tea ready, along with more of Maritza's culinary treats, brought tears to her eyes. She lingered in the car for a moment for fear he'd see how despondent she was and try to jump in and fix things for her. After a day like the one she'd just had, it would be too easy simply to let him.

Even though she'd taken the time to gather her composure, Harlan wasn't fooled. He took one look at her and reached out to gather her into his arms. She hesitated only an instant before accepting the comfort he offered.

"Bad day?" he asked.

"Is it that obvious?"

"To me, it is. Want to talk about it?"

She wrapped her arms a little tighter around his waist and rested her head on his chest. "No, but this is nice."

Too nice, she reminded herself sternly. Too easy. It was a dangerous trap. With a sigh, she pulled away. "Thanks."

"You could stay right where you are," he said. "These are mighty broad shoulders. Might as well make use of 'em, if you've got troubles."

''Nothing I can't handle,'' she said, and forced herself to step away from what he was offering.

When she would have turned away, his voice stopped her.

''Janet?'' he said in little more than a whisper.

She lifted her gaze to his and felt her heart skip a beat at the blazing heat in his eyes. She swallowed hard. ''Yes?''

''Jenny's off with Cody again. They're going to be a while. Care to take a chance on another kiss?''

She almost wished he hadn't asked at all, that he'd just swept her back into his arms without giving her any say in the matter. But she couldn't deny that a part of her was glad he'd reassured her of Jenny's whereabouts first.

''I can't,'' she protested halfheartedly, even as she swayed toward him.

He stroked a finger along her cheek. ''Talk about mixed messages, darlin'.''

She shook her head ruefully. ''I know. I'm pitiful.''

''Never pitiful,'' he argued. ''Strong, sassy, impossible, maybe, but never pitiful.''

His touch on her face lingered. There were a hundred questions in his eyes, but only one that really mattered: had she meant yes or no? Both, depending on whether he asked her head or her heart, she decided.

And just this once she was going with her heart. She stood on tiptoe to lift her lips to his. Her touch was tentative, but it was all it took to set passion blazing. So much tenderness. So much heat, she thought as he held her head still and plundered her mouth.

The rightness of it stunned her. He was everything she'd once been taught to hate by Lone Wolf—a Texan and a rancher. And yet, in his arms, as she was right now, she felt at home. At peace.

At least that was how she felt deep in her heart. Her head was another matter entirely. She had a hunch that struggle was far from over.

Chapter Nine

"Hot," Janet murmured eventually, backing away from Harlan as if he were a stove and she'd been standing over it too long. If she'd owned a hankie and it wouldn't have been a dead giveaway of how affected she was by his touch, she would have patted her brow with it.

"I'll say," he agreed, his eyes twinkling with amusement.

"I was referring to the temperature," she insisted as embarrassment made her face flush even hotter. At this rate she'd wind up as a little puddle of mortified genes right at his feet.

"Of course you were," he said perfectly innocently. "So was I."

"The weather, dammit!"

He nodded. "If you say so."

She turned her back on him and headed across the porch, trying not to mutter out loud about his impudence. On the way, she grabbed a glass of iced tea and held it against her feverish brow.

This attraction was getting out of hand. She was slipping into a pattern that had all the earmarks of surrender. It would be just her luck that she'd fall head-over-heels in love with Harlan Adams and then he'd discover that she was out to find a way to reclaim some of his land for the Comanches. He'd blow a gasket, blow her off, and they'd both wind up being hurt and feeling used.

She heard his booted footsteps as he crossed the porch to join her. He was moving slowly, almost as if he wanted to give her time to prepare. By the time he paused beside her, her nerves were jittery all over again. Damn, why did it have to be this particular man who made her feel like a whole, vibrant, sexy woman again?

"You still wrestling with yourself?" he inquired in that lazy tone that raised goose bumps up and down her spine.

"Wrestling, hell," she admitted. "It's all-out war."

He chuckled at that. "Good."

"You don't have to sound so complacent about it."

"Sure I do. That's the nature of an Adams man."

Despite herself, she laughed and shifted until she could look into his eyes. "Big egos, huh?"

"I prefer to think of it as self-confidence."

"You would. Arrogance by any other name is still a flaw, Harlan."

"I'm entitled to one serious defect, don't you think?"

She held back another urge to laugh. "Just one? That's all you're admitting to?"

"I'm not a fool, darlin'. I'm not admitting to a single one you haven't already discovered. You're searching so hard for more, I'd hate to spoil your fun."

"How altruistic," she retorted sourly, wondering when she'd become so transparent. Or was it just that Harlan had an innate knack for reading her, a knack that stemmed from fascination and concentration? Few men had ever studied her quite so intently, that's for sure. Barry had never even scratched the surface of her emotions. She couldn't decide whether to feel flattered or cornered that Harlan could.

He settled himself onto the porch railing, then pulled her between his thighs. She didn't even have the strength of will to resist.

The provocative position, the glitter of desire in his eyes, sent shivers of pure longing dancing through her. As dangerous as the reaction was, she couldn't have pulled back if her life depended on it.

He kept his hands loosely settled on her hips as if to convey she was free to go, if she chose...if she could.

"Your skin turns to fire when you're close to me like this," he observed.

"How polite of you to point it out," she said, but without nearly as much venom as she should have mustered. Besides, it was true. That was what had forced her away from him only moments before.

"Why does that bother you so much?" he asked. "Men and women have been attracted to each other from the beginning of time. It's natural."

"Sometimes the attraction's to the wrong person."

"You think I'm wrong for you?"

She nodded. "And I'm just as wrong for you."

"Why?"

She sighed, unwilling to spell it all out for him. "It's complicated. You'll just have to take my word for it."

Drawing in a deep breath, she leveled a serious look straight into his blue eyes. "If you can't, I'll have to stop coming around. I'll keep Jenny away, too. We'll find another way to pay for the repairs to your truck. I'll work it out with Mule."

"Your debt's not with Mule. It's with me," he insisted stubbornly.

"He's making the repairs, isn't he?"

"Forget the blasted bill," he said, his exasperation apparent in his tone. He lifted her aside and stood. "Your daughter stole my truck. I didn't call the sheriff because you agreed to let her work off the debt out here."

She stiffened at the reminder. "I wonder how the sheriff would feel about your taking the law into your own hands, devising your own brand of justice?"

He scowled at her. "You want to test him and find out?"

Janet had a feeling that—laws or no laws—he knew the justice system in Los Piños and could manipulate it far better than she ever could with her legal expertise and law school degree.

"Why are you making this so difficult?" she snapped. "Hasn't anyone ever turned you down before?"

A ghost of a smile played around his lips. "Haven't asked anyone until you came along, not for more than thirty-five years."

That sucked the wind right out of her sails. She reached up impulsively and placed her hand against his cheek. "Harlan Adams, you don't play fair."

"That's right, darlin'. I play to win."

Before she could reply to that, his mouth was moving over hers again, coaxing, persuading, claiming.

It was a hell of a kiss by anyone's standards. By Janet's, it was devastating. A bone-melting, breath-stealing crack of thunder deep inside her. It raised goose bumps from head to toe and had the hair on the back of her neck raised on end.

"I think I'd better be going," she murmured when it was over. As badly as she wanted to sound serene and unfazed, she couldn't seem to get her voice above a shaken whisper. She glanced around anxiously, trying to spot the purse she'd dropped somewhere.

"Without Jenny?" he inquired, laughter dancing in his eyes.

"Oh," she murmured. "No, of course not." She drew in a deep, supposedly calming breath. It didn't help a whit.

"How soon will she and Cody be back?" she asked a little desperately.

"Not for a while," he reported complacently. "You might as well settle back and relax."

Relax? It would take an entire bottle of tranquilizers to get her to relax as long as Harlan was in the vicinity. She didn't have so much as a single pill to her name. She sipped at the only available distraction, her iced tea, but it didn't go far in terms of settling her nerves or soothing the thirst that kiss had aroused.

"You look as if you could use a nice, cool shower," Harlan said after a bit.

Her head snapped up. "What?"

"A cool shower," he prompted, grinning. "Alone, if that's the way you prefer."

"Here?" she asked incredulously.

"Why not? It's a big house. There are lots of bathrooms. If I'd put in that pool the boys were always plaguing me to, I'd suggest that, but a shower is all I have to offer."

The offer might have been part generosity, part seduction, but Janet was intrigued just the same. Maybe an ice-cold shower would get her through the wait, she decided thoughtfully. It would wash away some of the hot day's dust and cleanse her wicked thoughts at the same time.

And maybe not. She weighed just how far she could trust Harlan to stay right here where he was, rather than following her inside.

Don't be an idiot, she lectured herself. Of course, he would stay here. The man was a gentleman...when it suited his purposes.

As if he'd read the temptation in her eyes, he said, "Use the bathroom in Luke's suite. It's the first one upstairs on the right. I think Jessie probably left some of that fancy, perfumed bubble bath she likes, if you'd prefer to relax in a tub for a while."

The suggestion conjured up images so steamy her brain should have been x-rated. "A shower will be fine," she said, bolting to presumed safety.

Inside Luke's suite, with the door locked, and inside the bathroom with *that* door locked, she leaned back against it and released a pent-up breath. Safe at last, she thought. What was yet to be determined, however, was whether she was hiding from Harlan's pursuit or her own increasingly dangerous longings.

Damn, but she was a stubborn one, Harlan thought to himself the following morning as he surveyed the disaster Jenny had made of his toolshed. Almost as stubborn as her mama.

Janet's abrupt retreat to hide out in Luke's suite until Jenny's return the night before had left him chuckling on the front porch. Frustrated as hell, but amused just the same. There'd been no mistaking how grateful Janet had been to be given a reason to escape his provocative company for a bit.

Jenny had shown up finally, looking for her mama. When Harlan had told her she was inside taking a bath, Jenny's shocked expression suggested she was making far more of that than she should have. Thank goodness Cody wasn't with her or he'd have had a few choice words to add to the conversation for sure.

Harlan had instantly regretted any inferences Jenny might have made, but he hadn't been able to think of any way to correct her mistaken impression without adding to the problem.

"Tell her I'm waiting in the car," she'd said stiffly, and stalked away, her back as straight and proud as any Comanche chief he'd ever seen pictured in the art museums around the Southwest.

"Sure you don't want a glass of tea or maybe some of the oatmeal-and-raisin cookies Maritza baked earlier?" he'd called after her. He'd seen his plans for an evening with the two of them vanishing in a puff of smoke. Janet was scared spitless of being around him and Jenny clearly resented whatever was happening between him and her mother.

The offer of cookies went unanswered, just one indication of how upset she'd been. When he'd relayed her whereabouts to her much cooler-looking, if no less rattled mother, Janet had grabbed her purse and taken off without so much as a goodbye.

"Well, that certainly went well," he'd muttered as he'd watched the trail of dust settle in their wake.

Apparently their evening hadn't gotten any better, if Jenny's sullen mood this morning was any indication. She wouldn't even meet his gaze, which made him wonder just what Janet had told her about their little set-to the night before.

At midmorning, as soon as she'd picked disinterestedly at the snack Maritza had prepared for her, she'd stalked out of the kitchen and disappeared, sparing him little more than a glare.

He hadn't seen her for another hour or so. Hadn't even looked that hard, truthfully. He'd figured she needed time to settle down and get her bearings again without him hovering over her with a lot of questions.

Then, not more than five minutes ago, he'd spotted her sneaking away from the toolshed with suspicious streaks of yellow paint on her clothes. It was not a good sign, he'd decided as he went out to the shed.

The shambles he found triggered an explosion that could have been heard in the next county. Toolboxes had been upended, yellow paint had been splattered hither and yon, and nuts, bolts and nails were scattered like birdseed all over the floor.

"Damn that girl's hide!" he bellowed, even as he wondered precisely what had set her off this time. He'd long since discovered that Jenny only acted out when she was feeling threatened in some way.

Taking off in the direction he'd seen her heading, he followed her trail all the way to the creek. He found her sitting at the edge, her feet in the water, tears streaming down her face.

He lowered himself to the ground next to her and waited, biding his time until she felt like talking.

"I don't care if you do send me to jail," she said eventually in a voice choked with barely contained sobs.

"Actually, I hadn't considered that possibility," he said. "I was thinking you could spend the rest of the day back there cleaning up the mess you made."

He looked her in the eye and saw thirteen years of hurt and loneliness there. "First, though, why don't you tell me what's on your mind?"

"Nothing."

"You just decided to tear up things inside the toolshed for fun?"

"So what if I did?" she said belligerently.

"I suppose everybody gets in a foul mood on occasion for no reason and needs to let off a little steam," he agreed, then slanted a look at her. "Just seems to me as if something must have set you off."

"Well, it didn't, all right!"

He shrugged. "If you say so."

For the next few minutes they sat there side-by-side in total silence except for the sound of birds singing in the trees overhead and the soft splash of the creek as it ran past.

"You just gonna drop it?" she asked, regarding him with a mix of surprise and wariness.

"I thought there was nothing you wanted to say. Of course, maybe if you tell me, you'll feel better. That's how it works sometimes. Sharing the load goes a long way toward making it seem a little lighter."

Her shoulders slumped dejectedly as she picked at the frayed edge of her cut-off jeans. "You'll get mad."

"So it has something to do with me?"

She nodded, looking miserable.

"Is it me and your mom?"

Her head gave an almost imperceptible little bob. "I think she likes you," she mumbled finally. "She says she doesn't, but I can tell."

Harlan considered the observation a promising sign. He didn't tell Jenny that. She obviously disagreed.

"Would that be so terrible, having your mom like me?" he asked instead, hoping to get to the root of her displeasure. Did she resent the possibility of a replacement for her father? Was it just him in particular she disliked? He had a feeling the answer might hold the key to his future.

"It's not that exactly," she admitted. "I mean, you're okay, I guess. A little bossy, but okay. It's just that my mom and me, we've been a team ever since the divorce. We don't need anybody else."

"Maybe I do," he said quietly.

The concept seemed to intrigue her. "What do you mean?"

"Just that it's been awful quiet around here the past year or so, ever since my wife died. My sons are all grown and living their own lives now."

"Maybe Cody and his kids could move in with you," she suggested, either in an attempt to be helpful or an attempt to get her and her mother off the hook.

He could have given some glib reply to that, but he decided she needed honesty from him. She needed to be treated like an adult, at least on this issue. "Oh, the truth of it is, Cody and I would butt heads constantly. And Melissa should be able to run her own house the way she wants without worrying about the way things were always done around here."

She nodded thoughtfully. "That could be a problem, I guess. So how come you like having me and my mom around so much?"

"For one thing, you're a pretty special kid, in case you didn't know. I knew it the second you climbed down out of that truck of mine, spitting mad and taking your own foolishness out on me."

He slanted a sideways look at her. She appeared to be listening intently, so he went on. "As for your mom, she's made me laugh again. That's mighty important. It's always seemed to me that folks weren't meant to go through life without a companion, someone who thinks they're terrific. I don't know a lot about what happened between your parents, but divorce is never easy. I think you and your mom deserve someone who'll put your needs first. And I could sure use someone to liven this place up."

Jenny looked torn between wanting him to feel better and her own distinctly opposite needs. "Maybe you could just play the radio real loud or 'Geraldo' and 'Oprah.' Wouldn't that work?"

He grinned. "It's not the same."

"You mean you just want people to talk to, stuff like that?"

"More or less."

"Oh." She seemed to be considering the idea, then she lifted her chin and stared him straight in the eye. "I thought you wanted sex with her."

The blunt and far too perceptive remark sent blood climbing up the back of his neck. He had to choke back a chuckle. "That's a whole other issue and one I do not intend to discuss with you, young lady," he said sternly.

"My mother and I talk about everything. She doesn't keep secrets," she said, regarding him with a sly look. "Not from me, anyway."

"I'll bet she'll keep this one," Harlan countered. It was beginning to seem to him, though, that there were too damned many people fascinated with his love life these days.

"So?" he asked. "What's the verdict? Do you object to your mom and me seeing each other?"

"Would you stop if I did?"

"Probably not," he admitted. "But I'd work like crazy to make you change your mind."

"Would you let me off this prison sentence you imposed?"

He grinned at the ploy. "Is being out here really so terrible?" He fixed a steady gaze on her. "Tell the truth."

"No," she said with an air of resignation. "It's just the principle of it. You get to boss me around and I have to take it."

"That's right," he said. "That's the way it works in the real world."

"Yeah, but in the real world you get paid. I'm doing slave labor."

He nodded. "Okay, maybe I didn't set up the rules quite right. How about we go back to the house and figure out how much you owe me for the truck—and the toolshed," he added pointedly. "Then we'll set a salary for your chores around here. You can pay me back out of your earnings each week."

"Will I have to pay you every dime?"

He chuckled at her negotiating skills. He'd raised one son who'd had the same knack for getting his way. He was head of an oil company now. He suspected Jenny could share a similar fate if she put that quick thinking of hers to good use.

"We can negotiate that," he suggested. "We'll work out an appropriate payment schedule. Of course, that might mean you won't be paid off at the end of summer. You might have to keep coming out here."

She weighed that for several minutes before nodding. "Okay."

He held out his hand. "Shall we shake on it?"

The instant they had solemnly shaken hands on their new deal, Jenny stood and whooped with undisguised glee. "I know exactly how I'm going to spend my money, too," she declared.

"How?" he said, anticipating a litany of CD titles and video games.

"I'm going to buy back Lone Wolf's land and give it to Mom."

He thought the plan might be a bit overly ambitious, given her debt and her likely wages, but who was he to discourage her. "And where is Lone Wolf's land?"

She grinned at him. "You're sitting on it."

Chapter Ten

This had been her great-great-grandfather's land? Harlan couldn't have been more stunned if Jenny had announced she and her mother had robbed a bank. He gazed around at the lush, verdant banks of the creek and beyond to the rolling landscape he'd always considered his home.

"You sure about that?" he asked, trying to piece together all of the implications. Was that why Jenny had stolen his truck in the first place, just to wrangle a meeting with him? Or maybe in some twisted way to get even with him for the perceived theft of her ancestor's land? It was certainly one explanation for the resentful expression he'd caught on Janet's face the day they'd gone riding over the ranch's acres.

It was several minutes before he realized Jenny hadn't answered. When he looked at her, he saw that she was scuffing the toe of her sneaker in the grass and looking guilty as sin. Since things like theft and destruction didn't stir that expression, he couldn't help wondering what had.

"Jenny?" he prodded. "How do you know that this was your great-great-grandfather's land?"

"Mom told me," she admitted, reluctance written all over her face. "I wasn't supposed to say anything, though. Please, don't say I told. Please."

There could only be one reason for keeping such a secret that he could think of. Janet had some cocka-mamie plan to right an old wrong and get this land back. He'd heard of court battles like that, efforts to reclaim Native American lands stolen by individuals or the government.

He didn't know of too many that had been suc-cessful, though. The government's treatment of Na-tive American rights might have been shabby, but there were probably legal documents a foot thick to prove that the Native Americans had been compen-sated for every bit of land taken from them.

The thought that Janet might try, though, was enough to make his blood run cold. The knowledge that she had insinuated herself into his life without ever saying a word about her intentions infuriated him. He would have sworn Janet Runningbear didn't have a duplicitous bone in her body. It appeared his judgment had been impaired after all.

"Don't worry," he reassured Jenny with icy calm. "I won't say a thing to your mother."

No, he was going to sit back and wait for her to make her move. He would be ready for her, though.

And he would make her regret the day she ever tried to tangle with Harlan Adams.

Later that night, alone in his den, he fought against the wave of disappointment rushing over him. He'd been so hopeful that Janet and her rebellious daughter were the answers to his prayers. Now it appeared that Janet, at least, was nothing more than a liar and a cheat.

He didn't like the prospect of sitting idle, waiting for her to strike. That wasn't his way.

And maybe he couldn't admit to all he knew and involve Jenny, but he could try to force Janet's hand. Maybe it was time he found out once and for all if it was him she was attracted to, or, as he was beginning to believe, the land she thought belonged to her.

With cold deliberation, he sat behind the desk where he'd kept White Pines books for so many years and plotted a strategy for making sure that not one single acre ever left Adams ownership. Janet Runningbear might be the smartest, slickest lawyer ever trained, but she was no match for him.

Except maybe, he thought, in bed. As icily furious as he was about Jenny's innocent revelations, he couldn't seem to tame the desire Janet aroused in him. Maybe sex was the way to force the issue. He could satisfy this growing hunger that had him aching to touch her morning, noon and night. A woman revealed a lot when she made love to a man. He was almost certain he would know once and for all what was really in Janet's heart, if he could just get past her emotional defenses.

He sipped on a glass of bourbon, pleased with his

plan. His pulse kicked up just thinking about it. There was nothing like the prospect for steamy sex or a good battle of wills to make a man feel alive. He had Janet to thank on both counts, he thought with a trace of bitterness. He'd have to be sure to express his gratitude when all was said and done.

Janet glanced up with surprise when the door to her office opened at midmorning and Harlan stepped across the threshold onto the threadbare carpet she couldn't afford to replace until business picked up. Something in his expression alarmed her. She'd seen him looking determined. She'd seen him defiant. Both traits were evident now, but there was a cold, calculating gleam in his eyes that was something new and not entirely reassuring.

"What brings you into town?" she asked warily.

"I thought maybe you and I could get a word alone here."

She hadn't noticed that he had all that much difficulty getting her alone at White Pines when he was of a mind to, but she just nodded. "Something important come up?"

"In a manner of speaking," he said, perching on a corner of her desk, his jeans-clad knees scant inches from hers.

It seemed to Janet that he was deliberately crowding her. In fact, it was just more evidence of his odd mood. He had been acting weird all day. She'd noticed it first when she'd dropped off Jenny.

Now that she thought about it, Jenny had seemed awfully subdued since yesterday evening, as well.

Had she gotten into more trouble? Was Harlan fed up with playing surrogate daddy? Had he come to tell her that he wanted to end their arrangement?

"Jenny's not giving you trouble, is she?" she asked, regarding him uneasily. Jenny, for all of her grumbling, would be heartbroken if her days at White Pines and with Harlan were over.

"None that I can't handle," he said.

The response relieved her mind on that score at least, but there was something. She was sure of it. "Then, what is it?" she prodded.

His gaze locked with hers. "I think we should go away together," he announced.

Oh, boy, she thought as the breath whooshed right out of her. This was the last thing she'd expected. Well, not the last thing, but certainly she hadn't anticipated such an invitation coming so soon. Janet felt her cheeks flame as she battled temptation and embarrassment.

"Go away together?" she repeated dazedly. "You and me? Why? I mean, we haven't even had a real date. Don't you think we're getting a little ahead of ourselves here?"

"We had dinner at your place. We've had dinner at my place. We've been on a picnic down by the creek. You don't call that dating?"

"No," she insisted. She didn't have a better name for it, but she'd been swearing to herself for days now that she was not dating Harlan Adams and that's the way she intended to keep it. "Even if those meals counted as dates, that's hardly a sufficient basis for assuming I would go off on some romantic tryst with you."

"I figured those kisses were a clue that you might at least consider the offer."

"Then you leapt to a wrong conclusion," she said adamantly.

An expression of pure frustration crossed his face. "Your daughter is asking me if I'm interested in having sex with you. My sons are practically salivating over every development in our relationship. I'd just like to get to know you someplace out from under their watchful eyes."

She stared at him with growing horror. "Jenny asked you about sex?" she asked with a sinking sensation in the pit of her stomach.

"Indeed she did," he said. "Not the workings of it, of course. Just whether that was the only reason I was interested in you."

"Oh, sweet heaven," she murmured. "I'm sorry."

He didn't seem to care about an apology. In fact, he seemed torn between exasperation and admiration for her child's audacity. She'd noticed that about him. Almost nothing threw Harlan Adams off stride. He was confident in a way that didn't require controlling other people. For all of the teasing she'd witnessed between him and his sons about his manipulation, she noticed that each of them had gone their own way, apparently with their father's blessing.

"I can't go away with you," she finally said with some regret. "I won't leave Jenny, for one thing. For another, I can't afford the damage to my reputation. I'm having enough difficulty getting the people in town to trust a woman lawyer, who's part Comanche, to boot, without giving them anything more to speculate about.''

Harlan's expression promptly clouded over. ''Are people still giving you a hard time? I thought that would be a thing of the past by now.''

''It's no worse than I expected,'' she repeated emphatically, regretting taking that particular tack with him again. She knew better than to get his white knight tendencies stirred up.

''Who's bothering you?'' he demanded, ignoring her low-key attempt to sidetrack him. ''I'll have a word with them.''

''No. You will not! We've been all through this. I will not have you fighting my battles for me. We're talking about my career. I can handle it.''

He seemed ready and eager to rush off and slay a few dragons for her, but he finally backed down at her adamant tone. It was another thing she liked about him. He didn't just listen to her. He actually *heard* what she was saying.

Somewhere in a corner of her heart she was beginning to recognize that Harlan Adams wasn't like any other man she'd ever known. And all of those sturdy defenses that had served her so well the past few years were slowly but surely beginning to topple.

''Let's talk a little more about you and me, then,'' he suggested, shifting gears so quickly it left her head reeling. ''Where do you see us heading?''

Janet wished she had prepared herself better for this moment. She had known a conversation like this was inevitable. Harlan wasn't the kind of man to be satisfied for long by evasive answers and rushed, skittish departures. She had no idea what had triggered this particular confrontation at midmorning in her office, rather than some evening out at White Pines, but apparently he'd reached a decision about the future and intended to put his plan into motion.

"I don't know where we're heading," she said, which was too close to the truth to suit her and too wishy-washy an answer to suit Harlan.

"You ever think about marrying again?" he asked.

She swallowed hard. "You mean, getting married to you?"

His gaze was riveted on her. "Or anyone," he conceded grudgingly.

Her throat went dry. She couldn't have croaked out a reply if she'd had one handy.

"Something wrong?" he inquired. "Cat got your tongue?"

An odd note in his voice triggered an alarm somewhere deep inside her. "Is there some reason you're forcing this issue now?"

"I just thought it was time to get our cards on the table." He studied her pointedly, then added, "All of our cards. Call the bet, so to speak."

Panic flooded through her. What exactly did he know? Had he somehow figured out her intentions about the Comanche lands? She'd been doing legal research in all her spare time, but no one knew about that, she reassured herself.

No one, except Jenny. Surely her daughter wouldn't have said a word. She knew how important silence was, especially when there was every chance in the world that nothing would come of her plans.

She studied Harlan's face and tried to guess what was going on behind that enigmatic expression. She had a feeling whatever decision she reached about that was critical. If she jumped to the wrong conclusion, said the wrong thing, it could ruin everything.

"My life's an open book," she said in what she hoped was an innocent-enough tone.

"Is it really?" he said, then shrugged. "I wasn't thinking so much of the past. I'm more concerned with the future."

"Harlan, I'm just a single mom struggling from day to day to make ends meet."

The comment sounded a little ingenuous even to her own ears. Harlan responded with a lift of his eyebrows, indicating that he wasn't fooled by it, either. Janet sighed.

"Okay, what do you want me to say?"

"How about the truth?" he said with a surprising edge in his voice. "Start to finish."

The last suggested for the second time in a matter of minutes that he knew something, or thought he did. "Harlan, is there something specific on your mind?"

"I've told you what was on my mind. It's your head that remains a mystery." He stood. "Why don't we go grab lunch and see if we can clarify a few things over a cold beer and some of Rosa's enchiladas?"

"The last time you and I went to Rosa's, I got the impression people were hanging on our every word and reporting it afterward. Why would you want to go there now?"

He shrugged. "I was hoping the beer would loosen your tongue."

She stared at him in exasperation. "I'm being as honest here as I can be," she protested.

"Darlin', if this is your idea of being candid, I'd trust you to keep my deepest, darkest secrets." He stepped behind her and pulled back her chair. "Come on. Let's see if a beer will work any magic or not."

"I hate beer."

"Then you'll drink it down right quick, sort of like medicine," he said, a glint of amusement in his eyes for the first time since he'd entered her office.

Janet still couldn't help thinking there were undercurrents here, deep ones, that she might never figure out. Something told her, though, that her future might depend on her trying.

A half dozen heads snapped up when Harlan escorted Janet through the door at Rosa's. Mule rolled his eyes in disgust.

"You two hooked up together again? Don't expect me to get involved in another poker game with the likes of you," the mechanic warned, scowling at Janet.

"Don't worry," Harlan informed him. "We're here for a little private conversation."

He passed right by his regular table and urged Janet into a booth all the way in the back. It wasn't quite out of the sight of prying eyes, but it was the best he could come up with under the circumstances.

"That was a little rude, don't you think?" Janet said when they were seated, a half dozen pairs of eyes staring at them. "Just the kind of thing that will stir up more gossip."

"Oh, will you stop fussing about gossip? Seems to me you have more important things to be fretting about."

"Such as?"

He reached across the table and touched a finger to her lower lip, all the while keeping his gaze locked with hers. "Such as the way your skin burns when I touch you like this."

He could feel her trembling even as she blinked hard and deliberately looked away. So, that much was real, he decided. She couldn't be faking a reaction like that, for devious purposes or otherwise. Which meant her reluctance to commit to anything more than the casual encounters they'd shared thus far was pure cussedness on her part.

Or perhaps a belated attack of ethical considerations, he amended. Maybe she'd decided she couldn't get any more involved with a man she intended to try to fleece out of his land. He supposed even would-be thieves had a code of honor they wouldn't breech.

He finally allowed his hand to drop away. "You trying to tell me that doesn't mean anything?" he chided.

"It doesn't," she insisted stubbornly.

"I don't believe you."

"Okay, I'm attracted to you," she snapped. "Is

that what you wanted to hear? Does it make your heart go pitty-pat? Is your oversize ego satisfied?''

He chuckled at her irritation. ''As a matter of fact, yes on all counts.''

She lifted the menu and pointedly retreated behind it.

''You two planning on arguing all afternoon or were you thinking of ordering lunch?'' Rosa inquired, not even trying to hide her amusement.

Harlan wondered with a sigh exactly how much she'd heard before she spoke up. He supposed whatever it was, his sons would know every word before nightfall. He wondered idly if Rosa's silence could be bought. He glanced up and studied her speculatively.

''Rosa, darlin', what would it take to keep you from telling Maritza or any of your other myriad relatives in Los Piños that I was even in here today?'' he asked.

Janet peeked around her menu, curiosity written all over her face. ''You're trying to bribe Rosa to keep silent?'' she demanded.

''You bet,'' he muttered grimly. ''Come on, Rosa, what will it take?''

The heavy-set Mexican woman shook her head as she regarded him with an expression of pity. ''You cannot buy loyalty, old friend.''

''I can't seem to get it, either,'' he grumbled. ''Whatever you heard here today, just forget it, okay? That's not so much to ask, is it?''

Rosa's expression was perfectly bland. ''But I heard nothing.''

Harlan sighed. "I'll bet."

Not trusting her one whit, he still dropped the subject and asked Janet what she wanted. When he'd placed the order, he leaned back and focused once more on the woman seated opposite him.

The color in her cheeks was high. That was probably a sign of guilt, he decided. She'd wound her hair into some sort of prim knot on top of her head, but she'd done it in a way that made a man's fingers just itch to tug it free. He considered it another contradictory message in a whole sea of them he'd been getting lately.

As irritated and suspicious as he was, he wanted her with a hunger that stunned him. He'd been comfortable in his marriage with Mary. He'd enjoyed the physical side of their relationship. There'd still been plenty of passion to it. More than a lot of people shared after being together more than thirty-five years, from what he'd heard.

But these feelings he was experiencing now were a far cry from that. His pulse quickened just at the prospect of seeing Janet. His body responded like some randy adolescent's at the most innocent touch. A kiss was enough to trigger a desire so thorough and overwhelming, it was a wonder he hadn't busted the zipper of every pair of jeans he owned.

None of those reactions had eased just because he now suspected her of trying to cheat him out of his ranch. Was that because on some level he couldn't believe that's what she meant to do? Was he thinking with his testosterone and not his head? He wouldn't be the first man to fall prey to that sort of foolishness.

He met her gaze and tried to read her intentions in her dark brown eyes, but in the restaurant's shadows they were more inscrutable than ever.

"Harlan, what's really bothering you?" she asked, sounding more worried about him than frightened for herself. She didn't sound like a woman with secrets she feared might have been uncovered.

"I told you, I'm trying to get a grasp on what the future holds," he said, making the response enigmatic enough to cover anything from their relationship to the future of White Pines.

"Is that something you need to figure out today?" she asked, amusement lurking in her eyes. "Couldn't you just take it day by day as it comes, the way most of us mortals do?"

"I've never much liked surprises," he admitted.

"So it's true, then," she teased. "You do like to control everyone and everything around you. Your sons and daughters-in-law were right about that."

The truth chafed, especially when it was being used to suit the purposes of someone who didn't want to reveal her own intentions. "What's wrong with wanting to shape your life, with wanting to take charge and make it the best it can be?"

"You miss out on the serendipities," she observed.

"Like Jenny stealing my pickup, I suppose."

She grinned. "It's true. If you didn't make it a habit to leave your keys in plain view, that wouldn't have happened. Maybe you're more open to risks than you know."

"I don't mind a few risks, when I've had time to weigh the odds," he countered pointedly. "For forty

years those keys had never been a temptation to anyone in Los Piños. Now those are odds worth taking
a risk on."

He looked her straight in the eye. "You seem like
a good risk to me, too."

She didn't seem pleased by the observation. "You
make me sound like a filly you might bet on in the
fifth race at Belmont."

He waved off the comparison. "That's just money.
I'm talking about fate here, Janet. Yours and mine.
You've been talking a lot about my willingness to
take risks. What about you? How do you feel about
serendipity?"

He watched her closely as she seemed to struggle
with the question. Whatever internal war she was
waging struck him as a pretty good indication that
she did have things to hide.

"I'm all for it," she said eventually.

"Oh, really? Then why aren't you seizing my offer
to take you away to some romantic spot for a few
days?"

She scowled at him. "I explained that."

"Not to my satisfaction."

She stood then and threw down her napkin. "Not
everything in this world has to meet your satisfaction,
Harlan Adams. You'd do well to remember that."

With that she turned and sashayed straight out of
Rosa's, ignoring the gaping expressions of Mule and
all the others following her departure. To his everlasting regret, Harlan's body turned rock-hard just
watching her go.

When she was finally out of sight, he sighed. That

woman's defiant streak was going to be the death of him yet. Worse, he didn't know a damn bit more about what was going on in her head now than he had before he'd forced this confrontation. Yep, it was just as he'd suspected. He was definitely losing his touch.

Chapter Eleven

"Mom, did Mr. Adams seem weird to you today?" Jenny asked as she watched the hamburgers she had frying on the stove for dinner.

"Weird, how?" Janet replied, even though she thought she knew exactly what Jenny was talking about. He'd struck her as weird, impossible, arrogant and a whole lot more. She was interested, though, in just which vibes Jenny had picked up on.

"Like he was mad or something. I don't know. He was just awful quiet, not bossy like he usually is. And he took off in the middle of the morning without giving me anything to do. He said I could just go into his library and read, if I wanted to."

"That must have been when he came into town to see me."

Jenny put the spatula down, turned and regarded her worriedly. "How come?"

Janet had been wondering the very same thing ever since he'd appeared on her office doorstep. Their lunch hadn't really enlightened her. Even though Harlan had plainly stated that he wanted to discuss their future, there had been those odd undercurrents, as if he were really looking for evidence of some treachery. She couldn't share that with her daughter, so she simply said he'd wanted to talk.

"About what?" Jenny persisted. "Me?"

The last was said with a plaintive note that Janet found worrisome. "Why would you think he wanted to talk about you? Have you been making trouble out there?" When Jenny remained silent, Janet's heart sank. "Okay, what happened?"

"Nothing."

"Jenny?"

"Okay, okay. Don't bust a gut. I did make sort of a mess of his toolshed yesterday," she finally admitted.

"I see."

"But I cleaned it up," her daughter said in a rush. "I even painted it. Bright yellow, in fact. It's awesome."

Janet couldn't work up much enthusiasm over the color scheme of the toolshed, especially since Jenny herself seemed to be the reason it had needed painting.

"Why did you wreck it in the first place?" she asked, even though she thought she already knew from what Harlan had mentioned about Jenny's questions to him. "Did it have something to do with your being worried that Mr. Adams and I might be sleeping together?"

Jenny groaned and turned beet red. "He told you, didn't he? Jeez, Mom, he swore he wasn't going to blab."

"He didn't blab, at least not the way you mean. It just sort of came out in a conversation we were having."

"About the two of you?"

Janet nodded.

"So, are you?"

"Are we what?"

"Sleeping together," Jenny said impatiently. "He wouldn't say exactly."

"And neither will I," Janet said. "That's not a subject that's any of your business."

"How can you say that? He's the enemy."

Janet grinned at Jenny's determination to cling to that label. Her daughter was even more stubborn than she was. She'd conceded days ago that Harlan was no more the enemy than some descendant of Custer's might be.

"You don't believe that any more than I do," she chided.

"You're giving up?" Jenny said, staring at her incredulously. "You're not going to fight him for Lone Wolf's land?"

"I'm still researching whether there's any legal way to get the land. Besides, I told you before that I don't have evidence that Lone Wolf's father was ever on Mr. Adams's land. We may never know for sure.

And the way things worked back then, it wasn't like the Comanches had deeds on file.''

"But I told him—" Jenny turned pale. "Whoops."

Janet felt as if she'd been whacked over the head by a two-by-four. Of course! That explained those odd undercurrents she'd felt with Harlan. With her thoughts in turmoil, the odor of meat burning barely even registered. At the moment the fate of the hamburgers was the last thing on her mind.

"You told him what?" she asked carefully.

"Nothing," Jenny muttered, backing away from the stove and clearly trying to put some distance between herself and her mother at the same time.

"Jennifer!"

"Okay, I might have let it slip that his ranch was sitting on Lone Wolf's land."

"You might have?"

"I did, all right?" she said belligerently. "I don't know what difference it makes. He was going to find out sooner or later anyway."

Janet clung to her temper by a thread. "But it might have been nice if he found out about it from me. Now he must think I've just been playing some sort of sick game by hanging around out there. He probably thinks we're out to betray him."

"Aren't we?" Jenny asked simply. "Isn't that why we're in this godawful state, instead of back home in New York, where we belong?"

With that she whirled and ran from the kitchen, leaving Janet to take the burned hamburgers from the stove. No longer the least bit interested in food, she dumped the frying pan, burgers and all, into the sink, then went out to the front porch to sit in a rocker and think.

Should she go out to White Pines first thing in the morning and tell Harlan everything? But, if he already knew most of it, why had he been trying to back her into a corner about their future earlier today? Why hadn't he been blasting her as the deceitful traitor she felt like? Would she ever understand the workings of this man's mind? Or any man's, for that matter?

And why, dear heaven, did it suddenly seem to matter so much to her that Harlan Adams not think ill of her? Was it possible that he had come to mean more to her than that elusive dream she'd formulated as a child and held on to so tightly ever since?

She could still recall Lone Wolf telling her about the Comanches known as Penateka or Honey-Eaters, who'd occupied a stretch of the Comancheria from Edwards Plateau to Cross Timbers. His telling had been further preservation of the oral history of his forefathers.

Even now she shook with indignation at his description of the 1840 meeting in San Antonio during which the Comanche leaders who'd come to discuss peace had been slaughtered in what had come to be known as the Council House Massacre. There had been nothing after that to indicate to the tribe that Texans could ever be trusted.

Slowly but surely settlers had been given more and more of the Comanche lands, until Lone Wolf's ancestors had been forced from Texas altogether. Could she ever achieve retribution for something that had occurred so long ago and even now seemed so complex? Everything she'd read indicated it would be difficult, if not impossible, to make any legal claim.

The questions kept her up most of the night. The answers didn't come at all.

In the morning, she didn't have a chance to act on any of the myriad possibilities that had occurred to her. When she and Jenny got to White Pines, Harlan was nowhere to be found. It was Cody who waited for them on the front porch.

"Come on, short stuff," he said to Jenny, who brightened immediately. "You and I are going out to look for stray calves this morning."

"Oh, wow!" Jenny said, clearly pleased to be asked to help her idol with such an important task. It was the first time Janet had seen a smile on her face since their argument the night before.

"Where's your father?" Janet asked Cody, hoping that her heart wasn't sitting in plain view on her sleeve.

He shrugged. "Beats me. He left me a note to take Jenny with me today. Didn't say where he was heading or when he'd be back. He took his plane, though. He might have had business over in Dallas or something."

"Oh." Janet fought against the tide of disappointment that washed through her as Cody headed over to the two horses he'd saddled and had tethered to a fence rail. She should have been relieved, but she wasn't. She brushed a kiss across Jenny's forehead, ignoring her daughter's embarrassed protest. "Have a good day, pumpkin. See you tonight."

"Yeah, Mom. Bye," Jenny said, already rushing off to keep up with Cody's long strides.

Feeling abandoned on all fronts, Janet stood where she was until Cody and Jenny had ridden off. Only after they'd gone did she admit to herself that she would rather have had Harlan screaming at her than ignoring her this way. There was little doubt in her mind that he'd deliberately made it a point not to be at home this morning.

Maybe he really had had unexpected business to take care of, just as Cody had suggested, she consoled herself as she drove into town. Right, she scoffed right back. Without telling Cody the details? No way. He was very careful not to step on his son's managerial toes. No, the truth of it was, he was avoiding her because his discovery of her treachery was eating at him.

She resigned herself to waiting until Harlan turned up again before settling matters between them. The delay wouldn't make much difference. She doubted she'd have any clearer an idea how to handle it hours or days from now than she did right this minute.

Harlan had spent half the night after his aborted meeting with Janet reading through every book in his library on the Comanches and their days in the southern Great Plains. Nothing he found there was conclusive proof that Janet's ancestral claim to his land was solid. In fact, it seemed to him that Lone Wolf's father had probably been a typical nomadic hunter, before being sent off to the reservation in Oklahoma.

It had been well into the wee hours of the morning

when he'd decided to do a little more investigating by going to Oklahoma to see what he could discover there. His meetings with folks at the Bureau of Indian Affairs and with tribal elders who agreed to see him were inconclusive, as well. He sensed that Janet would never find the proof she sought unless she hoped to stake her claim for all Comanches and not just for her great-grandfather and his descendants.

Still, the meetings had given him much to think about, a historical perspective on his own family's actions when they'd moved to Texas to flee the war that had destroyed their home in the South. In seizing an opportunity for themselves, had they stolen it from others? He found he could understand Janet's actions far more clearly now and he could do so without feeling the rancor of betrayal.

Perhaps, if Janet ever opened up to him, they could reach some sort of compromise. In the meantime, though, he'd decided that she enriched his life too much for him to walk away without fighting for their future. It was a decision weighed and reached with years of maturity, rather than the angry, instantaneous, hot-blooded reaction he might have had a couple of decades earlier.

Also, the more he thought about the desperate plea he had made to Janet to run away with him, the more he realized that she had been exactly right to turn him down. The place to court her was right in Los Piños, in plain view. He didn't ever want a soul to think he was sneaking around with her because he wasn't proud to be seen with her. There were too many people ready with quick bias for him to be adding to that sort of rotten speculation about her morals or his own.

As soon as he'd set down his plane at the local airfield, he marched straight down Main Street, walked into her office and hauled her off to have dinner at DiPasquali's.

"Harlan," she protested, even as she hurried to keep pace with him. "What about Jenny? She's going to be waiting for me at White Pines. She'll be worried."

"I called Melissa from the airport. Jenny will have dinner with her and Cody. Sharon Lynn and baby Harlan love having her around. You can pick her up there."

She halted in her tracks and scowled at him. "Do you always have to manipulate everything to get your own way?"

He grinned unrepentantly. "Always," he assured her. "Get used to it."

He linked her arm through his and gently, but insistently, escorted her the rest of the way to the restaurant. It seemed to him her footsteps dragged a bit reluctantly, but at least she didn't bolt on him.

Inside DiPasquali's, he directed her to a table right smack in front of the window, in plain view of anybody coming or going inside the restaurant or passing by on the street outside. She regarded him with a curious look, but sat where he'd indicated.

Gina DiPasquali joined them at once with their menus, winking at Janet as she handed one to her. If he hadn't already known about their conspiracy over that dinner at Janet's, he would have wondered what the two of them were up to.

"Are you thinking of having the lasagna?" Harlan inquired innocently, his gaze fixed on Janet's face.

Gina chuckled as Janet's cheeks turned pink. "Caught you, didn't he?"

"Before he'd taken two bites," Janet admitted. "Then he rubbed it in for the rest of the evening."

"I did not," Harlan protested, feigning indignation. "But I couldn't very well let you go on thinking you'd put one over on me, though, could I? It would have set a dangerous precedent. I might never have gotten the upper hand again."

"Who says you ever had it," she shot right back. "Besides, no gentleman would have embarrassed a hostess by pointing out what he suspected. You should have been oohing and aahing over my supposed culinary skills."

Gina rolled her eyes. "If you were counting on that, I could have told you not to bother. Harlan's only a gentleman when it suits his purposes."

"Besides which, you'd have felt guilty as sin if I offered high praise for a dish you knew you hadn't prepared," he asserted. "I was just saving you that."

"How considerate," Janet retorted a trifle sourly.

Gina apparently decided to let them resolve the issue of etiquette they were debating, because she stuffed her order book back into her pocket.

"You two can sit here and battle wits from now till the cows come home," she said. "Let me choose dinner tonight, so you won't have something more to quibble about. I'll have Tony fix you something special.''

''Perfect,'' Janet said.

Harlan decided she was apparently no more eager to choose from the menu than she was to cook in her own kitchen. It was a wonder she wasn't skin and bones.

When Gina had gone, he did an appreciative survey of Janet. Whatever her disinterest in food, she managed to have a perfectly rounded figure that could fill a man with lust. He dragged his attention away and stared at the ceiling in what was only a partially successful attempt to bring his hormones under control. The reaction only confirmed what he'd guessed earlier, that he couldn't walk away from her.

''Everything okay?'' she inquired with a half smile that was all too knowing.

He caught the undisguised mirth in her eyes. ''Fine,'' he lied. ''How about you? You looked put-out when I turned up at your office a little while ago. Something on your mind?''

''Just your habit of appearing without notice and expecting me to drop everything to accompany you. Haven't you ever heard of the telephone?''

''Sure, but it's harder for you to turn me down face-to-face.''

''What makes you think that?''

''Watching you stammer around for excuses a few times.''

''I never stammer,'' she retorted irritably. ''Still, I can't keep taking off at the drop of a hat, just because you get some whim to feed me.''

"You have a lot of work piled up?" he inquired doubtfully.

"That's not the point."

"Sure it is. No sense in you sitting around in your office pretending to be busy, when you could be having a nice meal with me."

"What about a nice meal with my daughter?"

"Who'd cook?"

She frowned at him. "You really do have a rotten streak, Harlan Adams."

"Just speaking the gospel truth. It's not even hearsay. Don't forget I saw the state of your kitchen that night and you never even dared to put that meal on the table. Makes me wonder how the two of you have survived this long. Must have been the takeout available from all those fancy New York restaurants."

She looked a little like a chicken who'd had her feathers ruffled by that comment, but she kept her mouth clamped firmly shut. Harlan watched the temper flare in her eyes, then slowly diminish before she finally seized on another topic.

"Where did you go so early this morning?" she asked in a perfectly neutral tone.

He grinned. "So, you did miss me. I'm gratified to hear it."

"I did not say I missed you. It was a simple question, Harlan. Just a little polite conversation, okay? If it's some big secret, just say so."

He got the impression he might be pushing her a little too hard with his teasing. He opted for giving her the truth, or at least a select portion of it. "I had some unexpected business to take care of."

"I thought Cody took care of all the ranch's business these days."

"Doesn't mean I can't stick my nose into it, when I'm of a mind to," he said. "By the way, did I mention you're looking particularly beautiful today. That red blouse suits you."

"Thank you," she said, but her gaze narrowed suspiciously. "You're up to something, aren't you?"

"I could ask you the same thing with more cause," he retorted, enjoying the unmistakable guilt that darkened her eyes.

He decided there was something to be said for tormenting her. Maybe he wouldn't tell her about that trip to Oklahoma, not until she came clean with him. Surely a man was entitled to some secrets from a woman who had the ability to tie him in knots without even trying.

Gina played straight into his hands by turning up just then with a platter of antipasto and two glasses of Chianti. It got them both off the hook, which was probably to the good, he decided as he watched Janet nervously shoving a couple of olives around on her plate. Let her stew for a bit.

"You get any clients today?" he asked after a while.

She looked up, her expression revealing unmistakable gratitude for the change to a more innocuous topic. "As a matter of fact, yes. Mule came by."

Harlan's mouth gaped. "What the devil did he want?"

"That's a matter of client confidentiality," she

said, obviously pleased that she'd not only stunned him, but stirred his curiosity.

"Well, I'll be damned. You sure he didn't want to get in a few quick hands of poker? He might have been running short of cash, since he's had that garage of his closed for so blasted long."

"Sorry," she said blithely. "I can't talk about it."

"Mule tells me most of his business anyway," he said, trying to coax her into telling, when he knew perfectly well that she was too ethical to ever say a word. He was enjoying aggravating her too much to stop just yet.

"Then you'll have to ask him about this," she retorted. "Now, stop prying."

"Just making polite small talk," he shot right back, echoing her earlier jab.

She rolled her eyes. He couldn't help chuckling at her exasperated expression. "You are a treasure, you know that, don't you?"

The compliment seemed to throw her off-balance. "Where did that come from?" she asked in a tone that said she didn't think she deserved it.

"Just an observation. A man's entitled to make one every now and again, isn't he?"

"Of course."

"Shall I make a few more?" he inquired, leaning forward and lowering his voice to a seductive whisper.

She swallowed hard and shook her head. "I don't think so."

He grinned. "How come?"

"Because I don't think this is the time or the place

to be discussing whatever it is you have on your mind.''

''Now that's an interesting bit of speculation on your part,'' he observed, trying to keep the amusement out of his tone. ''Just what is it you think I have on my mind that would be unsuitable for discussion in a public place?''

She blushed furiously. ''Never mind. Perhaps I was wrong.''

Harlan shook his head. ''Now, you don't strike me as a woman who admits lightly to being wrong. Maybe you ought to say what's on *your* mind. Could just be you're right on track.''

''Why are you doing this?'' she demanded. ''A gentleman—''

''We've already established that I'm no gentleman, not when it comes to affairs of the heart, so to speak.''

He allowed his gaze to sweep over her, lingering long enough to keep her color high and her nerves jittery. The game turned on him, though. The next thing he knew his own heartbeat was racing and the blood was rushing straight to a portion of his anatomy where its unmistakable effect could prove downright embarrassing. He wanted her with an urgency that drove out all other thoughts. Visions of taking her here and now took up residence in his brain and clamored for action.

Apparently he'd been wrong about one thing, though. He was just enough of a gentleman not to act on such a desperate, wicked longing. But Janet Runningbear could thank her lucky stars that he'd chosen DiPasquali's for dinner tonight instead of White

Pines. He doubted he'd have been anywhere near so restrained in the privacy of his own home.

He met her gaze and thought he read a mix of passion and uncertainty in those dark brown depths. Soon, he silently promised her and himself. He would claim her soon.

As if she could read his mind, an audible sigh eased through her. A sigh of satisfaction perhaps? Or maybe anticipation? Whichever it was, Harlan could only share in the sentiment.

To him the future was as clear-cut as a pane of glass or a ten-carat diamond. Whatever Janet Runningbear's original agenda had been in coming to Los Piños, he had a feeling it was only a matter of time and subtle persuasion before he'd have her seeing the years ahead as vividly as he did.

Chapter Twelve

The bouquet of flowers that arrived in Janet's office the next morning was so huge that the only surface big enough to accommodate it was her desk. She was still staring in astonishment at the arrangement of splashy yellow mums, vivid orange tiger lilies, Texas bluebonnets and fragrant white roses when the man responsible for sending it walked in.

She didn't get it. Why was he lavishing all this attention on her, now that he knew the truth? Why had he kept so silent about what Jenny had told him? Was he planning to set her up to take a tremendous fall? If that was it, it was a pretty diabolical plan; one she couldn't imagine Harlan resorting to.

She was still trying to puzzle it out when he came up behind her, spanned her waist with his hands, brushed aside her hair and planted a kiss on her nape.

"I see it got here," he said, sounding extremely pleased with himself.

"Just a few minutes ago," she said, unable to take her eyes off the lavish display. She couldn't quite decide whether to be awed or appalled. She settled for adding, "The flowers are beautiful."

He released her, stepped in front of her, then examined her face intently. Apparently her expression gave her away. He frowned.

"Too much?" he inquired.

"It's not that...exactly," she said, not wanting to trample on the sentiment behind the overdone gesture. She'd discovered long ago that men required all the positive reinforcement possible, if a woman expected flowers and candy not just for special occasions, but as impulsive gifts for no reason at all. This wasn't a habit she wanted to break, just to modify. And this was an improvement over that first floral excess he'd brought to the house.

She gestured helplessly at the arrangement's takeover of her desk top. "Where am I supposed to work?"

He nodded. "Definitely a problem." He settled an innocent look on her. "So, take the day off."

She couldn't help laughing at his mischievous expression and at the outrageous suggestion. "Was that why you sent such a huge bouquet, so I wouldn't be able to work?"

"Actually, no, but I'm a man who can think on his feet. I could see your dilemma right off and came up with what I consider to be the perfect solution—play hooky."

She studied him suspiciously. "Seems a little convenient to me that you turned up here just in time to make a suggestion like that."

"You've obviously been hanging around with too many criminals. You lack trust."

Janet perched on the only available corner of her desk and studied him intently. "Okay. If—and that's a very big if—I were to take you up on your suggestion, what exactly do you have in mind?"

"Lunch," he said at once.

"It's barely nine-fifteen in the morning."

"In Dallas."

She stared at him and tried to keep her mouth from gaping. "You want to go all the way to Dallas for lunch? Isn't that a little extravagant?"

He had a ready answer for that, too, apparently. "We could shop," he said without so much as a hesitation.

"For?"

He shrugged, his expression vaguely uncertain. "Beats me. I just figured all women loved to shop. And much as I love Los Piños, I can see that it's not exactly loaded with those fancy little designer boutiques, where a hankie costs an arm and a leg."

"I can't afford a boutique where hankies cost a hundred times what I'd pay for a pack of tissues."

"But I can."

She grinned at his persistence. "You want to fly to Dallas to buy me lunch and a hankie?"

"Or maybe a fancy outfit to wear to a party," he said, watching her with another of those exceptionally innocent expressions that wouldn't have deceived anyone with even half a brain.

Janet's gaze narrowed. "What party?"

"The one I'm throwing on Saturday night to introduce you to a few of my friends."

"Harlan, I told you I do not want you trying to drum up business for me."

He scowled, his exasperation apparent. "This isn't about business, darlin'. This is strictly personal."

For some reason she didn't find that nearly as reassuring as she should have. It struck her as being too...personal, she decided, using his own word to describe it. Too intimate. Especially given that unspoken subject hanging in the air between them. Why, why, why? she wondered again. What was he up to?

"I don't know—" she began, only to have him cut her off.

"It's no big deal," he reassured her. "There are a lot of people I owe for inviting me to dinner and stuff. I figured one big bash would take care of all those obligations. I can't have a big to-do without a proper hostess, can I?"

"And that's me?" she said skeptically. "The woman who can't cook a lick."

"I have Maritza and all of her relatives for that."

"You also have three very lovely daughters-in-law who would be happy to play hostess, I'm sure."

He waved off the suggestion. "I want a woman of my own."

She cringed at the possessive description, but let it pass. "Half the people in town barely say more than hello to me," she noted pointedly.

"That'll change when you're with me."

Knowing that he was right about that grated. "Harlan, I have to win people over myself."

"You will. I'm just opening the door, so they'll give you a chance to show 'em what a brilliant, witty, warm woman you are." He reached behind her desk and grabbed her purse. "Come on. You can think it over while we fly to Dallas."

"What about Jenny? What have you done with her since I dropped her off?"

"She's helping Melissa out with the kids today. I'm paying her ten bucks an hour to baby-sit. She says minimum wage is too cheap for the trouble those kids get into. Had to admit she was right about that."

Janet shook her head. "This is the oddest brand of punishment I've ever seen."

He shrugged. "So I'm lenient, sue me. Any more excuses?"

She was about to muster the last of her resolve and say no when she took a good, long look into his eyes. They were bright with excitement. He genuinely wanted to do this for her. How could she possibly disappoint him, when he'd already been so good to her and to Jenny? Besides, an unplanned trip to Dallas was exactly the sort of impulsive act she'd indulged in far too rarely.

"Okay, let's go for it," she said at last.

At the same time, she swore that she would do everything in her power not to take advantage of him. Lunch was one thing. A party outfit was something else entirely. She would buy that for herself, if she could convince herself that one of the dozens of cocktail dresses already in her closet from what seemed like another lifetime wouldn't do.

For a man who claimed not to know much about shopping, Harlan guided her around the best shops in Dallas with the ease and familiarity of an extravagant tour guide. He seemed to have his heart set on a particular kind of dress and, after trying on dozens, all she knew for certain was that it wasn't baubles, bangles or beads he was looking for.

"I think I know just the place," he said at last, and led her to a boutique carrying designer Western wear. He gazed around at the fancy Western-cut shirts and rhinestone-studded jeans and nodded in satisfaction. "Yep, this is it."

Janet shook her head. "You knew all along this was what you wanted me to wear, didn't you?" she accused.

"I wasn't sure," he claimed.

"Harlan, there is no comparison between those cocktail dresses and this," she said, gesturing to the displays. "Why'd you waste three hours taking me to those stores, so I could try on silk and lace?"

"I thought all women liked to dress up in pretty clothes. Besides, I thought you might find something you couldn't resist." He shook his head. "You're a tough nut to crack, though. I never once saw a glimmer of longing in your eyes."

"Because I wore those kinds of dresses to more social functions than I care to recall back in New York. My closet is crammed with them. If I never wear another one, it will be okay with me."

He chuckled at that. "That's another thing I love about you. You've long since figured out who you are."

Janet denied his assessment with a quick shake of her head. "You're wrong. I know who I don't want to be anymore. I don't want to be a big city lawyer, living in a pressure cooker. I don't want to go to parties because I might meet someone important," she said pointedly, then added with a touch of wistfulness, "But I'm still discovering who I am."

Harlan listened to all that intently, then asked softly, "Any room in the picture for a rancher?"

The direct question took her by surprise. Her heart thumped unsteadily as she considered all the implications of what he was asking. "Maybe," she said eventually, her gaze locked with his.

"That's good enough," he said quietly. "For now."

She finally forced herself to break eye contact by feigning a sudden interest in a fancy denim outfit.

"Janet," Harlan said, drawing her attention back to him. "If there's one thing I've learned the past few years it's that life is unpredictable and often far too short. Don't get the idea I'm going to leave you much room to maneuver for long."

Her breath caught in her throat at the silky tone. "Is that a threat?"

He touched his fingers to her cheek in a light caress that set off fireworks in her midsection.

"It's a promise," he declared, then winked. "Now, try on that outfit you've been eyeing since we walked in the door. And while you're at it, take a look at that skirt and blouse with the sparkly doodads on it.''

"Rhinestones?" she teased.

"That's the one. Looks perfect for square dancing.''

"We're going to be dancing on Saturday?''

"Darlin', you can't have a big to-do in this part of the world and call it a party, unless there's dancing.''

"I had no idea.''

"That's why you have me," he reassured her. "I'm going to see to it that you fit right in in no time.''

"I do so admire a man with a mission," she said as she grabbed the selected clothes off the racks and carried them into a nearby dressing room.

Inside the room, she shut the door and leaned against it, drawing in a deep breath. With every single minute she spent in Harlan Adams's company, she realized she was coming closer and closer to losing her heart. The day when she would have to choose between that and her own personal mission was clearly just around the corner.

On Saturday, Harlan fussed over every detail as the time for guests to start arriving neared. Maritza was beginning to mutter in Spanish, her tone suggesting it would be far better if he didn't try to translate. Her cousin Consuela, who'd been the original house-keeper at White Pines until Luke had lured her off to his ranch, finally backed him out the kitchen door by waving a dish towel in his face.

"Go, go. You stay out now," she ordered, barring the doorway. "You are only in the way in here."

"Damn, but you're bossy," he grumbled affectionately. "Who's running that house of Luke's? You or him?"

Her dark eyes flashed fire. "You remember that I can walk out before this affair of yours begins," she threatened, her own tone just as fond. "I will take Maritza and the others with me. How will you manage then, *señor?*"

"With my charm," he quipped.

She turned her gaze toward heaven as if praying for patience. "It will not feed this crowd you have invited," she reminded him. "Now, go and talk with your sons or play with your grandbabies."

"I'll go out and check to see if the tent's set up right," he said.

"No," she ordered at once. "The men have everything under control." She tilted her head at him. "I do not recall you making such a fuss over details in the past. This party is important to you?"

He nodded, feeling sheepish. "Silly, huh? We must have thrown a hundred parties in this house, but this is the first time I've ever been a wreck."

Consuela's expression sobered at once. "It is because you no longer have Mary by your side," she said sorrowfully. "I should have thought, Señor Harlan. You must miss her very much at a time like this."

That was part of it, he supposed. But he'd come to terms with his loss in the past few months. Though he was likely to miss Mary until the end of his days, he had moved on. No, this sense that he was standing

at the edge of a precipice and that the slightest mis-
step would send him over was due to another woman
entirely.

"No," he corrected softly. "It is because I want
everything to be perfect tonight."

Consuela's eyes widened. "For the *señorita,* yes?"
At his startled look, she explained, "Rosa told me
she has seen you together in town many times and
then Luke and Jessie described meeting her. They say
your eyes light up when you are in the same room.
You care for this woman?"

He nodded, even though that was a pale description
of his feelings. "Deeply," he admitted.

"Then Maritza and I will see that this party im-
presses her. Leave it to us, okay?"

He grinned. "Do I have any choice?"

"No," she conceded, and disappeared into the
kitchen from which she had just banished him.

Left at loose ends, he paced. When that failed to
calm him, he retreated to his office and fiddled with
papers, none of which caught his full attention. He
was trying for the third time to add up a simple col-
umn of figures when he realized he was no longer
alone. He glanced up and found not one, but six pairs
of prying eyes studying him with amusement.

"What's the matter with the bunch of you?" he
grumbled, staring sourly at his sons and their wives.
If he could have kept them away from this event, he
would have, but he hadn't wanted to send the wrong
message to Janet. He was very aware of how sensitive
she was about not being accepted in Los Piños, de-

spite the cavalier attitude she had expressed on the subject.

"We heard you were driving the entire staff nuts," Luke said. "Consuela thought you might need company."

"Consuela is a busybody." He noticed Jordan and Cody rolling their eyes. "And you two can be uninvited, you know."

"Us?" Jordan said innocently, exchanging a look with his younger brother. "What did we do?"

"We're giving him a taste of his own medicine," Cody retorted, clearly undaunted by the threat. "Looks like he can't take it."

Harlan heard the sound of footsteps clattering down the stairs. "Aren't those your little hellions I hear?" he demanded. "Damn, but they make a racket. Can't you control them?"

"Those are your precious grandchildren," Luke corrected. "And you're the one who said you wanted this to be a family event. How come, Daddy? You have big plans for tonight? Maybe an announcement of some kind?"

Harlan was startled by the suggestion, even though he could see how they might have leapt to that conclusion. "Don't go getting ideas. This shindig's just to let Janet get to know the family and some of my friends."

"How big's the guest list?" Jordan prodded, his expression entirely too smug.

"Two hundred, okay?" Harlan retorted, frowning at him. "Once I got started, I figured I might as well invite everybody at once."

"I hope Janet's not expecting an intimate little gathering," Jessie said worriedly. "I'll never forget that birthday party you threw for me when I was first married to Erik. I'd never seen that many people gathered together outside of a church revival in my entire life."

"Well, we'll know soon enough," Kelly stated. "She and Jenny are just pulling up." She grinned at her father-in-law. "Did you tell her to come early to play hostess?"

Harlan shook his head in disgust at their teasing. "Never mind what I told her," he said as he strode past them.

"He must not think we're up to the responsibility," Kelly said to Jessie and Melissa. "Think we should stage a protest?"

"I'm for it," Melissa teased.

Harlan turned back and glared at the lot of them. "If you all don't behave tonight, I'm disowning every one of you."

"I win!" Cody said with a whoop.

Harlan scowled at his youngest. "Win what?"

"We placed bets on how long it would take you to threaten to disown us. I figured less than ten minutes. Luke and Jordan thought you'd hold your temper longer."

"I was counting on Janet being here to keep him in line," Luke explained.

"Out of the will, every one of you," Harlan declared as he walked off and left them laughing.

Only after he was out of their eyesight did he allow himself to smile.

* * *

Harlan must have invited everyone within a hundred-mile radius, Janet decided as she stared at the throng of people filling their plates at the heavily laden buffet tables.

As if he sensed that she might be overwhelmed, he had stuck close to her side ever since her arrival, silencing gossip with a frown, introducing her to people who could bring her their legal business, shielding her from his sons' excessive teasing.

He'd left her just a moment before to greet the governor, promising to bring him back to meet her. The governor, for heaven's sake! At what Harlan referred to as a little backyard barbecue. Obviously he took such illustrious guests in stride.

To her, the sheer size of the event was daunting without even taking into account the importance of some of the guests. Her ex-husband would have had whiplash from looking this way and that to be sure he didn't miss anybody. The fancy New York parties they'd attended had been nothing compared to this assembly of Texas's rich and powerful.

"A little daunting, isn't it?" Jessie inquired, magically appearing by her side just when Janet was beginning to feel exactly that way.

"It's second nature to him, isn't it?" she replied, watching the ease with which Harlan escorted the governor from cluster to cluster. As many parties as she'd been to, she'd never been entirely comfortable with the small talk required.

"You wouldn't have thought that, if you'd seen him earlier," Jessie revealed. "He was like a kid throwing his first party and terrified nobody would come. Of course, in his case, I think you're the only guest he's been really worried about.''

Janet couldn't get over the idea that Harlan might have suffered a bad case of stage fright. ''He was nervous?'' she asked incredulously.

Jessie nodded. ''Because of you. He really wanted tonight to be special for you.'' She studied Janet intently. ''Are you two involved? I mean, happily-ever-after involved.''

Janet evaded a direct answer by asking a question of her own, ''What does he say?''

''Not a darn thing, really. It's driving all of us crazy.'' She grinned. ''I figure it serves Luke and his brothers right. On the other hand, I want to be in on the secret.''

''There is no secret,'' Janet assured her.

Jessie's expression turned serious. ''If he asks you to marry him, what will you say?''

Janet swallowed hard. It was clear that Jessie felt her question wasn't nearly as premature as Janet hoped it was. ''I can't answer that,'' she said. To soften the response, she added, ''And even if I could, you're not the one I'd be telling. Harlan would be the first to have an answer.''

Jessie nodded approvingly. ''Good. Now I know that all the bullying from these Adams men won't force you into a corner.'' She grinned. ''It takes a strong woman to put up with them. I think you'll do just fine.''

''Thanks for the vote of confidence,'' Janet said. ''But sometimes trying to say no to Harlan is like swimming in quicksand.''

"You ever need a lifeline, just let me know," Jessie offered. "The same with Kelly or Melissa. We've all been there." She glanced up and caught sight of Harlan approaching with the governor at the same time Janet did. "Whoops, I'm out of here. I voted for his opponent. I'd hate to have to admit that in front of Harlan."

Janet was still chuckling when Harlan reached her. She acknowledged the introduction to the governor and his wife with a smile and sufficient small talk to cover her nervousness. Fortunately, the band struck up a slower tune just then.

"That's my cue," the governor said, beaming at his wife. "Shall we?" As they headed for the dance floor, he said, "Call my office next week. I'd like to talk with you a bit about your interest in Native American affairs."

Janet stared after him openmouthed. "How did he know about that?"

Harlan shrugged. "I might have mentioned it. All that talk about Lone Wolf and his ancestors led me to think you might have a particular interest in the subject."

As if he thought he might have already said too much, he glanced toward the crowded dance floor that had been set up under the stars. "How about it? You willing to risk a turn around the floor with me?"

The request didn't give her time to wonder how a few comments about Lone Wolf had led Harlan to guess how deep her interest in Native Americans ran. Before she could even form a question, she was in his arms and they were swaying to the soft music.

The feel of his body pressed against hers made every inch of her flesh tingle. With her head tucked against his shoulder, she felt warm and secure and desired. His heat surrounded her, making her senses swim.

Suddenly she was no longer aware of anything but the provocative rhythm of the music and the feel of his muscles playing against her own. She could hear the steady sound of his heart pounding, feel the quickening of his pulse. A desperate hunger began to build deep inside her, a hunger that was clearly matched in the man who held her so tightly.

"You'll stay the night?" he asked out of the blue, his gaze searching hers.

"Jenny," she said, unable to manage another single word.

He nodded his understanding of her concern. "Not to worry. I'll speak to Cody. Melissa will think up an excuse to have her baby-sit. Will that do?"

"Yes," she whispered, sighing as she settled her head against his shoulder. She was grateful for his consideration, anxious to get this entire crowd on its way before she had time for second thoughts.

He leaned back and gazed down at her. "You want me to send everybody packing as badly as I want to do it?" he inquired, a teasing glint in his eyes.

"Yes," she admitted. "Isn't that terrible, especially when you've gone to all this trouble?"

"Wanting it isn't so bad," he claimed. "We'll just have to think of it as a test of character that we don't act on it." He winked at her. "Besides, a little anticipation isn't all bad. It'll just make the rest of the night all the sweeter.''

Janet regarded him skeptically. It seemed to her the next few hours were going to be the longest of her entire life. And if Harlan had a brain in his head, he wouldn't give her anywhere near that long to reconsider the decision she'd just reached in the provocative circle of his arms.

He leaned down then to whisper in her ear. ''Don't look so impatient, darlin'. You'll be giving folks ideas about what's on your mind.''

''No question about that,'' Luke said impudently as he tapped his father on the shoulder. ''I'm cutting in before you two make a spectacle of yourselves.''

''Go away,'' Harlan said, refusing to release her.

Janet chuckled as the two of them stared each other down. ''I think Luke has the right idea,'' she said, slipping out of Harlan's embrace. ''Go dance with somebody else for a while.''

Harlan frowned at his oldest son. ''You'll pay for this,'' he muttered irritably, but he did start off. He hadn't gone more than half a dozen steps before he turned back to Janet. ''You and I have a date, darlin'. Don't be forgetting it.''

''Not a chance,'' she promised.

She looked up to find Luke chuckling. ''What?'' she demanded.

''Another five seconds I'd have had to hose the two of you down.''

''I'm beginning to see why your father finds you so irritating,'' she muttered.

He laughed out loud at that. ''Jessie was right.''

"About?"

"You'll fit in just fine."

The approval behind the comment stayed with Janet for the rest of the seemingly endless evening. She was glad that Luke and Jessie thought she'd be right for Harlan. She couldn't help wondering, though, how they'd feel if they discovered what had originally brought her to Texas. Would they be as open and generous then? Or would they do everything in their power to see that she and Harlan never spent another single second alone together?

Chapter Thirteen

"We'll all meet here for a late breakfast," Harlan said to Jenny as she prepared to leave with Cody and Melissa and their kids after the party. He'd been trying to shoo people off for an hour now, to little avail. His sons particularly showed no inclination to go.

To Janet's surprise, though, Jenny didn't seemed particularly thrown by the change in plans. She was probably thrilled to be spending the night under Cody's roof. Fortunately her daughter had missed the earlier exchange of winks between Cody and his brothers when they'd learned that Harlan was sending Jenny home with Cody and his crew.

"You'll be back then, too, Mom?" Jenny asked sleepily as she climbed into Cody's car.

Janet nodded. "I'll be here," she promised.

Jenny yawned. "Okay. See you."

A moment later they were gone and Janet's heart climbed straight into her throat at the look of pure longing in Harlan's eyes. Despite the irreversible commitment she'd made to stay, despite her own yearning to make love to this incredibly gentle, thoughtful man, she was more nervous than an innocent bride on her wedding night.

She still had so many questions about why he seemed to have forgiven her for what must have seemed to him a hiding of the truth at least. That he still hadn't mentioned what Jenny had told him kept her from relaxing and falling entirely under his spell. She kept waiting for him to reel her in and then turn on her when she least expected it.

"What about the others?" she asked, delaying their return to the house.

His gaze never left her face. "What others?" he murmured distractedly, his attention clearly riveted on her.

"Jordan and Kelly, for instance," she said, though she was a bit distracted herself by the intensity of his gaze and the electricity arcing between them.

He stroked a finger along her cheek. "They've gone home. Slipped away a while ago, in fact."

Janet swallowed hard before managing to add, "And Luke and Jessie?"

"Upstairs in their suite." Her expression must have given away her trepidation, because he quickly added, "It's at the opposite end of this big old place from mine. Think of it as being like a fancy hotel. You wouldn't think twice about who was down the hall."

"But this room is occupied by your son and his family, not strangers."

He shrugged off her concern. "I promise you it's not a problem."

Janet disagreed. "How will they feel when they find out I've stayed the night?"

"For one thing, I don't think any of them had a doubt in the world that you would be here come morning. Besides that, you seem to be forgetting whose house this is."

"Hardly."

"Okay, but whatever Luke's opinion might be, he'll keep it to himself."

Janet chuckled at the unlikelihood of that. "Are we talking about the same Luke?"

"Stop fussing," he soothed, cupping her face in his hands. "If you want to put this off, just say the word. You'll have your own room for the night. I can even fix you up on a different floor, if you'd prefer. Give you a key for the lock, too, if it'll make you feel better."

She wrestled with the offer. Eventually, longing and a deep sense of inevitability overcame doubt. With Jenny staying at Cody's overnight, there might never be another opportunity like this one.

She reached up and covered his hands with her own. Her gaze locked with his. "If I stay here tonight, it will be with you."

Rather than seeming relieved, he tensed as questions darkened his eyes. "If? You aren't seriously thinking of driving back into town, are you?"

She tilted her head. A smile tugged at her lips at

the stark disappointment in his expression. She had another alternative in mind, one with which she was far more comfortable.

"I was thinking I'd have you take me," she said. She lowered her voice to a coaxing note. "My house might be a half hour from here, but it is totally deserted." Unspoken was the fact that there would be no ghosts in the bed or prying family members down the hall.

The tension in his shoulders eased the instant he caught her meaning. "Well, why didn't you say so?" he said, grinning. "I'll get my car keys."

"Mine are in my purse," she said, already reaching for them and handing them over. "Besides, with only my car parked out front, no one will ever guess you're there. No gossip."

"Better yet."

They rounded the house, laughing like a couple of kids sneaking off to make out. Harlan gunned the engine in a way that would have had Mule sulking for a month about his disrespect for what the mechanic had declared to be an almost-classic car.

Then he shot down the lane and away from White Pines as if he'd been celibate for a decade and had finally discovered he was about to get lucky. Janet found his eagerness both touching and very arousing.

The drive into Los Piños seemed to take an eternity, especially after Harlan placed her hand on his rock-hard thigh and covered it with his own. So much heat, she thought as her senses spun wildly. So much strength. So much barely contained passion.

His blatant desire fueled hers, until by the time they

reached her house, the last of her uncertainties had been stripped away. They rushed through her front door, barely taking the time for Harlan to kick it shut behind him before he dragged her into his arms. He kissed her with all of the pent-up hunger that had been held in check on the dance floor, on the long drive and for who knew how long before.

The kiss was commanding and all-consuming, wiping out every thought except for some primitive understanding of its wicked effect on her senses. Never in her life had she experienced such raw, untamed lust. She was suddenly trembling from head to toe with anticipation.

She was fumbling with the buttons on Harlan's shirt just as urgently as he was stripping away the blouse they'd searched all over Dallas to find just yesterday. Then his mouth was covering first one breast, then the other, teasing, suckling in a way that sent shock waves ricocheting through her.

His skin was on fire beneath her touch, but her own was hotter. The caress of his tongue cooled, then inflamed, then cooled again in a devastating cycle. A moan of pure pleasure escaped, shattering their previously silent, passionate duet.

The sound brought his head up, leaving her feeling bereft. As if he had suddenly found his bearings, he tucked her tightly against his chest and sucked in a deep, calming breath.

"Whoa, darlin'," he murmured softly, as if gentling a skittish mare.

"No," she pleaded. "Don't stop."

He chuckled at the urgency in her tone. "I will not

make love to you on the floor in the foyer," he said. "Not that I'm entirely sure I can get us both out of this tangle we've made of our clothes and into the bedroom."

If that was the only delay, Janet was more than willing to help. She shucked what was left of her clothing, kicked it aside and headed down the hallway stark naked. Only when she realized Harlan hadn't followed did she turn back. He was staring after her, looking stunned. The thoroughly masculine appreciation in his eyes made her knees go weak.

"You take my breath away," he said in a hoarse whisper.

"Ditto," she said in a voice only faintly louder. "If you get over here, though, I'll give you mouth-to-mouth resuscitation."

Amusement danced in his eyes at that. "You certified?"

"No," she admitted, then grinned. "I'll need lots and lots of practice."

Practically before the words were out of her mouth, he had joined her, scooping her up and carrying her into the bedroom with long, anxious strides.

"Then by all means, let's get to it," he said, lowering her to the bed, then settling down beside her atop the thick comforter.

The break had allowed just enough time for ardor to cool. To Janet's astonishment, it took little more than a sweeping caress of her bare hip with callused fingers to return it to a fever pitch.

But Harlan was clearly in no hurry now that they'd made it this far. He seemed intent on making each response linger, then build to a shattering crescendo before trying something new. In her head, Janet knew that this was the same body she'd lived with all her life, but under his gentle, tormenting ministrations it seemed entirely new and heart-stoppingly responsive.

She was filled with astonishment over each exquisite, devastating sensation. And when every nerve was vibrantly alive, when he finally, at long last, entered her with a slow, tantalizing thrust, she felt as if she'd finally discovered the true meaning of joy.

As their bodies played out this timeless ritual, over and over through the night, perfecting it, elaborating on it, exploring its every nuance, she wondered if she'd ever been alive before she met Harlan Adams or if she'd just been existing in some half-awake state, waiting for this moment.

Discovering such passion deep within herself should have been exhilarating, but in the silvery, moonlit darkness just before dawn broke she was overcome by an agony of indecision. She tried to compare these new, barely tested feelings for the man sprawled out half on top of her, his hand possessively circling her breast, with older loyalties to the grandfather she had adored.

If there hadn't been such a history in her family of mistakes, of choosing mates so unwisely, perhaps she could have reached a different decision. But neither her father nor her first husband had understood this gut-deep need she had to discover the Comanche side of her heritage. She doubted Harlan would be any different, especially when he realized that part of that discovery meant righting a century-old wrong if there was any legal means at all to do so.

Sighing, she resolved that this night would never be repeated. She knew with everything in her that it was a decision Harlan would never understand, one he would fight with all of his incomparable powers of persuasion. She also knew it was the only one she could make.

And knowing that broke her heart.

Harlan was the kind of man who usually snapped awake in an instant. He'd never had much interest in lingering in bed when there were chores to do and a ranch to run. Maybe the trait had been born of necessity decades ago, but it had become a habit he'd had no reason to break, not even when the whole day stretched out emptily ahead of him.

This morning, though, he seemed to be easing back into consciousness, sensation by sensation. First it was the heat that tugged at his senses. Then it was the sweet, sweet smell of some light-as-air flowery scent, layered with an undertone of dark, musky sensuality. And then, dear heaven, it was the soft-as-satin brush of skin against skin, a teasing caress that had his blood pumping so hard and fast he thought his heart might flat-out explode in his chest.

That woke him, all right! His eyes snapped open to gaze straight into sleepy, dark eyes that struck him as far more troubled than they ought to be after such an incredible night.

"You're looking mighty serious," he said, brushing Janet's hair back over her shoulders so he could drink his fill of the sight of those rose-tipped breasts. The peaks pebbled at once, even under such an off-hand caress. He might have lingered longer, intensified his touch, had Janet's gaze not seemed so fraught with worry.

"Regrets?" he asked.

"None," she swore.

Harlan wasn't convinced. "You sure?"

"I could never regret what happened between us last night," she said more firmly.

Though he was still doubtful, he decided he'd just have to take her at her word. "Then I think we ought to talk about making it permanent."

This time there was no mistaking the alarm that flared in her eyes.

"No," she whispered, touching a finger to his lips. "Please, don't say any more."

He couldn't take rejection so easily, not when he had his heart set on spending his future with this woman, not when he knew without a trace of doubt that deep inside that was what she wanted, too. He suspected he even knew what was preventing her from accepting his proposal.

"You don't even want me saying that I love you?" he said, keeping his tone light. "You don't want to hear that I won't settle for anything less than making you my wife, not after last night?"

A tear slid slowly down her cheek, even as she declined his proposal for a second time.

"I can't," she whispered.

"Of course you can," he insisted just as adamantly. "There's nothing to stop you, except some foolish willfulness on your part."

He knew as soon as the words were out of his mouth that they had been exactly the wrong thing to say. Whatever she was struggling with—and he was certain now that he knew what it was—he shouldn't have dismissed it as foolish or willful. A milewide stubborn streak would kick in over words like that. His own certainly would have.

"I'm sorry. I shouldn't have said that," he apologized at once.

"No," she said stiffly, retreating as far from him in the bed as she could and surrounding herself with layers of covers despite the room's more than comfortable temperature. "You shouldn't have."

Because he needed time to rein in his temper, Harlan stood and searched for his pants. When he'd yanked them on, he returned to sit opposite her on the edge of the bed.

"Can we discuss this?"

"I don't see why you'd want to," she said dully.

"Because this is too important for you to leap to a snap decision that could affect the rest of both of our lives, to say nothing of Jenny's," he explained, fighting to keep his tone even. "You know I care for her as if she were one of my own. You also know I've been a good influence on her."

She shot him a stubborn scowl. "I'm not going to get married again because Jenny needs a father."

"Then how about because you need a husband who loves you, almost as much as I need a wife who'll make me feel alive the way you did in this bed last night, the way you have every day since we met? Can you deny you felt the same way?''

''No, of course not. I would never lie to you about something that important,'' she told him. ''But I came here to find myself. You're such a strong man. From all I've heard, your first wife doted on you. You were her first and only priority. I'm afraid I'd turn out to be just like her, that I'd lose myself in being Mrs. Harlan Adams, rather than Janet Runningbear, a Comanche lawyer in search of her roots.''

''It's the last that's important, isn't it?'' he said, experiencing the bitter taste of defeat in his mouth. ''It's this thing you have about your great-grandfather.''

Her gaze narrowed. ''What if it is?''

''Why don't you tell me what really brought you to Texas?'' he commanded.

Her gaze faltered. ''I've told you a hundred different ways,'' she said. ''You haven't been listening.''

''You want to know what I hear? I hear you denying yourself a future you want because of some crazy notion that won't ever pan out the way you want it to.''

She frowned at that. ''Don't be so certain of that, Harlan. There's very little I can't accomplish if I set my mind to it. I won't let you or my feelings for you stand in my way. I can't allow that to happen. I will never be like Mary, so you might as well accept that and move on.''

It was quite likely the only argument she might have made that he didn't have a ready answer for. Words were too easy for a fear like that, especially when he couldn't deny that Mary had given up a part of herself the day she became his wife.

He resigned himself to taking a little time to show Janet that that had been Mary's choice, not his. He was ready and eager to have a strong and independent woman at his side. He was no young kid who'd mistake independence of spirit with a lack of love.

Patience, unfortunately, was not one of his virtues. More, he suspected that that would solve only part of the problem. Janet was still struggling with her conscience over her desire to get her hands on the land that she felt had belonged to her ancestors.

Until she could tell him about that herself, until they could work it through together, it would always stand between them and happiness. She'd almost said the words a moment ago, he was sure of it, but something had kept her silent. Whether it was fear of his reaction or a desire not to hurt him, he couldn't be sure.

"Okay," he said eventually. "I'll let it slide for now, if I must."

He walked around to the other side of the bed where she still sat huddled under the covers. He determinedly tucked a finger under her chin and tilted her face up until their eyes clashed.

"But I won't give up on us. I'll pester you until you see what I see, that we belong together."

A clearly reluctant smile tugged at the corners of her mouth. "That ought to scare the hell out of me," she said, then gave a little shrug of resignation. "But for some crazy reason, it doesn't."

"That's because you know I'm right," he said with satisfaction.

"I do not," she insisted.

"Argue all you want, but the end result will still be the same," he informed her. "Now get dressed so we can sneak back to White Pines before the whole gang figures out we're missing."

"It would serve you right," she muttered as she strolled off to the shower. "You're the one they'd taunt unmercifully. They're very polite to me."

"They won't be, once they know you're going to be family."

"I am not going to be..." she shouted, then sighed audibly. "Oh, never mind."

Harlan grinned as the bathroom door slammed behind her. Yes, indeed, no matter what she thought, no matter what kind of struggle she put up, it was only a matter of time.

Facing the entire Adams clan around the breakfast table—except for the youngest babies, who were being watched upstairs—was a heck of a lot more intimidating than their first meeting had been, Janet decided after several awkward minutes ticked by. Their fascinated gazes kept shifting from her to Harlan and back again. Only Jenny and the older grandchildren seemed oblivious to the undercurrents. Their unrestrained chatter was all that made the situation bearable.

The minute everyone had finished eating, Harlan said, "I had Consuela's brother put up the wading pool out back. Jenny, why don't you take the little ones out to play in that and keep an eye on them?''

Jenny surveyed him speculatively. ''My usual rates?''

''Yes, you little entrepeneur,'' he said with contradictory fondness. ''I'll pay you your usual rates.''

''Great! I'll be able to buy more CDs, if we ever get to a town with a decent music store,'' she said with a pointed look in Janet's direction.

''Maybe next weekend,'' Janet replied distractedly. She was too worried about the inquisitive expressions on Cody's, Jordan's and Luke's faces to pay much attention to Jenny's normal grumbling about the lack of shopping in Los Piños.

The reply seemed to satisfy her daughter, because she took off readily with the younger children.

''Well?'' Luke said, his gaze fixed on his father.

Harlan tried to stare him down. ''Well, what?''

''Isn't there something you two want to tell us?''

''No,'' Harlan and Janet replied in chorus.

Luke and Jessie exchanged a look filled with amusement that was promptly caught by the others.

''You know something, don't you?'' Cody guessed. ''Come on, big brother, share.''

Harlan's gaze narrowed. ''I don't know what you think you know, Lucas,'' he said, ''but if you've got any decency in you, you'll keep it to yourself.''

''He has a point,'' Jessie said, laughter dancing in her eyes. ''I mean, we don't know for sure where they were going when they went sneaking off in the middle of the night.''

Janet groaned and buried her face in her hands, sure

that her complexion must be a fiery shade of red. "That's it. I'm out of here," she declared, shoving her chair back and practically racing from the room.

"Now look what you've done," Harlan chided, sending his own chair scooting across the floor with a clatter. "When I get back, I want you out of here. Maybe the whole blasted lot of you ought to think about moving to Arizona or Montana, anywhere that's far away from here."

If she hadn't been so embarrassed, Janet might have chuckled at his blustery tone. As it was, she just wanted to disappear herself. She was already outside when he caught up with her.

"I'm sorry," he said. "You know what big mouths they have. I told you so myself before we came back here this morning."

"It's not that," she said miserably. "It's just so sweet the way they tease you. I know they wouldn't do that, if they didn't want something to happen between you and me. I feel as if I'm letting all of you down."

"Only for the moment," he reminded her with that trace of stubbornness that proved he still hadn't accepted that her no meant an emphatic *no*.

She lifted her chin and leveled a look straight into his eyes. "No, Harlan. Not just for the moment. I meant what I said back at my house. There is no future for us, not unless you mean it to be no more than friendship."

"I won't settle for that," he said with surprisingly little rancor. She knew why when he added, "And in time, neither will you."

Chapter Fourteen

Jenny's presence was the only thing that gave Harlan any peace of mind at all in the days after Janet had fled from White Pines. The fact that she continued to turn up every morning reassured him that there was hope. It enabled him to be patient.

Not that the teenager had suddenly turned into a saint or even a staunch advocate of his relationship with her mother, but she was showing signs of weakening. Her belligerence was sported more for effect than any real attitude on her part. He decided one afternoon to call her on it.

She'd thrown a fit not an hour before over some inconsequential task he'd asked her to do. She'd saddled Misty after that and taken off. He guessed he'd find her at the creek.

Sure enough, she was sitting on the grassy bank, her bare feet dangling in the cool water.

"If you wanted to come down here, all you had to do was ask," he said, dropping to the ground beside her.

She regarded him with disbelief. "You'd have let me come?"

"You know I would. You also know I would have come along. You just figured you ought to raise a ruckus so I wouldn't get too used to the more mellow Jenny, isn't that right?"

She slanted a look at him. "You think you're pretty smart, don't you?"

"I know I am. The question is, are you ready to admit it?"

She sighed heavily. "If you're so smart, how come Mom's dropping me off at the end of the lane again? It's her idea this time," she added, so there would be no mistake.

"Because she's sorting through some things."

"She's behaving like a ninny, you mean."

He grinned. "Is that what I mean?"

"Seems that way to me." She met his gaze evenly. "Are you in love with her?"

"Don't you think that's between her and me?"

"Not if I have to live with her while you two are figuring things out. I think I deserve to know what's going on." She shot him a sly look. "I could help you, you know. Mom listens to me."

Harlan hid a smile. "Is that so? What would your intercession on my behalf cost me?"

Jenny blinked. "Hey, wait a minute," she protested. "That's not the kind of thing I'd charge you for."

"Then that would be a first," he said dryly.

"Look, you don't want my help, it's no skin off my nose. You don't seem to be doing so great on your own, though."

"Trust me," he said. "I can handle this without any help from you." He studied her curiously. "But can I assume from what you're saying that you would approve of your mother and me getting married?"

She looked reluctant to make that big an admission, but finally she shrugged. "I suppose it would be okay."

He grinned. "Thanks for the endorsement."

"Would it mean I could stop doing chores and get an allowance?"

"I doubt it."

"Oh." She regarded him intently. "But you would want me around, right?"

"You bet," he said. "It's definitely a package deal. You comfortable with having me as a stepdaddy?"

To his astonishment, Jenny shifted and threw her arms around his neck. She didn't say a word, but the dampness of fresh tears on his neck told him all he needed to know. He had himself a daughter.

Janet was feeling besieged. Not by Harlan, bless his heart. To her surprise he was giving her all the space she'd claimed to crave. No, it was his family that wouldn't leave her in peace.

Every son, every daughter-in-law made some excuse or another to pay a call, to proclaim all of Harlan's virtues, to try to wheedle from her a reason for her reluctance to accept the proposal, which they had somehow discovered he'd made. She had the same answer for each of them: "Does your father know you're here?"

And when the reply was consistently no, she suggested that they talk with him if they had questions about the relationship. "He knows why I won't marry him," she repeated over and over.

Unfortunately, Jessie wasn't as easily dissuaded as the others. She popped in two weeks after that disgraceful scene Janet had caused by running out of the dining room at White Pines. The minute she'd walked through the door, she settled into a seat opposite Janet and showed no inclination at all to leave.

"I'm not going to talk about it," Janet declared for what must have been the hundredth time, hoping just this once to stop any questions before they started.

Jessie nodded. "That's understandable," she soothed.

It was, perhaps, the hundredth time Janet had heard that, too. Everyone who'd dropped by had said the same thing, then proceeded to butt in just the same.

"It's private," Jessie added, indicating a deeper understanding than most.

"Exactly."

"Harlan's probably done more than enough bullying himself without the rest of us getting in on the act."

"Precisely," Janet said.

To her relief, Jessie appeared willing to give up. She even stood, to indicate an imminent departure.

"Let's go to Dolan's and have a milk shake," she suggested.

Janet blinked. "What?"

"A thick, chocolate milk shake," Jessie added temptingly. "Come on. I never get anything like that at the ranch. Consuela's a great cook, but lately she's constantly worried about killing Luke with too much fat. There hasn't been so much as a pint of ice cream in the house in months. I have to sneak over here to Los Piños to get a milk shake, if I want one."

"And just this morning you decided you had a hankering for one and drove...what? Two hours? Three, just to get one?" Janet said skeptically, not believing for a minute that Jessie couldn't have whipped one up right in her own kitchen if she'd really wanted to.

"It's amazing the cravings that come on when a woman least expects them," Jessie said. "Chocolate milk shakes..." Her expression turned innocent. "A man, same difference. Once the idea's planted in your head, you might as well give in to it."

That sneaky little reference to men triggered all of Janet's alarm systems. "Are you suggesting that I should go ahead and marry Harlan, because he's like some sort of addiction I won't be able to break?"

Jessie regarded her with another innocent look. "I was talking about milk shakes. You're the one who brought up marriage." She tilted her head inquiringly. "Has it been on your mind a lot lately?"

"If I didn't like you so much, I'd tell you to go fly a kite," Janet muttered, but she stood. "As it is, though, now you've got me craving a milk shake, too. Let's go."

They walked down the block to Dolan's Drugstore and headed for the counter. Melissa popped out of the store room. She'd worked there before her marriage to Cody and still filled in several days a week to keep from going stir-crazy on the ranch.

"Hey, you two, what brings you in in the middle of the morning?" Melissa asked. "Jessie, I didn't know you were coming to Los Piños today."

Janet thought the greeting sounded suspiciously cheery, as if they'd plotted this little gathering. When Kelly strolled in not five minutes later, she knew it.

"Okay, what's going on?" she demanded.

"That's what we want to know," Kelly said, propping her elbows on the counter and leaning forward intently. "Harlan's been grumbling like an old bear for the last week. Jordan, Cody and Luke are practically busting with curiosity, but he refuses to say a single word to any of them. Cody told Jordan you've been dropping Jenny off at the end of the lane again."

"I had no idea everyone was so fascinated with my habits," Janet said irritably.

As if she sensed that Janet was about ready to bolt, Jessie laid a soothing hand on top of hers. "Look, we all like you and we love Harlan. You seem to make him happy. He's crazy about Jenny. I doubt the two of you would have gone sneaking off and tearing down that lane in the middle of the night, if you weren't more than fond of him. So, what's the deal?"

"It's complicated," Janet summarized.

"Nothing's too complicated it can't be worked out, if two people love each other," Melissa declared, distributing milk shakes without even being asked. "I can vouch for that."

"Me, too," Jessie said.

"And me," Kelly added. "We had three of the most reluctant bridegrooms in Texas and look at us now. We're all deliriously happy."

"Well, most of the time," Jessie amended. "After all, those Adams stubborn streaks didn't vanish overnight."

Two "Amens" greeted the comment.

"Anyway," Melissa said. "You clearly have Harlan in the palm of your hand, yet you're throwing away the chance to marry him. How come? Is Jessie wrong? Don't you care about him?"

"I love him," Janet forced herself to admit to these three women who were clearly so concerned with their father-in-law's future that they'd ganged up on her. "That's why I can't marry him."

"Huh?" Kelly said blankly. It was echoed by the others.

Janet pushed aside her practically untouched shake. "I can't explain. Not to you, anyway. I can't even make myself tell Harlan all of it."

"Are you still married or something?" Melissa asked, eyes wide.

Janet grinned. "No, it's nothing like that."

"Then you can work it out," Jessie said confidently. "Just tell him what's on your mind. Harlan loves to fix things up for the people he cares about."

Kelly nodded. "He doesn't lay on some heavy guilt trip like a lot of men would. He just takes care of things."

Janet wondered if she could bring herself to tell Harlan that she had wanted the very land he was living on. If she did, would he ever believe that she was marrying him for any reason except to get her hands on that land? It didn't seem likely.

"At least think about it," Jessie prodded. "You won't regret marrying Harlan."

That had never been her fear, Janet thought. She was far more concerned that Harlan would regret marrying her.

That night, now fully aware that her every move was being scrutinized by fascinated relations, she drove all the way up the lane at White Pines to the house to pick up Jenny. She had almost managed to convince herself to lay all of her cards on the table and tell Harlan everything. She would test Jessie and Kelly's theory that Harlan would somehow make everything right and forgive her.

When she arrived, he was nowhere in sight. Maritza answered the doorbell.

"You are here for Jenny, *sí?* She will be back soon, I think."

"Actually I'd like to speak with Mr. Adams if he's available," she said.

"He's in his office. Come, I will show you."

She led Janet down the hall and pointed to a heavily carved door. "In there. You would like me to tell him you are here?"

"No, I'll knock. Thanks, Maritza."

She stood outside the door for several minutes summoning up her courage before finally rapping softly. "Harlan?"

"Janet, is that you? Come on in," he called out so eagerly that she was immediately consumed by another bout of guilt.

He was on his feet and halfway across the room by the time she had the door open. His expression made her heart skitter wildly. There was so much hope there. So much love.

"I wasn't expecting to see you today. You've been making yourself scarce."

"I had some thinking to do." She looked into eyes so blue they reminded her of the summer sky. "Thank you for letting me do it in peace."

He looked as if he wanted to reach for her, but he shoved his hands into his pockets instead. "Reach any conclusions?"

"Just one, thanks to Jessie, Kelly and Melissa. I have to tell you the truth about something."

His eyebrows rose. "Sounds serious."

She nodded.

"Then come on over here and sit." He gestured to a big leather chair in front of the fireplace, then settled into the one beside it.

Janet liked the arrangement. She didn't have to look directly into his eyes while she talked. She began slowly, telling him about the summer she had spent with Lone Wolf. Then she repeated all of the stories he had told her about their ancestors being forced out of Texas.

"I resolved then that I wanted to make it right. I came here wanting to get that land back. If I could have found a legal way to do it—which I couldn't, by the way—I would have taken White Pines from you,'' she summarized.

There, it was all out in the open. She glanced over at him to gauge his reaction. To her astonishment, he smiled.

"I know," he admitted without batting an eye. "I've known for some time now."

"You've known," she repeated blankly, then wondered why she was so surprised. Of course he would have put all the pieces together. He hadn't become a successful rancher without knowing how to read people. What she couldn't seem to absorb was the fact that he had taken the discovery so well. Where was the ranting and raving she'd anticipated with such dread?

"And you still wanted to marry me?" she asked, bemused.

"How could I blame you for thinking of Lone Wolf and wanting to make amends for what happened to his father?"

"Why didn't you say anything?"

He shrugged. "Because you needed to figure out you could trust me enough to tell me the truth."

Tears stung her eyes. "Oh, Harlan."

"Hey," he protested, "don't start crying. I won't say I wasn't mad as a wet hen when I first figured out what was going on after Jenny spilled the beans about where Lone Wolf had once lived. Then I did a little research of my own. I discovered you had cause to come here and do what you were doing. I'm sorry you couldn't figure out a legal way to do it."

"But you see, then, why we can't get married," she said. "I just wanted you to know that it's not because I don't love you. It's because you'll never know for certain if it's you I want or White Pines."

"Darlin', my ego's in no danger of being deflated by uncertainty," he said, waving off that argument dismissively. "You'd never marry a man you didn't love. There's never been a doubt in my mind about that."

She refused to accept that. It was too easy. She deserved his hatred or, at the very least, his disdain. Yet he was still claiming he wanted to marry her.

"I have to go," she said, leaping to her feet and heading for the door.

He stepped in front of her. "Not without saying yes to my proposal. All our cards are on the table now. There's no reason to say no."

"I can't," she insisted, guilt and confusion tumbling through her. How could she say yes, when she didn't deserve the love of a man like Harlan?

"Mom!" Jenny wailed from the doorway.

Her gaze shot to her daughter. "How long have you been standing there?"

"Long enough to know you've flipped out completely. I can't believe you'd do something like this." With that she whirled and ran from the room.

Janet stared after her in shock, then turned back to Harlan. "I have to go after her."

He nodded. "Go. But this isn't over, Janet. Not by a long shot."

Jenny refused to say a single word during the entire drive home. She huddled against the passenger door and stared out the window, her expression sullen. Janet felt as if they were right back where they'd been when they'd first arrived in Texas. All of the progress she and Jenny had made over recent weeks had disappeared in an instant back in Harlan's study.

When they got home, Jenny headed straight for her room.

"Jennifer, get back here."

"I'm not in the mood to talk."

"Then you'll listen," she said. But once Jenny had reluctantly sprawled in a chair in the living room, she had no idea what to say. She wasn't even entirely sure why her daughter was so furious. She could hazard a guess, though.

"Look, I know you like to think of Mr. Adams as the enemy," she began. "But he's not. And there's no need for you to concern yourself that I'll marry him, anyway, because I turned him down."

Jenny shot her a look of disgust. "Jeez, Mom, don't you think I know that? I heard everything."

"Well, then, why are you acting as if I've gone over to the enemy?"

"You've got it all wrong. I think you're making the worst mistake of your life, if you don't marry him."

Janet's mouth dropped open. "What?"

"I know why you're turning him down, though. It's not because of all that stuff about Lone Wolf and the land."

"Of course it is," Janet insisted.

"It is not. Not really. He told you that stuff didn't

matter to him anyway. You're saying no because of your own stupid pride.''

The accusation stung, not because it was unjustified, but because somewhere deep inside it rang all too true. ''I don't have any idea what you're talking about,'' she said stiffly.

''Oh, puh-leeze!'' Jenny retorted. ''When you left Daddy, you swore you'd show him you could stand on your own two feet. You're afraid if he hears you're marrying some rich guy, he'll think you've sold out.''

Before Janet could gather her wits to react to that, Jenny went on.

''Do you think it even matters to him what we're doing?'' she said with adolescent bitterness. ''He never calls. He never comes to see us. The only time you hear anything at all is when he sends a child support check. I think you'd tear that up, if you could.''

It was true. Only the awareness that the money belonged to Jenny kept her from doing just that. Every cent was in an account in her daughter's name, meant for her college education.

''So what's your point?''

''Just that you're afraid if you marry anyone, much less a guy like Harlan Adams, Daddy will see it as an admission that you couldn't make it on your own. Like he really cares,'' she said with more of that angry sarcasm Janet had never heard before.

Feeling both bemused and under attack, she asked carefully, ''Do you want me to marry Harlan?''

''I want you to be happy, Mom. It's all I ever wanted. And Harlan's a pretty cool guy. I knew that the minute he caught me after I stole his truck. He didn't freak out, like some guys would have. I've been pretty rotten sometimes since and he hasn't hated me for that, either.''

She shrugged. ''Maybe I was testing him, to see if he'd be like Daddy and abandon me just because I wasn't behaving suitably.'' The last was said in precisely her father's judgmental tone.

Janet sighed heavily. At last the reason behind Jenny's behavior for the past few months was coming clear. She'd lost her father, even when her behavior had been exemplary. She'd been testing, not just Harlan, but before that, Janet herself, to see if they would abandon her at the first sign of trouble. Now her gaze was fixed anxiously on Janet's face. ''So, will you at least think about it?''

''I'll think about it,'' she promised.

She did little else for the next twenty-four hours. By morning, she thought she had figured out a way to prove to Harlan that it was him—and him alone— she loved.

Chapter Fifteen

When Harlan turned up to take Janet to lunch the next day, he sensed right away that something had changed. He couldn't tell exactly what it was, just a bit more color in her cheeks, maybe a glint of confidence in her eyes.

"I have some papers here for you to sign," she said when he walked through the door.

He frowned at her businesslike tone. Was she about to get into the land ownership issue, after all? Had she found some blasted loophole she hadn't admitted to the last time they'd talked?

"What sort of papers?" he asked suspiciously.

"It's a legal agreement."

His wariness doubled. "Who are you representing?"

"Myself."

His heart slammed against his ribs. So it was about the land.

"Suing me, are you?" he asked, keeping his voice light, when he wanted to lay into her at the top of his lungs for spoiling everything, for not trusting him to do what was right.

Her mouth curved into a sensuous smile that made his heart go still. If that smile had anything to do with a land deal, he'd eat his hat. But what, then?

"You'd love that, wouldn't you?" she taunted. "You're never one to back down from a good fight."

"Gets the juices flowing, that's for sure." He reached for the papers and began to read. His eyes widened at the first line. "A prenuptial agreement? What the hell is this for?"

"It's an agreement between you and me, before marriage, guaranteeing that I won't take a dime of your money if the marriage ever breaks up."

"Like hell!" he exploded, too furious to even think about the fact that she was apparently agreeing to marry him. He didn't like the terms she had in mind. He didn't like 'em one damned bit! "I'm not going into a marriage thinking about how it's going to end. The day you and I get married it will be forever, Janet Runningbear, not one of those blasted things where one of us skedaddles at the first hint of trouble."

To his astonishment, she chuckled. "I had a feeling you were going to say something like that, so I made a few alterations from the traditional prenup agreement. Perhaps you should read the details."

He was about to rip it to shreds when a phrase

caught his eye. Something about guaranteeing that White Pines would remain with his sons.

"What's this?" he asked.

"Just putting what's right in writing," she said. "I want to be sure there's never a doubt in your mind about why I'm marrying you. Read the rest. See how it suits you."

The next paragraph legalized his adoption of Jenny as his daughter. He couldn't have been more flabbergasted if they'd let him win at poker. He searched Janet's face for proof that this wasn't some sort of diabolical hoax.

"She's sure about this?" he asked, not able to control the hint of wonder in his voice.

"She and I talked it over this morning. It's what she wants. She wants to be your daughter." Her gaze caught his. "If you'll have her."

Tears stung his eyes. "It would make me proud to have her call me daddy. Your ex-husband, though, he won't mind?"

"He'll have to be consulted, of course, but I don't see why he would, especially if it would let him off the hook with the child support he sends so grudgingly."

He couldn't believe that everything was finally coming together just the way he'd imagined. He cupped Janet's face in his hands. "You're dead serious about this? You're not going to back out of this on me, are you?"

She shook her head. "Not a chance."

"You know we're going to be butting heads every now and then. That's just the way of marriage."

"So I've heard. Your daughters-in-law have informed me what it's like to be married to a stubborn Adams."

"Traitors," he muttered, but he was smiling. He knew he owed the three of them for making Janet take a second look at his proposal and forcing her to shed her conscience of that secret she'd been keeping. He had a feeling he might owe Jenny, too. She'd promised to intercede in his behalf and it looked as if she had.

He studied Janet intently, not quite able to believe that she was almost his. She was so beautiful she took his breath away. He'd be counting his blessings till the day he died.

"How soon?" he asked.

"How soon what?"

"When can we get married? You want a big to-do or can we sneak off and keep it from those brats of mine?"

"It doesn't have to be big, but I want those wonderful children and grandchildren of yours to be there. We're going to start this off as a family," she insisted. "No more secrets. Understood?"

"Don't look at me with those big brown eyes of yours," he accused. "I'm not the one who was hiding what I was up to. You knew from day one what I wanted from you."

She grinned and looped her arms around his neck. "And what was that?"

"This," he said, and settled his mouth over hers. He ran his tongue along the seam of her lips until they parted. The taste of her was sweet as peppermints and far, far more intoxicating.

"If you hadn't said yes soon," he declared when his breathing was finally even again, "I'd have had to kidnap you and haul you off to some justice of the peace."

"And what if I still hadn't been willing?"

"I'd have used all of my considerable influence to see that the ceremony came off anyway," he declared, liking the immediate flare of temper in her eyes.

"You can't expect to bully me into giving you your way, Harlan Adams."

"Who's talking about bullying?" he said, closing a hand gently over her breast and teasing the nipple until he could feel it harden even through the silk blouse and the lacy bra he knew was underneath. "There are other ways to tame a skittish filly."

His expression sobered then. "I love you, Janet Runningbear. I'll make you happy. For all my teasing and taunting, you can count on that as a solemn promise."

"I love you, too, Harlan." The smile she turned on him then was radiant. A bride's smile. "It ought to be downright fascinating, don't you think?"

"What?"

"Our marriage."

He grinned back at her. "I'm counting on it."

Janet stood at the back of the church barely a week later and fussed with her white antique lace dress.

"Are you sure I look okay?" she asked Jenny for the thousandth time.

"You look beautiful, Mom. Every hair is in place," she added, anticipating Janet's next question. She twirled in her own dark rose dress. "How about me? Do I look grown-up?"

"Too grown-up," Janet declared, wondering where the time had flown.

It seemed only yesterday that her daughter had been small enough to rock to sleep in her arms. And yet she wouldn't go back for anything. Jenny was going to make her proud one day. She was bright, spirited and intrepid. With Harlan as a father, she could be anything she chose to be.

Lone Wolf would have been satisfied with how far his descendants had come and how far they would continue to go, she thought. Perhaps she had fulfilled her promise to him, after all.

"Isn't it time yet?" Jenny asked. "What's taking so long?"

"Blame me," Harlan said from the doorway to the church, taking them both by surprise.

"Harlan," Janet protested. "You shouldn't be back here. It's bad luck."

"You and I have one last detail to settle before you walk down the aisle," he said, pulling a thick packet of papers from his pocket and handing them to her.

Janet regarded him warily. "What's this?"

"It's one of those prenuptial things you seem to like so much. I ripped up yours," he said, handing her the shreds of paper as proof. "I set out a few terms of my own."

Janet allowed the remains of her prenuptial agreement to filter through her fingers, then took Harlan's papers with a hand that trembled. She wasn't sure what last-minute fears might have driven him to clarify the status of things between them in writing.

"Read it," Harlan insisted, putting an arm around Jenny's shoulders and giving her a squeeze as Janet began to scan the familiar legal language.

She'd read no more than a clause or two before her gaze shot up to meet his. "This isn't a prenuptial agreement at all. It's a will."

"I knew a fine lawyer like you would see that right off," he taunted.

"You're putting Jenny into your will as one of the heirs to White Pines?" she whispered, incredulous.

"She'll be my daughter," he said firmly. "She's entitled to her share, not just as my daughter, but as a descendant of Lone Wolf's."

Tears welled up in Janet's eyes. "The land should belong to your sons. They were raised on it."

"'Just putting what's right in writing'," he insisted, quoting her. "If things had gone differently a hundred years ago, maybe you'd have been raised on this land. Maybe Jenny would have been born here. I just see that paper as bringing things full circle."

"She'll probably put a shopping mall on it," Janet threatened.

Harlan winced, but stood firm. "That'll be her choice," he said, gazing fondly at Jenny, who was staring at the two of them in stunned silence. "Thanks to you, she has a good head on her shoulders and good, decent values. She'll make us both proud."

Oblivious to wedding day conventions, which had already been shot to blazes anyway, Janet threw her arms around his neck and kissed him. "Oh, Harlan, I do love you."

He grinned. "It's a darn good thing, 'cause there's no way you'd get out of this church today without saying 'I do'. I can't wait to walk down that aisle in there, so the whole world will know how proud I am to be your husband."

"Even if I don't change my name from Running-bear to Adams?"

He winced. "Even then," he conceded. "You've worked hard to be who you are. I guess you've earned the right to call yourself whatever you want, as long as it's me you come home to at night."

"Count on it," she said softly, then took his hand. "Since we've already made a mishmash of tradition, how about walking down that aisle with me to stand before the preacher?"

"Mom!" Jenny protested with a wail. "What about me?"

Janet grinned. "You can still go first. You'll probably have to revive the organist. She won't know what's going on."

"That's exactly why I'm so anxious to get started on this marriage," Harlan declared, winking at Jenny. "With your mom around, there's no telling what'll happen next. I expect there will be surprises in store for all of us."

The ceremony wasn't nearly as tospy-turvy as their arrival for it, Harlan reflected late that night while

Janet was changing into some fancy negligee he was going to take pleasure in stripping right back off.

He let his mind wander over the days and weeks since she'd come into his life and counted each minute among his blessings. He was so engrossed in his memories, he never heard a thing as she apparently managed to sneak up behind him and circle her arms around him.

"I love you, Harlan Adams," she whispered.

At the sound of those sweet words, a tremendous sense of peace stole through him. They were going to be so damned good together. Family had always been the most important thing on earth to him. Now, after losing his beloved Mary and his son, Erik, both in terrible tragedies that had taken them too soon, his family circle was going to grow once more. His life was once again complete.

"I love you, Janet Runningbear. And I love the daughter you've brought into my life."

Her eyes lit with a teasing glint. "Who knows, Harlan? Maybe I'll give you another one before we're done."

It was a good thing she slid into his lap and kissed him then, because he was too darned flabbergasted to say a single word. A father again? What an astonishing, incredible idea! One thing for sure, any child they had together was bound to be a hellion.

He could hardly wait.

Epilogue

By golly, if Janet didn't go and make good on her promise. Barely nine months to the day after their honeymoon, Harlan found himself pacing the hallways at the hospital waiting for her to give birth. The whole danged family was there, fussing and carrying on, teasing him unmercifully about getting a second chance at parenthood.

"Maybe this time you'll get it right," Cody teased.

"There's not a thing about the way I did it the first time that I'd do over," he shot right back, then sighed heavily. "Except with Erik. I'd do that over if I could."

Luke put his arm around him. "Daddy, Erik made his own choices."

Jessie stood on tiptoe to kiss his cheek. "That's right. It's time to let it go. Besides, this should be a happy occasion. We should be concentrating on the new baby, not sad memories."

Jenny, who'd been standing impatiently in the corridor outside the delivery room for the past hour, came up in front of him and scowled. "I just don't get it. What's taking so long? And why aren't you in there with her?"

"Because he'd be telling the doctor what to do, that's why," Cody chimed in. "The delivery room staff signed a petition to keep him out."

"But you took those classes with Mom and everything," Jenny protested. "Now she doesn't even have a coach in there with her. If I'd known you were going to chicken out, I'd have taken the classes."

Just then a nurse appeared in the doorway. She zeroed straight in on Harlan. "Mr. Adams, your wife is asking for you."

His breath caught in his throat. "The baby?"

"Should be here any minute now," the nurse said. "She says you'll probably only have to suffer through a contraction or two."

When his sons heard that, they hooted. "Now we know," Jordan taunted. "Janet was terrified you were going to faint in there, wasn't she?"

"We reached an agreement is all," Harlan said defensively.

The truth of it was, Janet had fought like a demon to keep him from seeing her in pain. He'd fought just as hard to be in that delivery room. He'd missed out on the birth of his sons, because that was the way of the world back then. He'd regretted it more than he could say. This time he wanted to be there for the miracle, just one of many to come into his life since the day he'd met Janet and Jenny.

As promised, he walked through the door of the delivery room just in the nick of time. Janet's face was bathed in sweat, but the smile she turned on him was enough to fill his heart to overflowing. He clasped her hand.

"I hear you're doing great," he said.

"So they tell me," she said, suddenly clenching his hand in a grip so fierce he thought for sure the bones would break. "This is it."

"Sure is," the doctor agreed. "That's it, Janet. Come on. Just a little more."

Harlan's incredulous gaze was fixed on the doctor, watching his concentration, then the smile that slowly spread across his face just as he lifted their brand-new baby into the air.

"It's a girl," he announced. "A big one, too. Pretty as her mama."

If there'd been a chair close by, Harlan would have collapsed onto it. Tears welled up in his eyes as he turned a tremulous smile on Janet. "A girl," he repeated softly. "Another daughter."

"I promised, didn't I?" Janet whispered.

He leaned down and pressed a kiss filled with gratitude and love to her lips. "Thank you for my two girls," he murmured. "Most of all, thank you for loving me and making my life complete."

Just then a nurse approached carrying their daughter in a pretty pink blanket. "Here she is, Mr. Adams. Would you like to hold her?"

An awe unlike anything he'd ever before experienced spread through him as he took that precious bundle into his arms and gazed down into his daughter's tiny, scrunched-up face.

"She is so beautiful," he said, barely getting the words past the lump in his throat. "What are we going to name her? Have you decided?"

"I had a thought, but I wasn't sure how you'd feel about it," Janet said.

"What?"

"I was thinking of naming her Mary Elizabeth," she said, watching his face intently.

He was stunned by the generous, unselfish gesture. "Wouldn't you mind naming her for Mary?"

Eyes shining, she reached for his hand. "It's something I'd like very much to do for you and your sons. I was thinking we might call her Lizzy."

He gazed down at the child in his arms and grinned. "Lizzy, huh? What do you think?"

Mary Elizabeth Adams opened her tiny mouth and wailed. There was no telling if that was a sign of approval or dissent, but Harlan took it as a positive reaction. He smiled at Janet. "Lizzy, it is."

"So," she said, as they wheeled her and the baby to her room, "do you think there are any more surprises in store for us?"

"You bet," he promised. "They're around every corner."

* * * * *

THE LITTLEST ANGEL

Chapter One

Angela hadn't wanted to come home like this, with her belly the size of two watermelons, and not one single proud accomplishment she could claim. She'd always meant her return to be triumphant, proof that she could succeed on her own without relying on the Adams name that meant so much in one little corner of West Texas. She'd envisioned a banner across the porch and a barbecue in her honor in the backyard and her name in lights, if Grandpa Harlan had his way.

Instead, it was the dead of night and no one even knew she was coming. Until she'd driven down the last stretch of deserted highway, anticipation mounting with every mile, she hadn't known for sure herself if she would have the courage to face her family. The car had settled that for her. It had conked out less than a mile from home. She sat in the rapidly chilling air and shivered, wondering if fate was on her side this time or just out to humiliate her further.

Home. The word had always conjured up a barrage of images for her, some good, some bad. Over the last six years the bad ones had faded until only the special memories remained. With her birthday tomorrow and Christmas just a few days away, it was no surprise that it was the holiday memories that came back to her now in a flood.

The celebrations always began early and lasted through New Year's, with everyone—aunts, uncles, cousins—traipsing from home to home for one party or another, but always, *always* ending up at White Pines. Grandpa Harlan insisted on it. He claimed he could spoil his grandkids rotten in his own home on Christmas Day if he chose to, while anywhere else he might have to show some restraint.

Rather than feeling deprived that her birthday was so close to Christmas, Angela had always felt as if all of the holiday trimmings made the day more special than it would have been at any other time of the year. Other kids got cakes and a single party. Angela's celebration included a huge tree, blinking colored lights, endless music and nonstop parties that went on for days.

She'd missed that while she was away, missed it when she'd noted the occasion all alone in a college rooming house already deserted by students who'd headed home for the holidays. Last year she'd almost forgotten it herself. She was too caught up in love, too excited about sharing her first Christmas with a man who really mattered to her.

Now, though, the memories were as vivid as if she'd never left. Even from her stalled car way out here on a lonely Texas highway she imagined she could see the lights twinkling on the ceiling-scraping Christmas tree, smell the aroma of Consuela's fresh-baked sugar cookies and bread mingling with the scent of fresh-cut pine. She could almost hear the sound of carols being played at full volume, while her dad chided her mom that she was going to deafen all of them.

She sighed as she remembered the angel of shimmering gold that was ceremoniously placed on top of the tree each and every year and the pride she'd felt when that duty had been given to her. At five she'd been too small to reach the top, so her father had hoisted her up on his broad shoulders so she could settle that frothy angel onto the tree's highest branch. Then and only then, in a room that had been darkened for the ceremony, did they switch on the lights, always too many of them, always so magical that she and her mom had gasped with delight, while her dad had grinned tolerantly. The same ceremony had been repeated at White Pines, where as the oldest grandchild she'd always been the one who'd put the angel on her grandfather's tree.

So many wonderful traditions, she thought now. How could she have run away from all the warmth and love in that house? she wondered in retrospect.

Rebellion, pure and simple. She had chafed at all the bright expectations and what she now suspected had been imagined pressures. Like all families, hers had only wanted what was best for her.

It was just that the Adams men, particularly Luke and her grandfather, had a tendency to think they were the only ones who knew what was best. No two men on earth could be more mule-headed once they'd charted a course of action, for themselves or someone they loved.

Ironically, they had rarely agreed on what that course should be. One plan would have been hard enough to fight, but two were impossible. Angela had wanted to decide her future for herself, and leaving— choosing a college far from Texas where the Adams influence didn't reach—had been the only way she'd seen to do it. She'd limited contact to occasional calls, an infrequent e-mail to her computer-literate father.

Now, with snow falling in fat, wet clumps and the roads turning into hazardous sheets of ice, she sat in her idled clunker of a car less than a mile from home and wondered if anything else could possibly go wrong. Even as the thought crossed her mind, she glanced quickly heavenward.

"Not that I'm tempting fate, You understand," she said wearily. "But even You have to admit my life basically sucks these days."

She was twenty-two, unmarried, unemployed and no more than a week or two from delivering a baby. She was virtually back on a doorstep she'd vowed she wouldn't cross again until she'd made something of herself and done it totally on her own without the Adams power and influence behind her. If she'd taken one thing away from Texas with her, it had been the fierce Adams pride, the determination to buck everyone and chart her own path.

She supposed, in a manner of speaking, that she had. She had made a royal mess of things. No other Adams that she knew of had gone so far astray. She'd skated through college with grades no higher than they had to be. She'd lied about who she was and run away more times and from more places than she could count. Rather than upholding the noble Adams tradition, she'd thumbed her nose at it. Oh, yes, she'd made something of herself, all right, but she wasn't especially proud of it, and this was hardly the triumphant homecoming she'd once envisioned.

The only thing she had going for her was the absolute certainty that the two people inside would welcome her back with open arms and without making judgments. Luke and Jessie Adams accepted people for who they were, flaws included. That went double for their only child, the daughter they adored. They would be relieved that she'd finally realized that her heart and her identity were all wrapped up with the tight-knit family who'd been patiently waiting for her all this time.

As she huddled in the rapidly cooling car, she recalled the oft-told story of the joy with which she'd been welcomed into the world twenty-three years ago tomorrow. She had been born in the middle of a Texas blizzard with no one around to assist her mother except Luke Adams, her uncle at the time and the man who became her father. Luke had been blind drunk that night, but he'd sobered in a hurry when faced with the immediacy of those shattering labor pains. He had risen to the occasion like a true Adams hero.

From an early age Angela understood that they both considered her to be their Christmas blessing, a miracle on a cold and bitter night. With her natural father dead, her birth had brought Luke and Jessie together, helped them to overcome the anguish and guilt they'd felt at having fallen in love even before her father's fatal accident. Just as her name implied, she was their angel. Living up to such a lofty label had been daunting.

Admittedly, though, their expectations for her probably hadn't been half as exalted as she'd imagined them to be. She hadn't done a lot of listening before breaking the ties with home. At the first opportunity, she had fled Texas, first to attend college, then to roam the country in search of herself. It was time, she had thought, to do something totally outrageous, to discover what she was truly made of. Being angelic was a bore. She wanted to be wicked or, if not actually wicked, at least human.

Unfortunately, even after four years at Stanford and a year on her own the answers still eluded her. Over the past few months she'd had plenty of empty nights to examine her past. She was human, all right. The very human mistakes were mounting up.

She'd made the worst miscalculation of all in Montana with a rancher named Clint Brady, a low-down scoundrel if ever there was one, she thought bitterly. Her mound of a belly was testament to that. She wasn't looking forward to the hurt and worry that her parents would try their best to hide when they saw her and realized just how much trouble she'd managed to get herself into. She hated the thought of the heartbreak she would read in their eyes.

She was less worried about the reaction of her incredible grandfather, Harlan Adams. When it came to family, he was thoroughly predictable. He would probably set off fireworks to celebrate the birth of his first great-grandbaby. If he had questions about the baby's conception, he'd keep them to himself.

For the time being, anyway, she amended. As meddlesome as he was capable of being, he wouldn't be silent for long. By year's end he'd probably have a lynch mob searching for the baby's father, assuming he could get Angela to name him, which she had no intention of doing. Not even Clint Brady deserved to face the rancor of the Adams men, once they'd been riled up.

In addition to Luke and her grandfather, there were Cody and Jordan. They might be wildly different in some ways, but they all shared the Adams gene for pure cussedness and family loyalty. Clint wouldn't have a prayer against the four of them. He'd be hogtied and married to her before he could blink. She would have no more say in the matter than he did.

To her chagrin, just the thought of Clint and her wild and reckless behavior in Montana made her blood run hot. Until she'd met him, she'd had no idea that passion could be so overwhelming, so completely and irresistibly awe inspiring.

Nor had she known how quickly passion could turn to hatred and shame.

She was glad now that she'd lied to him, that she'd

faked a whole identity so that she could pretend for just a little while that she wasn't Luke and Jessie Adams's little angel. It had been liberating to pretend to be Hattie Jones, a woman with no exalted family history to live up to, a woman who could be as outrageous as she liked without regrets.

The decision to lie had been impulsive, made in a darkened country-western bar where she'd stopped to ask about a waitressing job that had been posted in the window. Clint had had the kind of lazy smile and sexy eyes that made a shy, astonishingly innocent college graduate imagine that all sorts of forbidden dreams were hers for the taking.

The job had been forgotten as she'd succumbed to newly discovered sensuality she hadn't even been tempted to test with the boys she'd met at Stanford. By the end of the night they were lovers. By the end of the week, she had moved in with him. She supposed that there was yet more irony that after all her running, she'd wound up with a rancher, after all.

More than once in the blissful days that followed she had regretted the casual lie she'd told when they met. More than once she had vowed to tell him the truth about who she was and where she came from, but Clint had been the kind of man who lived in the here and now. He didn't talk about his own past. He never asked about hers.

As weeks turned into months, it seemed easier to live with the lie. She liked being devil-may-care Hattie Jones, who flirted outrageously and never gave a thought to tomorrow. She liked the way Clint murmured her name in the middle of the night, as if he'd never before heard a word so beautiful.

In Clint's arms she was ecstatically happy. His ranch was a fraction of the size of her father's or her grandfather's, the days were long and exhausting, but none of that mattered, not at night when they made magic together. She found peace on that tiny Montana spread and something she had thought was love.

Then she'd discovered she was pregnant, and all of the lies and secrets between them—most of them admittedly her doing—had threatened to come unraveled.

When Clint had reacted in stunned silence to the news they were expecting a baby, that famous Adams pride had kicked in with a vengeance. She'd shouted a lot of awful, ugly things and he'd responded in kind. Even now the memory of it made her shudder.

If he'd been that furious over the baby, she couldn't imagine what his rage would be like once he discovered that she'd lied to him from the start. In her entire life, no one had ever made her feel so low. Nor had she ever before wanted to hurt a person so deeply that he would never recover from it. Words were their weapons and they had used them well.

Angela hadn't waited for tempers to cool. She'd loaded up her car and hit the road before dawn, determined to put Clint Brady and Montana far behind her.

That had been nearly seven months ago. She'd been in a lot of cities since. Few of them had even registered. She had no more than vague memories of cheap hotels and back-road diners.

She wasn't exactly sure when she'd realized that Clint was following her. It had been almost a sixth sense at first, a nervous knotting in the pit of her stomach, a prickly sensation scampering down her spine. She was too hurt, too sure that she'd been wrong to get involved with him, too ashamed of her age-old predicament to let him catch her. What was the point of one more argument, anyway? It was best to put him in the past, along with all the other mistakes she'd made. A fresh start beckoned from around every curve in the road.

To her surprise, Clint hadn't given up easily. He'd nearly caught up with her in Wyoming, cutting short the part-time waitressing job she'd taken to get gas money to move on. Warned about the man who'd been in earlier asking questions about her, she'd slipped out the diner's back door just as Clint came through the front.

The narrow escape had made her jittery for days. She hadn't felt secure until she'd managed to trade her beloved blue convertible in for cash and a sensible beige sedan so old she hadn't even been born the year it was made. No car that old should have been expected to survive the kind of journey she'd taken it on.

She had moved quickly on to Colorado, then doubled back north to Cheyenne, looped up to South Dakota, then headed west to Seattle, enchanted by the idea of living by the water.

In Seattle she'd found a one-room apartment in an area called Pill Hill for all the hospitals clustered together. For the first time she had searched until she landed a halfway decent job as a receptionist. She'd found a kindly obstetrician to make sure she was doing all the right things for the baby she'd already learned to cherish. She'd vowed that the baby would never have to pay for the mistakes she'd made. Oddly enough, though being Angela Adams had daunted her, being a single mom did not.

In Seattle she'd even made a few friends, older, married women who invited her over often for home-cooked meals and the kind of nurturing concern she'd missed since leaving home. She took endless walks along Elliott Bay, bought fresh produce and fish at Pike's Place Market, sipped decaf cappuccino in every Starbucks she passed.

Clint seemed to have lost her trail or else he'd just given up and gone home, satisfied that he'd made a noble attempt to find her. No doubt that enabled him to sleep well enough. By then, he was probably sharing his bed with some other woman. At any rate, she'd felt it was safe to linger in Seattle. Contentment seemed almost within her grasp. She couldn't bring herself to admit that she was disappointed that he had given up.

Maybe, if it hadn't been for the Seattle weather, she could have made it work. But as summer gave way to fall and then to a premature winter, all that rain and gloom had finally gotten to her. She began to miss clear blue skies and the kind of heat that baked the earth.

When she packed up and moved on, she told herself her goal was merely sunshine. The undeniable truth was, she was heading straight for Texas, toward home.

For better or worse, she was going back to become Angela Adams again. The spirited Hattie Jones had died in Montana. Like it or not, Angela Adams was a Texan through and through. Her baby would be, too. The heritage she had abandoned for herself, she had no right to dismiss for the baby. It should be up to her child to decide someday if being an Adams was too much of a burden.

Not that she ever sat down and listed all the pros and cons for going home. The choice was instinctive. She'd hardly even needed a map to guide her south along the Pacific Coast and then east. If she'd stopped to reason it out, she probably would have found a hundred excuses for staying as far away from Texas as she could.

She'd developed a bad case of jitters near the end and wound up in Dallas, bypassing the turn to the south that would have taken her home much sooner. For days she'd lingered, wandering around the stores that had been decorated for the holidays, pretending that maybe this would be the final destination. It was close enough to home for an occasional visit, but far enough away to maintain her independence.

This afternoon, though, she had gotten into her car and impulsively started driving, taking familiar turns onto back roads and straight highways that were unmistakably leading her back to Los Pinos. Her static-filled radio had crackled with constant threats of an impending blizzard, but she hadn't once been tempted to turn back or to stop. Not even the first flurries of snow or the blinding curtain of white that had followed daunted her. Home beckoned by then with an inevitability she couldn't resist.

It was ironic, of course, that it had been on a night very much like this that her mother had gone into labor practically on Luke Adams's doorstep, had delivered Angela in his bed, with his help.

That had worked out well enough, she reminded herself as she tried to work up the courage to leave the safety and comfort of the car for the bitter cold walk home. Their marriage was as solid and secure as a bank vault.

Maybe that was why Angela had run from Clint Brady, had kept on running even when she knew he was chasing after her, even when she realized that it was possible that he wanted her back. She had seen what it could be like for two people who were head over heels in love, who faced problems squarely and grew strong because of them. She wanted nothing less for her child. If she couldn't offer the baby that, then she could at least make sure there was a wide circle of family around to shower her son or daughter with love.

As if in agreement, her baby kicked ferociously. Boy or girl, she thought defiantly, the kid was definitely destined to be a place kicker in the NFL. She rubbed her stomach and murmured soothing words, then drew in a deep breath.

Exiting the car to face an icy blast of air, she shivered and drew her coat more snugly around her.

"Okay, little one," she whispered as excitement stirred deep inside her, overcoming dread or at least tempering it. "This is it. Let's go home."

Chapter Two

Clint Brady had always possessed the kind of charm that could get him out of jams and, just as easily, into trouble. It was a blessing and a curse. Recently, he'd spent a lot of time regretting that he'd wasted a single ounce of it on Miss Hattie Jones. She'd been nothing but trouble.

Drawn to her blue eyes and dark auburn hair, enchanted by her from-the-gut laughter, seduced by a body that curved and dipped like a Rocky Mountain road, he'd tossed aside common sense and set out to get her into his bed. There'd been half a dozen years age difference between them, but he'd dismissed that as if it had been no more than a minute.

Even when half of what she'd said hadn't added up any better than his books at the end of the month, he'd dismissed reason and run with his hormones. He should have been old enough and smart enough to know better, which just proved how wrong things could go when a man started thinking with something other than his brain.

Even so, for the better part of a year, he hadn't regretted his decision. That choice had set them off on one heckuva steamy ride. Hattie had been like no woman he had ever known before—sweetly vulnerable one minute, a wickedly sensuous vixen the next. His life had been filled with an incomparable mix of unexpected laughter and impromptu sex. They hadn't been able to get enough of each other. They'd learned to strip faster than a cook could shuck an ear of corn.

Yet for all of Hattie's spontaneity in the bedroom, she'd had a head filled with commonsense advice and straight thinking. He'd admired that almost as much as he had her generosity in bed.

For a man who'd never known the meaning of permanence, not when it came to relationships, anyway, he had actually started to think about forever. The prospect had scared him worse than the first time he'd crossed paths with a bear and twice as badly as dancing away from a rattler.

Right square in the middle of his panic, she'd dropped the news that she was pregnant. She'd stared at him over a candlelit dinner and said the words straight out, as blunt as a dare and twice as challenging. He figured there wasn't a man on God's earth that would blame him for being temporarily stunned into silence.

Women, on the contrary, obviously expected a more immediate and more joyous response. Before he'd been able to gather his wits, before they could have anything resembling a rational discussion of their options, Hattie had come completely unglued. She'd hurled a bunch of accusations in his direction, then added that she was no more interested in commitment than he was. She'd verbally blasted the hard life she'd had living with him and had followed that almost immediately with the intentionally cruel announcement that she'd be giving the baby up for adoption and that he'd be the last man on earth she'd allow to claim any child of hers.

Shaken by her venom, Clint had shouted good riddance as she'd flown out the door. The echo of car doors slamming had been as sweet a sound as he had ever heard.

Naturally as soon as she was gone, though, he'd calmed down and changed his mind. He hadn't been able to stop thinking about a little blue-eyed, red-haired girl or boy who'd grow up to take over the small ranch he owned in Montana. He'd finally have the family he'd always secretly longed for, but had convinced himself was out of reach as long as he was living such a hand-to-mouth existence. With a few hours of peace and quiet to soothe his frayed temper, the sound of wedding bells hadn't seemed nearly so discordant.

Unfortunately, Hattie was long gone by the time he came to his senses. He had been fool enough to figure that she would come back when she calmed down, that they would work it out. In all the months they'd been together, he'd somehow missed the fact that Hattie had a temper to match that red hair of hers.

By dawn he'd begun to realize that he'd misjudged the depth of her fury. By noontime, he was calling himself every kind of fool for letting her get away. By four he was on the road, chasing down a trail that was already growing cold. No one in town had seen her go. She hadn't even stopped for gas.

He spent two blasted weeks he couldn't spare playing cat and mouse with a woman who clearly didn't want to be caught. When she ducked out the back door of a diner in Wyoming just as he came in the front, he blistered the air with a string of curses that could have been heard clear back in Montana. It was pure luck he'd been able to get a grip on himself before the sheriff had shown up to check out the lunatic on the premises.

He told himself he'd had it, that she didn't matter, that the world would keep on turning if he never set eyes on her again. He no longer allowed himself to picture his baby at all. It hurt too much to think that he'd never even know if he had a son or daughter.

Back home with spring just around the corner, he worked the ranch every day until his back ached and sweat poured off his brow. He collapsed into bed each night, exhausted, but with his mind still alive with images of Hattie and his body aching for her touch.

Then, despite his best efforts to keep them at bay, the images of their baby flooded in, the child he would never know if he left things as they were. He'd grown up fatherless, the youngest in a long line of kids and apparently the straw that broke his father's back. His dad had left the day he was born. His own brothers and sisters had resented him from the beginning, had blamed him for their dad's leaving. Only his mother had cared that he was alive. She was the only one with whom he'd kept in touch. It was easier on all of them if he kept his distance.

No one on earth knew better than he what it was like to wonder, what it was like to yearn for a father's smile, for a sense of identity that only a father could give. No kid of his should have to go through that. No kid of his would ever have a minute's worry that he was unlovable, that it was his fault that his dad wasn't around.

And so he'd started the search all over again, picking up a clue here, another there, using a private detective when he could afford one, his own instincts when he couldn't. At least once a month he was on the road, following a lead, showing a snapshot of a smiling Hattie, sitting on a low-hanging branch of a tree, skirt hitched up to her thighs. That picture had grown faded and blurred from handling, but her smile was still enough to make his heart ache.

He was way past desperation now. By his calculations the baby was due any minute and there were times it seemed he was no closer to finding Hattie than he had been seven months ago. The trail of slim leads from the last detective had ended in Dallas where she'd been spotted at a cafe. It was a huge city with lots of nooks and crannies a woman could hide in, if she was of a mind to, which Hattie certainly was.

Depressed by the needle-in-a-haystack enormity of the task facing him, Clint took refuge in a diner, the sort of cheap, inconspicuous place he'd discovered

Hattie was drawn to. The too-bright lights glared off yellowing Formica and scarred chrome that had been polished until it managed a faint sparkle.

The tired colored lights on a tiny artificial Christmas tree winked on and off erratically, reminding him that it was a season of joy and wonder. The place smelled of stale grease and fresh coffee. The jukebox mourned lost love. If crying had been in his nature, Clint would have wept.

"Hey, sugar, you look like a man who needs a drink worse than he needs the kind of grub you'll get in this place."

Clint looked up from the laminated menu and found himself staring into sparkling brown eyes. Unruly blond hair had been partially tamed into a luxuriant ponytail. Lush, upturned lips, which would have made his pulse race a year ago, did little more than draw a returning smile now. The tag on her pocket said her name was Betsy.

"Betsy, are the burgers juicy and big?" he asked.

"Big enough to shut down half a dozen arteries before you can say bypass surgery," she responded.

"Is the coffee hot and strong?"

"Sugar, it'll make the hair on your chest curl," she said, her gaze pinned on that particular part of his anatomy as if she could see straight through his shirt.

Clint nodded. "Then I'm in the right place, after all. Two burgers and keep the coffee coming." He glanced around, assured himself that he was the only customer, then added, "And I'll double your tip if you pull the plug on that jukebox."

"What's the matter?" she inquired with a touch of feigned indignation. "You don't like country?"

"Under the right circumstances, I love country music."

Her expression radiated understanding. "It's just that you're so low-down, you don't want to be reminded of it."

"Exactly."

She silenced the jukebox and left him alone after that, except to bring his food and refill his coffee cup half a dozen times. The last time, as the clock ticked on toward midnight, she lingered.

"Sure you don't want to talk about it? I've got nothing to do tonight but listen."

Clint couldn't see the point in talking, but he couldn't much see the point to keeping silent, either. He poured out the whole sad tale, while Betsy clucked and sympathized.

"So, let's see this woman who has you all tied up in knots," she said eventually. "You have a picture of her?"

He dragged out the snapshot and pushed it across the counter. Expecting no more than a glib comment about Hattie's beauty, he wasn't prepared for the quick, indrawn breath or the suddenly cautious expression.

"What did you say her name was again?"

"Hattie," he told her. "Hattie Jones."

"No way," Betsy said, then clamped her lips together as if she'd already said too much.

"You recognize her, don't you?" Clint demanded,

his hopes soaring for the first time in months. "Has she been in here? Did she work here?"

"Heck, no," she said as if the idea were totally preposterous.

The reaction startled him. He'd always thought Hattie was a high-class woman, but she surely wasn't above an honest day's hard work in a diner.

"What, then? How do you know her? What name's she going by now?" he asked. It would be no surprise to discover she'd taken an assumed name. Nothing about Hattie surprised him anymore, including the fact that she was quicksilver fast at slipping away from him.

"Her own, I imagine."

"And that would be?"

Betsy stared hard, straight into his eyes. "What'd you say you wanted with her? Give me the bottom line."

"I told you before, we have some unfinished business. That baby of ours needs a daddy and I intend to be one."

"You aiming to marry her?" Betsy prodded.

"That's one possibility," he conceded, though he wondered if that particular answer wasn't out of the question. Hattie had made her opinion of him plain as day by running from him time and again.

"And the others?" Betsy asked.

"We'll work something out about the baby." Clint offered up a full-wattage smile, the kind he'd been told was irresistible to women. "Come on, Betsy. I saw that book you were reading. You're a sucker for a happy ending, aren't you? Help me out here."

Betsy appeared to weigh his response before saying, "I hope to hell I'm not making a mistake."

"You're not," Clint reassured her, then held his breath and waited. He thought he'd won Betsy's trust, but he was equally certain that something about Hattie was making her hesitate. Did she have a new boyfriend the size of a Dallas Cowboys linebacker? Or had she simply sworn Betsy to secrecy? Whatever the explanation, he saw the wariness in Betsy's eyes give way to determination.

"Her name's Angie," she said evenly. "Angela Adams."

She said it without the slightest hint of uncertainty that would come with recent acquaintance. In fact, she said it with the confidence of someone who'd known her long and well. Better than he had, maybe.

"Angie Adams," he repeated, testing the name on his tongue. "You're sure?"

"Sugar, she and I went all through school together, first grade right on through graduation. Of course, that's when I quit, but last I heard Angie was going off to some fancy college in California." Her brow creased. "Stanford, maybe. That was five, no, almost six years back. She'd be out by now."

If Hattie had been to Stanford, then Clint had a degree in nuclear physics. She'd been looking for a job in a low-class bar the night they'd met. He doubted Stanford gave out degrees in waitressing.

"It can't be the same person," he insisted.

"Then Angie has a twin," she replied just as adamantly.

"You haven't seen her recently, have you?"

"Not since graduation. Seemed like she couldn't put enough distance between herself and home."

"What about her family? Are they here in Dallas?"

"Heck, no. They're over in Los Pinos. They practically own the whole town and most of the land surrounding it. Her granddaddy was the biggest rancher in the state till he turned the family spread over to her Uncle Cody. Her daddy's the second biggest. Her Uncle Jordan owns an oil company."

Hattie? Clint thought incredulously. Hattie, who'd been having a tough time scraping together food money when he'd met her?

Suddenly, though, dozens of tiny evasions began to make sense. Her familiarity with ranching, despite her claim that she'd never set foot on one, took on new significance. She'd pitched in with chores as if she'd done them before, but she'd sworn she was just a quick study. He'd been too glad of the willing help to cross-examine her. Now it seemed as if his tendency to live and let live had been a big mistake. He should have started asking questions the day she appeared in that bar.

If she'd lied about her name and her background, what else had she lied about? Who the hell was Hattie Jones, after all? Had she even been pregnant when she'd left or had that been just another in the series of lies? Maybe she'd just been testing the depth of his affections and he'd failed the test, so she'd moved on to greener pastures.

Then again, she was awful close to home. If she'd been avoiding it for all these years as Betsy claimed, what would bring her back if not the impending birth of a baby? An heir to all this Adams wealth that Betsy had been describing? There was only one way he could think of to get answers.

"Can you tell me exactly how to get to her parents' place?"

"Better yet, I'll show you," Betsy offered. "I've got a whole week off and I was planning on heading over to Los Pinos for Christmas as soon as my shift ends at one. My car's been conking out on me a lot lately, though. If I can hitch a ride with you, I'll take you straight to their front door."

She winked at him. "And just in case things don't work out, I'll point the way to my folks' place. It's not as fancy as theirs, but you'll be welcome."

Clint didn't want to give her any false expectations. Betsy was a nice woman, but she was no Hattie. Who knew, though? Once he'd decided whether or not to strangle the woman who'd walked out on him, a straight shooter like Betsy might start looking pretty good.

"Let's see how this turns out," he said. "If this Angie Adams is the right woman, I'll owe you."

"Sugar, it's not your wallet I'm interested in." Her expression turned resigned. "But a few bucks is all you're likely to part with, isn't it? You really do have it bad, don't you?"

He wasn't about to admit just how bad. He settled for offering a warning. "Betsy, you don't want anything to do with a man like me. Just ask your old friend Angie. I'm sure she'd be eager enough to tell you all my flaws."

"Sugar, working in a place like this, I learned a

long time back to be a good judge of character. You look just fine to me. Besides, Angie never did know when she had it good. Wait till you see that spread she grew up on. If she could turn her back on that, she doesn't have the sense the good Lord gave a duck. You'd be better off with a woman who appreciates you.''

There was a time, Clint thought, when no one had appreciated him better than Hattie had. It was his fault that that had changed. In one lightning-quick moment of frozen panic, he'd destroyed all they'd had together. He was willing to accept responsibility for that much, anyway.

Or was he entirely to blame? Maybe Hattie was just the kind of woman who had to keep on moving on, who'd instigate a fight so she could go. Maybe she was just a natural-born liar. Could be he wasn't the first man she'd run out on or the first one she'd lied to.

After months of feeling angry and lonely by turns, he was about to find the woman who'd tied him in knots. He'd settle things with her once and for all. For the first time they would put all their cards on the table and decide where they stood. He'd find out if she was even capable of telling the truth.

He hoped so. He really did, because no conniving, lying woman would get the chance to raise a child of his. If he didn't like what he discovered, their baby would be going back to Montana with him. She could bet the whole fancy Adams ranch on that.

Chapter Three

Coming home had been a hundred times worse than Angela had anticipated and a thousand times better.

She had seen first shock, then joy register on her parents' faces as they'd realized who was ringing their bell and waking them out of a dead sleep. If she'd kept her old key, she could have crept in unnoticed and greeted them over breakfast in the morning, when she had her own emotions under better control. As it was, she'd dragged them out of bed, stunned them first with her return, then dismayed them with a refusal to answer a single question about the baby she was so obviously carrying. The tearful reunion had taken on a confrontational tone very quickly.

"Dammit, I want to know who's responsible for

the condition you're in,'' her father had bellowed loudly enough to raise the rafters.

"I am,'' she had replied quietly.

He glared at her. "Unless things have changed a helluva lot more than I realized, you didn't get pregnant on your own. Where's the father of this baby? Are you married?''

Angela regarded him in stoic silence.

"Luke, that's enough,'' her mother had said eventually, when it was clear they were at a standoff.

As always, her touch on his cheek was more effective at quieting him than her words. Angela had always envied them that, the ability to communicate with a touch, a glance.

"Can't you see she's worn-out and shivering?'' her mother had chided. "It must be below freezing outside. Come into the kitchen right this second and let me make you some hot chocolate.''

"I'd rather have tea,'' Angela said, casting a wary look at her father's grim expression as he followed them into the kitchen. "Herbal, if you have it.''

"Of course I have it,'' her mother said as she filled the teakettle with water and put it on the stove. "Consuela insists we keep wild blackberry tea in the house just for you. It was always your favorite.''

"How is she?'' Angela asked, smiling, relieved by the chance to change the topic. "I thought for sure she'd be retired by now. She must be what? Eighty-something?''

"Eighty-two and as spry as ever. She wears me out and she flatly refuses to retire,'' her mother said. "She says she won't have someone else in her kitchen. She'll be over the moon in the morning when she finds out you're home. She's been baking your favorite cookies for the past week. She swears something told her you'd be back this year. Nothing we said could dissuade her.''

Guilt rippled through Angela. Consuela had been far more than a housekeeper. She had been the grandmother Angela had never had. She'd taken a terrible chance not staying in touch with her. At Consuela's age anything could have happened and Angela would never have known.

''I'm sorry I haven't been in touch, especially this past year. I'm sorry I didn't let you know I was coming.''

''Nonsense. It doesn't matter. You're here now.'' Her mother glanced at her father. ''Isn't that right, Lucas?''

His stony expression softened just a fraction. ''Of course we're glad you're home, angel. We've missed you.''

Tears welled up in her eyes at the hurt she heard in his voice. ''I'm sorry,'' she said, her own voice choked. ''I'm sorry for everything.''

''Oh, baby, you don't have anything in the world to apologize for. You may not believe it, but we both understood exactly why you felt you had to go. Didn't we, Luke?''

''That's true enough. We didn't like it, but nobody knows better than we do what it takes to be an Adams in these parts,'' he said, his expression wry. ''I fought it in my way. Your uncles fought it in theirs. You just ran a little farther than the rest of us.''

"The bottom line is we love you," her mother said. "And we are both very glad you're home again where you belong." She hesitated. "You are here to stay, aren't you?"

Angela wished she could claim that she was just passing through, that she had a home and a life of her own to get back to once the holidays were over, but she couldn't. "If you'll have me," she said, no longer able to control the tears that had been threatening ever since she'd crossed the threshold.

Her father reached over and brushed the dampness from her cheeks. "There was never any doubt about that. Never."

Angela could feel their love warming her, chasing away all the fears and loneliness of the past few months. Once she had felt smothered by that love, choked by the overly protective nature of her whole extended family, from Grandpa Harlan and her strong-willed uncles right on down to the two people in this room. Not anymore. She realized now just how desperately she had been longing for this kind of unconditional acceptance. For the past couple of months her nesting instinct had been kicking in with a vengeance.

After her father's initial outburst, her parents had held their questions about the baby she was expecting. They had filled her with hot tea and thick ham sandwiches and a half-dozen Christmas cookies before sending her off to bed in the room that hadn't changed a bit since she'd left it behind. Consuela had kept it swept and dusted, but the old concert posters were still on the walls, and her menagerie of stuffed animals still tumbled across the bed.

She'd heard her parents' whispers as they'd gone off to their own room and known that the reprieve from questions wouldn't last forever. It wasn't in her father's nature to let one of his own be hurt without taking action to see that it never happened again. Even as he'd fallen silent after her mother's soft reproach, Angela had noticed the stubborn, determined jut of his chin. Her mother's intervention had only managed to delay the inevitable until this morning.

As Angela stood at the foot of the steps and tried to work up the courage to enter the dining room for breakfast, she braced herself for the new barrage of questions that he'd been forced to hold back the night before. She vowed to tell them as little as she could get away with. She ought to be very good at evasions by now. She'd been practicing long enough. She'd perfected the technique in Rocky Ridge, Montana.

She drew in a deep breath and stepped into the dining room. Her mother and father looked up when they heard her, and smiles spread across their faces.

Before she could even summon up a returning smile, she was enveloped in the arms of a plump Mexican woman whose once-black hair had gone almost completely white. There were new lines carved into her olive complexion, but her dark brown eyes sparkled as merrily as ever.

"Ah, *niña*, you are home," Consuela murmured, stroking Angela's hair back from her face as she had when she was a child. A rapid stream of Spanish that was part welcome, part chastisement followed until

Angela laughed and pressed a finger against the housekeeper's lips.

"Despacio, por favor," she pleaded. "Slowly, Consuela. I've forgotten every bit of Spanish you taught me."

"Then you must practice," Consuela said briskly. "It will be good for the baby, too. He will grow up bilingual."

"He?" Angela said, grinning at the assumption.

"Of course. I know these things." Consuela scowled at Luke, who hadn't bothered to hide his skepticism. "You laugh? Did I not predict the sex of every child ever born in this family, starting with you and your brothers?"

"That was easy. No girl had been born in the Adams clan for a hundred years," Luke teased.

"And what of Cody's daughter? Or your stepsister?" Consuela countered indignantly. "They were not so easy to predict, yes?"

"Okay, okay, I surrender," he said. "You know these things."

"Indeed," Consuela said. "Now, *niña,* what can I fix for you? Waffles, eggs, a Spanish omelet, perhaps?"

"The omelet," Angela said eagerly, her hands on her swollen belly. She grinned. "And the waffle. For the baby."

"Of course," Consuela said, bustling off to the kitchen to work her magic.

Angela sat down opposite her mother, aware of the worried glances she kept casting at her husband. Apparently she was anticipating the flood of questions,

just as Angela was. Only Consuela seemed willing to accept her condition as a simple fact of life and not cause for an inquisition.

"Where have you been for the past year and a half?" her father asked oh, so casually, in what for him was a dramatic show of diplomacy. "Aside from an occasional call to say you were OK, we haven't heard so much as a word from you since you graduated from college. You never gave us so much as a post office box, so we could contact you."

"I was traveling most of that time," she said. It was the truth as far as it went.

"Obviously you stayed in one place a little too long," her father retorted.

"Luke!" her mother said sharply.

He scowled. "Dammit, we have a right to know the truth."

"Only if Angela wants to tell us," her mother countered. "She's a grown woman."

The unfamiliar dissension between the two of them set her nerves on edge. Worse, she hated being the cause of it. "I can't tell you," she said with regret.

"What do you mean you can't?" Luke demanded, bellowing again. "Don't you even know who the father of the baby is?"

Angela stared at him in shock. "Of course, I know."

"Then is it asking too much to expect you to tell us?"

"It is if you're going to go ballistic and start making trouble," she shot back. "I'm here. The father's not. That should pretty much settle things."

"Nothing's settled, as far as I can tell. I'd say that trouble you're afraid I'll stir up is already here. I'm just trying to figure out how to clean up after it."

Angela trembled at the sound of barely contained rage in his voice. It was exactly what she'd anticipated, what she'd feared she would be stirring up by coming home.

"Maybe I should go," she said softly.

"Absolutely not," her mother snapped, adding in a rare display of temper, "Luke, that's enough. Let's everybody calm down."

Her father looked as if he were ready to explode. "Fine. You get the truth out of her, then," he said, throwing his napkin onto the table and stalking out.

"Don't mind him," her mother apologized. "He's just worried about you. We both are."

"There's no need to worry. I'm fine."

"Sweetie, if you were fine, you wouldn't have been on our doorstep, half-frozen in the middle of the night. I know you. You came home because you felt you didn't have anyplace else to go. You have too much pride to have come home otherwise."

The all-too-accurate assessment brought the sting of tears to her eyes. "Maybe I just missed you."

"Maybe you did, but that alone wouldn't have been enough to get you back here, not after you made such an issue of staying away," her mother said dryly. "Now you can tell *me* what's going on, or you can tell your father, or you can keep it all bottled up inside."

Angela grinned ruefully. "Those are my only choices?"

"Unless you'd rather tell your grandfather," her mother retorted. "No doubt he'll be on his way over as soon as he hears you're back. He's expected tomorrow, anyway. I doubt I'll be able to keep him away. He's been just itching to put a private eye on your trail for the past year and a half. When he sees you're pregnant, there won't be a place on earth the father of that baby can hide."

Angela thought of Clint's efforts to track her down. He was a pure amateur compared to her grandfather, but he'd done a pretty good job of it just the same. "He hasn't exactly been hiding," she admitted. "He's been trying to find me for the last seven months."

Her mother's gaze narrowed. "But you've been determined to elude him? Why? Did he abuse you?" she demanded, her voice barely above a horrified whisper. "If that man harmed you in any way—"

"No," she said hurriedly. "He never laid a hand on me."

Obviously relieved, her mother's expression softened. Her gaze fell on Angela's stomach. "Oh, really?"

"I meant he never hurt me, not physically."

"Why did you run then?"

"He didn't want the baby," she said simply.

"Are you sure about that?"

She recalled in vivid detail the humiliation of sitting across that candlelit table from Clint, praying for a whoop of joy, even a smile, only to see that stunned, blank expression on his face. "He all but said it when I told him I was pregnant," she said.

"He all but said it," her mother repeated with a sad shake of her head. "Darling, if he was so anxious to be rid of you and the baby, why has he been chasing after you all this time?"

"I don't know."

"Don't you think you should try to find out? Don't you owe it to your child?"

"It's too late."

Her mother looked skeptical. "Tell me one thing, then. Did you love him?"

"I thought I did," Angela admitted softly, then forced her gaze to meet her mother's. "I was wrong. I just want to put it all behind me."

For a moment it looked as if her mother was going to argue, but then she nodded. "Well, you've certainly always known your own mind. If that's what you want, I'll do my best to keep Luke and your grandfather from stirring things up."

"It's what I want," Angela said firmly and without the slightest hesitation. Even as she spoke, though, a little voice deep inside shouted, "Liar." She'd heard that same accusation so often the past couple of years that she was able to ignore it one more time.

Four in the morning or not, if he'd had his way, Clint would have started pounding on Angela Adams's front door the minute he and Betsy got to Los Pinos, but she had persuaded him to wait until a more reasonable hour. She'd also promised to make a call to the ranch to see if the lady in question was, in fact, back home again. Small town or not, her parents hadn't heard any gossip about it yet, though there'd apparently been plenty of speculation over the years about Angela's disappearance.

A half hour ago, after he'd managed to catch a couple of hours sleep in a guest room at Betsy's parents' house, she had made the call. She'd quickly confirmed that Angela had arrived home unexpectedly just the night before. She hadn't dared to ask whether the prodigal daughter had arrived home more than eight months pregnant. Still, Clint couldn't help believing that he had found his "Hattie" at last.

Now he sat outside the gate to the ranch and tried to bring his temper under control. The sight of a decrepit beige sedan half-buried in a snowdrift a half-mile back only raised his hackles more. He'd lay odds that was the car she'd been driving.

He told himself repeatedly that there was no point in charging in and getting the whole family riled up. Betsy, who'd proved time and again to be one of the most sensible women he'd ever met, had convinced him that a man in his position didn't want the whole lot of Adams men squared off against him, especially on their home turf.

So he was cooling his heels and hopefully his anger. He'd spent the past couple of hours envisioning this confrontation, envisioning the way Hattie's eyes—no, *Angela's,* dammit—would widen with shock when she realized she'd been found out. He could hardly wait.

He put his pickup in gear and drove up the winding lane to the impressive house. It seemed to ramble forever, dwarfing his own ranch. Barns, stables, everything in sight was spit-and-polish perfect.

Hands jammed into his pockets, he forced himself to walk slowly up to the front door, fighting intimidation over his surroundings every step of the way.

His control wasn't quite strong enough to prevent him from leaning on the doorbell. He could hear the impatient chime echoing through the house.

"I'll get it, Mom," an all-too-familiar voice called out.

The sound of that sweet voice sent goose bumps chasing down Clint's spine. Up until now he supposed a part of him had been holding out hope that Betsy had been wrong, that Hattie was Hattie and that there'd been no monumental lie between them. Now there was no denying the truth. He'd been played for a fool.

After taking a look around at her daddy's spread, he could imagine just how pitiful his own ranch had seemed to her. No wonder she'd been so eager to put it behind her. What stumped him, though, was why it had taken her so long to hightail it back to her daddy's place.

When the door swung open, he got exactly the shocked reaction he'd been hoping for, but he doubted it was any greater than his own. Even though he'd known she should be in the final month of her pregnancy if she hadn't lied to him about that, too the reality of it stunned him.

With her formerly svelte body swollen with his baby, she was more beautiful than ever. Curves that had been intriguing enough before were lush and gloriously feminine. He couldn't seem to tear his gaze away from her stomach, where both of her hands had settled protectively. Instinctively he reached out to touch her, to feel this growing child she'd kept from him, but she jerked away and tried to slam the door in his face.

Fortunately she was a little too ungainly to be as quick as she needed to be to prevent him from slipping inside. He caught the toe of his boot in the crack of the door, then wedged it open until the rest of him could follow. He closed it securely, while she eyed him as warily as if he'd been a rattler already coiled for striking.

"Hello, Hattie. Looks like we have some things to talk about." To his everlasting irritation, his voice shook when he said it. She still had the power to make him weak-kneed and crazy with desire. He had wondered if she would, had prayed that she wouldn't. At best, he'd wanted to be consumed with hatred, at worst, ambivalent. He hadn't wanted to be practically struck dumb with longing. Add to that her ability to rile him, and it was a wonder he managed to get a word out at all.

"Not here," she whispered urgently. Her eyes pleaded with him. "Please, Clint. I'll meet you in town. Just give me an hour."

He shook his head. "I'd like to accommodate you, I really would, but you have this nasty habit of taking off on me. I don't think I'll chance it this time."

Just then a woman who looked like an older version of Hattie came down the hall and into the foyer. She was tall and slender and radiant. She had the kind of self-possession and grace that attracted men and made women envious. Her glance shifted from Clint to her daughter, then back again. Apparently even she could sense the crackling tension in the air.

"Angie, is everything okay?"

Clint figured he'd let Hattie field that one. He fixed his gaze on her and watched the color bloom in her cheeks. Her shoulders sagged.

"Mother, this is Clint Brady," she said eventually. "The man I told you about."

Mrs. Adams's friendly expression vanished at that. "I think you should leave," she said, her voice stiff and formal. "You've caused enough pain."

"I swear to you that I don't want any trouble, ma'am, but I'm not leaving. Not until Hattie and I settle a few things," he said politely, but firmly.

His vehemence clearly took her aback. Apparently few people argued with her, confirming Betsy's description of a family used to being in control not only of its own destiny, but of most of the world around it.

She quickly regained her composure, then glanced at her daughter, her expression vaguely puzzled. "Hattie?"

Clint's lips curved as he observed Angela's unmistakable discomfort. "I guess you forgot to tell your mother some of the details."

"Clint, please," she begged.

Her mother took pity on her, even if Clint's patience was too far gone for him to.

"I think it's best if you go. You don't want to be here when my husband gets back," Mrs. Adams insisted. "He has a quick temper and these circumstances call for some preparation."

Clint shrugged. ''I figure your husband and I prob-ably want the same thing about now...'' He looked straight at Hattie. ''Answers. I'm not leaving here without them.''

Hattie sighed. Resignation spread across her face. ''It's OK, Mother. I'll deal with this.''

''Are you sure? I can call your father.''

Hattie shook her head. ''It's not necessary.'' She stared at him pointedly. ''Clint's no threat to me.''

Her mother backed down with obvious reluctance, leaving Hattie to lead the way into a living room that was almost the size of his whole ranch house. The money spent on the furnishings would have kept his place afloat for a year. The holiday decorations were as spectacular as any he'd ever seen in a department store, all gold and glitter and candlelight even at mid-morning.

Clint and Angela stared at each other uneasily. He was trying to assess exactly where to begin. She looked as if she were girding for battle.

An older Mexican woman appeared almost at once, bearing a silver tray laden with coffee and freshly baked cinnamon rolls. There was also a cup of herbal tea, the wild blackberry kind he knew Hattie favored. Somehow he felt reassured by that small bit of evi-dence that she was still the same woman he'd fallen for in Montana.

''Thanks, Consuela,'' Hattie said distractedly.

''Thank you, ma'am,'' Clint said. ''That coffee smells mighty good.''

''You need anything else, you call, *niña*,'' she said to Hattie, then gave Clint an assessing once-over. Apparently whatever she saw pleased her, because she left the room with a satisfied smile on her lips. It appeared he had one person in his corner. Judging from Hattie's lack of welcome, he probably ought to count himself lucky that no one so far had aimed a shotgun his way.

"How do you do that?" Hattie said.

"What?"

"Mutter half a dozen words and charm the socks off a woman? First Mother backs down and Consuela practically swoons."

"It's a gift," he declared. He tried smiling at her. "Used to work on you, too, as I recall."

She didn't bat an eye. "That was then. This is now. How'd you find me?"

"Pure grit, *Hattie*."

"Drop the Hattie," she said irritably. "Obviously you've figured out by now that it isn't my real name."

"OK, Angela." He regarded her speculatively. "Something tells me, though, that around here they probably call you Angel."

The flood of color in her cheeks told him he'd hit the mark, but she ignored the observation.

"Maybe the more important question is why did you bother?" she asked.

Her expression was a mix of curiosity and an even deeper resignation. She actually looked vulnerable, more vulnerable than he could ever recall Hattie looking when she'd been dancing up a storm and flirting with half the men in Montana.

"You're having my baby, unless you lied about that, too, *Angela*."

"That didn't seem to matter to you when I told you," she reminded him.

"That was then. This is now," he mimicked. "I've been trying to catch up with you since the day you left."

"I repeat, why?"

"Because no child of mine is going to grow up without a father," he said simply, his gaze locked with hers. A shudder seemed to wash over her, even as a spark of pure defiance lit her eyes.

"It's not your decision," she retorted.

"Yes," he said softly. "It is. As of this minute, I'm making it mine."

Chapter Four

Angela had her hands clenched so tightly in her lap that even her bitten-to-the-quick nails were cutting into her flesh. Clint Brady was the most arrogant, the most infuriating, the most insufferable man she had ever had the misfortune to cross paths with. He was going to make a pest of himself. She could feel it. His words flat-out guaranteed it. She had run out on him, which perversely made him want both her and the baby.

The truth was, though, he hadn't wanted either one of them when she'd been right under his nose and more than willing to stay. This display was just male pride kicking in, nothing more. She couldn't allow herself to get caught up in an emotional tug-of-war, not when Clint would eventually tire of it and leave.

She couldn't work herself up over his threats and taunts. If she did, she'd be an emotional wreck.

Reasoning that out made her feel marginally better, despite the grim glint in his eyes and the stubborn jut of his chin.

Unfortunately, she also had the awful, gut-sick feeling that once he got over his desire to throttle the man, her father was going to take to Clint the way bears took to honey. They spoke the same testosterone-laden language. Add to that their dedication to ranching and the two of them were like two peas in a pod.

It was ironic, really. She had run away from Texas to escape all that stubborn, macho nonsense. Until just this instant, with Clint scowling at her and insisting that he had rights here, she hadn't noticed that he was cut from the same cloth as all the Adams men she'd left behind. Just her luck.

"Go back to Montana," she pleaded one last time. "I'm home. I'm surrounded by my family. You don't need to worry about me or the baby."

"Maybe you should let me decide who needs worrying about," he said.

He said it in that sexy, laid-back tone she had once found incredibly seductive. Now it was merely patronizing and irritating. She wondered for a minute if his potent effect on her had finally worn off, but one long glance at him told her the emphatic answer to that. Her blood practically sizzled and she seemed to have no ability whatsoever to stop it.

Fixing her gaze on sun-streaked brown hair that needed trimming just to be respectable, blue eyes with a look of pure mischief in them and sensual lips capable of turning kissing into an art form, she knew she was far from over him. Just looking at him sent a jolt of desire slamming through her.

While she caught her breath, she realized that he was studying her just as intently.

"You look a little pale," he concluded. "Aren't you getting enough rest?"

"My color has nothing to do with exhaustion. I just keep getting an image of you with a bullet in your heart when my father finds you here," she said dryly.

"I had no idea you cared."

"Oh, for pity's sake, that wasn't a declaration of undying love. I'd feel the same about some poor, hapless animal walking past a hunter's shotgun."

He grinned. "Would you really? I guess that puts me in my place."

She glared at him. "Don't you dare mock me."

His expression sobered at once. "OK, I admit, we are getting a little far afield here. We have plans to make. Exactly when is the baby due?"

She saw little point in not telling him. It didn't take a genius in math to calculate the date with some degree of accuracy. Clint certainly ought to have the starting point pinned down well enough.

"Two weeks," she admitted grudgingly. "Though first babies are a little unpredictable, according to the doctor."

"Good, that gives us enough time, then."

She regarded him suspiciously. "Enough time for what?"

"To plan a wedding, of course."

Angie's mouth dropped open. If he'd suggested brushing up on his medical skills so he could deliver the baby himself, she wouldn't have been any more stunned. "A wedding? You and me? Have you completely lost your mind?"

He paused, his head tilted thoughtfully, then said, "Nope. I don't think so. What kind of wedding do you want? Huge, I imagine, though it may be a little late in the day to try to pull that off. How about New Year's Eve? Something small and intimate. That ought to suit your sense of the romantic. Maybe right here in the living room, if your parents wouldn't object. The room could be lit with lots of candles." He glanced around deliberately. "We're already halfway there on that score."

Angela stared at him incredulously. He was serious. She recognized that stubborn glint in his eyes all too well. If she didn't stop him, he'd be ordering the rings and the flowers. Poinsettias in honor of the season, no doubt. The room would be a sea of red. She shuddered at the image.

Maybe if he'd said one single word about love, she would have catapulted herself straight into his arms. Instead, he'd set off warning bells. She saw the scheme for exactly what it was: a way to stake a legal claim on her baby. Well, she wouldn't be a party to it, and that was that.

If Clint Brady really wanted to be a father to this baby, then he was going to have to prove it, not with an impulsive wedding, but over time. Weeks, at the very least. Maybe months. As furious as she was, maybe even years.

"Forget it," she said softly. "No wedding. Obviously you've been sitting around the past few months with guilt weighing on your mind. That's OK. I always knew you were an honorable man. Now you've tracked me down and done the noble thing. You made me an offer of marriage, and I appreciate the gesture. I truly do. But it's not necessary. You can go on back to Montana and live your life exactly the way you want to with no commitments holding you back."

Before she could say another word, he had crossed the room and hauled her up off the sofa—no easy task, in her present condition. "Shut up," he murmured just before his mouth closed over hers.

His lips tasted like deep-roast coffee and felt like black velvet, sensuous and seductive, as they teased, then plundered. Clint had always known how to make a kiss memorable, and he was at his best this morning. Or maybe it was just that she'd been longing for another of his kisses for far too long. At any rate, this one was a doozy. Her resolve melted, right along with most of the muscles in her body. She felt like a limp noodle by the time he released her. A restless yearning had begun inside her, and she knew exactly where that was likely to lead unless she stopped this craziness. They'd be in front of a preacher by nightfall. Her father would encourage that notion right along.

"Oh, my," she murmured before she could stop herself. So much for a display of resolve, she thought irritably.

"At least that hasn't changed," he said with obvious satisfaction.

"No," she conceded because there seemed to be

little point in lying about it. His arms were just about the only thing between her and collapse and they both knew it.

She looked him square in the eye. "But it doesn't matter."

"Oh, it matters," he taunted. "It seems to me it's the only thing that does."

"Of course, you would say that. All that ever mattered to you was the sex. OK, I agree. We had spectacular, fireworks-caliber sex. Time stood still. The world rocked on its foundation. Adam and Eve would have envied us our total lack of inhibitions. So what?"

"So what?" he repeated softly. "You think that's unimportant?"

"In the overall scheme of things, yes," she said defiantly, even though that kiss had been potent enough to prove otherwise.

"Liar."

Angela shrugged. "I've been called worse, especially by you."

Clint sighed and for the first time he looked the slightest bit guilty. "Look, I know I didn't respond exactly the way you wanted me to when you told me about the baby."

Months of nursing hurt pride kept her temper up. "That's an understatement, if ever I've heard one."

"You took me by surprise, that's all. We hadn't talked about the future. We hadn't talked about the two of us, much less about a baby. You knew—"

"Did you or did you not say that a baby was the last thing you wanted?"

"I did, but—"

"Did you or did you not say that marriage was out of the question?"

"I did, but—"

She was on a roll now and had no intention of pausing for any of his fast-talking rationalizations. She'd been stewing over that night for months now. It felt good to have another chance to throw in a few more digs at his lousy behavior.

"Did you or did you not mean every low-down, spiteful, mean word you uttered that night?" she demanded.

"No."

That single word, spoken with soft vehemence, slowed her down. She regarded him skeptically. "Oh, really?"

Clint sighed. "OK, yes, at the time, I meant it."

"I rest my case."

"I didn't know we were having a damned trial here," he practically shouted.

Two worried faces promptly appeared in the doorway. "It's OK, Mom," Angela said hurriedly. "You and Consuela don't have to stand guard. Clint and I are just finishing a discussion we started several months ago."

Clint's cheeks turned a dull red as he apparently realized that every word they'd spoken had been overheard, that more than likely their kiss had been witnessed by two very interested parties.

Good, Angela thought. She was on her turf now. Let him suffer a little embarrassment and humiliation. Let him suffer the tortures of the damned, for that matter. In fact, she would have welcomed the arrival of her father just about now. She might even load his shotgun for him.

Even though Angela thought she'd made her dismissal of their observers plain, her mother stepped into the room, followed by the housekeeper. Obviously nobody intended to listen to a word she said this morning.

"Maybe we should all sit down and discuss this rationally," her mother suggested, a worried gaze locked on Clint.

"If you would like a New Year's Eve wedding, *niña*, I could have everything ready," Consuela offered eagerly. "It would be my joy."

Had everybody she knew turned deaf all of a sudden? Angela wondered irritably. "There is not going to be a wedding, not New Year's Eve, not ever," she said, her voice rising with each word. "Haven't I made myself clear? Clint will be leaving, going back to Montana, and that's final."

"I don't think so," Clint said quietly.

Consuela beamed at him, then chided Angela, "Maybe you should listen to him, *niña*. He seems very sincere."

"Oh, yes," Angela snapped. "He's about as sincere as a snake in the grass."

"Has she always been this stubborn?" Clint inquired as if she were no longer in the room.

Her mother smiled, clearly more than halfway ready to succumb to his charm, won over by his call for a wedding, even if it had come belatedly.

"Wait until you meet the rest of the family," she

said. "She comes by it naturally. In fact, if you wouldn't mind a word of advice—"

That was it. That was the final straw. "Mother, I do not want you giving Clint Brady advice," Angela practically shouted, hoping that sheer volume would succeed, when nothing else had.

Her mother went on as if Angela had spoken in a whisper. "You might let her cool down a little, get used to the idea. I'm sure she'll be in a more receptive frame of mind in a few days. You could stay with us. You'll be able to meet the rest of the family. With the holidays coming, everyone will be here for a few days. And, of course, today is her birthday, so we'll be pulling together a last-minute party just for us, to celebrate. You can't miss that."

Clint Brady here, under the same roof? No way. Either her pragmatic mother was trying to make the best of an awful situation or she was getting back at Angela for running away from home in the first place.

"I do *not* want him in this house!" Angela insisted.

Despite the vehemence and shrill, escalating volume of her words, she had the distinct impression they were falling on deaf ears. Consuela leaped up and bustled off to ready the guest suite. Clint thanked her mother for the invitation and accepted without so much as a by-your-leave look in Angela's direction. She might as well have been invisible, she thought, thoroughly disgruntled by the turn of events.

Since no one seemed to give two hoots about what she thought, she hefted herself up off the sofa again and marched out of the room without a backward glance. If she hadn't been thoroughly exhausted from running, if she'd had anyplace else on earth to go, she would have fled the ranch and Texas and the overwhelming presence of Clint Brady.

Unfortunately, as she had all too recently discovered, there was apparently nowhere she could hide that he wouldn't find her. If there was going to be a grueling standoff, it might as well be where she could sleep in her own bed.

Luke Adams had the look of a man on a mission. Standing beside his pickup with his single piece of luggage, Clint observed Luke warily as he approached, hands jammed in the pockets of his jeans, a scowl etched in his rugged features and fire blazing in his eyes. He guessed it was going to be a tricky conversation.

They were about the same size and, despite the difference in their ages, probably equally fit. Ranching toughened a man at any age, and Luke had the look of a man who didn't leave the hard tasks to others. They had that in common, Clint thought optimistically. That and Angela, though he doubted her father would view the latter as a subject on which there could be much agreement.

"You're Brady?" Luke asked, regarding him distrustfully.

Clint offered his hand. Luke Adams ignored it. Clint guessed it was because he was scared to death if his hands came out of his pockets, one of them would land squarely in the middle of Clint's face. Clint couldn't blame him entirely for the reaction.

"I know this looks bad," he began.

"Bad?" Luke snapped. "Son, I figure you've got about thirty seconds to do some very fast talking to keep me from ripping you apart."

"I think I understand how furious you must be, but I swear to you that I am trying to get your daughter to marry me," Clint said. "I'm trying to do right by her and the baby."

"Shouldn't you have been thinking about that nine or ten months ago, before she wound up pregnant?"

"Nine or ten months ago the only thing on my mind was trying to keep my ranch afloat," Clint said honestly. "I figured I wouldn't have a whole lot to offer a woman, if it went under and I lost the land. Then Angela hit me with the news that she was pregnant and I panicked. I know I was wrong. Hell, I knew it even while we were still shouting at each other, but before things could calm down, she split. I've been chasing after her ever since, trying to put things right."

He realized that despite his anger over the discovery of all her lies, that was what he still wanted. He shook his head ruefully. "That woman moves faster than any oil slick and she's twice as slippery. Until now I've barely caught sight of her since the night she stormed out of my house."

Luke pinned him with a penetrating look. "Why'd you bother chasing her at all, if catching her was so much trouble?"

It was the same question Angela had asked, but Clint wasn't any more certain of the right answer now than he had been a few hours earlier.

"Because I wanted to do the right thing by her.

Your daughter's a hell of a woman. And that baby, well, I may not have what you have here, but I am its daddy. I figure a child has a right to know the man responsible for bringing it into the world.''

To his surprise something in Luke Adams's expression softened. The harsh, down-turned lines around his mouth eased up just a fraction. It was not quite a smile, but Clint felt relieved nonetheless. The tension in the air lessened. The first step toward a grudging respect had been taken—or at least he hoped it had.

''Even though she swears she wants no part of you, are you planning on sticking around?'' Luke asked.

''Until I can talk her into marrying me,'' Clint vowed. He hadn't thought much beyond that. His first goal had simply been to make everything nice and legal. He'd figured that would be tricky enough without worrying about what the next step might be. He wanted an honest claim on that baby, if the matter ever wound up in court. He kept that particular motive to himself. After what Angela had done to him, he figured he was entitled to one devious act. A gambler would call it hedging his bets. Luke Adams probably wouldn't see it that way.

As it was, his declaration drew a full-fledged smile from his prospective father-in-law. ''It won't be easy,'' Luke informed him. ''She seems to have made up her mind to do this her way.''

''I can be very persuasive when I have to be,'' Clint said with more confidence than was probably justified. Angela had shown some evidence of being able to resist his charms. That had been an unexpected turn of events. He'd thought that breezing in here and staking his claim was going to be easy. He wasn't exactly disturbed to find he'd been wrong. He loved a good challenge as well as the next man. It kept life interesting, especially if a woman like Angela was involved.

"We'll work it out," Clint promised.

Luke seemed to find his self-assurance amusing. "Good luck," he said. He started toward the house, then turned back, his expression sobering. "Just one more thing. I don't know the details of what went on between the two of you in the past, but you hurt that girl of mine again and this time you'll be answering to me. Do we understand each other?"

The warning was as plain as a six-shooter pointed at the gut. Clint's respect for Luke Adams tripled in that instant. Here was a man who fought for what was his, who fiercely protected those he cared about. He was exactly the kind of man—the kind of father— Clint intended to be.

"Perfectly," he said quietly. "We understand each other perfectly."

The only problem he foresaw was getting the message through to Angela.

"Mother, how could you invite that man to stay here?" Angela demanded as she paced her room in pure frustration. She was already feeling claustrophobic just thinking about his presence, and this house was five times the size of the one she and Clint had shared in Montana.

"It seemed the sensible thing to do, dear," her

mother said blandly as she calmly folded the laundry Consuela had done earlier in the day. "You don't want him roaming all over the countryside talking about this situation with everyone he happens to meet, do you?"

"So this is some sort of bizarre protective custody to keep him from damaging my reputation?"

"Exactly."

"I have news for you. My reputation is bound to suffer the minute anyone gets a good look at me." She regarded her mother warily. "Or do you intend to lock me up here, too, until I do the right thing?"

"Of course not. You're perfectly free to come and go as you like, but I would say a little discretion is called for. You need to think long and hard about how you want to handle all of this. If you're determined not to marry Clint, then you'll have to decide what you're going to tell people, starting with the family."

Angela sighed. "I am not ready to see the family yet." She figured she might not be ready until her baby hit puberty.

"Well, you'd better get ready in a hurry because everyone is coming here tomorrow for our annual pre-Christmas party," her mother retorted, severely cutting into Angela's preferred timetable. "Someone is going to have to explain what's going on."

"I could hide in my room," she said wistfully, but without much hope that her mother would agree to such a cowardly plan.

"And what do you propose I say about Clint?" Her mother's eyes twinkled. "Or were you planning on locking him in here with you?"

"Mother!"

"It is an interesting thought," her mother said, then added slyly, "He is a very handsome man."

"What does that have to do with anything?"

"I imagine that's how you got into this predicament to begin with."

"Mother!"

"Sweetie, he's gorgeous. You're carrying his child. It doesn't take a genius to figure out you were sleeping together."

"I do not want to discuss this with you," she said, flushing with embarrassment.

"OK," her mother said cheerfully. "But I saw something in your eyes when you looked at him that reminded me of another woman."

"Who?" she asked, curious despite the instinct that told her to drop the subject of her very primal and unmistakable reaction to Clint Brady.

"Me. It was exactly the way I used to look when I caught a glimpse of Luke. I could no more help it than I could control the setting of the sun. It was plain as day to anybody who saw me. Jordan and Cody saw it. Luke saw it. Even your natural father was aware of it. I was the only one so deep in denial that I didn't recognize what was happening."

"My father knew about you and Luke?" Angela had always wondered about that, but it wasn't something her mother had ever discussed.

"Erik knew how we felt. He also knew we'd never acted on it and that we wouldn't. After he'd had his accident, when he knew he wasn't going to survive, he gave me his blessing. He was an incredible, generous man." She brushed away the tears dampening her cheeks, then smiled. "He would have loved you so much. And he would have been very proud of the gesture you made by studying education the way he always wanted to."

Neither of them mentioned her failure to follow through and actually go into teaching. "It seems so strange to me to think that Luke isn't my natural father," Angela said instead. "I've always known it, of course, but on some intellectual level. It never really registered in my heart."

"Because he's been there literally from the beginning. He adores you."

"Were he and my father very much alike?"

"Not at all. Your father was the quietest and gentlest of the brothers. He was never suited for ranching, but Harlan bullied him into trying. I'm not sure he's ever entirely forgiven himself for that. If he'd allowed your father to follow his own dream, Erik would never have been on that tractor the day he died."

She patted Angela's hand. "Enough sad memories for now. You have difficult decisions to make. I have only one word of advice for you."

"Only one?"

"OK, three. Follow your heart."

Angela knew the advice was well meant. She knew it was sound. The only trouble was that the last time she had followed her heart, she had gone and fallen in love with a man who didn't believe in happily ever after.

She knew, too, that even though Clint was trying to bulldoze her into marrying him now, he no more

believed in love than he had on the night she'd
walked out of his house. It reminded her of some sort
of deathbed conversion to religion. Say whatever it
took.

She didn't trust the turnaround. She knew better. If
anything, Clint's view of love and marriage was probably more jaded now than ever before. He knew that
their whole relationship had been built on one huge,
gigantic lie. She knew something else, as well, and it
terrified her. Clint Brady wasn't the kind of man
who'd forgive that kind of betrayal easily. If he was
proposing, there was a reason for it, and it for darn
sure wasn't love.

Chapter Five

In retrospect, her birthday dinner had been an extremely civilized affair, Angela concluded as she helped Consuela carry the last of the dishes into the kitchen. Clint had even sounded sincere when he'd joined in wishing her a happy birthday.

She smiled grimly. It might have taken him aback if he'd known what she'd wished before she'd tried to blow out the candles on the cake Consuela had baked. Not that it mattered a hoot now. One candle had remained stubbornly lit, so apparently even the gods were in on the conspiracy to keep Clint around.

At any rate, her father and Clint had gotten along better than anyone could have anticipated. They'd spent most of the meal comparing notes on ranching. No blows had been struck. No harsh words had been exchanged.

Every time Angela had been tempted to interrupt or to snap out a sarcastic retort, a warning look from her mother had silenced her. In the end, she'd left the table so frustrated, she'd been ready to spit.

"Your young man—" Consuela began as they entered the kitchen.

"He is not my young man," Angela retorted automatically, hoping to end that particular notion right now.

The housekeeper ignored her. Persistence was as ingrained in Consuela's personality as her smile. She'd had years of dealing with Luke and the other Adams brothers to practice.

"He will make a very good father," she said. Her defiant expression dared Angela to argue with her about that.

"You don't even know him. How can you be certain of a thing like that?"

"Because he treats you well."

"Excuse me? He all but threw me out of his house when I told him I was pregnant."

"No, *niña*," Consuela corrected gently. "I think you ran because you got insulted that he did not react as you wished. That is your way. You run from things rather than facing them, just as you ran from your home years ago."

The hard-truth assessment was a little too accurate, and Consuela did have the proof of Angela's rebellious departure from Texas on her side.

"Whatever," Angela said dismissively. "The point is, a few months ago he didn't even want this baby." Even as she said the words, she rubbed her belly soothingly as if to apologize to the baby for its father's reaction.

"There are many things men do not know they want until we show them," Consuela said. "Lucas could not admit he wanted your mother and you until he almost lost you both. Perhaps it was the same with your Clint."

"*My* Clint is just the kind of man who wants what he can't have. I guarantee you that if I said yes to this crazy wedding nonsense, he would take off before the ceremony."

"Care to test that theory, angel?" a taunting voice inquired from the doorway.

Angela whirled around to find herself face-to-face with the man in question. "I really wish you would stop sneaking up on me."

He grinned. "I came in to see if you and Consuela needed any help cleaning up. You shouldn't be doing dishes on your birthday."

"I thought you and my father were off somewhere discussing breeding or something."

"Breeding is a touchy subject around here these days," he said dryly. "We've been talking about water rights. It's a much safer topic."

"Very funny. I'm so delighted that you two are getting along so famously."

He regarded her with obvious amusement. "You don't sound delighted. You sound miffed. Why is that, I wonder?"

"I don't give two hoots if you and my father become bosom buddies," she said vehemently.

"You sure about that, angel? Weren't you sort of hoping that he'd blow my head off?"

"The prospect did hold a certain appeal, yes," she admitted.

"*Niña!*" Consuela protested, sketching a cross over her chest. "You should not say such a thing. A lady is always polite to her guests."

"He is not my guest. He's mother's. I didn't want him here, remember?"

Clint grinned at the obviously distraught house-keeper. "I guess the gloves are off."

"Oh, go suck an egg," Angela snapped.

Consuela regarded her with stern disapproval. "That is not the way you were brought up to behave, *niña.*"

She blushed at the rebuke, but she was too angry to let the matter drop. She stared at Consuela in disgust. "For goodness' sakes, isn't anybody around here going to take my side? Clint's been here less than twenty-four hours and everyone is treating him as if he were the prodigal son back from the range wars or something."

"Perhaps we just see what is not so plain to you," Consuela said. "Now go along. I will finish up in here. You two need to talk." She faced Angela. "And to listen," she added pointedly.

Angela sighed.

"Well?" Clint said, when she made no move to do as she'd been told. "Do you feel like going for a walk?"

"Not really," she said stubbornly.

He chuckled, then said, "It's snowing."

Immediately, just as he'd intended, an image of another night filled her head. They had left the bar where they had met and walked aimlessly through the small Montana town of Rocky Ridge. They had said little as they strolled along, thrilling to new sensations and content merely to have hands clasped. They had walked for an hour or more, both of them afraid to break the spell of unexpected intimacy that had captivated them.

Clearly uncertain of where things would go from there, Clint had walked her back to her car. Standing there, his hands on her waist, he had bent his head oh, so slowly and kissed her. It had been the sweetest, most innocent of kisses, but it had been the start of something incendiary.

As he pulled away, his eyes locked with hers, and she had felt the delicate touch of something cold and damp against her cheek. A snowflake. It had melted against her heated flesh practically before she realized what it was. It took another and another before it had registered.

"It's snowing," she had whispered, delighted, her face turned up toward the sky.

"Nothing's more beautiful than sitting in front of a fire and watching the snow fall outside," Clint had said. "Would you like to share that with me?"

The answer had been easy and as inevitable as that kiss. By dawn, in front of a blazing fire, they had become lovers. And outside, the ground had been covered with the first snow of the season, a fairy-tale dusting of white that had turned the world into a wonderland.

There had been more snow that winter, blizzards, in fact, but none had been as memorable as the one that had fallen on that first night she had spent in Clint's arms.

She gazed into his eyes now and saw that he was daring her to recapture that magic.

"I'll get my coat," she said quietly and started from the kitchen. She turned back, still defiant, but a little sad. "It won't be the same, you know."

His lips curved at her tone. "Maybe not," he agreed. "Maybe it will be better."

"Are you warm enough?" Clint asked. The minute they'd gotten outside, he'd started wondering if he'd made yet another foolish mistake dragging Angela out on such a bitter cold night. When he'd noticed the snow falling, it had taken him back to another time, another place, when things between them had been far less complicated. That night had been about discovery and beginnings. Perhaps tonight would be about a new beginning for the two of them, one built on a more solid foundation.

"I'm fine," she insisted yet again, her face turned up to the sky.

Snowflakes landed on her cheeks and melted in rapid succession. They caught in her eyelashes. She looked as ecstatic and as shatteringly vulnerable as if they had just made love. Clint wanted to kiss her so badly his body ached. He forced himself to hold back. Kissing had been the start of their problems. It wouldn't solve them. As the feisty Consuela had insisted, they needed to talk more than anything else at the moment. Unfortunately he had no idea where to begin. The emotions ripping through him were complex and conflicting.

He could start with his outrage over her running off. Or he could yell about the risks she'd taken traveling alone, especially these last couple of weeks with the baby almost due. Or he could demand an explanation for the monumental lie that stood between them. That last angered him more every time he thought about it.

Hattie Jones, indeed! Had she merely plucked the name out of the air on the spur of the moment? He imagined that more than one woman meeting a man for the first time in a bar might fib about her identity until she knew precisely with whom she was dealing. But wouldn't an honest woman come clean when the flirtation turned into a relationship? Why in hell had Angela perpetuated the lie until the day she'd left him? He had the feeling that any answer she had for that would only infuriate him more, would perhaps deepen his disdain beyond repair.

"Go on," she said, breaking the silence.

He regarded her blankly. "What?"

"Yell at me. Tell me what an idiot I was to run away. Tell me what a jerk I was for pretending to be Hattie Jones for all those months."

"I'm the one who feels like a jerk," he grumbled, hitting on what galled him most, his own stupidity. "Why didn't I see that you were lying?"

"What man would suspect that a woman he'd been sleeping with for the better part of a year wasn't who she'd claimed to be?" she retorted. "I wanted you to think of me as Hattie Jones. I wanted to be Hattie Jones, at least for a while.''

"I just have one question, why? Why did you lie? Not that first night, but later. Why did you keep lying?''

For a minute he thought he was going to get a flip response, some quick and easy explanation that would diminish the magnitude of what she'd done. Instead, her expression turned thoughtful and the silence dragged on. He let it.

"I suppose I just wanted a chance to be somebody else,'' she said eventually.

He stared at her in amazement. "Why? What on earth was wrong with being Angela Adams?''

She closed her eyes and sighed. "I know it doesn't make any sense to you. Just look around. I grew up on an incredible ranch. My parents are the best. There was no possible way on earth for me to be dissatisfied, right?''

"But you obviously were,'' he said, trying to make sense of it. He would have given anything to have grown up in a place like this with a family like hers. Instead, he'd had to scramble for every penny he'd earned. His dream of owning his own spread had seemed impossible once. He had made it happen. He didn't resent the difficulties he'd faced or the comparative ease of her past. It was just the way life was. A man could let it make him bitter or make him strong. He'd opted long ago for strong.

He saw that she was still struggling to put her thoughts into words and conceded that even though none of what she was saying made any sense to him, she was genuinely troubled. There was no mistaking that.

"Not dissatisfied," she said finally. "I felt smothered. There's a whole long story about how I was born, right here in Luke's bedroom, as a matter of fact. Luke isn't my natural father. His brother was."

Clint tried to hide his shock, but failed. The relationships here at least had seemed so straightforward, but obviously they were anything but. She shrugged.

"It's complicated," she said in what was an apparent understatement. "Anyway, everyone credits my birth with getting Luke and my mother together. I was supposed to be some sort of Christmas blessing."

She held out her hand and caught a snowflake, watching it melt before she spoke again. "It's weird growing up as part of some sort of family legend. I always felt as if so much was expected of me. The truth was, no matter how hard I tried, I would always be mortal, just another human being with lots and lots of flaws, when I was supposed to be an angel. Maybe if I'd had sisters named Faith, Hope and Charity, the pressure wouldn't have seemed so intense."

Clint chuckled, even though he could see that she was half-serious. He'd had six brothers and two sisters. The pressures she'd felt as an only child were an enigma to him.

"Don't laugh," she said. "Just being born an Adams comes with all sorts of baggage. Grandpa Harlan figures because we carry the name, we're all destined for something important. He also figures he gets to decide what that will be. Just ask Luke. He was the first one to rebel. Then Jordan. Even Cody bolted for a while. Only my dad tried to please him by going along with Grandpa Harlan's divine plan. It killed him.''

Clint was stunned by her words. "Killed him? How?''

"Granddad wanted him to be a rancher, so he tried, when what he really wanted to do was teach. He was always distracted. His head was always in some book. You know yourself, a rancher can't afford to be distracted. Too many things can happen in the blink of an eye. Who knows what he was thinking about, but the tractor he was riding here on Luke's ranch ran into a ditch and overturned. He died a few hours later.''

She sighed sadly. "You would have thought Grandpa Harlan would learn from his mistake, but he's still as meddlesome and controlling as he ever was. So is Luke. They are the most wonderful, best-intentioned men in the universe, but I couldn't breathe under the weight of all those expectations.''

"So you ran off and became Hattie Jones,'' Clint surmised. He'd heard of people moving, settling in someplace new to reinvent themselves, but a whole new name and identity? Wasn't that carrying it a little too far?

"Not at first. Actually, other than choosing Stanford instead of the University of Texas, my first act of rebellion was relatively mild. I studied English lit and education, instead of agriculture.''

She smiled briefly. It seemed a little wistful to him.

"I meant to be the teacher my father had wanted

to be,'' she added. ''I messed up at that, too. I graduated from college by the skin of my teeth, applied for my first teaching job and got cold feet. I knew in my gut I had no business at all being in a classroom trying to shape little minds, not when my own was such a mess.''

''Is that when you came to Montana?''

She nodded. ''Rocky Ridge was the first town I'd driven through that appealed to me. When you see Los Pinos, I think you'll understand why. Ironically, the two places are very much alike. Anyway, I walked into that bar on pure impulse to apply for the waitressing job posted in the window and there you were. It wasn't just that you were the sexiest thing I'd ever laid eyes on. You looked dangerous, harder and tougher than the men I'd met at school certainly.''

She reached up and touched his hair. ''All that shaggy, sun-streaked hair and those devilish blue eyes. You were flirting outrageously with me, and I felt as if you were my first and best chance to be a whole new person, a woman who was exciting and sensual and wicked. With you I could be anybody I wanted to be.''

Clint wasn't sure why, but the explanation chilled him. He didn't want to be anyone's act of rebellion. People who stuck together ought to bring out the best in one another, not the worst.

''I'm glad I could oblige,'' he said with a surprising edge of bitterness. ''You played the game well. Hattie was a real sexy invention. We had some good times.''

She frowned ever so slightly at his words. "You say that as if the good times were all in the past."

"I think maybe they were," he said slowly. He gazed into her eyes, searching for the woman who had once intrigued him so. A man would have to be a fool to try to perpetuate something that had only been make-believe. Sometimes it was smarter just to concede that the game was over and call it a draw.

"What are you saying?" she demanded.

It appeared to him that there was a touch of panic in her voice. A day ago that might have delighted him. Now it hardly seemed to matter.

He wanted to tell her that coming here was a mistake, that trying to convince her to marry him was a mistake, but that would ruin his long-range plan for getting custody of his child. "Just that you can't recapture the past," he said instead. "I thought you could, but I was wrong."

Her eyes darkened with hurt, but he noticed she didn't try to argue with him.

"Then you'll be leaving, after all?"

He thought he detected a blending of hope and despair in her voice, but he was too upset to figure out what was going on in that mixed-up mind of hers. He shook his head. "Not a chance, sweetheart. I meant what I said about that wedding. That baby of ours is going to have my name."

"Why? You can't possibly care about the child of a woman you despise."

Despise was too strong a word, but he didn't correct her. "I care about *my* child, though. Make no mistake about it, angel, this baby is mine."

Now there was no mistaking the genuine panic in her expression. "Meaning?"

"I will fight you for him," he declared, then amended, "or her."

He saw her shudder as the words registered and knew he had shown his hand too soon. He regretted that, but it wouldn't change anything. Maybe the fight would be fairer if they both knew where they stood. Fairness was a lot more than she deserved.

"You can't," she protested.

"Watch me," he said and walked away.

"You can't win," she shouted after him. "Not here. The Adams name means something here in Texas."

"And Jones?" he taunted. "Does the name Hattie Jones mean anything?"

That silenced her. He was halfway back up the lane toward the house when he heard the rustle of her coat against denim, the crunch of ice beneath her boots as she followed him. He wasn't sure why, but he waited for her at the door.

That was a mistake, he realized at once, when he saw the sheen of tears on her cheeks. Then he told himself that the dampness was merely snowflakes melting. A woman as coldly calculating as Hattie Jones—or Angela Adams—couldn't possibly be crying.

Angela was holding back sobs by the time she closed the door to her room behind her. She would not let Clint Brady see that he had hurt her. She would not let him see that she was terrified of his threat to take the baby. But behind that closed door, she let her fear and anguish flow unchecked. Still in her coat, damp now with snow, she huddled on her bed, clutching a pillow. She had botched things again. She had tried to be open and honest with Clint—albeit belatedly—and he had taken her words and twisted them into something ugly.

He would use them against her, if he had to. She had seen that much in his hard expression. She had watched his pride kick in and she had shuddered. Months ago she had seen that his pride was a more than even match for any Adams.

She knew exactly what would happen. He would go into court and portray her as a woman unfit to be a mother, a woman who had committed the ultimate betrayal by pretending to be someone else entirely. He would describe her behavior in Montana as something wanton and sinful and she would be helpless to deny it, because that was exactly what she had meant it to be. Hattie Jones had been outrageous and deceptive, because those were traits that Angela Adams had been forbidden in her nice, protected world.

What had she been thinking? That wasn't who she was, not really. Just look how quickly she had done the traditional thing and fallen in love with the man. Just look at the perfectly normal expectation she'd had back then that they would get married and raise the baby they'd conceived in love together.

In the end she'd even messed up being outrageous. Now everyone was going to know about her foolish mistake. Her parents. Grandpa Harlan. The whole damned world, if Clint had his way. She couldn't let that happen. She had to find some way to compromise with him, some way to win him back. She had to smooth things over until tempers cooled.

Only a few hours ago he'd been determined to marry her. He'd wanted the baby to have his name. Obviously he wanted to do things the traditional way, just as she had from the very moment she'd discovered she was pregnant with his child. He wanted to behave honorably, because down deep that was the kind of man Clint Brady was. She had recognized that in him from the beginning. Maybe it was why she had felt so free to behave as she had, because she had known she could trust him not to harm her in any way.

He'd never taken back his proposal, not even when his temper had flared. Maybe his motives weren't as innocent and pure as he had wanted everyone else to believe, but he hadn't retracted the words. She could use that to her advantage.

She got slowly out of bed and changed into her nightgown. She washed away the last traces of her tears. There would be no more, she resolved.

She smiled at herself in the mirror. She had learned a few tricks as Hattie Jones. It was time she made them pay off for her. Once, Clint hadn't been able to resist her. Whatever her name, she was still that same woman.

Before anyone knew that his interest in marriage was totally self-serving, she was going to make absolutely certain that they were walking down the aisle. She was going to protect her role in her baby's life…no matter what Clint had in mind for the future.

Chapter Six

"So, where's my precious angel!"

Angela heard her grandfather's booming voice all the way upstairs and sighed.

"Not yet, please God," she whispered. She wasn't ready to see him yet, wasn't prepared to see even a hint of judgment in his eyes. She wasn't ready to explain the baby she was expecting. She certainly wasn't prepared to explain Clint, not with things so terribly unsettled between them.

Nor could she rely on her parents to smooth the way. It wouldn't be fair to expect them to give answers to so many difficult questions, when she didn't know the answers herself.

"Not yet," she pleaded again.

Apparently God had other ideas. She heard her grandfather's two-at-a-time tread on the steps, then the sharp, impatient rap of his knuckles against her door.

"You in there, darlin'?"

Resigned to the inevitable, she drew in a deep breath, plastered a bright smile on her face and threw open the door.

"Grandpa," she said and felt herself scooped into an awkward, but exuberant bear hug.

After a minute he set her back on her feet and stepped back. "Let me get a good look at you." His gaze traveled over her mound of a belly, then came to rest on her face. His eyes were troubled, but his beaming smile never faltered.

"You look pretty as a picture," he declared. "Impending motherhood obviously agrees with you."

"You should have seen me the first month," she said, thinking of the nausea that had been a constant companion. There had been mornings she hadn't wanted to budge from bed, much less see herself in a mirror.

"I wish I had," he said at once, "instead of you being away in who-knows-where all by yourself."

Sensing the likelihood that a lecture was about to begin, she hurriedly said, "My turn now."

She quickly scanned him from head to toe. Other than a few more gray hairs and a slight stoop to his shoulders he looked as fit as ever. He was one of those men who wore his age well and would until his nineties, God willing. He was almost in his eighties now and barely looked sixty.

"You haven't changed a bit," she told him.

"You're every bit as handsome as you were the day I left."

He winked at her. "Love," he confided. "I highly recommend it at any age."

Angela grinned at the allusion to the woman who'd turned his whole outlook on life upside down. "How is Janet?" she asked.

"Perfect. Wonderful," he enthused, eyes sparkling at the thought of her. "She's downstairs with your mama. She's as anxious to see you as I was, but she shows more restraint. She still says I haven't got a lick of patience or any understanding whatsoever of privacy."

Angela grinned at him. "I guess there are some traits not even love can change. Not in an Adams man, anyway."

His expression sobered. "So when are you going to make me a great-granddaddy?"

"The way I feel right now, it can't be soon enough. Another week or two is what the doctor told me before I left Seattle to come home."

He shook his head. "I can't believe it. Me with a child in her teens and a great-grandbaby on the way. Talk about a couple of curve balls. Life's thrown me some doozies. Not that I'm complaining. I wouldn't have it any other way."

She grinned at his expression of delighted disbelief. "How are my cousins?" she asked, referring not only to the teenager her grandfather and Janet had had together, but to Janet's daughter Jenny. It was Jenny's theft of Grandpa Harlan's truck that had brought them together in the first place. As a child, Angela had always thought Jenny's rebellious ways fascinating. She'd envied the daring teenager. In the end, it appeared she'd outdone her.

"Jenny's going to be teaching school soon," he said proudly, apparently oblivious to the irony. If his reaction to Erik's desires had been half so approving, perhaps Angela's natural father still would have been alive.

"As for Lizzy," he went on, "she is the most beautiful child ever born and the smartest."

"Don't you let Luke, Cody and Jordan hear you say that," Angela chided. "You'll hurt their feelings. They all think they were gorgeous and sexy from day one."

"Those three have hides like an elephant," he said dismissively. "My talk's not going to faze them. Besides, they were never as cute as Lizzy. She's her daddy's girl. Top of her class every year."

Amused by his bragging, she teased, "Don't you suppose just maybe she inherited some of her intelligence from her mother? Janet is an attorney, after all, and a very good one." In fact, Janet Runningbear Adams had built a national reputation for her work on behalf of Native American causes.

He grinned. "Much as it galls me, I suppose I can share some of the credit with her." He looped an arm around Angela's shoulders. "Come on down and see them. Jenny's not here yet, but the others are waiting. Lizzy was ecstatic when we told her about the baby. She's tired of being the youngest. Cody and Jordan should be turning up soon with their broods. You won't believe how grown-up all my grandbabies are.''

The thought of facing them all made her palms sweat. Overwhelming uncles, rock-steady aunts and rambunctious cousins. It promised to be too much.

''You go on ahead,'' she suggested. ''I'm not quite ready.''

Ignoring her hesitance, he declared, ''You look fine to me. Another touch of powder on your nose isn't going to make you one bit prettier.''

''It's not that. I…'' She gazed into his eyes, pleading with him to understand.

His expression softened at once. ''You're scared, aren't you?'' he said bluntly. ''Or ashamed. Which is it?''

When she said nothing, he captured her face between his work-roughened hands and met her gaze evenly. ''Darling girl, there's no need to be. Family's all that's important to us. Everyone here has made more than their share of mistakes. Everyone here loves you, no matter what. Don't you know that by now? All that matters to us is that you're home again.''

She nodded, tears welling up. Maybe it was his words, maybe her wacky hormones, but she felt like bawling. ''I'll be there in a few minutes, I promise. I'm not going to duck out the back door.''

His eyes twinkled. ''What about that tree by your bedroom window? You thinking of climbing down that the way you did when you were a girl so you could sneak off to see your friends?''

She laughed at the memory, as well as the impossibility of resorting to such an escape now. She patted her belly. "Like this? I don't think so. I'll be down to face the music, and I'll use the stairs like a proper, grown-up lady."

"You'd feel braver with me by your side," he said lightly. "Nobody's going to mess with my darlin' girl with me around."

She grinned at that. "You can't protect me from everything, Grandpa."

"I can sure as hell try," he said fiercely. "I love you, angel. Don't make any mistake about that."

She stood on tiptoe and kissed his weathered cheek. "I love you, too. And I didn't realize until now just how much I'd missed you."

He cast one last worried look in her direction, then retreated downstairs. Angela stared after him for what seemed an eternity, trying to work up the courage to join everyone.

"Facing your family's harder than you expected, isn't it?" Clint said, exiting the guest room across the hall.

"Is it necessary for you to spy on me?" she snapped, then recalled that she was supposed to be trying to win the man back, not offend him. "Sorry. It's just that seeing Grandpa Harlan shook me more than I'd expected it to. He acts as if I haven't done anything wrong, when I know perfectly well he must be furious."

"More likely with me than with you," Clint suggested. "Want to go downstairs with me and protect me?"

She glanced up at him with astonishment and saw

the sympathy and understanding in his eyes. She knew perfectly well he wasn't one bit terrified of her grandfather or any man. Despite their battle the night before, he was offering her his support. She thought she had never loved him more than she did at this moment. It really was too bad that everything between them had gotten so messed up. At heart he was a decent, sensitive man. Maybe if she'd remembered that and given him time to adjust to the idea of being a daddy, things would never have gotten so out of hand.

For just a moment she allowed herself to imagine the way it could have been. Arriving home as Clint's wife, their first baby on the way, would have turned the holidays into something unforgettable.

Instead, there was bound to be an endless amount of tension and strain as everyone tiptoed around the subject of their relationship. She didn't envy Clint his role as an outsider, not with everyone bound to feel especially protective of her. He had no idea what he had let himself in for by accepting her mother's invitation to stay on through the holidays.

"I wonder if he knows yet that you're here," she murmured thoughtfully.

"I doubt it. I haven't heard any explosions since he arrived, have you?"

"My father might have warned him."

"Oh, somehow I doubt that," he said with a wry expression. "Your father would probably be delighted if your grandfather took one look at me and ripped me to shreds. Luke can't do it himself because we declared a truce yesterday."

She studied him curiously. "I wondered about that. How did you win him over?"

"I didn't say I'd won him over, just that we'd agreed not to brawl. I'm on probation. He's waiting for me to make just one tiny mistake and then, I guarantee it will be his pleasure to chase me all the way back to Montana."

She regarded him impishly. "One tiny mistake, huh?"

He scowled at her. "Don't go getting any ideas, angel. I have no intention of treading on anyone's toes until I can claim my child."

She ignored the subtle reminder of his threat. She would deal with that when the time came. Instead, some thoroughly outrageous instinct, probably left from her days as Hattie, made her link her arm through his. Now was as good a time as any to start her scheme to win him back.

"Let's go," she said with a wink. "Let's see just how much trouble I can get you into, if I try."

There wasn't so much as a twinkle in his eyes when he met her gaze evenly. "That works both ways, sweetheart. You'd do well to remember that."

The deliberate taunt jangled her nerves, just as he'd obviously intended. It reminded her that she was playing games with a master.

At the top of the stairs, before Clint's quick retort had evened the score, her promise of troublemaking had seemed like a fine idea. She'd expected to sail into the midst of her family with restored confidence.

Instead, standing in the doorway to the living room with a circle of inquisitive faces staring at them, she realized she'd miscalculated. Walking into that room on Clint's arm hadn't been the masterstroke she'd anticipated. It had simply quadrupled the speculation and added to the pressure. Now it wouldn't be just her folks and Consuela anticipating a wedding, but this whole roomful of relatives. Why hadn't she seen that she should have locked the man in a closet until after New Year's?

Since she couldn't seem to find her tongue, it was Clint who worked his way around the group, introducing himself with an ease that she found thoroughly annoying. Why wasn't he feeling the same kind of intimidation that she felt? This was her family, after all. Right this second he seemed more at home than she did.

He slowed when he got to her grandfather. She saw the two men taking each other's measure. Everyone seemed to be holding their collective breath, waiting to see what Harlan Adams would do or say to the man who had gotten his grandchild into the fix she was in.

Her grandfather's expression was unreadable, but he was the first to hold out his hand. "Welcome, son. It's good to have you with us for the holidays."

The palpable tension in the room eased.

"Thank you, sir," Clint said with just the right amount of deference. "I've heard quite a lot about you. It's a pleasure to meet you at last."

Who's lying now? Angela thought bitterly. Up until the day before yesterday, Clint Brady hadn't even known this family existed, yet he was treating them all as if they were people he genuinely cared about getting to know.

Worse, they were falling for it, toppling like dominoes under the warmth of his natural charm.

She sighed and tried to be grateful for the fact that his presence had shifted some of the attention away from her for the moment. She was able to slip from the room and head for the kitchen to get her bearings before yet another carload of exuberant Adamses showed up.

She was surprised to find the kitchen deserted. There was no sign of Consuela, even though preparations for that night's feast were well underway. Expecting the housekeeper to return at any second, she filled a glass with milk and sank down into a chair at the table where she had spent many an afternoon as a girl talking out her problems, sometimes with Consuela, just as often with her mother. This room had heard a lot of secrets over the years.

When the door swung open, she glanced up and saw that it was her step-grandmother who'd followed her. Angela's smile was genuine as she surveyed the tall, slim woman with the shoulder-length black hair and sparkling brown eyes. She had always admired the strong, feisty lawyer who'd stolen her grandfather's heart. Janet Runningbear Adams exuded the kind of quiet serenity Angela wished she could attain. It had taken a woman with amazing self-confidence to stand up to Harlan Adams strong will and become his partner in life, as well as his mate.

Janet rested a hand on her shoulder, when Angela would have risen to hug her. "Stay where you are. I know how difficult it is to get up and down at this stage of pregnancy. Are you feeling OK?''

"As well as any blimp could be expected to feel,'' Angela told her. "Did you come in here looking for Consuela? Or a snack, maybe?''

"Actually I came to see you.''

"Oh?''

"It was your grandfather's idea that we have a talk. He got it into his head last night after he spoke to your father and heard that Clint was here. Naturally he practically shoved me out of the living room just now, instead of letting me wait a bit.''

Angela regarded her warily. "What did he want you to talk to me about?''

"He thought you might need some legal protection.''

"Legal protection? From Clint? You mean like a restraining order or something?''

Her incredulity made Janet smile. "Actually, I think he was thinking more along the lines of a pre-nuptial agreement.''

"Oh.'' Given the lack of real wedding plans and her own financial circumstances, the idea struck her as just as ludicrous. Besides, she'd always thought that starting a marriage by figuring out the financial ins and outs of ending it showed a certain lack of faith in the relationship.

"Why on earth would he think I needed something like that?''

"I'm not recommending it,'' Janet said hastily, clearly reacting to the defensive note in Angela's voice. "Your grandfather and I had quite a few words over that very subject when we got married. We ripped up a lot of paper, but a prenuptial agreement does serve a purpose. It can protect what's yours or his.''

''You may not have noticed, but I don't have a lot,'' Angela said dryly. ''My savings account is virtually empty. So's my checkbook. As for Clint, his ranch is hardly the kind of place that needs protecting from my greedy little grasp.''

''But you're an Adams,'' Janet reminded her as if that alone explained the need for such an agreement.

''He's hardly likely to try to steal my name.''

Janet grinned. ''No, but you stand to inherit this ranch. You have a sizable trust fund from your grandfather that will be yours in another couple of years.''

Neither of those things had ever crossed her mind, maybe because she'd figured her parents and grandfather would live forever. ''Clint not only doesn't know about that, he wouldn't care if he did,'' she said with absolute certainty.

''Are you so sure? I was under the impression that there was a time when he wasn't the least bit interested in marrying you or claiming his baby. Now he turns up here and does a one-eighty. Maybe that's honestly motivated,'' Janet said reasonably. ''Maybe not, but you ought to be sure before you risk everything that will one day be yours.''

Angela shuddered. ''I don't know. That seems so cold and calculating. It's not like Clint at all. Besides, none of this ever mattered to me, anyway.''

''Possibly not, but you should think about this baby you're carrying. You should protect what's yours for your child's future. Will you at least consider what I've said?''

Angela nodded reluctantly. Janet reached across the table and squeezed her hand. ''If there's anything else you need to talk about, I'm available, not as a lawyer, but as a friend. Remember that. Sometimes it takes an objective outsider to help sort things out.''

''You're hardly an outsider,'' she reminded her.

''I wasn't born an Adams,'' Janet said wryly. ''In the end it makes a difference. An Adams is single-minded when it comes to family. On occasion I have to remind Harlan that there are two sides to most stories.''

Angela grinned. ''I imagine you do. Thank you. Maybe one of these days when I figure out what all the questions are, I'll see if you have any answers.''

''Bottom line? There's really only one question and I think you already know what that is.''

Angela sighed. ''Do we love each other, I suppose.''

''That's the one.''

''Any insights?'' Angela asked wistfully.

''I haven't seen the two of you in the same room long enough to tell yet.'' She winked. ''Give me until tomorrow. I'll share my matchmaking insights with you, though to hear Jenny tell it, I'm really lousy at it.''

That said, she left Angela alone again with her thoughts. All of the things she had to consider were beginning to give her a headache. If she'd thought she could manage it without getting caught, she would have slipped back up to her room and hidden out there until the holidays were over.

The distrust between her and Clint had just escalated to another level, fueled by Janet's suggestions that he had somehow discovered her potential net worth and decided that maybe being married wouldn't be so terrible after all.

At this rate, would they ever be able to rediscover the feelings that had drawn them together so many months ago? Or were they destined always to be at cross-purposes, always trying to second-guess motives?

Angela sighed heavily. She'd been exposed to a lot of very strong marriages over her lifetime. Jordan and Kelly, Cody and Melissa, her own parents, Grandpa Harlan and Janet. All of them had shown her the power of love. She believed in it with all her heart. She also knew that trust was at the core of each and every one of them.

Over the last few days the seeds of distrust had been sown between her and Clint, intentionally or inadvertently. It didn't really matter which. The point was, could any couple overcome that kind of obstacle? The sad answer, it seemed to her, was no.

Clint knew he was on display. Hell, he was on trial. So far he thought he'd managed to hold his own. Harlan Adams was an even tougher nut to crack than his son, but Clint thought he seemed at least willing to wait and see if Clint could prove himself worthy of an Adams.

The irony of it all wasn't lost on him. If he'd

known everything he knew now about her family on the day he'd met Angela, even he would have said he was out of his league. But he hadn't fallen for Angela Adams. He'd been caught up in a blazing romance with Hattie Jones, whose background had been kept a mystery and whose heart was as generous as any woman's on earth.

That was what made him crazy now. He kept remembering all of Hattie's best traits and questioning which of them existed in Angela. Had any man ever been presented with such a complex puzzle to sort out? If so, he'd like to meet him and discover how he'd done it without losing his sanity in the process.

When another carload of family members turned up—Cody and Melissa and their kids, if he'd gotten the names straight—he took the opportunity to slip away from the ensuing chaos and hunt for Angela. She'd vanished again, though he was pretty sure this time that she'd gone no farther than the kitchen. He'd noticed that she seemed to retreat there an awful lot. It must have always been some sort of haven for her. That suited him just fine, since the warm room and the sympathetic housekeeper drew him, as well.

Sure enough, Angela was sitting at the table, eyes closed, a half-empty glass of milk on the table, her feet propped up on another chair. He noticed that her ankles were swollen. Since she was either asleep or simply oblivious to his arrival, he slid into the chair closest to her feet and lifted them into his lap. He massaged them gently, regretting all the exhausting days she must have spent when he hadn't been around to perform this simple act of kindness for her.

Her sigh of pure pleasure sounded genuine. Slowly she opened her eyes and stared at him in surprise. "You?"

"Who'd you think it was?" he inquired, chuckling at her disconcerted expression.

"I don't know. Consuela maybe."

"I'm disappointed, angel. I thought for sure you'd recognize my touch."

"It's been a long time." Her gaze caught his and lingered. "A very long time."

"Some things a man never forgets," he said. "I guess it's different for a woman."

"Not really," she admitted softly.

The response and the hint of intimacy hovered in the air between them, too fragile to test. Clint was wise enough for once to keep silent. He contented himself with the sighs his ongoing massage earned him.

"I suppose I can't put it off any longer," she said eventually.

"What?"

"Joining the others."

"There are more here now," he advised her. "Your uncle Cody, I believe. I skipped out before meeting him and came to look for you."

She grinned. "Two Adams men didn't alarm you, but three began to seem like impressive odds, I guess."

"Something like that." He gave her a lazy smile. "Or maybe I just missed you."

"I wish I could believe that," she said almost wistfully.

"Then do. It's true."

She regarded him with blatant skepticism. "True or convenient," she muttered.

His fingers stilled against her soft skin. "Convenient?" he asked, his tone lethal.

There was a flash of pure panic in her eyes, but it quickly gave way to defiance. "Yes, convenient," she said firmly. "You're up to something, Clint Brady. There's not a doubt in my mind about that."

"Sweetheart, unlike you, I laid all my cards out on the table. I intend to marry you and give my child my name."

"And then?" she asked distrustfully.

"Well, I suppose we'll just have to take things as they come after that."

She scowled. "Now that's the part that has me worried."

"It shouldn't." He slid his hand up her leg, beneath her slacks. The skin was soft as silk and warmed to his caress. "We were always very, very good at improvising."

An obviously reluctant smile tugged at her lips. "Yes," she conceded eventually. "Yes, we were."

Chapter Seven

Clint had grown up in what he considered to be a large family, plenty of brothers and sisters to make holidays chaotic, if stressful, even a handful of cousins on his mother's side to fill up the house. He'd always thought that was one reason he'd moved to such a small town in Montana and chosen an isolated ranch. He'd longed for some peace and quiet.

He now knew with absolute certainty that the one thing he would never get with Angela in his life was peace and quiet, not on holidays spent in Texas, anyway.

By three in the afternoon he'd lost count of the number of people who'd arrived for the pre-Christmas party. Harlan Adams presided over the celebration with as much pride as any clan patriarch in a state filled with larger-than-life men. He commanded the respect not only of his sons, but his daughters-in-law and of all the grandchildren. They deferred to him in most matters, teased him unmercifully about others and always, always showed their love with every word and action.

Clint knew it took an incredible man to earn so much adoration. He'd never had a male role model of his own. He'd thought when he first met Luke Adams that Luke might be the man to emulate. Now he realized that Luke was simply his father's son: a strong, honest man shaped by a strong, honest father. Cody and Jordan were, as well. Parenting such fine men was a legacy Harlan Adams could be proud of.

Watching their interaction made Clint feel the kind of gut-deep envy that he'd never before experienced as child or adult. Sure, as a kid he'd wanted a dad around for the simple stuff, a father-son dinner at school, a game of catch in the backyard, an afternoon of fishing. He'd regretted not having something that even his own brothers and sisters had experienced. But he hadn't felt this wrenching sense of having missed something powerful and meaningful in his life.

He had no idea what kind of man his father had become when he'd left them, but the fact that he'd gone said quite a lot about his character. It was obvious to Clint that his father hadn't come from the same sort of stock that Harlan Adams had. Even if he'd stayed, his influence on Clint's life probably wouldn't have been as sharply defined as Harlan Adams's had been on his sons.

It was rare for Clint to feel that he wasn't another

man's equal, but in this crowd he began to have his
doubts. His own code of ethics was decent, his own
brand of loyalty deep, but he wasn't at all sure it
measured up to what he was witnessing at this family
gathering.

Having doubts about himself always made him
edgy. As a kid he'd taken swings at anyone who'd
suggested he was less than they were. As an adult
he'd learned to avoid situations that would put him
at a disadvantage.

Now, feeling decidedly edgy, he retreated outside
after Consuela's gargantuan feast. He figured it would
be hours before anyone even noticed he'd gone. If
they did notice, they'd probably be relieved since his
presence had created more than one awkward, stressful moment.

Angela surely wouldn't miss him. She was finally
and totally caught up in her reunion with her family,
just as she should be. Whatever questions anyone had
raised had been silenced, probably by stern admoni-
tions from on high. In the absence of such probing,
she had relaxed. Her smile had come more frequently,
twisting his insides with the innocent beauty of it. He
thought she looked happier than he'd ever made her.
That made him edgy, too.

"Too overwhelming?" she asked, suddenly appearing at his side as if he'd conjured her up. Her hair
was whipping around her face in the icy wind. That
same wind had put patches of color in her cheeks.
She was desperately tugging at her coat, trying to
close the ever-widening gap over her expanding
tummy, but it was a losing battle.

He smiled at the futile effort and drew a responding scowl.

"You try adding an inch a day to your waistline and see how long clothes fit," she grumbled.

"You shouldn't be out here," he said curtly. "The sun's about to go down and the temperature's dropping."

"I needed some air and a chance to let my face muscles relax."

He grinned at that. He'd felt much the same way himself. Still, he couldn't resist the urge to taunt. "Too much smiling?" he inquired. "Didn't I read somewhere that it takes fewer muscles to smile than it does to frown?"

She chuckled. "Have you been reading those beauty magazines I left behind?"

It was closer to the truth than he wanted to admit. She'd cluttered the whole darn ranch house with her romance novels and her magazines. After she'd gone, he'd felt closer to her when he'd glanced through them. Silly nonsense, for the most part, at least when it came to the magazines.

The books had been another story. Some of those writers could weave a fascinating story, and the steamy sex in a few of them had left him downright hot for days afterward. He'd regretted not peeking at them when Hattie had been around to satisfy the urges they stirred.

"You have, haven't you?" she demanded, laughing. "I don't believe it."

He feigned a scowl. "Don't let it get around, angel. You'll ruin my reputation."

She eyed him speculatively and he could see evidence of the insatiable Hattie in her expression. She had always been as eager as he to make love, as anxious as he for a stolen caress or a passionate kiss.

"Exactly what other tidbits of useful information did you pick up from your reading?" she asked.

Suddenly enjoying the game, he reached over and tucked a wayward curl behind her ear. He lingered to trace his thumb across her lower lip and felt the shock of his touch jolt through her. The flare of yearning in her eyes was unmistakable. Once upon a time he'd seen it often. That kind of longing was heady stuff for a man who'd always been odd man out with his own family. To have someone want him so desperately fueled his masculine ego and filled his heart. Only after she'd gone had he realized just how much he'd come to depend on it. Now she was openly offering him a chance to grab just a small taste of what they'd once shared.

"For starters," he said quietly, his gaze pinned on hers, "I learned that sometimes a kiss is more devastating than sex, that the brush of a finger across a woman's lips can make her toes curl." He studied her quizzically as he suited action to words. "Is it true, angel?"

She swallowed hard, but never took her eyes from his. The bold look further inflamed him as he waited to see if she'd respond honestly or lie.

"It seems to be," she said. "But I think one experiment is hardly scientific."

Smiling to himself, he traced the outline of her mouth, lingering at the dip in the top lip, then skimming the bottom lip lightly with his fingernail. She trembled.

"Two for two," he said with satisfaction. "Enough yet?"

"Not nearly enough," she insisted.

"The experimenting's getting dangerous," he warned.

"You scared?" she taunted.

"No, but maybe you should be."

"Nothing scares an Adams," she retorted.

He laughed. "That's definitely one part of your heritage you never denied. You were always game for any risk."

"So were you. Some said it was what made us a good match," she said.

"Still feeling intrepid?"

"Always."

He slowly lowered his head until his mouth hovered over hers. "Still?"

With her gaze pinned to his, she simply nodded.

The touch of their lips set off a familiar blazing heat. Clint was no longer aware of the biting cold of the wind. Inside, his body temperature shot up. Perspiration broke out on his brow.

When Angela settled into his embrace, her lips molded to his, he felt as if he could strip naked, make love to her right here and right now, and never even notice the frozen ground beneath them. She could make him hotter faster than a wood stove set on high. Always could.

"Hey, Justin, is there steam rising from Angie?"

Reality slammed into him at the comment. Angela

went absolutely still in his arms. He guessed the whispered question came from young Harlan Patrick, Cody's son. He was twenty or so and had a smart mouth and a young man's fascination with sex. That much had been evident from the moment he arrived.

"Maybe we should douse them with water," Jordan's son, Justin, whispered back. "That's what Dad does to the cats when he catches them going at it."

"You do and you are going to be two very uncomfortable young men for the rest of your visit," Clint said. Angie shivered or so he thought. He glanced down and realized she was laughing and trying to keep her two cousins from catching her at it. She buried her face against his chest.

Justin and Harlan whirled to take off, but Clint released Angela with some reluctance and placed himself squarely in their path, one hand firmly on each boy's shoulder. He regarded them steadily. "Now here's the deal, guys. You keep very, very quiet about what you saw and I will keep my mouth shut about the cigarettes you were sneaking."

Despite being plenty old enough to smoke the two teens exchanged guilty looks. They knew how vehemently their grandfather objected. Harlan had gone on about it earlier.

"Are we agreed?" Clint asked.

"Oh, yeah," Justin said fervently. "Even at my age Dad would knock me from here to Dallas if he knew I was smoking."

"From here to Kansas," Harlan concurred. "We never saw a thing, Mr. Brady." He dared a glance at

his cousin. "Sorry, Angie. We didn't mean to interrupt."

"Yeah," Justin said. "You guys go back to doing
whatever it was you were doing when we showed up.
Not that we noticed or anything."

"Later, guys," Clint said. "And ditch the cigarettes."

They took off running. Away from the house, Clint
noticed with amusement.

"How'd you know they'd been smoking?" Angie
asked when they were out of earshot. "I never
smelled a thing."

"Guesswork," he admitted. "They looked guilty
as sin when your grandfather was talking about cigarettes. My brothers and I used to sneak out and try
to catch a smoke after some family gathering, so we
could feel grown-up. It was my mother who caught
up with us the second or third time we tried it. She
was not pleased. She threatened to shred the tobacco
like a salad and make us eat it for dessert, if she ever
caught us with a cigarette again. She said if we were
going to put that foul stuff into our bodies, we might
as well chow down on it. Said it would kill us quicker
that way."

"Did she do it?"

"Never had to. We'd gotten the message."

She studied him, her expression thoughtful. "You
never talked much about your family when we were
together," she said.

"Neither did you," he pointed out.

"*Touché.* Maybe we should start all over again,
pretend we just met."

He glanced at her protruding belly. "That's a little hard to do, don't you think?"

Suddenly she gasped and grabbed her stomach.

"What?" he demanded at once. "Are you okay? Sweet heaven, you're not going into labor, are you? It's too soon, isn't it? Have you even seen a doctor since you got here?"

"Whoa. Relax." She grinned. "Your kid was just making his presence felt. I think he's practicing for the NFL already."

"You're convinced it's a boy?"

"No, but Consuela is. She's almost never wrong." She regarded him shyly, then took his hand and placed it on her stomach. "Here, feel."

For several seconds he felt nothing at all, then suddenly he felt the *thump* of a very solid kick. The rush of feelings that came over him was mind-boggling. For the first time, the baby was a reality, not just part of some grand lie that stood between them.

"A field goal kicker, for sure," he said, feeling the unexpected sting of tears in his eyes.

He'd missed months of this. He'd been cheated of hearing his baby's heartbeat for the first time, of seeing Angela's body change to accommodate the child she was carrying. OK, so that was partly his fault, but she was the one who'd impetuously taken off. She was the one who'd kept on running.

"Damn you," he said softly.

She stared at him in shock. Her eyes filled with hurt and confusion at the harshness of his words. "What?"

"You've robbed me of so much."

Never one to take an accusation lightly, she scowled back at him. Temper flared in her eyes. "You had a choice," she reminded him stiffly. "You could have reacted like a man and accepted responsibility from the beginning."

It was the same old story, dragging them back to square one. Clint sighed. If he were entirely honest, he'd have to admit they shared the blame. There was more than enough to go around. Even so, he couldn't resist one last dig.

"Is that all you expected, for me to accept responsibility? I never questioned that this was my baby. Not once. I was always under the impression what you really wanted was for me to declare my love and marry you."

"It's the same thing," she said defiantly.

"Not quite, angel. And if you were being entirely honest, you'd admit that back then you and I were nowhere close to sorting out our feelings for each other. You didn't even trust me enough to tell me the truth about who you were."

Her lips compressed into an angry line before she snapped, "Don't talk to me about honesty, Clint Brady. You've never once owned up to what you're really doing here."

He went absolutely still at the unspoken accusation behind the words. "Meaning?"

"Just how did you find out who I was and where to find me? Was finding out that I came from a wealthy family enough to drag you down here after me?"

She had hinted at as much earlier, but Clint still

couldn't believe his ears. The unfairness of her charge apparently never crossed her mind. Quick-tempered retorts came into his head, but he knew if he spoke even one of them, ugly words would start flying fast and furiously. Their tempers had always been their downfall. There was no such thing as a quiet, rational conversation between Hattie and him over even a small difference of opinion. They shouted whatever came to mind at full volume.

When the dust settled, there were always hurt feelings and fences to mend. He suspected it was the one area in life that didn't improve with practice. He suspected the cuts just went deeper and the fences grew harder and harder to mend. Maybe it was time to break the cycle and find a new way of getting along. Since he didn't have an imagination vivid enough to figure out how to do that on the spur of the moment, he decided some distance was called for.

"Go back inside, Angela," he said abruptly, backing away from her. "It's too damned cold for you to be out here."

"I will not," she said, digging in her heels literally and regarding him with fire in her eyes. "You don't make decisions for me."

"Oh, for pity's sake, can't you do one thing because it's sensible and stop worrying about the fact that the suggestion came out of my mouth?"

With that he scooped her up in his arms and headed for the house. After a moment of stunned silence, she blistered the air with protests loud enough to wake the dead. Half the family was standing in the kitchen watching by the time he deposited her unceremoniously on her feet inside the door. Thank heaven no one laughed or she probably would have grabbed the carving knife lying in plain sight by the turkey and come after them.

He turned on his heel, then, and struck off for a very long walk. He glanced at the sky, hoping for signs of an impending blizzard. He'd figured no less than a foot of snow was likely to cool his temper anytime tonight.

He'd been walking for the better part of an hour, his face chilled, his hands jammed into his pockets, the wind cutting through his coat, when he saw Luke Adams walking slowly in his direction. He had the feeling Angela's father would either go or stay at a signal from him. He gave the older man a curt nod that was apparently accepted as welcome enough.

"I suppose you'll be wanting me to leave now," he said eventually.

He thought he caught a glimpse of Luke's smile in the moonlight.

"Not unless you want to," Angela's father said. "You're going to have to make up your own mind what the best solution is to this. You and Angela. If you decide to stay, we'll welcome you. If you decide to go, we'll look out for Angela and the baby."

"And hate my guts for the rest of your days," Clint concluded.

"Hating is a waste of time and energy," Luke said.

He said it with such passionate conviction that Clint stared at him. "You ever hated anyone?"

"Myself for a long time," Luke said candidly. "My father for a bit."

The response stunned Clint. If Luke could hate a man like Harlan Adams, then there was no word for the depth of his own feelings toward his father. "You hated your father? How'd that happen?"

Deeply felt sorrow seemed to etch new lines in Luke's rugged face. "I figured between us we killed my brother," he explained, echoing the story that Angela had told Clint earlier. "I also resented the hell out of the fact that he was trying to control my life. Jessie was the one who made me see that the only thing in life that really counts is family. When you love people, you work out your differences, no matter how difficult it is or how long it takes. I was never a big talker, so it was always harder for me."

"I know what you mean," Clint said. "I always figured actions ought to speak loudly enough."

"I'd say yours do," Luke said with a grin. "They were loud and clear earlier tonight."

"Sorry," Clint apologized again. "That woman can make me angry quicker than you can set off a rocket on the Fourth of July."

"So I noticed, but that wasn't what fascinated me so."

"Oh?"

"What I saw was a man who cared enough about a woman to make sure she was in out of the cold, even when he was mad enough to throttle her. That's the kind of man I could respect." He gave Clint a direct look. "It's something to think about, isn't it?"

Before Clint could respond, Luke headed for the barn and left him with nothing but his thoughts for company.

At least there was one member of the Adams clan that didn't think he was here with an ulterior motive, he concluded bitterly. Too bad it wasn't Angela.

Where she'd gotten the nut-brained idea that he was after the Adams fortune was beyond him. He hadn't even known she had a dime to her name when he'd traced her to Dallas and met Betsy. If he was an ambitious, money-hungry kind of man, would he have been scrambling to make ends meet on a broken-down ranch in Montana? There were far easier ways to make a buck.

He just happened to love ranching. He liked the exhausting work and the never-ending challenges and the intellectual stimulation of figuring out how to better his herd from year to year. It might never make him rich, but fulfillment was all he was after. It was enough to have something of his own, something he could take pride in. If Angela hadn't seen that much in their months together, then she hadn't really known him at all. And it was damned sure he hadn't known her.

"Well, that was certainly humiliating," Angela said, when she'd finally calmed down enough to speak. Most of the family had discreetly slipped away, leaving her in the kitchen with two of her cousins and Consuela.

"I thought it was romantic," Sharon Lynn said with huge eyes and an exaggerated sigh.

Sharon Lynn was less than a year younger than Angela, but she'd stayed in Los Pinos her whole life, surrounded by family, content with running Eli Do-

Ian's Drugstore, where her mother had once worked and where her mother and Cody had carried on much of their highly irregular and high-volume courtship. Maybe that explained why she thought that Clint's he-man act was so romantic. She wasn't worldly enough or liberated enough to know better.

"You want him, you can have him," Angela snapped.

Her cousin laughed. "Not on your life. I'm not wasting my energy chasing after a man who's already hooked."

"Besides, she already has eyes for Kyle Mason," Dani said. She gave Angela a sympathetic look. "Are you okay?"

"Just peachy."

Dani, who was now a veterinarian in town, urged Angie toward the kitchen table. "Sit down. Your hands are like ice." She glanced around the kitchen until her gaze found Consuela. "Could you make her some tea, please?"

Angela accepted the tea and the solicitude. Dani hadn't been born an Adams. She'd been adopted by Jordan when he and her mother, Kelly Flint, had married. She was older than Angela by four years, but it seemed to Angela that something had changed in her cousin.

Angela studied her intently, trying to figure out what it was exactly. Once exuberant and outgoing, Dani now seemed shy and quiet, even as she managed to take charge of the situation. Obviously her veterinary training had enabled her to cope well with unexpected emergencies, but there was a vulnerability about her that was out of character.

When she handed the cup of tea to Angela, her worried gaze shifted away the instant Angela made eye contact with her. Angela put the cup on the table and caught her cousin's hand. "You OK?"

Dani's responding smile seemed forced. "Hey, you're the patient, not me."

"It must be nice having a patient who can tell you what's wrong for a change," she teased. "I'm just cold. It'll pass." She sobered and added quietly, "There's something else going on with you."

"Don't be silly. I'm perfectly fine."

Sharon Lynn stepped in and circled an arm protectively around Dani's waist. She met Angela's gaze evenly. "Let it go," she said quietly, but firmly.

Angela was taken aback by the fierce joining of forces. The cousins had all been close growing up. There'd been no way around it, with family gatherings as common as Texas bluebonnets in summer. They'd never taken sides back then. In fact, the girls had all been amazingly compatible, practically as close as sisters. Had things changed since she'd been gone? Was she now viewed as an outsider? Were there secrets that would never be shared with her?

"I'm sorry if I pushed," she apologized.

Dani gave her hand a quick squeeze. "Don't worry about it." Her expression turned briskly professional and her gaze warmed. "How are you feeling now? Better?"

"I'm warmer," she said.

"But still unsettled," Dani guessed. "Clint strikes

me as the kind of man who could keep a woman unsettled.''

''He is a royal pain in the—''

''Whoops,'' Sharon Lynn said with a laugh. ''Don't get her started again. There won't be enough chamomile tea on earth to calm her down.''

''Maybe you should go upstairs and rest,'' Dani said.

''No,'' Angela protested.

''A few more weeks and you'll be begging for rest,'' Dani warned.

''Not with me around,'' Consuela said. ''I cannot wait to hold this child in my arms. Angela will have to fight me for a chance to take care of the little one.''

''You're still spoiled rotten, I see,'' Sharon Lynn said to Angela, even as she reached up and squeezed Consuela's hand. She eyed her cousin speculatively. ''Have you ever actually held a job?''

''Don't be mean,'' Dani said.

The familiar bickering made Angela smile, even though she was the butt of the teasing. ''Actually, I've held quite a few jobs.''

''Couldn't keep one, huh?'' Sharon Lynn taunted.

''You just wait until this baby is born. I'll take over the soda fountain for you one day and my milk shakes will have the residents of Los Pinos weeping.''

''Have you ever actually worked a soda fountain?'' Dani inquired skeptically.

''No, but I worked a bar. How different can it be?''

''My customers are sober,'' Sharon Lynn pointed out. ''They know what they're getting.''

Angela grinned at her. ''Oh, how I've missed you

two. Nobody could ever put me in my place the way you do."

"Not even Clint?" Sharon Lynn asked.

The back door slammed open just then, caught by the wind as Clint tried to enter. "Not even Clint what?" he asked, his gaze fixed on her.

"Not a thing," Sharon Lynn said.

"See you," Dani said, dragging her cousin out of the room.

Consuela snatched up a silver coffee service and slipped out behind them.

"*Et tu, Brute?*" Angela muttered.

"I do not know this Brute," Consuela said, then leaned down to whisper, "Talk to the man, *niña*. Do not stop talking until you have reached an understanding. *¿Si?*"

Angela glanced up into Clint's stormy eyes and shuddered. She had the distinct impression that quiet conversation was the last thing on his mind.

Chapter Eight

"Are you planning to apologize?" Angela asked Clint, figuring that a preemptive strike was called for.

"Me? You were the one throwing insults around," Clint shot right back, his blue eyes as stormy as a hurricane-tossed sea.

"Maybe we should take turns," she suggested cheerfully. "I'll apologize for making disparaging insinuations about your character, and you can apologize for being a dyed-in-the-wool macho jerk."

His gaze narrowed at the deliberate insult. "You're not off to a very promising start with that apology."

"Sorry." She smiled. "Best I can do."

"Let me get this straight. Are you admitting that you know perfectly well that I'm not after the family fortune?"

She thought about that for a minute. It was apparently about fifty-nine seconds too long, judging by the increasingly furious expression on his face. His righteous indignation did carry some weight with her. He'd never been an especially good actor. His emotions were always right out there in plain view. If he'd ever lied to her, she was pretty sure she would have known it. Of course, he'd probably thought the same of her. Maybe both of them were just plain lousy at character assessment.

"OK, I admit it," she said eventually.

He regarded her skeptically. "Say it like you mean it, angel."

"I know you didn't come here because of my family's money," she said solemnly.

"Mind telling me who sowed that idea in your head in the first place?"

Now that was tricky turf. She didn't want him to realize that her grandfather had been speculating about his honesty. They seemed to have built a good rapport in a very short time. She didn't want to force Clint's pride to kick in. It would destroy that relationship before it ever got a decent chance.

She bit back a sigh. No matter how she fibbed to herself about wanting Clint to back off and leave, the truth was she liked having him here, liked seeing him slowly becoming a part of the family. Getting along with Grandpa Harlan was a huge part of that. Perhaps her grandfather had had his doubts about Clint, but she wanted to believe Clint could prove to him there had been no merit to those doubts.

"It was just the only thing I could come up with

to explain your persistence,'' she told him, skirting the truth by a wide margin.

He studied her intently for some time, then shook his head. "I never thought I'd say this, especially given recent evidence to the contrary, but you're a terrible liar, angel. If you came up with that notion all on your own, then I'm Billy the Kid.''

The irony of the remark wasn't lost on her. "I guess I used to be more convincing, huh?''

"Much more convincing,'' he agreed. "So, 'fess up. Who was it?''

She debated lying again, then decided there wasn't any point to it. He was the kind of man who'd nag at it and sooner or later, he'd figure out the truth. Maybe it would be better if she told him. She settled for an explanation that was true as far as it went and left her grandfather out of it.

"Janet, actually.''

"Janet,'' he repeated, his expression more thoughtful than furious. "I should have known. Was she advising you to protect yourself from my greedy clutches?''

"Something like that.''

"She was just thinking like an attorney, I suppose.''

"Exactly.''

His gaze clashed with hers. "Unless your grandfather was the one who put the idea into *her* head. Was he?''

"Does it really matter?'' Angela asked hurriedly. "The bottom line is Janet was looking out for my best interests the way any good attorney would.''

"Did she want you to insist on a prenuptial agreement?"

"As a matter of fact, yes."

"Not a bad idea," he said calmly enough, though his eyes were once again turbulent. "Did you agree?"

"We're not getting married so what's the point?" she retorted.

"Let's just say we were, would you want the agreement?"

"Yes," she said instinctively, then hastily retracted it. "No. Dammit, Clint, I don't know what makes sense."

"You really don't trust me, do you?" he asked, sounding more defeated than angry.

"Do you trust me?" she shot back.

His grin was rueful. "Maybe not, but there's one big difference, darlin'. I've never betrayed you the way you betrayed me. I may have been a fool back in Montana, I may not have responded to your announcement the way you'd been expecting, but I have never betrayed you or lied to you. I accepted you at face value. Apparently you can't say the same."

She swallowed hard against the tide of hurt that washed over her at his charge. She couldn't deny it, either. He was right. He had far more reason to distrust her than she did him.

"Where does that leave us?" she asked, suddenly exhausted by the tension of the past few hours.

He leveled a look straight into her eyes, a look filled with questions and regrets. Then he sighed. "I wish to hell I knew, angel. I wish I knew."

* * *

Clint left the kitchen feeling more hopeless than he ever had in his life. To her everlasting credit, his mother had raised a houseful of optimists. She had refused to blame his father for walking out on them. She had never said a harsh word about the man who had left her to cope with all those children and a mountain of debts. She had just taken his departure as one more challenge to make them all stronger.

All of them had grown up believing that with just a little effort life could be better than it had been. He wouldn't say his brothers and sisters were over-achievers, but they were undaunted by a good challenge. They'd heard the old adage about turning life's lemons into lemonade so often, none of them could drink the stuff.

He'd been the same until today. He'd been fortunate enough to go a lifetime without being distrusted. Back home, folks knew the Bradys were honest, if poor. In Montana, he'd paid off every debt he owed, including the ranch. As of last month, it was his free and clear. If he gave his word, he kept it. No one had ever had cause to worry about the kind of man he was.

Now these people who didn't know him at all found his motives suspect. He supposed it was natural enough that they would worry about one of their own, that they would think first of protecting Angela, but the instinctive lack of trust in him cut just the same. Worse, he had no idea how to rectify it. Words weren't the answer. And actions, the kind of actions that would deepen respect and engender real trust, took time, time he didn't have.

Sooner or later he would have to head back to Montana. He had a good foreman there looking after things now, but he couldn't rely on Hardy Jenkins shouldering the burden of running the ranch forever.

As he trudged up the stairs, it seemed he carried the weight of the world. Maybe he'd feel better with a good night's sleep. Maybe in the morning he'd have the answers that eluded him tonight.

He was halfway to his room—it was a damn suite, actually—when the man most on his mind exited a room down the hall. Harlan Adams smiled, his expression totally open and free of guile. Maybe he was already overcoming his suspicions, Clint thought hopefully.

"You aren't sneaking off to bed at this hour, are you?" Harlan asked.

"I was considering it," Clint admitted. "I've got some thinking to do."

"Not when there's a poker game about to start downstairs in Luke's office," he insisted. "Son, that would be downright foolish. Nothing takes a man's mind off his troubles better than a game of cards. You haven't played poker until you've played with us. Before the night's out, one of us is bound to bet the whole damn ranch."

"With my luck, I'd win it," Clint muttered under his breath. That would really win the family over, he thought.

"Never can tell, you might," Harlan said, proving his hearing was as sharp as ever. He looped a powerful arm around Clint's shoulders and propelled him back downstairs.

"Almost lost my own spread to Janet once," he confided. "That woman can play poker. She's got a sneaky side to her nature. Jenny's the same way. They even won over old Mule, God rest his soul."

"Mule?"

Harlan grinned. "Cantankerous man, but the best danged card player in Los Pinos. Mule had vowed never to play cards with a woman, but those two changed his mind. He said the kind of gumption and daring they had with a lousy pair of deuces was downright scary."

"Will they be playing tonight?" Clint asked, trying to imagine the fierce competitiveness of husband against wife and daughter. From what he'd observed of Janet and Jenny, it ought to be amusing.

"Hell, no," Harlan declared fervently. "I can't have the two of them showing me up in front of my own boys, can I? Besides if Jenny ever gets her hands on another share of White Pines, she's threatened to put a Bloomingdales on it. I can't have that, even if she does swear that without a few fancy department stores around she'll move back east one day, just so she can spend a decent day shopping."

"And you believe her?"

"Did once," he claimed. "I'm not so sure anymore. Not since she's discovered Nieman-Marcus. Of course, with Jenny you never know quite what to expect. She's a lot like her mama that way, lively and unpredictable."

To Clint's amusement, he actually sounded as if he considered it possible that one day Jenny would impulsively erect a huge store on his property just so she could shop. It also seemed as if it didn't bother him all that much. Before Clint could analyze how a man could be so blasé about losing his land, they reached Luke's office.

"Look who I've roped into joining us," Harlan announced as they entered.

"Ah, another lamb to the slaughter," Cody retorted. "Do you have any card sense at all?"

"I've played a game or two," Clint said.

"Which probably means he won half of Montana playing poker," Jordan assessed.

"It was blackjack, actually," Clint said, only partially in jest. He hadn't won his land that night, but he'd won the down payment for it.

"Does everybody have their deeds tucked away in a vault back home?" Luke inquired dryly as he poured Clint a shot of whiskey and set it in front of him.

"Are you kidding? Kelly won't even tell me where she has ours for safekeeping," Jordan replied.

"Melissa either," Cody added.

"Janet and I don't have secrets," Harlan boasted. "I know precisely where the deeds are."

"Sure you do," Luke taunted. "In her office, locked in *her* vault."

"Okay, okay, enough of this nonsense," Harlan grumbled. "Who's dealing?"

"We'll cut for it. High card deals," Luke said, shuffling the deck one last time.

Clint pulled a ten and figured that was the end of it. He waited for one of the others to come up with an ace or even a jack. Instead, the ten took it and Luke handed him the cards, along with a warning.

"We take this seriously, son. No fancy games and nothing wild."

"Except our manners," Cody said. "As the night wears on, we forget everything our mama taught us."

"We get drunk," Harlan translated. "One of us tries to stay sober enough to haul the others up to bed."

"Who's turn is it?" Cody asked.

"Yours," Luke and Jordan taunted, removing the tumbler of whiskey in front of him.

"I think Clint ought to do it," Cody protested.

"And have him see us at our worst and remember it? No way," Harlan said. "We might end up with our faces on the front page of the Dallas papers."

Clint stiffened at the suggestion that he'd resort to blackmail. It was only part of the rowdy teasing he was sure went on all the time with these men, but it cut a little too close to the accusations he'd all too recently been discussing with Angela. Thievery, blackmail, what would be next?

He glanced across the table and saw that Harlan was observing him with a steady gaze. He thought there was a message in that gaze, but he was damned if he could read it.

"Five-card draw," he said quietly and dealt the cards.

Luke won the first hand, which had the rest of them accusing Clint of stacking the deck to win over his prospective father-in-law. When Luke won the second hand as well, a hand dealt by Jordan, the men went silent.

They played now with a fierce intensity, the same way they did everything else. They'd played for a couple of hours when the cards began falling Clint's way. The chips stacked up in front of him. He had a nice bundle, when Harlan glanced at his watch and declared the evening over.

"That's it, boys. It's after midnight and I'm getting too old for this nonsense."

"Janet got you on a limited budget?" Luke teased.

"Nope, I just know when a man's on a roll. If the rest of you can't see it, then stay here and lose a few more dollars. I'm going up to my nice, warm bed and my nice, warm wife."

"Ah," Luke said. "Now that's a concept I can embrace." He, too, stood up.

"I guess that's it, then," Jordan said. "Congratulations, Clint. Nice playing. I think I hear Kelly calling me, too."

"Melissa's been calling to me for the past hour, but you haven't seen me dashing off to bed," Cody protested. "Besides, you guys, what about poor Clint? He doesn't have a wife upstairs."

"He can rectify that anytime he wants to," Luke responded dryly.

"I wonder about that," Clint said sorrowfully. "Angela doesn't seem inclined to make an honest man of me."

"Are you asking for our advice?" Harlan asked eagerly, clearly ready to sit down again if called upon for some wisdom about the battle of the sexes.

Clint laughed at the four men who were poised to stay and help him out with courting Angela. "Thanks, anyway," he said. "I have the feeling you all would just get me in more trouble than I'm in already."

"You're probably right," Cody said. "Not a one of us can claim our courtships were smooth sailing."

"And none of us learned a darned thing from our mistakes," Jordan added. "You go with your own instincts, Clint. You're the one she's in love with. Even I can see the way she looks at you and Kelly claims I'm clueless on emotional issues. You must have been doing something right up there in Montana."

After they'd gone, as Clint made his way upstairs, he tried to remember exactly what he'd done to impress Hattie Jones. About the only thing he recalled with any certainty was seducing her on the night they'd met. It wasn't a tactic he could try with the woman eight and a half months pregnant.

Or was it? He paused at the top of the steps and stared at the closed door opposite his own. Was Angela lying in bed wide awake, tormented by thoughts of lovemaking the way he'd been night after night? What would she do if he slipped quietly into her room and settled himself into bed beside her, if only to hold her close until morning? How long would it take her to wake the household? He envisioned a whole line of very shaky guns aimed in his direction. Drunk as they all were when they'd parted, at least one of them was still bound to hit him if they accidentally fired.

Even with that image sharply defined in his head, he reached for the doorknob and quietly turned it. He stepped into the room and closed the door behind him, then waited, his heart thundering in his chest, to see if his movements had disturbed her.

"You might's well come all the way in," she said as if she'd been wide awake and expecting him. "What's the matter? Did you lose your way back to your own room?"

His eyes adjusted to the room's darkness and his gaze sought out the bed. Though the covers were tangled, there was no sign of Angela in it. Besides, even through his alcohol-induced haze, he grasped the fact that the bed was on his left and her voice had come from somewhere on his right.

"Angel?"

"Yes," she said, her amusement plain. "I'm over here, by the window."

He saw her then, seated in a rocking chair beside the huge bay window. A faint trail of moonlight shimmered over her. She had brushed her hair out of its usual careless knot so that it fell in glorious waves to her shoulders. Against the creaminess of her skin and the stark white of her nightgown, her hair shimmered like a cascade of garnets, dark red and mysterious and sensual. Quite simply, she took his breath away.

"You truly do look like an angel," he whispered, awestruck as always by her beauty.

"And you look like a man who's spent the evening in a saloon," she retorted dryly. "You're weaving a bit, cowboy. Sit down before you fall down. Did you have a good time with the Adams card sharks?"

"I did, indeed. I won."

He thought her eyes widened a bit in surprise at that.

"Really?"

He pulled his winnings from his pockets and allowed the bills to flutter into her lap. There was a satisfying heap of them when he was done.

"My, my," she said, fingering a fifty. "Must have been pretty high stakes."

"High enough," he agreed. "But nobody bet their ranch."

"You sound disappointed."

He regarded her sadly. "Not that again, angel. I don't want your money. I don't want your land. How many times do I have to say it before you believe me?"

She regarded him speculatively. "What do you want, then?"

"You," he said without hesitation. "Just you."

Moonlight caught the sheen of tears in her eyes. The sight of them distressed him. "Are you crying?" he asked, kneeling in front of her. He brushed the dampness from her face. "Don't cry, darlin'. Please don't cry."

"It's okay. I just wish…" Her voice trailed off.

"You wish what?"

She reached toward him and her fingers sifted through his hair, then came to rest on his cheek. "I just wish you meant it."

"I do mean it," he insisted. "From the night we met, I've wanted you. There's never been another woman like you. You make me…"

"Crazy?" she supplied.

"Angel, angel," he protested, "where's your sense of romance?"

"Sleeping," she said briskly. "That's what we ought to be doing, too. Everyone will be heading out at the crack of dawn. And tomorrow we start all over again at White Pines."

Clint stilled. He hadn't considered the possibility that everyone might go off somewhere for Christmas. Where would that leave him? Was he expected to head on home? Maybe linger back here alone? Or were they automatically assuming he'd be coming along?

He wondered if he could convince Angela to stay right here with him. They could have their own private holiday celebration, maybe even sort out where they were going without all the well-meaning interference. He was about to suggest just that when he realized that she was describing the last Christmas she'd spent with the whole family.

"It was just like today, only better. There were tons of presents, because everybody has always gone overboard. Consuela and her cousin Maritza, who works for Grandpa Harlan, fixed enough food to last for a month. Grandpa waited to put up his tree until we all got there, so we could decorate it together. We sang carols while we did it, then we all traipsed off to midnight services." She sighed. "It was wonderful. Year after year we had the exact same tradition."

"And you've missed it, haven't you?"

"More than anything else we do," she admitted. Her gaze caught his. "Will you come with us? Will you share it with me this year?"

The invitation pleased him more than he cared to admit. "If that's what you want."

"It is."

"Someday soon, though, you and I are going to have to sit down and talk, all by ourselves, without any interruptions or distractions. The baby's going to be here any day now and we have to get things settled."

"No," she said sharply.

He stared at her. "What do you mean, no?"

"I will not make any sort of a decision about anything just because we have a deadline staring us in the face. Whatever happens between us, whatever conclusions we reach about the future will be made when the time is right and not a minute before that."

Clint stared at her in frustration. "Dammit, I want this baby to be born with my name."

"That's what I wanted seven months ago, and you were in no big hurry to accommodate me."

He stood up and began to pace. "So this is payback? You're going to punish the baby, make the kid start life without his father's name, just because you want to get even with me? How can you be so cruel and heartless?"

"Of course that's not what I want," she snapped. "But I will not marry you just so the baby can have your name. I'll put your name on the birth certificate. You'll have your claim to paternity, but any relationship between you and me is going to have to be based on something else, something just between the two of us." Her flashing eyes clashed with his. "Is that clear enough?" she demanded.

"Oh, it's crystal clear," he muttered as he headed for the door. He paused to take one last shot. "Since you have Janet covering all your legal angles, maybe it's about time I found an attorney of my own."

He heard her sharply indrawn breath across the room. Good, he'd struck a nerve.

"Clint, no," she protested, sounding panicked by his impulsive threat.

He refused to back down. Meeting her gaze evenly, he said, "Good night, angel. Sweet dreams."

He closed the door softly behind him, even though he would have preferred to slam it shut. That would have awakened the whole household, though, and he was in no mood to explain the latest argument he and Angela had had.

It seemed lately as if every time they tried to talk, it disintegrated into some sort of name-calling argument. Hadn't he concluded not more than a half hour earlier that it was time for actions, not words? There was no time like the present to get started, with his ire roused and his inhibitions weakened by whiskey.

He threw open the door and crossed the room in three angry strides. She had risen from the rocking chair and stood halfway between it and the bed, her gaze startled. Without a word, he pulled her into his arms and delivered a kiss meant to take her breath away.

She gave a soft yelp of surprise, then a soft sigh of pleasure as he peppered kisses across her face. He found the hem of her gown and lifted it, his fingers sliding over silky flesh that had filled out into lush, provocative curves.

When he reached her belly, he slowed and the nature of his touch changed to one of awe. Her skin was stretched taut, and beneath the surface, he felt the stirring of his child. His mood altered in a heartbeat. All of the anger dissolved. Lust gave way to something tender.

With a sigh that was part dismay, part frustration, he rested his forehead against hers.

"I'm sorry," he said, his breathing ragged.

"No, I am."

"We can't go on like this, fighting until our nerves are raw. We'll end up saying something one of these days that we can't take back."

"I know."

"Maybe we should put some distance between us, think about this," he suggested.

"Not again," she said.

The fierceness of her reaction startled him. "No?"

"Absolutely not. You're not running and neither am I. We will settle this, Clint. Let's just take one day at a time. Let's enjoy Christmas and maybe the rest will take care of itself." She rested her hand against his cheek, then smiled. "After all, it is the season of miracles."

Chapter Nine

Angela wasn't sure what had possessed her to invite Clint along to White Pines. She was asking for trouble, no doubt about it. Maybe she'd been persuaded because she didn't think she could shake him any easier than a horse could rid itself of a burr under its saddle. Maybe it was simple politeness.

More than likely, though, it had something to do with sentiment. They had spent the previous Christmas together, and despite all her reminiscing the night before about past holidays with her family, Christmas with Clint in Montana had been one of the most incredible of her entire life. She smiled to herself just thinking about it.

They had gone out the day before Christmas, tromped through a foot or more of hard-packed snow until they'd found the perfect tree. Clint had chopped it down and hauled it back to the ranch, grumbling all the way about the size of it. He'd sounded exactly the way her father did every year, which had made her homesick. In some peculiar way, it had also re-assured her. Seeing similarities in the two men she cared most about suggested that her judgment wasn't all bad.

Since an earlier search of the house had turned up not one single strand of lights or an ornament, Angela had gone into town after the tree was up and gathered everything she could think of to decorate the ceiling-scraping monster of a pine. Clint had taken one look at the bags of cranberries, packages of popcorn and yards of ribbon and shaken his head.

"I don't know, darlin'," he'd said, his expression doubtful. "This is looking an awful lot like work."

"You just wait," she'd promised. "We are going to have the most spectacular, old-fashioned Christmas tree you've ever seen. Start popping the corn, okay? I'll get busy with the cranberries."

They had sipped hot chocolate and played carols on the stereo as they'd worked. They'd eaten as much popcorn as they'd strung, but by evening the tree was crisscrossed with strands of white and red. Colorful red and green bows added a festive touch. Clint had flat-out balked when she'd wanted to add candles in place of lights.

"Enough's enough," he'd declared. "I don't want the ranch to burn down in the name of having some Christmas decorations straight out of 'Little House on the Prairie.' I'll go get lights, if you insist on having them."

"The store's sold out," she said, disappointed by his reaction.

He'd leaned down and kissed her. "Trust me, Hattie. I never make a promise if I don't think I can deliver."

She had started cooking while he was gone, sure that this was one promise he wouldn't be able to keep. She'd consoled herself by making every dish she remembered from Christmas dinners back home: turkey with corn bread stuffing, cranberry relish, mashed potatoes, gravy and two gigantic pumpkin pies.

It was dark by the time Clint had gotten home and the house was filled with the familiar scents of pine and cinnamon and roasting turkey. He'd stood in the doorway, shaking the snow from his coat, and sniffed appreciatively.

"It smells like Christmas in here."

She had grinned. "It's true what they say, the sense of smell does bring back memories, doesn't it?" She eyed the bag in his hand speculatively. "Lights?"

He'd tossed it to her. "Enough to rival some big-city skyscraper at night," he declared.

Eagerly she had opened the bag and found a half-dozen strands of tiny white lights, six hundred in all. Her mother would have been in raptures.

"Oh, this is going to be wonderful," she'd said, already imagining it. "I can't wait to see it."

Putting the lights on after the fact had been tedious and at times hilarious as they'd gotten tangled up in popcorn and cranberries, but the results had been worth it. The tree simply glowed, sparkling like a night sky with a million stars.

"You really get into this Christmas stuff, don't you?" Clint asked, watching her.

"Sure. Don't you?"

He'd shrugged indifferently. She'd tried to question him about his own holiday memories, but he'd cut the conversation short and won her silence by saying that the memories they made together were the only ones that mattered to him now. The sweet remark had brought tears to her eyes.

Clint had reached in his pocket then and handed her a small, gaily wrapped package.

Surprised, Angela had stared at it. "What's this?"

Clint grinned sheepishly. "What does it look like?"

"A Christmas present? For me?"

"It is Christmas, isn't it?"

"Yes, but—"

"You thought I'd forgotten."

"Something like that."

"Aren't you going to open it? Or would you rather wait until morning?"

"No, no, now is fine." She hadn't been sure she would be able to stand the suspense until morning.

Her fingers fumbled with the ribbon, which had been so artfully tied it was evident that a store clerk, not Clint, had been responsible for it. "It's beautiful."

"If you're that impressed with the wrapping, I can't wait to see your expression once you get it open," he'd said dryly.

"At this rate I may never get it open. My hands are shaking."

He'd reached out and clasped them between his, stilling her efforts. "Hattie, it's not a big deal. It's just a present, a token really."

Eyes tearing, she had gazed at him. "It's a big deal to me. It's the first present you've ever given me."

"Are you worried about my taste?"

"No, absolutely not. Anything you picked out will be special to me."

He'd let her finish unwrapping it then. The flat velvet box made her heart thump unsteadily and once again she was all thumbs as she tried to lift the lid. Inside, against a white satin pillow, rested a gold pendant, a tiny Christmas tree with winking jewels as decorations. A diamond sparkled at the top.

"I thought maybe it would remind you of our first Christmas together," he'd said, looking awkward and uncomfortable at the sentimental gesture.

"Nothing you could have gotten me would have meant more," she swore to him. "Nothing." Eyes shimmering with unshed tears, she gazed at him. "Help me put it on."

It was his turn to fumble as he tried to manage the small clasp. When the necklace was secure, she gazed at herself in the mirror. The emerald, ruby and sapphire chips twinkled gaily against the soft gleam of gold as the pendant rested against her bright green sweater. He stood behind her in front of an oval mirror, his hands on her shoulders, as she'd admired the necklace. Lifting her gaze, her reflected glance caught his.

"Merry Christmas, darlin'," he'd whispered.

"Merry Christmas."

Now, thinking of that moment and the love she had been so sure she had seen shining in his eyes, she reached up and touched the pendant resting against her skin. She had worn it ever since, no matter the season, because it had reminded her of the man she had fallen in love with one lonely winter in Montana.

Could they recapture what they had felt that night? Or could they only move on to create new memories? When the new year began, would they still be together or would they have resolved to go their own separate ways, connected only by the child they had conceived together?

Her baby stirred restlessly in her womb as if he, too, was anxious to know the answers to those questions.

"I want us to be a family," she murmured, admitting it for the first time in a very long time.

Whether that was possible, though, was up to Clint. If he couldn't love her after what she'd done, if he couldn't forgive her for pretending to be the mythical Hattie Jones, then she would have to let him go.

"And we'll be just fine," she promised her child.

The baby kicked in apparent protest.

"We will," she repeated fiercely, her hands on her belly. "But I won't give up without a fight, little one. I promise you that, too."

This was the first Clint had actually seen of the town of Los Pinos. It was miles beyond Luke's ranch and beyond the home where he'd spent the night with Betsy's family. Gazing at the quaint, unpretentious stores and homey restaurants, he felt immediately at ease.

There was nothing fancy about the Texas town. It was practically a mirror image of the one he'd left behind in Montana. No wonder Angela had gravitated toward Rocky Ridge and felt at home there.

"I know," she said at a look from him. "I see the resemblance, too. I saw it that first night I stopped in Rocky Ridge. Felt it, too. The people are the same, warm and friendly. I still don't know why you wanted to stop here, though, instead of going on through to Grandpa's."

"You said your family does Christmas up big. I want to contribute my share."

She regarded him with obvious puzzlement. "You mean like some champagne or a couple of pies?"

He chuckled at the suggestion. "Knowing your grandfather, I'm sure he has the food and beverages pretty much under control. I was talking about presents."

"That's not necessary," she protested. "You don't even know the family that well. There's no need to be buying presents. No one will expect it. I only picked up a few last-minute things before I left Dallas."

"I want to," he insisted stubbornly. "You can help me pick out the right things." He glanced at her worriedly. "Or are you too tired? If this is too much for you, you can settle down in one of the restaurants and wait for me. The Italian one looks nice. I can smell the garlic clear out here."

"You are not sticking me off in some restaurant

while you shop," she retorted. "I love picking out gifts. I can get a few more myself. Where do you want to start?"

He glanced up and down the street. There weren't more than a dozen stores, all decorated brightly. "You pick. You know what they stock better than I do."

"Let's start at Dolan's," she decided.

He glanced across the street at the shop with a dusty, ancient display and a forlorn string of colored lights drooping across the window. "The drugstore?" he asked doubtfully. "I'm not settling for cheap perfume and some boxes of stale candy, darlin'."

"Don't let the window fool you. It's been that way since way before I was born. Eli Dolan never saw any need to change it. Sharon Lynn runs the place now and she's stubbornly stuck with tradition. But it has the best milk shakes I've ever had. Made from scratch with real ice cream."

"Angel, we're supposed to be shopping, not eating."

Her expression turned sly. "The baby's starved and milk is very good for his bones."

He grinned at the ploy. "Oh, in that case, we absolutely should have a milk shake."

A bell over the door tinkled as they entered and half a dozen people seated at the old-fashioned soda fountain turned to stare.

"You're on display, cowboy," she said with a wink as she led the way to the counter.

Clint endured the stares, nodded at the introductions and stewed when the stares transferred themselves pointedly to Angela's oversize belly. It was one thing for the family to be watching the two of them speculatively. It was quite another to have the whole darned town ready to spread gossip.

"Maybe this was a bad idea," he muttered, just as Sharon Lynn emerged from a back room with a beaming smile.

"Hey, you two," she said cheerfully. "I'll bet you're here for milk shakes."

"You bet," Angela said eagerly, "chocolate."

Sharon Lynn caught Clint's eyes. "You, too?"

Caught now, he gave in to the inevitable. "Absolutely."

"I thought you'd be over at White Pines by now. Janet called earlier. She said you were expected any minute."

"Mom and Dad probably are there. We got sidetracked by a little shopping," Angela said.

Sharon Lynn leaned over the counter. "I don't see any packages."

"Because this was our first stop," Clint said. "Sustenance for the ordeal ahead."

"Ah, I see. Then I'd better make these shakes double thick. The stores are jammed and everyone's patience is frayed. Christmas Eve shoppers tend to be desperate. You'll need your strength to compete with them."

One by one the other customers drifted away, either anxious to finish their own last-minute shopping or eager to spread the news that Angela Adams was back home with a mysterious stranger in tow and a baby on the way.

"Don't worry about them," Sharon Lynn told him when Angela had left them alone to use the rest room. "They're harmless. The Adams clan has been giving this town something to talk about for years now. It's practically a tradition."

"I should have thought about that before I subjected her to this, though."

"Forget it. We've long since learned to be thick-skinned, since we seem destined to provide so much entertainment. Angela's not upset. Why should you be?" She regarded him speculatively. "Unless you really care deep down about her feelings?"

"Of course, I do."

She beamed as if he'd confessed to something far more telling. "That's a start," she said, giving him a peck on the cheek before going to wait on a wide-eyed customer who was staring at them from the cosmetic counter across the store.

When Angela emerged from the back, he smiled at her ready-for-anything expression.

"You look as if you're preparing to charge into battle," he teased.

"Have you ever shopped on Christmas Eve before? It's full-scale warfare."

"Even in Los Pinos?"

"Especially in Los Pinos. One of the other traditions around here is that everyone waits until the last minute to shop, so they can brag about how insane it was. I've seen people kicking and shoving to get the last electric razor."

"That bad, huh?"

"Worse," she insisted, then grinned. "But you

have an edge. Practically nobody will argue with a pregnant lady.''

''I just knew you were going to come in handy,'' he responded, then held out his hand. He studied her intently. ''You're sure you're up to this?''

''Lead on. I can't wait.''

Clint had never shopped for quite so many people before, not when he had a decent amount of money in his bank account and a heart that was suddenly full of Christmas spirit. Nor had he ever been accompanied before by a woman with a zealousness for a good bargain and the taste of an aristocrat.

They made four trips back to his pickup to deposit bundles of leather gloves, silver money clips and enough silk scarves to perform the dance of the seven veils. On the last trip, he suggested once again that Angela take time out and wait for him.

''No way,'' she argued. ''I'm just getting warmed up. There's a sale at Geoffrey's we haven't checked out.''

''You misunderstood, angel. That wasn't a suggestion. That was an order. Go have another milk shake. Rest. Gossip with your cousin. Geoffrey's, whatever that is, will wait.''

''Geoffrey's is a dress boutique,'' she said distractedly. Her gaze clashed with his. ''Why are you so anxious to get rid of me?''

''It's Christmas Eve and I'm shopping. Why do you think?''

Her expression brightened as his meaning finally registered. ''Oh.''

He saw her reach instinctively to her neck and

guessed that she was wearing the pendant he'd given her the year before. He'd been wondering about that. He had noticed the gold chain and thought it was the same one, but he hadn't been able to detect whether the tiny tree was on it or whether it had been exchanged for something else. She always wore it carefully tucked beneath her blouse. Her unconscious gesture now was very telling. He gathered she hadn't wanted him to see that she was sentimental about anything connected to him.

Ah, well, let her have her secrets, he thought with a smile.

"Are you going to wait in the drugstore or in the truck?" he asked.

Her eyes sparkled mischievously. "Maybe I have shopping of my own to do."

"Then we'll meet back here in twenty minutes?"

"Twenty? You can pick out a present for me in twenty minutes?"

He enjoyed the fact that she sounded disgruntled. "I was thinking of grabbing the first suitable thing I came across," he teased. "Maybe a huge bottle of that perfume I saw Sharon Lynn selling to a customer earlier."

"I'm sure whatever it is will be lovely," she said as primly and politely as any child who'd ever anticipated a doll only to receive socks and underwear.

"I'll do my best," he said cheerfully. "Twenty minutes, OK?"

"Fine. Don't get all bent out of shape if it takes me longer."

He noticed that she pointedly headed off in the direction of the hardware store. He also noticed that she kept glancing back over her shoulder to try to see where he was going. He waited until she finally went inside, her expression grimly determined, before moving swiftly up the block himself and going around the corner to a store he'd spotted earlier. He'd deliberately ignored it then, preparing for this moment and hoping that Angela wouldn't guess his destination.

It took him only a few awe-struck moments to make his selection and to arrange for a delivery to the ranch. At the mention of White Pines, the middle-aged clerk became even more accommodating.

"This is for Angie, then? I heard she was expecting a baby any minute."

The grapevine hadn't wasted a second, he noticed. "True enough."

"So," the woman said, "are you the proud daddy?"

Clint figured it wasn't any big secret, not at this point. "That's right."

"You're a lucky man. Angie was always a doll. I taught her English all through high school. I just moonlight here during the holidays. She had a real gift for understanding literature. I always thought she'd teach one day. I heard that's what she studied at college."

Since she seemed to have more facts than he did about Angie's educational history, Clint kept silent. The clerk handed him his receipt. "You have a real nice Christmas and tell Angie I said hello. Mrs. Grayson. She'll remember. Tell her I'd love to see her if she gets a minute while she's home."

"I'll be sure and tell her," Clint agreed. "Merry Christmas."

He made one more stop en route back to the car and tucked that gift in his pocket. He was leaning against the side of the pickup in nineteen minutes. He noticed there was no sign of Angie.

He finally spotted her lugging an ungainly bundle down the block. She could barely see around it.

"What on earth?" he asked, taking it from her and hoisting it into the bed of the truck. It wasn't as heavy as he'd expected, but it was the most oddly shaped package he'd ever seen. His curiosity stirred, despite his long-standing disinterest in gifts of any kind. Except for the gathering of relatives, holidays hadn't been a big deal at his house. Gifts had been practical, not sentimental or lavish. He'd never even seen, much less received anything that looked quite like this.

"Do I get a clue?" he asked, eyeing the giant red package with its huge green bow.

She grinned. "Do I?"

"I don't think so."

"Then neither do you."

"Just answer one question, then. Is it likely to explode?"

"Probably not," she said, her expression thoughtful. "Not if you drive very carefully."

"You know, angel, you're a real cutup."

"So they say."

He thought about passing along the message from her old high school teacher, then thought better of it. If he mentioned Mrs. Grayson, it was entirely possible that Angela would know where she moonlighted during the holidays. She might have been doing it for years. He would pass along the greetings tomorrow.

"Are you finished now?" Angela asked.

He glanced at the mound of packages tucked behind the seats of the truck. "I think so. I have something for your parents, all the aunts and uncles, the cousins and both housekeepers. That should do it, right?"

"Unless you're into pet toys, yes."

"Pets?"

"Dani has managed to foist off several kittens over the years. The main house is crawling with them, because Grandpa Harlan has always been a sucker for one of her sob stories. Uncle Jordan set a limit of two at home and he claims he's not happy about that, but I notice every time we're over there that one cat or another is always in his lap. Fortunately Dani's animal hospital also sells pet supplies and toys, so we buy them wholesale."

He shook his head. "Forgive me, but I think I'll skip presents for the cats."

"I'll forgive you," she said readily, then regarded him slyly. "Dani's a whole other story."

He sighed. "Where's the clinic?"

She grinned. "Just two streets down to the left. She'll be thrilled to see us."

"How many cats are we talking about?"

"Hard to say. The little devils multiply like rabbits."

"You'd think she'd do something about that. She is a vet, for goodness' sakes."

"She's also a soft touch. Every kid in town knows

they can get a free kitten from her that's up-to-date on all its shots. She's the town's own personal animal shelter. There's no need for a pet store in Los Pinos.''

Following Angela's directions, he pulled up in front of a small white house with dark green shutters. An old-fashioned white sign hung from a wrought-iron pole. A half-dozen cats lazed in patches of sunlight on the sloping front porch.

''The clinic entrance is on the side,'' Angela told him. ''We can go in through the house and catch her in her office. Judging from the number of cars along here, half the pets in town have been overindulging in Christmas goodies. The waiting room will be a mess. Besides, family does have its privileges.''

A harried-looking Dani barely waved at them as they slipped into the back of the clinic.

''Shopping for the cats,'' Angela called over the racket of barking dogs, howling cats and an occasional protesting screech from what sounded like a parrot or maybe a myna bird.

''A lot of pets get boarded here over the holidays,'' Angela told him. ''I tried helping out once when I was in high school and Dani was still assisting Doc Inscoe during vacations from veterinary school. I couldn't stand it. Too much commotion. She's in heaven, though, and that's what matters. It was the only thing she ever wanted to do.''

She led the way into what struck Clint as a pet store boutique. It was filled with elegant little sweaters for puppies, outrageously expensive leashes, dog houses that looked like mansions and a more varied assortment of toys than he'd ever imagined existed.

"Dani tends to indulge her animals. She thinks everyone else should, too. It's her little eccentricity, but we love her, anyway."

While he was still gaping in amazement, she zeroed in on several inexpensive little kitty treats hanging from an artificial tree like decorations. She gathered up a supply.

"I'll total up the cost at home and you can pay her when you see her," she said, dumping her selections into a bag and handing it to him.

"Are you sure this isn't a setup to get me arrested for shoplifting?" he inquired as they headed back through the house without so much as a parting wave for the clinic's owner.

"She won't even remember we've been here," Angela assured him. "Your money will come as a huge and welcome surprise."

Clint shrugged. "If you say so."

He added this package to all the others, then helped Angela into the truck. "Is this it? Anything else you want to do here in town?"

She shook her head.

Clint started the truck, then glanced over and caught the faraway expression on her face.

"What is it?"

"It just sank in. You and I are actually going to White Pines. Together."

There was something in her eyes and in her voice that told him not to make light of that. "That means even more to you than me showing up at your folks' place, doesn't it?"

She nodded. "I can't really explain it. Our ranch is home, but White Pines is…" Her voice trailed off.

"Is what?" he prodded.

"Something special," she said eventually. "Our history, I guess. Just wait. You'll see. Grandpa's ranch is like no place else on earth."

Given the fact that her own family's ranch was pretty spectacular, that was saying something. "Big?" he asked, trying to pin it down.

"Our place is bigger actually. Luke was trying to make a statement. It's not the house or even the land. It's a feeling that comes over all of us there, a sense of our own history maybe. Home is home," she said, clearly struggling to explain so he would understand. "White Pines is our heritage."

Heritage wasn't something that had meant much to Clint growing up. He'd hoped to change that with his own small ranch. He'd envisioned it as a legacy he could pass on, one that would flourish and grow with succeeding generations. It was clear that Harlan Adams and the generations preceding him had already endowed Angela and the others with that kind of meaningful legacy.

For one fleeting instant of doubt, he wondered if he would ever be able to offer her anything that would compare to it.

Chapter Ten

Clint and Angela's belated arrival at White Pines was greeted with amazement. Most of the family had already settled in and started helping Consuela and Maritza with the final preparations for tonight's family celebration and tomorrow's traditional open house but they all came out to help with the bundles that Clint had managed to amass in Los Pinos, exclaiming over the sheer number of them.

"I told you you were going overboard," Angela told him.

"What'd you do, son? Buy out the stores?" Grandpa Harlan asked with a grin.

He shot a look Angela's way, then said, "We tried, sir. Angela wore out too quickly."

"Very funny," she retorted. "Everything's

wrapped. The presents can go straight under the tree.''

''Except for the cat toys,'' Clint reminded her dryly.

''Oh, no, you didn't,'' her mother protested. ''Tell me you did not make Clint buy gifts for all of your grandfather's cats.''

''What can I say? He was feeling generous.''

''And you took advantage,'' her mother chided, regarding Clint with sympathy. ''Shame on you, Angela.''

''Just doing my bit to keep Dani's business afloat,'' Angela insisted nobly. ''She'd give away the store unless she's changed drastically.''

Silence fell at what should have been no more than an innocuous comment. To Angela's confusion her mother rushed to change the subject.

Angela put her hand on her mother's arm to prevent her from leaving. She let the others lead Clint inside. As soon as they were out of earshot, she asked, ''Mom, what's going on with Dani? I sensed something the other day, but Sharon Lynn hushed me up. Now everybody here gets all quiet when I so much as mention the possibility that she's changed.''

''Sweetie, she's had a rough year, that's all,'' her mother said, looking decidedly uncomfortable. ''I'm sure she'll tell you about it one of these days.''

''Why don't you tell me and save her the trouble?'' Angela suggested. ''It might keep me from putting my foot in my mouth over and over again.''

''It's her story to tell or keep to herself.''

''Someone hurt her,'' Angela guessed. ''Badly.''

Her mother sighed. "Yes. Very badly. She lost three people she loved very much. Now let it go. Christmas is not the time for Dani to be thinking about the past. The best gifts you could give her are your love and support."

"And no questions," Angela surmised.

"Exactly."

She relented and kept the burgeoning questions to herself. She followed her mother inside. The rest of the family was gathered in the huge living room discussing the best place for the mound of gifts Clint had bought.

"We can't put them under the tree," Jenny protested. "It's not even decorated yet. We'll be stepping on them." Her dark eyes glinted with mischief. "I say we open them now."

"Nice try, you little sneak," Angela teased. "You always did want to open something on Christmas Eve. Next thing we knew you had half your presents open. It's time you learned to wait until morning like the rest of us. You're supposed to be grown-up, the oldest of all of us. It's about time you set an example."

"What's the fun of being grown-up at Christmas?" Jenny complained, poking at a particularly lumpy package with evident curiosity.

"You get to discover the joy of anticipation," Angela told her, then glanced at Clint. His steady gaze stirred its own brand of anticipation deep inside her. Aside from a couple of stolen kisses and a few fleeting, if very promising caresses, he'd barely touched her in too many months now. She knew all about the slow build of anticipation. Judging from the hunger she saw burning in his eyes, so did he.

She wondered idly if they could sneak in a kiss or two if she showed him the way to his room now. Her grandfather promptly put an end to that idea by suggesting a tour of the ranch before dark. Angela knew when it came to a competition between her and a herd of cows, it was a real toss-up which one would win. Clint reacted with predictable enthusiasm. Naturally Cody and Luke had to go along. Jordan stayed behind to make business calls.

"On Christmas Eve?" her grandfather grumbled. "What's wrong with you, boy? Don't you ever take a vacation?"

"When I do, it won't be to sightsee on a ranch I grew up on," Jordan retorted, grinning to soften the remark. "I'll whisk my beautiful wife off to a deserted beach in the Caribbean. You go chase after your cows. While I'm sitting in here by the fire, I promise I'll think of all of you out there freezing your butts off for no good reason."

After they'd gone and the women had retreated to the kitchen once again, Angela was left with her uncle. She wondered if Jordan would be any more forthcoming about Dani's troubles than her mother had been. Tales of his bemusement at becoming the adoptive father of a precocious five-year-old when he'd married Kelly were part of family legend. It was evident to anyone, though, that Jordan had taken to fatherhood and to Dani with the same kind of dedication that had built his oil empire.

"Uncle Jordan, can I ask you something before you make those calls?" Angela asked.

He glanced up distractedly from the pocket-sized computer that held the numbers of his important business contacts. "Sure, angel. What's up?"

"I'm worried about Dani. She hasn't seemed herself since I got back."

Normally the most tranquil of her relatives, Jordan suddenly looked mad enough to wring somebody's neck with his bare hands. "Leave it be," he said curtly.

"But—"

"Dammit, I said leave it alone," he thundered. "She's been through enough without dragging it all up again, OK? The holidays are going to be especially bad as it is, thanks to that fool idiot she fell for."

His fury stunned her into momentary silence. "I'm sorry," she said quietly, beginning to get the picture, though far from all of it. "I didn't mean to upset you."

His expression softened. "No, I'm the one who's sorry. I shouldn't be taking it out on you. I know you're just concerned about her. Please, please, just don't ask her about it. Can you promise me that?"

"Of course," she said at once.

To herself, though, she vowed to get at the bottom of Dani's troubles. The two of them had always been especially close. Four when Angela was born, Dani had prided herself on helping to care for her messy baby cousin. As they had grown up, Dani had always been as eager as she to get into mischief.

"You two are just natural-born trouble," her

grandfather had said on more than one occasion. He'd always said it with more pride than venom, though. Grandpa Harlan admired spunk, even when it made mincemeat of the discipline their parents favored. They knew to save their most daring enterprises for visits to White Pines.

"What happened, Dani?" she murmured as she climbed the stairs to the room she'd always used on visits to White Pines. "What or who hurt you so?" Every instinct told her this went way beyond a simple broken romance.

For the first time since his arrival in Texas in search of Angela, Clint felt his old confidence soaring. Ranching was something he knew and loved every bit as much as the men who were riding over White Pines land with him. Like them, he appreciated the beauty of the land. Like them, he understood the complexities and hardships of the business and the excitement of mastering the daily challenges.

"You have an impressive operation here," he told Harlan and Cody.

"It wasn't always that way," Harlan told him. "My ancestors hadn't run the ranch the way they should have. It took a lot of time and hard work and pure cussedness to make it what it is today."

"You should have seen us trying to drag Daddy into the computer age," Cody said. "He still thinks those new-fangled machines will be the downfall of us all." He grinned at his father. "Am I quoting you accurately?"

"Pretty much," Harlan said. "I still say you're in

a hell of a fix when the electricity goes out and everything you need to know about your operation is lost in some danged machine.''

''That's why we have back-up disks and battery-powered laptops,'' Cody responded.

''More money wasted that could have been spent on a new bull for the herd,'' Harlan insisted.

''See what I mean?'' Cody said. ''He'd be happy if we still did the books in an old ledger.''

''Come up to my place,'' Clint suggested. ''I'm lucky if my receipts ever get entered into a ledger. By the time I get back to the ranch house at the end of the day about all I can cope with is falling into bed. You'd be in heaven.''

''He would,'' Luke agreed. ''What about it, Daddy? Want to go and rough it at Clint's? You can reminisce about the good old days.''

Harlan scowled at his sons. ''Now the two of you are trying to run me off my own place. That's the trouble with sons, Clint. Now daughters,'' he said with a sigh, ''they're something else again. They give a man comfort in his old age.''

Luke and Cody exchanged a look.

''He must have forgotten about Jenny stealing his pickup and crashing it into a tree,'' Cody said.

''And the time she ransacked the tool shed and splashed paint all over it,'' Luke added. ''Then there was Lizzy's nosedive from the barn rafters. Broke her arm in two places.''

''Selective memory,'' Cody agreed. ''I hear it happens a lot in old folks.''

''You think your sisters were trouble, maybe we

should start dredging up the grief you all caused me," Harlan shot right back. "Let Clint weigh that and see whether he'd rather Angela delivered a girl or a boy."

Luke's expression softened at once. "Girls are a blessing," he admitted. "Angela could always light up a room. I'd come home at the end of an exhausting day and one smile on that little girl's face would cheer me right up."

"Indeed," Cody chimed in. "Sharon Lynn has been a joy compared to that brother of hers. Harlan Patrick must take after Daddy. He surely doesn't take after me."

"Who are you trying to kid?" Harlan demanded. "That boy is all your own worst sins come home to haunt you."

Clint chuckled at the nonstop and obviously affectionate banter. "Do you all ever let up on each other?"

"Never," Luke said.

"Why should we?" Cody asked. "Daddy acts as if we've made his life a torment, but there's another side to that story we could share with you."

"Never mind," Harlan said hurriedly. "We'd better be getting back and cleaned up before the women get dinner on the table. We'll never hear the end of it if we're late for Christmas Eve supper."

"Who cooked the turkey?" Cody asked worriedly. "Maritza or Janet?"

"I'm going to tell Janet you asked that," Harlan swore. "You'll be lucky if you get out of here in one piece."

"When was the last time you ate anything she cooked?" Cody retorted.

His father grinned. "Not since I married her, I guarantee you that. When we were courting, I had to be polite. Fortunately, most of the time she had the good sense to try to sneak food in from some restaurant and pretend she'd fixed it."

"Now who's telling tales?" Luke asked. "Isn't a husband duty bound to gloss over all his wife's flaws in public?"

"This isn't public, Luke," Harlan declared. "Clint's practically part of the family."

"Well, I still say we should be setting an example for him," Luke protested. "The first time he gives away any of my daughter's little idiosyncrasies, I can just about guarantee there will be fireworks."

"Your daughter has idiosyncrasies?" Cody asked, feigning astonishment. "Since the day she was born, you've had us believing she was perfect."

"She is," Luke said quickly, then grinned. "For the most part." The grin quickly shifted to a scowl when he faced Clint. "That's something I can get away with saying, son. You can't. Just a word of caution."

"Believe me, that's advice I won't have any problem taking. I've seen your daughter's temper at close range." He gestured to a tiny slash over his lip. "Have the scars to prove it, too."

"She hit you?" Harlan asked incredulously.

"With a skillet," Clint claimed, though the truth was even more humiliating. He'd actually walked straight into the danged thing while she was waving it around as a threat. "It pretty well ended the last discussion we had before she tore off and disappeared on me."

"You must have riled her pretty good."

Clint realized he'd just waltzed himself straight into a dangerous trap. Maybe they suspected the fight had been over Angela's pregnancy, maybe they didn't. It wasn't a topic he particularly wanted to discuss with them.

"The same way you all rile your wives, I suspect...by disagreeing with them," he said.

The response drew the expected laughter and the potentially tense moment dissipated. They were still laughing when they walked inside.

Angela looked up from the pie crust she was filling with pumpkin and promptly caught Clint's eye. She looked worried. He walked over and brushed a kiss across her lips, plainly startling her.

"There's nothing to worry about, angel. We were just doing a little male bonding."

"That's what worries me," she responded.

"Shouldn't you be sitting down to do that?" he asked, deliberately changing the subject. He reached for a chair. "Sit."

"It's easier if I stand."

They scowled at each other in a stubborn test of wills. Clint finally shrugged. "Suit yourself. I'm going up to shower and change."

"Supper's in an hour," she called after him.

"Then you'd better get upstairs, too. I've never known you to take less than that to get ready."

"Uh-oh," Luke and Cody muttered in unison.

"I'm out of here," Harlan said, patting Clint on the back as he passed. "Good luck, son. If you figure a way out of this one, let me know."

Their wives vanished right along with them, leaving Clint with only Consuela and Maritza to run interference. The two housekeepers took one look at Angela's stormy expression and muttered something in Spanish that sounded dire. Then they, too, retreated.

"Take it back," Angela said, advancing on him with a spoon covered with pumpkin.

"You wouldn't want me to lie now, would you?" he taunted, edging around the table and trying to keep it between them. He figured he was safe enough. She wasn't half as quick as she'd been the time she'd caught him off guard with that skillet.

"Who spends twenty minutes just polishing his boots?" she demanded. "And another twenty in the shower?"

"Do the math, angel. That still puts me ahead of you."

"We haven't even gotten to the amount of time you spend shaving and admiring yourself in the bathroom mirror."

"Are you suggesting I should grow a beard to save time dressing?"

"No. What I am suggesting, Mr. Brady, is that you are a bald-faced liar."

"Takes one to know one."

She paused at that. The spoon, which she'd been waving threateningly, drooped to her side. From across the room he couldn't be sure, but he thought there might be tears in her eyes.

"Angel?"

"What?" she asked with a telltale sniff.

"Don't cry."

"I am not crying, even if that was another particularly low blow."

He circled the table to reach her, ready to take her in his arms and kiss away the tears. She whapped him on the butt with that damnable spoon. When she would have done it again, he wrenched it away from her and pulled her into an embrace that stilled her frantic movements.

Gazing down into her upturned face, he saw that he had been right about the tears, but there were also glints of laughter sparkling in her eyes now as well.

"Got you, didn't I?" she said with obvious pride.

"Only because you're sneaky. Truce?"

She sighed and slid her arms around his waist and rested her head against his chest. "Truce," she murmured.

Clint felt a rare and unexpected surge of contentment steal over him as he held her.

"Think we can keep the truce through New Year's?"

"I doubt it," she said honestly.

He grinned. "Me, too."

She sighed again. "Clint?"

"Yes."

"Do you think that means we should give up on any idea of a future together?"

"Just because we can't go ten minutes without arguing?"

"Yes."

"I don't see why, as long as we have sense enough to stop and listen to each other occasionally. Some relationships are just plain volatile. It keeps the adrenaline pumping."

"Are you saying we're excitement junkies?"

"I suppose." He regarded her curiously. "Do your parents argue?"

"All the time," she admitted.

"Have you ever doubted their love for each other?"

"Never."

"See there," he said. "Maybe they'll tell us how they make it work."

"Sex," Angela said without hesitation, then blushed. "I mean I don't know this for a fact or anything. It's not something we discussed. Haven't you noticed, though, that they're always touching, always stealing a kiss when they think no one's looking?"

"Like us," Clint pointed out.

"At least the way we used to be," she said thoughtfully.

"You can't steal a kiss from someone who's run off to another state, angel."

She met his gaze evenly. "Point taken. No more running," she promised. "I swear to you that I will stay right here and try to work things out."

"You're making a commitment?" he asked, surprised by the renewal of the vow she'd made before coming to White Pines.

"A commitment to try," she amended. "It's not going to be easy, you know. There's a mountain of distrust between us."

"Our baby deserves nothing less than our best efforts," he responded. "He deserves to know that we've done everything possible to give him a real family."

"Everything," she echoed.

Clint pressed a kiss against her forehead. Anything more and neither one of them would have been ready for dinner on time. Of course, time wasn't the only thing frustrating them at the moment. This baby of theirs was a built-in warning to cool down.

As they went upstairs hand in hand, he couldn't help wondering, though, whether Angela would remember her promise tomorrow when she saw one of the gifts he had bought for her. Maybe he ought to give it to her now, when she was in such an amenable mood. In his experience it was best to capitalize on moments like these to pin her down about anything. A day from now, even an hour from now, the winds might be blowing another way entirely.

Chapter Eleven

Male bonding, indeed, Angela thought irritably. They'd probably been out there conspiring to get her married to Clint with the least amount of fuss. They'd probably been indulgently listing all of her idiosyncrasies and giving Clint advice on how to cope with them. Men! Especially Adams men!

She hurriedly took her shower and rushed to get dressed in a half hour, just to make the point that she could move quickly when the situation called for speed.

She thought back over the conversation they'd just had. The truce she and Clint had declared was just dandy. It would make the holidays peaceful.

But, she resolved, that didn't mean she wouldn't put him in his place occasionally. After all, the women in this family had to take a stand once in a while or be completely run over by their stubborn, willful and thoroughly unpredictable mates.

Goodness knows, she would never have guessed that both her father and her grandfather would take such an immediate shine to Clint, despite their natural protectiveness of her. They seemed to understand the man who'd tracked her down all the way from Montana. They talked the same language—ranching and testosterone. Clint was becoming one of the family before she could spit. On the one hand, she could see the benefits of that. On the other, it was darned annoying.

To her surprise, Clint seemed to be settling in quite nicely. He was showing no inclination to duck out and run home, no matter how she infuriated him. He seemed to have made up his mind to stick this out.

In fact, instead of being scared off, he seemed to be endlessly fascinated with everything about her and her family. And, if the truth be told, he also seemed every bit as intrigued by her swollen body as he had been on the day they'd met, back when she'd actually had a figure to brag about. For a woman who was feeling especially ungainly that alone would have been enough to endear the man to her.

She was also beginning to understand just how deeply she'd hurt him by taking off as she had. His anger over having missed so much of her pregnancy appeared genuine. Her heart just ached, thinking about all they could have shared if she hadn't denied them the chance by running away. Every time she turned around she saw fresh evidence of the kind of devoted father he would be, the kind of father any child would be blessed to have.

In fact, to her very deep regret, she was beginning to weaken. She was beginning to recall just why she'd fallen in love with the man in the first place. He was kind and gentle and amazingly patient. For the most part, anyway.

His touches made her sizzle from the inside out. And his kisses could have ignited a bonfire in a soaking rain.

But that didn't mean she would marry him...if that was what he was after with this truce. He hadn't actually said the words, not lately, not since that impulsive declaration he'd made when he'd first arrived. His entire focus seemed to be on the baby she was carrying.

In the dead of night, when she was feeling restless and uncomfortable, she couldn't shake the very real possibility that his child was all he really wanted, that when the baby came he'd fight her for custody. He'd hinted at that often enough. In fact, he'd virtually threatened her with the possibility.

Still, in the past couple of days, aside from an occasional verbal dig, they had pretty much managed to put all her lies behind them. The truce had sealed their pact to leave the past in the past. It was either a terrific start or the greatest lie of all, made to lull her into a false sense of complacency. Was it possible he meant only to win her trust, then abandon her, as she had him?

As she ran a brush quickly through her hair and dashed on a hurried dusting of makeup, she wondered if the risks of this truce didn't outweigh the benefits. Maybe it would be smart to start building a wall between them, one that would protect her when the inevitable time came for him to go, and the fighting started over their child.

She wasn't sure she would be able to bear that kind of ugly battle. She feared, too, that when the whole truth came out about how she'd deceived Clint, her family would desert her and support him. They were all honorable people and Clint was bound to have their sympathy on his side.

She was an Adams, though, she reminded herself sternly. That still counted for something. Even if every one of her relatives disapproved of what she'd done, they would back her in any kind of struggle for her child. She had no choice but to believe that they would fight to claim an Adams heir, no matter the circumstances of his conception.

She looked at her watch and grinned. Forty minutes precisely. She cast one last glance in the mirror and nodded approvingly. The dark green velvet maternity dress she wore was the perfect foil for her pale skin and auburn hair. The pendant Clint had given her rested between her breasts, drawing attention to their new lushness. She concluded she looked about as sensual and provocative as it was possible for an eight-and-a-half-months-pregnant blimp to look.

She also squared her jaw and stiffened her resolve. She would maintain Clint's truce, because she had promised, but she would keep her own defenses squarely in place.

"Remember that," she said sternly as she reached

for the knob to open her door with fifteen minutes to spare.

Confident that she'd done the impossible in getting ready so quickly, she hurried downstairs and walked toward the living room.

To her chagrin, Clint was there before her, wearing a well-tailored suit and silk tie that had her gaping. He was a handsome man in denims and flannel. In a charcoal gray suit with his hair tamed, he was devastating. She couldn't help wondering if he'd brought that suit along because Christmas was coming or because he intended it to be his wedding suit. Her pulse fluttered wildly and her determination flew out the window. It either proved just how weak her resolve was or how extraordinarily potent he was.

His gaze locked with hers and she gravitated toward him across the room as if he were reeling her in with some invisible line.

"You look incredible," she admitted. "I've never seen you in a suit before."

"There's not a lot of call to wear one when I'm out with the cattle." His gaze swept over her appreciatively. "You've never put on such a fancy dress before, either. The color becomes you. You should wear it all the time."

It was the longest and prettiest compliment he'd ever paid her. Another brick thumped out of her recently erected and still-uncertain wall of defenses.

"Would you like something to drink?" he asked. "Harlan's brought in some nonalcoholic champagne just for you."

"I'd love a glass," she said, hoping it would take

him a very long time to pour it. She could spend the time gathering her composure.

"It's a good sign when you can get a man to wait on you," Sharon Lynn teased, coming over to stand beside her. "It means he's totally, thoroughly smitten."

"Does Kyle Mason wait on you?" Angela asked, then regretted it when she saw the sad expression on her cousin's face.

"He doesn't even know I'm alive," Sharon Lynn confessed irritably, then sighed. "It's humiliating. I've tried flirting. I've tried making him double-rich shakes when he stops by the drugstore. I've even considered asking him out, but my pride balks at that."

Glad to have her own relationship sidelined as the topic of conversation, Angela asked, "Who is he? He didn't go to school with us, did he?"

"No. He's new to the area. He turned up about six months ago."

"And just how often does this Kyle Mason come into Dolan's?"

"Every day or so," Sharon Lynn said.

"And where's his ranch?"

"About thirty miles north of Los Pinos. He bought the old Carlson spread at Cripple Creek."

Angela grinned. "Doesn't that strike you as a long drive to take so frequently if the man hasn't noticed you? Unless, of course, he's addicted to milk shakes," she added.

Sharon Lynn paused, her expression thoughtful. "I never thought about that. Do you think that's possible?"

"Likely, in fact. Maybe he's just shy," Angela suggested. "And the Adams name might be intimidating to a newcomer around here. Could be you're going to have to take the initiative. Call him right now and invite him to the open house tomorrow."

"I couldn't," Sharon Lynn protested.

"Why not?"

"Last-minute invitations are so tacky."

"Not to someone who's been waiting and waiting for you to make a move."

"He probably has plans."

"Stop making excuses, Sharon Lynn," Angela chided. "You won't know unless you call. At least it'll signal him that you're interested."

Her cousin's expression brightened. "I'm going to do it," she said, heading determinedly for the privacy of Grandpa Harlan's office.

"What was that all about?" Clint asked, reappearing with the champagne.

"You didn't listen in?"

"Of course not. It sounded like private girl talk."

Amused by his sudden burst of discretion, she said, "It was. I was just trying to shove my cousin off an emotional bridge."

"Uh-oh," he said uneasily. "Are you sure there's going to be somebody underneath to catch her?"

"Pretty sure."

"What if she gets the wrong answer and it ruins her holidays?"

She scowled at him. "Do you always have to look at the dark side of things?"

"Just being realistic."

Before Angela could worry herself into a tizzy over having inadvertently set Sharon Lynn up for a miserable holiday, her cousin dashed back into the room, her face aglow.

"He said yes," she practically shouted across the room. Oblivious to the curious glances from her parents and everyone else, she threw her arms around Angela. "Can you believe it? He said he would love to come. He didn't even hesitate."

"Obviously he'd been hoping for this."

"I was so sure he would have other plans. I know of at least three women in town who have been pursuing him like crazy."

"Other than you?" Angela teased.

"I have not been pursuing him," Sharon Lynn protested. "I have been very demure."

The thought of the exuberant Sharon Lynn as demure was enough to bring a smile, but Angela managed to keep a straight face. "Well, it looks as if that tactic has paid off, then," she said.

"Thank you for prodding me into doing something, anything, to get this relationship off dead center."

"Speaking of dead center," Clint interjected, his hand on Angela's shoulder. "Could I speak to you for a minute privately, before we go into dinner?"

She stared into his serious eyes and gulped. Either he was going to lecture her on interfering in Sharon Lynn's life or he had something much more personal in mind. She was well aware of the gaps already created in her defenses after no more than a few minutes in his company. A little time alone and she might as well kiss her resolve goodbye.

"Can't it wait?"

"Not really."

She heaved a sigh and gestured toward her grand-father's office. "Let's go in there. We'll be able to hear when the others start into the dining room."

With Sharon Lynn's fascinated gaze following them, they slipped away. Clint closed the office door firmly behind them. The soft click of the lock sent goose bumps dancing up her spine.

Vaguely alarmed, her gaze flew to his face. "What on earth was that for?"

"I don't want to be disturbed. There's only one way I can think of around here to manage that."

She instinctively backed up a step. "You're making this sound awfully serious."

"It is."

She saw him reach into his pocket, but even then his intentions didn't register. Not until he withdrew a small square package wrapped in gold did she begin to get an idea of what was on his mind. If he'd been determined to hit on a surefire way to destroy her resistance, this was it.

Angela swallowed hard and eyed that package as warily as if it were a rattler. "Shouldn't we wait until morning for presents?" she asked without much hope of him taking the suggestion. Obviously he'd planned the timing of this moment very carefully.

"Not this one," he insisted, holding it out in the palm of his hand. He grinned at her. "Take it, angel. It won't bite."

She plucked it out of his hand as gingerly as if it

might explode. She fingered the curling gold ribbon, but made no move to untie it.

"Come on," he urged. "Open it."

She lifted her gaze to his. "I'm afraid to," she admitted candidly.

He regarded her with obvious astonishment. "Why?"

"I don't think I can explain it."

"Try."

"If..." She drew in a deep breath, then tried again. "If it's what I think it is, it will change things."

"Forever," he agreed.

She sighed and closed her eyes. "That's what I was afraid of. Clint, we just declared a truce. It's too soon to ask for anything more."

He regarded her with amusement. "It's not as if we just met, angel. This day has been a long time coming. Too long, some would say, including you, I thought."

If only he had done this back in Montana, she thought, then chided herself for being unreasonable. She hadn't given him a chance to. That didn't change the fact that it felt all wrong now.

"I know what you're trying to do," she began.

"Oh, really?" he said wryly. "What am I trying to do?"

"Make things right. Be responsible."

"And that's so terrible?"

"Clint, the timing is all off."

"What the hell is that supposed to mean?" he demanded, amusement giving way to exasperation.

She struggled for an explanation, but none came to

her, none that would make sense to him anyway. "I can't explain. I'm sorry." She held out her hand, the unopened present still resting in her palm.

After an endless hesitation, he reached for the package, his disappointment plain. "Maybe you're right," he said halfheartedly. "I just thought..."

"I know what you wanted to do," she said. "And it was a lovely gesture, something I'll remember every single Christmas Eve as long as I live." She smiled, a little too brightly, probably. "I'm sure you can get your money back. The stores in Los Pinos have very lenient return policies."

That familiar headstrong look was back in his eyes. "I'm not taking it back to the store, angel. Just so you know, I'm going to do everything in my power to see that you accept it sooner or later."

She shuddered at the grim determination in his voice. If only he'd sounded like a man in love, instead of a man on a mission, she thought wistfully. Then it might have been almost impossible for her to say no.

Clint was disappointed, but not broken by Angela's refusal to so much as look inside that box, much less accept the proposal he'd been planning all day. Maybe it had been premature. It was just that he was so blasted anxious to get things settled once and for all. He wasn't used to being so out of control, to having anyone tie him in knots the way she did. He'd hoped to seize control back again.

Which, of course, was exactly the problem. They both wanted to set the ground rules and determine the pace of this relationship. What neither of them seemed willing to admit was that a third person was really in charge, that baby of theirs. If Clint had to hog-tie Angela and drag her in front of a minister, they were going to be man and wife when that baby was born.

As soon as he and Angela had rejoined the others, he realized that he'd made a mistake in asking for that moment alone with her. He should have caught up with her upstairs or waited. Now he'd raised expectations that the two of them would be making an announcement over dinner. He could see the anticipation in Harlan's eyes and the anxiety in Luke's and Jessie's. Jessie's gaze kept drifting to Angela's left hand as if she were expecting to see an engagement ring there.

"Dinner is ready," Maritza announced, saving him and Angela from the speculative glances.

"Luke, why don't you escort your daughter in tonight?" Harlan suggested. "Clint, you take Jessie."

Clint met Jessie's eyes and caught the spark of amusement.

"He wants to give me time to cross-examine you," Jessie said. "Subtlety is not Harlan's strong suit."

"You can always ask me anything. I'm an up-front kind of man. It saves wear and tear on the emotions."

"OK, then. Did you ask Angela to marry you tonight?"

"I did," he confirmed. "She said no."

Jessie sighed. "I thought as much. I just don't understand that daughter of mine. I can see perfectly plainly that she is crazy in love with you. She's just being stubborn, like a typical Adams. She got a double dose of it, too, with Erik's genes and Luke's influence.''

"Being an Adams can't be all bad," Clint teased. "You signed on for it twice."

"True," she admitted with a rueful grin. "I suppose I'm every bit as stubborn as they are. I hung in there with Luke when he flatly refused to admit how he felt about me. I hope you'll do the same with Angela."

"I don't have a choice. She's carrying my child."

Jessie studied him worriedly. "Is that what you've been telling her?"

"More or less. Why?"

"Well, no wonder she turned you down," she said, regarding him with dismay.

"I want that baby of mine to have my name."

Apparently he'd raised his voice, because several of the others glanced their way.

"My father left us the day I was born," he said more quietly, but just as fiercely. "I grew up thinking it was my fault he was gone. I will not allow that to happen to a child of mine."

Jessie rested her hand on his. "I know you mean well. I can see that you're desperate to do right by your baby, but what about Angela? How do you feel about her?"

As he was about to respond, she silenced him with a touch of her finger against his lips. "Don't tell me. Tell her."

The message was plain as day and Clint wondered how he could have been so blind to the obvious up until now. Of course Angela wanted to know how he felt about her. The only trouble was, he wasn't sure of that himself.

Her betrayal loomed between them and no matter how hard he tried, he couldn't seem to get beyond it. He was still attracted to her. He still wanted her. He understood the importance of forgiveness, but he wondered if he was capable of it.

He was quiet through most of dinner, wrestling with his conscience and his heart. He could have been eating sawdust for all the attention he paid the meal.

Beside him, Angela was just as quiet. She spoke only when she was asked a direct question, and the others, sensing that she was in turmoil, asked her very little.

Fortunately, the Adamses were a boisterous crowd. They more than made up for the silence of two of the guests. Only when the time came to decorate the tree did they insist on sweeping Clint and Angela into the midst of the activity.

"I'm a little tired," Angela protested. "I'll just sit here and supervise."

"Not a chance," Justin said, hauling her to her feet. "You're the only one who likes as many lights as I do. The others would stop after a couple of wimpy strands."

Clint observed in amusement as Angela and Justin wrapped at least eight strands of brightly colored lights around the tree. Watching them reminded him of her excitement just one year ago when he'd managed to find all those lights for their first tree together.

"Plug it in," Angela commanded now. When the lights blinked on, her eyes lit up. "It's beautiful."

"It's blinding," Sharon Lynn declared. "We won't even be able to see to put the rest of the ornaments on."

Angela rolled her eyes. "OK, OK. Turn 'em off, Justin. Let's finish decorating before we have the final lighting ceremony."

Tall and awkward, with the stretched-out lankiness of adolescence, Jordan's son practically upended the tree as he reached for the plug.

As Clint grabbed the tree and righted it, his gaze caught Angela's. Suddenly they were connected as surely as if they'd hopped aboard a time travel machine and zoomed back twelve months. He could see the memory in her eyes. Her expression softened, her complexion glowed and her lips curved into the faintest suggestion of a smile. He remembered it all as if it were yesterday.

"Let them finish," he suggested softly, holding out his hand. "Before one of them tangles a strand of garland around your neck and chokes you."

"Hey," Justin protested. "We're not that clumsy."

"Couldn't prove it by me," Harlan Patrick taunted. "Who dropped one entire box of ornaments when we were carrying them down from the attic?"

Justin shot back a rude remark.

"Maybe I'd better sit down," Angela said, taking Clint's outstretched hand.

Though there were plenty of chairs in the room, Clint led her to a love seat so he could sit beside her. As carols played on the stereo and the cousins bickered and laughed, he felt a longed-for contentment steal over him again. When he turned Angela and settled her back against his chest, she didn't protest. Instead, to his relief, she sighed happily.

"Glad to be home?" he asked quietly.

She nodded. "But I miss Montana, too."

"You do?" Clint asked, surprised by the admission.

"Just the two of us. It was magical." She gazed up at him, her expression wistful. "I thought we were starting our own traditions."

"I thought so, too."

"Who would have thought so much would happen to change everything?"

"It doesn't have to," he said. "We can have that again, if we want it badly enough. Do you?"

Before she could answer, they were surrounded by cousins.

"Come on, Angie. You have to put the angel on top of the tree. It's tradition," Harlan Patrick said.

She gazed at Clint, her expression clearly torn.

"Go," he told her. "Traditions are meant to be carried on."

He sat back and watched as the others handed her the gold and white angel for the top of the tree. She handled the obviously expensive, obviously old angel with such tenderness that it brought an unexpected sting to Clint's eyes. There had been no such traditions in his family, no such sentiment. His mother had tried, but there were often too many divisions and old hurts to make the holidays anything but stressful. He'd stopped going home after a while.

He watched nervously as Justin helped Angela up the small ladder at the side of the huge tree, then steadied her as she reached for the top branch. She settled the angel firmly in place, then stepped down.

Someone with a magician's sense of timing turned on the tree lights at precisely the same moment as someone else doused the other lights in the room. There were audible gasps of delight, then applause.

"The best tree ever," Harlan declared.

"You say that every year, Grandpa," Justin teased.

"And every year it is the best," his grandfather retorted. "This year's best of all because the angel's back on top."

Angela stared at her grandfather. "I don't understand."

"He wouldn't let us put it on while you were gone," Sharon Lynn explained. "He said it was your job."

"I begged and begged," Lizzy complained, "but Daddy said we'd just have to wait till you came home again to see the angel back on the tree."

"Oh, Grandpa," Angela said, throwing her arms around his neck.

"Now, don't go getting all weepy on me, girl. You'll mess up my suit before church," he protested, looking pleased just the same.

Clint fingered the ring box that was still in his pocket and tried not to feel an overwhelming sense of defeat. How could he compete with this much love, with this family?

He realized then that Angela's gaze had sought out his. Their eyes met and lingered. His heart thundered in his chest at the desire and longing he thought he saw in her face. For just that instant, anyway, it seemed that no one else in the room mattered.

Possibilities stirred to life again inside him. Confidence soared. He found himself smiling. After all, this was the season of miracles, wasn't it? She'd said that herself not so long ago. Maybe one really was possible for the two of them.

Chapter Twelve

Angela hadn't been inside a church since she'd left home. It wasn't that she'd lost her faith; maybe it was just one more act of rebellion. At any rate, when she walked back into the small, candlelit church she'd attended for most of her life, she felt a sense of peace stealing over her. Subconsciously she reached for Clint's hand. The warmth of his grasp was even more reassuring.

Throughout the familiar Christmas Eve service, she was all too aware of the man beside her, his deep voice blending with hers as they sang the joyous hymns: "Silent Night," "The First Noel," "Joy to the World." Each one brought back memories of past holiday seasons; each one stirred thoughts of one particular Christmas in Montana.

Ever since that moment when their gazes had

locked back at White Pines, she had felt as if she and
Clint were caught up in a spell. It was as if some
unseen hand were drawing them closer and closer,
insisting that they search their hearts for answers to
the dilemma they faced.

She wanted to love him again, as freely as she had
in Montana, without so many complications.

But life was filled with unexpected and unalterable
twists and turns. Coping with them, in the end, would
make them and their love stronger. She couldn't go
back to being Hattie Jones, no matter how desperately
she wanted to recapture that carefree time in her life.
She was about to become a mother, with all the re-
sponsibilities—and joys—that entailed.

It would be so much easier to share the demands
with someone, she thought wistfully, so much more
meaningful to share the joys.

She stole a glance at the man beside her. Every line
in his face, every expression on his lips was as dear
and familiar to her as if they'd spent a lifetime together, rather than a few short months. Here was
someone who wanted to take on that duty, who was
eager to be a father to his son or daughter. On that
score at least, she had come to trust Clint without
reservation over the past few days. He loved the baby
she was carrying as deeply as she did.

Tell me what to do, she prayed. *Please show me
the path to take.*

There were no blinding messages in response, no
signals in the night sky as they made their way home
again. Maybe, as she had accused Clint of doing earlier, she was rushing things, trying to force a resolu-

tion when the only real answers would come with time. Patience, never one of her virtues, was absolutely necessary with so much on the line.

At home, when everyone else climbed up the steps to their rooms, Clint lingered at the foot of the stairs, his steady gaze on her.

"Sit with me awhile," he suggested. "By the tree."

As tired as she was, she was unable to resist the appeal of the invitation, the draw of the man uttering it.

The lights were still on, blinking reds and greens, blues and golds, a magnificent display of shimmering Technicolor. Leaning back in his arms, she half closed her eyes to soften the effect into something reminiscent of an Impressionist painting.

"What is it about a Christmas tree that makes us feel as if we've been touched by magic?" she asked.

She could tell from his thoughtful expression that he took the question seriously, and she loved him for that. Some men would have laughed it off as romanticized nonsense. Clint had always taken her most whimsical statements seriously, though. He was also capable of wicked wit or off-the-cuff philosophy. Their conversations had never been boring.

"It takes us back to childhood, maybe," he said. "Back to a time when we were truly innocent and filled with anticipation."

"Back to a time when we were greedy little brats, you mean."

He laughed. "I was trying for a positive spin."

"Do you ever think about what our baby will be like?"

He seemed startled by the shift in topic. "You mean boy or girl?"

"No, I mean the kind of person he or she will grow up to be. Does it scare you, thinking about what the world is like and how to protect him?"

"Or her," he reminded her. "Now, having a girl scares me more than a boy. I figure I won't want any daughter of mine to date until she's ninety for fear she'll run across a man like me."

"What's wrong with you?"

"You, of all people, have to ask?"

"You're strong. You're decent. You're intelligent. Any woman would be lucky to have you," she declared with feeling, then recognized the irony.

"May I remind you that a very short time ago you turned down my proposal before I could even get it out of my mouth," he said, obviously aware of the irony, too. "I'd rehearsed the darned thing, too."

"Want to say it now?" The suggestion was made only half in jest. A part of her wanted a chance to say yes, even if common sense told her to stay silent.

He studied her intently, then shook his head. "Not right this second, angel. I can't take being humiliated twice in one night."

"I'm sorry."

"Don't be sorry. I was being impulsive. You were trying to use good sense. Marriage isn't something to jump into for the wrong reasons."

He rested his hand on her belly, and Angela felt her pulse skitter crazily. His expression turned awestruck as the baby shifted inside her. When he lifted his gaze to hers, she was almost certain she detected the sheen of unshed tears.

"Though this is a pretty darned good reason for getting married, if you ask me," he said quietly.

It was, Angela agreed to herself. But it wasn't the one she desperately wanted to hear. She could have told him that, probably should have, but she didn't. She wanted him to recognize their love on his own, to admit to it without any prodding from her...if he could.

"I think I'll go up to bed now," she said instead. She stood up, then bent down to drop a kiss against his cheek. "Good night, Clint. Merry Christmas."

He captured her face between his hands and kissed her back, slowly, persuasively until her knees were so weak she could barely stand. If he'd meant to make a point, if he'd meant to remind her that the passion between them burned hot even now, then he had.

"Merry Christmas, angel," he murmured. "See you in the morning."

With her blood pumping fast and furiously through her veins, she regretted the decision to leave, but pride wouldn't let her turn back. That was the trouble with the two of them, she concluded. They both had pride to spare, but no one with whom to spend the night.

Christmas morning dawned cold and bright. Sun glistened on a fresh covering of snow that had fallen after they'd gotten home from church the night before. Clint had caught a glimpse of it when he'd finally gone up to his room.

He'd stood by the window for an eternity, staring out at the stark, rugged terrain of White Pines softened by its blanket of white. Oddly enough, he'd felt no envy. His own ranch might be smaller, less ostentatious, but he owned every acre of it free and clear. He could take pride in the work he had done to make it a thriving cattle operation, one that would grow over time.

Was it enough to offer a child, though? Especially a child who could have at least some small stake in all this someday? He didn't like the doubts that kept creeping in when he least expected them. He didn't want to think about going home without his son or daughter.

He didn't want to think about going without Angela.

It was strange. He had come to Texas in search of Hattie—or more precisely, the child he'd fathered—but he'd found a different woman entirely. Not just in name, but in demeanor and more. To be sure, her body had changed with the child she carried, but it ran deeper than that. Hattie had been flirtatious and loving and generous, but he'd never seen the strength in her that he saw in Angela. She was prepared to face the uncertain future on her own, if she had to, without him.

His own feelings had changed over the past few days, as well. He'd come after a child. His child. He'd stayed, at least in part, because of a woman. She intrigued him in ways that Hattie never had.

Only one thing had stayed the same; the hunger she could build in him with just a glance. The skim of her fingers across his flesh, the touch of her lips, and he was achingly hard and hot as a branding iron.

Those thoughts of permanence and forever were coming more and more frequently, buoyed by the notion that the foundation was more solid. His attraction to her had deepened into something that could last through time. And this time, he thought, they had the truth on their side. They had a fresh chance to get it right.

He thought about what Jessie had told him earlier about a woman needing to know that a man wanted her for herself and not for the baby she carried. Maybe it was time he admitted that, put his heart on the line. Not doing so up until now had been a coward's act. When Angela had turned his proposal down she'd refused an offer only slightly better than a business proposition. If he told her he cared, if he confessed to loving her, it would be him she was rejecting. Little had ever frightened him before, but that did.

He'd had a lot of months to toughen his pride. He'd had that final scene between them to play over and over again. He'd had the night she'd given him the slip in Montana to reinforce all of his fears that the woman he was chasing didn't want him. Just as his father hadn't. Old insecurities that had festered for years came back to haunt him.

He had no proof, none at all, that her feelings toward him had changed. Not really. Oh, she had returned his kisses with a matching ardor. She had sent glances his way that could steam up a mirror two rooms away. That should have been reassurance enough.

But Angela was unpredictable in ways that Hattie hadn't been. Telling her how he felt still seemed risky. The knowledge she would have after such an admission would give her a certain kind of power over him, and he didn't like giving anyone around him an edge they could turn against him.

He'd wrestled with the dilemma most of the night. By dawn the answers were no clearer than they had been.

He could sense that others were stirring. He'd checked with Consuela the night before, and she'd assured him that his gift for Angela had arrived and been safely hidden. It would be under the tree by this morning. Just thinking of it made him smile.

He rushed through his shower, dressed in another suit and struggled with another damnable tie. He'd be glad when the holidays ended and he could go back to wearing comfortable denims and flannel shirts again. He'd noticed that the other men had been complaining good-naturedly about their own fancy clothes the night before. Except for Jordan. He was a man who looked as if he'd been born to wear pinstripes. He was as relaxed in Armani as the rest of them were in their Levi's and Wranglers.

He thought of that soft, green velvet dress that Angela had worn the night before. It had taken every bit of his strength to keep from caressing the fabric and the woman wearing it. He supposed wearing a fancy suit once in a while was a small price to pay to see the women gussied up in velvet and silk and diamonds. Seeing the pendant he had given her nestled between her breasts had made him smile.

Pausing outside Angela's door now, he listened for sounds of her stirring, but heard nothing. He realized why, when he got downstairs. She was in the living room with her grandfather, Justin and young Harlan. They were all dressed up and staring avidly at the mound of packages under the tree.

"Merry Christmas, everyone," Clint said, not even trying to hide his amusement.

"Merry Christmas, son," Harlan said. He eyed Clint hopefully. "Did you hear anyone else stirring up there?"

"Not really. I just heard you all coming downstairs."

Four faces reflected obvious disappointment. Clint noticed that Angela's gaze was fixed on the huge, wrapped package tucked back in one corner. From its size, Clint guessed it had to be the one he'd bought for her. He picked out the huge, lumpy present she'd chosen for him, then returned his gaze to her.

"Curious, angel?" he inquired, taking a seat beside her.

"It's Christmas morning. Of course I'm curious."

"We could open just one package each," Harlan suggested. "Wouldn't be anything wrong with that, would there?"

"Grandpa, you know the others would kill us," Justin said. "The rule is we wait until everybody's up."

Harlan grinned. "Then the two of you go upstairs

and raise a ruckus. Let's see if we can't get this show on the road.''

When the two young men had raced off, Angela regarded him sternly. ''Grandpa, you're worse than they are.''

''There's nothing like the spirit of giving to perk up a man's day. I'm old. I have the right to indulge my kinfolk.''

''Who are you trying to kid?'' she teased. ''You want to see what everyone got for you.''

''Watch it, girl, or that present with your name on it just might vanish before we get to the unwrapping.''

''He always threatens us like this,'' Angela told Clint. ''The man threatened to take back my teddy bear one year.''

''You told me the one you had at home was bigger. I figured you didn't need two. Also thought you needed to learn something about gratitude. You learned your lesson, didn't you?''

She grinned at him. ''Yes, Grandpa,'' she said dutifully. ''I think I'll go tell Consuela and Maritza we want to eat breakfast before we open packages. I'll suggest a nice, long, leisurely breakfast, pancakes, waffles, the works.''

''Oh, no, you don't,'' he said, catching her hand when she would have sashayed past him. He turned his gaze on Clint. ''Take her for a walk, will you? Keep her out of mischief until the others come down.''

Clint glanced outside worriedly. ''I don't know, sir.

It looks awfully cold and slippery out there. There's more snow coming down, too.''

"Traitor," Harlan taunted. "I guess I'll go up and see if my wife is awake."

"Let her sleep if she's not," Angela said. "Yesterday was a long day. Today will be, too."

"Then she can catch up on her beauty sleep tonight, not on Christmas morning."

When he'd gone, Angela shook her head. "He always was the first one up on Christmas morning. He said he loved seeing our faces when we sneaked down the stairs to see if Santa had come."

"Who was second?" Clint asked.

"Me," she admitted. "Jenny always tried to act blasé and Dani was a sleepyhead. I didn't get any real competition until Sharon Lynn was big enough to get down the stairs by herself."

"Which just shows that some things never change," the woman in question said, yawning as she joined them. "Has anyone made coffee yet?"

"There's a pot on the buffet in the dining room," Angela said.

"I'll get it," Clint offered. "I could use a cup myself. Angel, what about you? Is there decaf?"

"I already have my herbal tea," she told him, lifting the mug to demonstrate.

He left the two of them poking at packages. They were still at it when he returned with the coffee and a huge tray of freshly baked sweet rolls Consuela had told him were meant to tide them over until after the presents had been opened.

One by one the others straggled down the stairs, as

Angela and Sharon Lynn waited impatiently. Harlan was grumbling when he returned, decrying Janet's determination to shower and dress before joining them.

"I've given that woman enough fancy robes to stock a lingerie shop. Couldn't she have worn one of them?" he complained.

"Maybe she figured that once this day gets rolling, she wouldn't have another chance. No woman owns a robe that's fancy enough for greeting guests. What time are people expected for the open house?" Angela asked.

"Noon, same as always."

"How many?" Clint asked.

"Not too many this year," Harlan said. "A hundred or so."

The whole town of Rocky Ridge wasn't much bigger than that, Clint thought. Yet Harlan was more nonchalant about entertaining for such a crowd than Clint would have been at fixing dinner for four. Of course, with Consuela and Maritza on the job, he probably had very little to do except stay out of the way.

It was twenty minutes before Janet came downstairs. A cheer went up.

"Finally," Harlan said, feigning exasperation. There was too much love shining in his eyes for the comment to have much bite to it. She settled on the carpet at his feet and rested her head against his thighs. His weathered hand settled gently on her head. There was no mistaking how they felt about each other, Clint thought, envying them.

Lizzy deemed herself Santa and parceled out packages with enthusiasm. For all of the insistence on waiting until everyone was downstairs, there was no organized system to the opening. Everyone shredded paper as fast as they could. Shouts were exchanged. Thanks were hollered back and forth. The excitement in the room was palpable.

Clint was startled when the first gift was pressed into his hands, stunned when several more were added. He was relieved that he'd insisted on shopping for everyone, including the cats who were getting tangled up in the scattering of ribbons as they chased wads of wrapping paper.

He saved Angela's present to him for last, then laughed aloud when he saw the huge teddy bear she'd chosen. "For me?" he inquired. "Or the baby?"

"It had your name on the tag, didn't it?" she responded, then grinned. "But I know you're the sort of man who'd want to share with his baby."

"We'll see," he said, settling the bear beside him in the crook of his arm. "I kind of like this guy. He snuggles up and doesn't talk back."

"Watch it," she warned, laughing.

Whether it was the gift's placement in the corner or Lizzy's unerring sense of the dramatic, Clint's present for Angela was the last one delivered. It took help from Justin to drag it across the room.

Angela stared from the huge box to Clint and back again. "What on earth?"

"You won't know until you open it," he teased.

She studied the package intently. "You didn't bring this home yesterday."

"Nope," he said complacently, amused by her perplexed expression.

"How'd it get here?"

"I had it delivered."

"From where?"

"Darlin', just open the thing."

"Yes," Harlan said. "Hurry up. We're all waiting to see what's inside."

Encouraged by everyone, she began enthusiastically tearing away the wrappings. As he'd instructed, though, the box was plain. It revealed absolutely nothing about the contents.

"Want some help?" he asked, moving to her side and taking his knife from his pocket. He opened it and cut through the tape that sealed the flaps, then sat back and waited for her reaction. The entire room had fallen silent, and all eyes were on Angela as she peered inside.

She lifted out sheets of recycled packing paper, one after another. Clint watched her face intently and knew the precise instant when she saw the gift.

"Oh, Clint," she whispered, eyes shining. "It's beautiful."

"What is it?" Harlan demanded, trying to peer over her shoulder. "Let me help."

He lifted out an exquisite hand-carved cradle and set it gently beside Angela. Made of cherry wood, it was intricately detailed and polished to a warm shine. A puff of yellow bedding with teddy bears lined it. Clint imagined that giant teddy bear Angela had given him standing watch over the cradle and his child. It was as if they'd been on the same wavelength in some way.

"Son, that's a mighty fine gift," Harlan said, clapping Clint on the back. "Mighty fine."

Just then Angela gasped and clutched her stomach.

"Baby?" Harlan asked, regarding her worriedly. "Are you OK?"

"Honey, what is it?" Jessie said, rushing over.

Clint hunkered down beside her. "Angel, what's going on?"

He didn't like the way she looked one bit. Her complexion was pale, her eyes stricken as she met his gaze.

"I could be wrong," she said, "but I have a feeling that cradle arrived in the nick of time."

Clint stared at her, his heart slamming against his ribs. "What are you saying?"

"Unless I'm very much mistaken, I am about to have a baby."

Chapter Thirteen

If she hadn't been quite so panicky, Angela might have been amused by the stunned reactions to her announcement. Clint went absolutely white. Her father and grandfather, normally the most unflappable men she knew, started barking orders, most of them contradictory.

Her normally calm mother finally shouted over the commotion. "Enough!"

Angela grinned as everyone fell silent and stared at her mother. No one in the room knew any better than Jessie about the unexpected arrival of a baby. She hunkered down beside Angela and smiled reassuringly.

"You OK?"

"Just surprised."

"It could be false labor," Kelly offered helpfully.

The suggestion was echoed by Janet and Melissa.

"Clint, why don't you get her a glass of chipped ice?" her mother suggested.

Visibly grateful at being given an assignment he could cope with, Clint practically raced from the room. He came back with a glass of chipped ice and two excited housekeepers. Maritza and Consuela arrived chattering in Spanish, aprons flapping and hands waving.

"Harlan, how are the roads?" her mother asked. "Can we get her to the hospital?"

"I'll check," he said promptly. "If not, I'll call the snowplow driver and have him clear the way ahead of us. I pay enough taxes to get a few special privileges."

Just then another pain ripped through Angela. She latched on to Clint's hand and cursed a blue streak. He stared at her in shock.

"Oh, don't look at me like that," she grumbled when she had caught her breath. "I swore I wasn't going to do this."

"Do what?" he asked.

"Have this baby close to Christmas, much less on Christmas Day. Good grief, we'll be celebrating everything at once. My birthday, Christmas, everything."

"You should have thought about that before you got pregnant when you did," her mother said dryly.

"I should have thought about a lot of things before I got pregnant," Angela said, then cried out with another pain.

"How close?" she asked, panting. "Damn, I knew

I shouldn't have ignored that backache during the night.''

"Three minutes," her mother replied. "Harlan, forget the hospital. She'll never make it. Let's get her into one of the bedrooms. Dani, you come, too.''

"Me? Why me?" Dani asked, turning pale. She looked as if she wanted to flee.

"Just come, please," Jessie said.

When Clint had carried Angela upstairs and settled her into bed, her mother turned to the obviously wary Dani. "Honey, you've got the most experience delivering babies of anyone in this room.''

Angela wasn't sure whose wail was louder, her own or her cousin's.

The last bit of color washed out of Dani's face. "Me? I've delivered litters of kittens. I've delivered puppies. I've even delivered baby bunnies. Under duress, I've even managed to help out with foals and calves, but I have never delivered a child," she protested. "I really, really don't think this is the time to start.''

"I agree," Angela said emphatically. In fact, the very idea horrified her. It was ludicrous, insane, totally out of the question. Fortunately, Dani seemed just as appalled as she was. Surely her well-educated, professional cousin could make them see reason.

Sweat beaded on Angela's brow as her body was wracked with another labor pain. Panicked, she clutched Clint's hand and demanded, "Get me to a hospital, damn you. I am not having this baby with the help of a veterinarian, even if she is the smartest, nicest cousin on earth. The baby will wait, if I have to hold it in with both hands.''

''I don't know,'' Clint said worriedly. ''He seems a little impatient to me. The roads are an icy mess. Snow's still coming down. You heard what your mother said. Maybe we'd better play it safe.''

Angie panted, trying to ease another pain. As soon as she had breath to spare she glared at him and at her cousin. ''I want a real hospital and a real doctor. No offense, Dani.''

''None taken. Nothing would please me more than to accommodate you and turn you over to a real doctor,'' Dani said fervently. ''Maybe Grandpa can get his helicopter pilot to swoop in and take you.''

''Not in this storm,'' Clint insisted. He squeezed Angie's hand. ''Darlin', we have to be sensible.''

''You should have thought of that nine months ago,'' she declared. ''That was the time for straight thinking and protection.''

Clint grinned. ''Angel, that particular horse is already out of the barn. Let's deal with the crisis at hand, OK?''

''Maybe we should just get my father in here. He has more experience at delivering babies than any of you do. He brought me into this world.''

''I'm not sure how much help he would be,'' her mother retorted. ''The last time I saw him, he was sitting in a chair with his head in his hands muttering something about history repeating itself.''

She gazed up and found Clint hovering a few feet away from the bed. He looked so worried and ill at ease that she would have shipped him off to join the

446 THE LITTLEST ANGEL

others if she'd had the heart. Instead, she figured what he really needed was something to do.

Resigned to making the best of a lousy situation, she called out to him. "Clint?"

He was by her side in an instant. "What? Are you OK? What can I do?"

"Help me breathe," she said, thankful that she'd at least had the sense to take the Lamaze classes in Seattle before she'd left. Of course, the coach she'd planned on having was still in Seattle, too, but hopefully Clint would be a quick study.

"Here's the deal," she said, and explained what she needed him to do. The explanation took a long time because she kept having to stop for the increasingly severe pains.

After a particularly bad contraction, Clint said, "That's *it*. No more babies. I don't ever want to have to go through this again."

"You?" all three women protested in a chorus.

He grinned sheepishly. "Okay...Angela. I won't let *her* go through it again." He gazed at her mother worriedly. "Are you sure this is the sensible thing to do?"

"Sensible or not, we don't have a choice," she said, then looked to Dani, who'd just returned after finally conceding defeat and going off to scrub up for the impending delivery. "Do we?"

"Afraid not," Dani said irritably. "I'd say this Adams is about to make an entrance, like it or not. Aunt Jessie, can you find a blanket and some towels? Sterilize some scissors, too. And hurry, for goodness' sakes."

"Of course. I'll be right back." She feigned a scowl at Angela. "Don't you dare have this baby while I'm gone. I want to be right here when my grandbaby comes into this world."

"Then I think you'd better hurry," Angela said, her voice catching, then altering into a muffled scream. She didn't know a lot about the duration of labor. What she'd read said first babies tended to take a long time arriving. Hers didn't seem inclined to play by the rules. Typical of an Adams.

"Pant," Clint ordered. "Pay attention, darlin'. You remember the drill."

Fortunately she did recall there was more to it than panting. Since it was obvious everything else she'd just taught him had flown out the window. He watched her intently, then nodded. He grinned sheepishly when the pain had passed.

"Now I remember," he murmured.

With the next contraction, Dani murmured, "Here we go. Push, Angie. Do it," she said more sharply. "Push now."

"I am pushing, you lousy, no-good animal doc."

"Don't knock the help, kiddo, or Clint will find himself in my place."

"Be nice," he said hurriedly. "Dani's your best shot at getting this baby delivered with professional assistance."

"Oh, I think you could handle it, just as well as she could," Angela shot back. "How many calves and foals have you delivered?"

"A few."

"More than a few," she reminded him.

"Then get down here and take over," Dani pleaded. "I have absolutely no ego here. I'll take whatever help I can get."

Clint released her hand and was about to move when Angela latched on to it again and let out a shout that shook the rafters.

"Oh, my," Dani murmured. "Come on, Angie. Once more with feeling. That's it. Come on. Do it *now!*"

Angela felt as if her insides were being torn apart. Then suddenly, barely an hour after the severe pains had started, it was over. She tried to lift herself on her elbows. Clint was on his feet.

"My baby," she whispered urgently. "I don't hear anything. Dani?"

Just as panic was setting it, she heard a feeble cry, followed by a lusty wail.

"That's more like it," Dani said triumphantly. She took one of the towels that Jessie had brought in just that second and wrapped the baby. Her expression triumphant, she walked to the head of the bed.

"Angie, Clint, may I present your son."

"A boy?" Clint whispered, gazing awestruck at the chubby, red-faced newborn Dani placed in Angela's arms.

"Told you so," she said, her eyes filling with tears. "Oh, Clint, he's beautiful."

"Handsome," he corrected, grinning. "Boys are handsome."

"Not ours. He is absolutely beautiful."

"He is, sweetie," her mother said. She turned and

hugged Dani. "You were terrific. I'll never be able to thank you enough."

"We won't be able to thank you enough," Clint said.

"No problem," Dani said, then sank into a chair as if her legs had suddenly turned to water. "I don't ever, *ever* want to do anything like this again, do you hear me? I've never been so terrified of messing up in my entire life."

"Now she tells us," Angela teased.

She glanced at Clint. "I have an idea." She beckoned to him and whispered. Clint nodded.

Angela grinned. "OK, then. Don't fall apart now, Dani. Come here and officially meet your new godson," she said.

"Oh, sweetie, you don't have to do that," Dani said, but her eyes were bright with unshed tears. She rubbed the back of her fingers across the baby's soft cheek. "But I'm glad you did. Have you decided on a name?"

"I have," Angela said. "Clinton Daniel Adams."

"Brady," Clint amended, a determined scowl on his face. "Clinton Daniel Brady."

"Do you see a ring on my finger?" Angela asked, looking at her mother and her cousin. "Either one of you? Is there a ring here?"

The two women exchanged a look.

"Bye-bye," Dani said. "Glad to be of help."

"Call us if you need us," her mother said, brushing a kiss across her forehead. "You were great, sweetie."

"You're abandoning me?" she protested. "How can you do that? I just had a baby."

"Clint's here."

"Yes, but he has his own agenda at the moment. I want somebody who's on my side."

"We are," her mother insisted. "That's why we're going. You two need time alone with your baby."

It wasn't the prospect of being alone with her child that scared the daylights out of her. Clinton Daniel was the kind of miracle it would take a lifetime to study and appreciate.

No, what terrified her was the glint of pure cussedness she saw in Clint's eyes. He'd been possessive and determined enough before. Now there was no telling the lengths to which he'd go to claim his son.

For a long time after Dani and Jessie left Angela's bedroom, Clint couldn't form a coherent thought. He kept staring at the tiny infant, who was now wrapped in a huge yellow blanket. His son. Practically bald except for a few strands of soft blond fuzz, eyes as big as saucers staring solemnly back at him, a tiny pink bow of a mouth. He was in awe of him.

"Would you like to hold him?" Angela asked.

"I...um, I don't know," he said warily. "What if I do something wrong?"

"Are you planning to drop him on his head?"

He stared at her aghast. "Of course not."

"Then you'll do just fine," she said, holding the baby up in the air for Clint to take.

He gingerly accepted the baby and his tangle of

blanket. His gaze locked on his son's face as if he were mesmerized.

"Hi, kiddo," he said softly. Everything else in the room faded into the background as he concentrated on this tiny gift from God.

"I'm your dad," he said. "You and I, we're going to have a great time together. I have this little spread up in Montana and one day it's all going to be yours. I'm going to teach you every single thing I know about ranching."

"You might have to wait just a bit for that," Angela said dryly. "At least until he can walk."

"You're never too young to know that there's a plan and what your part in it will be," he insisted. "It makes a kid feel secure."

"You never had that, did you?" she asked.

He glanced at Angela, surprised by her accurate guesswork. "My mother did the best she could. Besides, the past's over and done with," he said, his gaze never straying from the beautiful face of his boy. "This child right here, he's the future. He's all that matters now."

"You can't build your whole world around a baby," Angela argued.

Something in her voice, a surprising hint of testiness, alerted him that her mood was rapidly disintegrating and that he was the cause of it. Suspecting he knew why, he glanced at her. "You OK?"

"Just peachy."

"Did I forget to mention how you fit into this future?" he inquired, giving her a lazy grin.

"Don't try to charm me, Clint Brady. All you care about, all you've ever cared about is your baby."

The accusation confirmed his own guesswork. Her feelings were hurt by what she perceived as his priorities. "That's not true, darlin'. You've just given me the most precious gift on God's earth and you will always have a place in my heart for that."

"I didn't have this baby to accommodate you," she grumbled, reaching for their son. Staking her own claim, he imagined. Clint reluctantly put the baby back into her arms. Her expression softened at once.

"He is precious, isn't he?" she whispered.

"He is, indeed, though I have a feeling you and I had better enjoy him while we can."

"Meaning?"

"I think I hear a thundering herd on the steps. My guess is we're about to have company. That boy's going to get passed around like a football."

"Over my dead body," she said, visibly tightening her embrace. "They can look, but nobody's getting this baby out of my arms today."

Before Clint could stake his own claim in what was becoming a knee-jerk reaction of possessiveness, there was a hard knock on the door, followed by a muffled burst of excited chatter. He supposed they might as well give in to the inevitable.

"You ready, angel?"

Her expression was clearly torn. "Not really," she said finally, "but I suppose it's only right to share on Christmas morning."

Clint opened the door and found Jessie trying to hold off the entire Adams clan.

"One at a time," she said forcefully. Then at a plaintive look from her husband and her father-in-law, she relented. "OK, two. Luke and Harlan, you can go in."

Clint grinned at her. "You think you can keep control of this mob by yourself?"

"You ever seen a mother bear protecting her cubs?" she retorted.

"I get the picture. Call if you need backup."

"You call if you can't budge those two men out of there in five minutes."

Clint went back into the room just in time to see Angela handing their son up to her grandfather.

"Your first great-grandbaby," she said.

As he cradled the infant, Harlan's expression was filled with the kind of fierce pride and tenderness that Clint had once longed to see in his own father's face. He thought he saw Luke surreptitiously wipe a tear from his cheek before he took his own turn holding the baby. This was the kind of tight-knit family, bound by love and respect, that he'd always wanted. If Angela would only say the word, he would be a part of it.

"How're you feeling?" Harlan asked her.

"Like I've been run over by a truck," Angela admitted. "But I've never been happier. He's perfect, isn't he?"

"The most beautiful baby boy I've ever seen," Harlan declared.

"Grandpa, you say that every time there's a new baby."

He winked at her. "But this time I mean it." He

turned and held out a hand to Clint. "Congratulations, son. He's a fine-looking boy. He'll do the Adams name proud."

"With all due respect, sir, he's a Brady."

Harlan shot him a look of understanding. "Well, of course, he is. But he's an Adams, too, and we take pride in our own, no matter what name they carry." He turned back to Angela. "Now I don't want you fretting about not having this baby in a hospital. I've called the Doc and he'll be here in an hour or so to check him out. He'd already got his sled out to come to the open house, so he said he'd just start a little earlier."

"Thanks, Grandpa." She smiled at her father, who was totally absorbed in studying Clinton Daniel's perfect little face. "You know what, Daddy?"

Luke tore his gaze away from his first grandchild. "What, darlin'?"

"I'm glad I had him at home. Now I know what it must have been like for you and Mom."

Luke grinned. "Darlin', you don't know the half of it. Dani is the next best thing to an M.D., compared to me. She was also stone-cold sober. Your mama got a rotten bargain when she stumbled up to my doorstep that night."

Angela shook her head. "I don't think so. I think that's the night we really became a family, even if it did take you a while to accept the inevitable."

Luke put Clinton Daniel back in her arms, then kissed her. "I love you, baby. Now your Grandpa and I had better get out of here before your mother comes in after us."

"Could you ask her to give us a second before she sends in the next round?" Clint asked. "There's something I need to say to Angela."

"No problem," Luke said, giving his shoulder a reassuring squeeze. "You just let Jessie know when you're ready for more company."

After Luke and Harlan had left, Clint sat down on the edge of the bed, hip to hip with the woman he wanted so badly to be his wife. He reached out and gently brushed a fingertip across his son's cheek. His skin was so soft, just like his mama's.

"Clint?"

Her expression was questioning. He looked directly into her eyes and for a moment he lost his train of thought. She could do that to him, rattle him so badly he'd be tongue-tied. He swallowed hard and tried to collect his thoughts.

"There's something I should have said before," he said eventually. His gaze strayed to the baby nestled in her arms, then back to her. "Thank you. Thank you for my son. Thank you for not giving him away, the way you threatened to do."

For an instant he thought he saw disappointment flicker in her eyes, but then it vanished.

"He's my son, too," she said quietly. "I know what I said in Montana. It was awful and it was cruel. I have no excuse, except that I was upset." She smiled, but it was clearly forced. "Just like you said, though, that was in the past. I can't change it. I just want you to know that I will always take very good care of him."

"We will, angel. *We* will take very good care of him."

"And just how are we going to do that with you in Montana and me in Texas?"

Clint wanted to declare flatly that she was going to marry him and come back to Montana with him, but the stubbornness he saw simmering in her eyes warned him off making that particular declaration.

"We'll work it out."

"I will not have this child bounced back and forth between two states," she warned.

"Neither will I."

"Which leaves us with what choice?"

"I haven't got all the details figured out just yet," he admitted.

"Well, do let me know when you think you have a plan," she snapped.

"Don't be sarcastic, darlin'."

"Go tell Mother to let the others in," she said through clenched teeth.

"Are you upset, angel?" he inquired sweetly, delighted with the reaction. If he could keep her stirred up and off-kilter just a little longer, maybe he could come up with a surefire way to get her to tumble straight into his arms.

"Upset? Me? Of course not."

"Then relax your jaw before you grind all your teeth to nubs," he advised. "Your family will get the idea that you and I are having a little squabble on what should be the happiest day of our lives."

"We aren't having a little squabble," she said. "I am trying very hard not to kill you."

"Shh," he whispered. "You don't want the baby to hear you saying a thing like that about his daddy."

She regarded him sourly. "My hunch is he'll hear a lot worse before all is said and done."

Clint turned away before she could catch him grinning. The new tactic was working very nicely, he thought, very nicely indeed.

Chapter Fourteen

Clint was sticking to her like a damned burr. He was about as annoying, too, Angela thought irritably.

Maybe if he'd looked at her once, really looked at *her,* she would have felt better. Instead, he couldn't seem to take his eyes off his son.

She told herself she was glad he was so enchanted with the baby, so taken with fatherhood, but it might have been nice if just once he'd kissed her or squeezed her hand or even run a fingertip across her skin the way he did across the baby's. Every time she witnessed that trembling, awestruck touch, she was so jealous she could spit. How pitiful was that?

She glanced up as he came into her room. His gaze skimmed across her, then aimed straight for the cradle beside the bed. When he realized it was empty, then and only then did his gaze settle on her.

"Where is he?"

"Grandpa's got him downstairs showing him off."

"Again? I thought most of the state was here yesterday for the open house. They got a look at him then."

"I'm not sure, but I think he's just showing Consuela and Maritza that he can already make the baby smile."

"Didn't your mother say that was just gas?"

"Try telling that to Grandpa. He's sure Clinton Daniel is very advanced for his age," Angela said with a grin. She waited for Clint to make up an excuse and go chasing after his son. Instead, he pulled a chair up beside her bed and sat down.

"How're you feeling, angel?"

"Better than I expected. I'd be downstairs myself, but everyone insists I should be resting. Another twenty-four hours of this and I'll be stir-crazy."

"Maybe you should be thankful there are a dozen people around who are eager to take the two a.m. feedings."

She regarded him skeptically. "Are you relieved?"

Clint grinned sheepishly. "No. I want to do it myself. I jump up the minute I hear him so much as whimper, and I run smack into a traffic jam outside your door."

Angela chuckled. "You'd think I'd have the inside track. After all, I am in the same room, but even if I get to him first, someone plucks him right out of my arms and tells me to get my rest."

"They wouldn't be able to do that if you were breast-feeding," Clint said thoughtfully.

Angela hadn't even had time to consider that. Too many people had been trying to take charge in typical Adams fashion.

"You know, you are absolutely right. Everything's happened so fast, I haven't been thinking straight." She glanced at her watch and saw that it was just about time for another feeding. "Will you go down and retrieve our son?"

His expression was so eager, she wanted to laugh.

"I'll be back in a heartbeat," he promised.

"Don't let anybody talk you out of this," she warned. "They'll try."

"I'll tell them I have my instructions," he promised. "Then I'll grab him and run like hell."

Angela wished like crazy that she could be there to watch Clint repossessing his son. Nobody stood in Clint Brady's way when he was after something.

Suddenly, though, her amusement faded. Would it be like that when he decided he wanted to take the baby away from her for good? That possibility slipped into her head when she least expected it. It had been frightening enough before the baby was born, but now that he was here, now that she'd held him in her arms, she wasn't sure she could bear the thought of losing him.

By the time she heard Clint coming in the door, tears were tracking down her cheeks. He was babbling nonsense to the baby so intently that he didn't notice at first that she was crying. When he did, he stopped dead and stared.

"Angel? What is it? What's wrong? Did something happen while I was gone?"

"My baby," she pleaded, holding up her arms. "Please, I have to hold him."

He gently placed the baby in her arms, then studied her with bemusement. "Darlin', are your hormones going wacky or is something else upsetting you?"

Unwilling to explain the fear that had suddenly overwhelmed her, she shook her head. "I'll be fine. Just leave me alone with the baby."

Clinton Daniel began to whimper. Nothing she tried seemed to soothe him, which sent more tears cascading down her cheeks. Obviously she didn't know the first thing about being a good mother. Clint wasn't blind. He would see that and use it against her. Even now he was scooping the baby up and rocking him gently. The baby quieted at once, more proof that Clint would be the better parent.

"Mind telling me what upset you?" Clint asked mildly.

"It's nothing. I'm fine," she said, blotting her tears with a tissue and fighting for composure. "Let me have him. He's fussy because he's hungry."

Clint studied her worriedly. "Are you sure? Maybe this isn't the time to change the routine."

"It's hardly a routine," she said testily. "He's only twenty-four hours old."

Clint ignored her and glanced at the baby. "He's asleep again," he said softly as he placed him in his cradle. When the baby was settled, he pulled the chair a little closer to the bed. "OK, angel, tell me what's been going on in that head of yours?"

She sniffed and cursed the combination of hormonal swings and genuine terror. "Nothing."

"Tell that to someone who'll buy it."

"Clint, just go away. I'm fine."

He studied her intently, then sighed. "You aren't, by any chance, panicking that I'm going to run off to Montana with the baby, are you?"

Alarmed that he could read her so easily, she tried to feign shock. "Why would you say that?"

"Wild guess."

"Well, you can just take your guesses and go fly a kite."

He nodded, but didn't budge. "That's a productive approach."

"Are you suddenly into soul baring?" she countered. "Since when?"

"Maybe I just wised up and realized it would be smart to put all the cards on the table so there'd be no room for misunderstandings."

"Did this epiphany happen overnight?"

He grinned at her sarcasm. "No, it's been coming on for a few days now."

"OK," she said agreeably. "You go first."

"I'm not the one with the attitude."

"Maybe not, but I have a feeling my attitude might improve if you just this once said what was really on your mind. Try it."

He squirmed uncomfortably and remained as tight-lipped as ever.

"It's not so easy when the shoe's on the other foot, is it?"

"No," he conceded. "OK, I will tell you what's on my mind."

Now that he'd made the commitment to open up,

Angela got a queasy feeling in the pit of her stomach. Maybe this was a really bad way to go. Maybe she wasn't ready to hear what was going on in his head.

"I've been trying to figure out a solution to our dilemma," he said.

His response took the option of silence away from her. "Any luck?" she asked warily.

"OK…as I see it, we have three choices. Well, one of them really isn't an option, but I'll lay it on the table. We could get married, baptize our son and head back to Montana together," he suggested, ticking it off on his fingers as if it were as unimportant as an item on a grocery list.

"Or, two, we could go into court and fight over custody and wind up with some judge deciding which one of us gets to keep him. Or, three, I could leave him here with you, forget all about him and let you raise him as an Adams."

She knew with absolute certainty that this last wouldn't be an option he would ever consider. As for a custody fight, as painful as it would be, she might have gone for that if it hadn't been for the whole Hattie Jones debacle. If that came out, well, the outcome in court might very well be a toss-up. She couldn't take that chance and Clint knew it.

"Are you trying to blackmail me into marrying you?" she inquired.

"Of course not. If you have other options you'd like to throw out here, by all means go ahead."

She considered and dismissed a few that were so outrageous not even she could think of a credible way to explain them.

"OK, what if we just worked out our own custody arrangement and had a lawyer draw it up?" she suggested hopefully.

He shook his head. "Now, you see, here's where I have a problem with that. I want my son with me. I don't want him bouncing from state to state, especially now when he's just a baby."

"We could wait—"

"Until he's older? I don't think so. I'm not going to miss one single second of watching him grow up."

Nor was she. The path kept twisting right back to marriage, Angela realized. A loveless marriage. Well, loveless on his part, anyway. She might not trust him worth two hoots, but she loved him anyway, for reasons that would never make a lick of sense to her. She sighed.

"I'll think about it," she said eventually.

He nodded. "Don't take too long, angel. Time's running out."

At the warning, her temper flared. "Don't threaten me. I can always take the baby and run again. It took you eight months to find me this time. I'll make damned sure it takes longer next time."

Clint seemed startled by her threat and her vehemence. Then his gaze narrowed and his eyes darkened. "Now it seems to me that's how we got messed up in the first place, with you making wild threats and refusing to listen to reason. Don't even think about running again, angel. Something tells me this time I wouldn't be searching all alone."

"Meaning?"

"Meaning that your father and grandfather would be looking for you right alongside me."

"They'd never join forces with you," she protested, but without much conviction. They would and she knew it. Clinton Daniel was an Adams and they would never ignore his existence or do anything to keep his father—a man they clearly liked and respected—out of his life. Besides, tough as they were, they were also a couple of old romantics. They believed in happy endings. For some reason they had evidently gotten it into their heads that she and Clint belonged together.

She sighed. If only Clint felt the same, she thought wearily. If only they could recapture the emotions they had felt when they'd first met. Now, though, whatever feelings they had were colored by betrayal and fear and distrust. She wondered for the hundredth time if even love could overcome all that.

Clint had found the entire conversation with Angela about their future unsettling. As casually as he'd tried to introduce the subject of marriage, he'd been feeling anything but casual. If he'd been hoping for a sudden acknowledgment of the inevitable, though, he'd been sadly disappointed. She wasn't about to give him an inch. He did have her thinking, though, and that was something.

He gave himself until the first of the new year to make good on his scheme for getting Angela to admit she loved him. After that, with her or without her, he was going to have to head back to Montana. The thought of leaving her or his son behind made his stomach churn. His plan had to work. He was counting on it.

After another two days of sly hints and devilish taunts, he concluded that he had to be losing his touch. Just when he was dead-on certain that Angie was weakening, that she'd say yes to a proposal, she slammed on the brakes and put enough distance between them to keep him in a constant state of frustrated arousal. The woman was driving him crazy. One thing was certain, a lifetime wouldn't be long enough for him to figure her out. Meantime the clock was ticking and he was fresh out of ideas.

He'd lain awake half the night trying to assess his progress. As near as he could tell, it pretty much added up to zero.

When he staggered downstairs at the crack of dawn for some of Maritza's potent, eye-opening coffee, he found Luke there ahead of him.

"You look like something the cat dragged in," Luke observed, his expression amused. "Coffee?"

"Please."

"Baby keep you awake?"

No, it wasn't his son who was responsible for his lack of sleep. It was the kid's stubborn mother. He shook his head.

"Angela, then?"

"Bingo."

"I don't want to meddle, but if you'd like to talk about it, I can certainly listen."

The only fathers Clint had ever known well were the ones in this family. Unless he'd very much misread them, meddling was their middle name.

"Thanks, anyway, but I think I'd better handle this on my own."

Luke nodded and regarded him thoughtfully. "You told me when we first met that you intended to marry Angela. Is that still your intention?"

"Yes."

"Have you asked her?"

"I've asked her, I've told her, now I'm trying to torment her into it by avoiding the topic completely."

Luke grinned. "I'd say that's your best bet."

Clint regarded his prospective father-in-law hopefully. "Do you honestly think it'll work?"

"In this family, reverse psychology is about the only thing that does. From the time she was an itty-bitty thing, Angie has been dead-set on going her own way, just the way I did. She couldn't wait to get away from Adams territory so she could prove she was her own woman."

"But she came back."

Luke nodded. "Exactly my point. We just had to be patient and wait for her to realize this was where she belonged."

"And that took how long?"

"Six years," Luke admitted.

"I am not waiting six years to claim my son," Clint exploded. "Can you see me commuting from my ranch to here every blasted month just to get a look at them? How am I supposed to convince her of anything from hundreds of miles away?"

"Maybe your absence will do the convincing."

"We were separated for seven months. You've

been around since I caught up with her. Do you see any sign that she's mellowing?''

"Seven months is a drop in the bucket. Like I said, Angie's stubborn. We all are.'' He smiled. "But I think she's worth waiting for, don't you?''

Clint muttered a curse. "Yes,'' he conceded eventually, "but I still think it's a lousy idea. She may decide she can get along without me just fine.''

"That is a risk,'' Luke agreed.

Clint shook his head. "It's not one I'm willing to take.''

"I do have one other idea,'' Luke said, "but I'm not sure how well it will sit with you.''

"Try me. I'm a desperate man.''

"You could come to work with me.''

Clint stared at him. "Here? In Texas?''

Luke grinned. "That is where my ranch is.''

Clint was shaking his head before the words were out of Luke's mouth. "That's very kind of you, but no, I can't do that. My place is in Montana. I can't let it fall idle, and I can't expect my foreman to go on running it by himself forever.''

"Let him hire somebody to help, or let him buy you out.''

"Not a chance,'' Clint said vehemently. "I've worked all my life to own a spread of my own. I'm not walking away from it.''

"If you marry Angie, my ranch would be yours one day, anyway.''

"No,'' Clint said. "It would be hers. I appreciate your offer, but I can't accept it,'' he repeated.

"Don't be stubborn," Luke said impatiently. "One of you has to break this impasse."

"And you think I'm more likely to bend than she is?" he asked with reluctant amusement.

"Experience would suggest it," Luke concurred. "Just don't rule it out. It might be the bargaining chip you need."

"You're giving Clint bargaining chips?" Angela asked from the doorway. She was clearly exasperated with the pair of them. "Who's side are you on, anyway, Daddy?"

"Just trying to get you two off dead center," Luke said cheerfully. He stood up and dropped a kiss on his daughter's forehead. "Talk, darlin'. Nothing's solved by silence. I ought to know."

Angela sighed as he left, then shot a wary look at Clint. "Tell me about this bargaining chip."

"It's not an option," Clint said. "Are you sure you feel up to being downstairs?"

"If I'd had the baby in a hospital, they'd have kicked me out days ago. Obviously the greatest medical minds in the world don't regard childbirth as a debilitating illness."

"That isn't what I asked. Can't you ever give a straight answer?"

"My, my, you are testy this morning. Daddy must have struck a nerve."

"I could do without the dime-store psychology."

"There's a shrink in Los Pinos who charges more. Care to try her?"

"You know, angel, you are trying my patience."

She didn't appear worried about that. "So?"

"It's a very dangerous path to take," he warned.

"Really? What happens if I test your patience? Will you storm off to Montana?"

So that was her game. He regarded her with sudden amusement. "It's not going to work, angel."

"What?" she asked, her expression all innocence.

"I'm not going to blow a gasket and abandon you here, even though that appears to be what you'd like me to do. Nor are you going to goad me into a display of temper that will have your family taking your side against me."

"Oh, well," she said with a shrug. "It was worth a shot."

She began to load a plate up with waffles and fruit. When she would have skirted past him and taken a seat on the opposite side of the table, he snagged her hand. The gesture caught her off guard. It took only the slightest jerk to have her tumbling straight into his lap. He caught the precariously tilting plate in one hand and set it safely on the table. His other arm circled her waist and held her secure.

There was fire in her eyes, when he met her gaze.

"Clint Brady, don't you dare."

"Dare what?" he inquired lazily.

Color bloomed in her cheeks. "Whatever you were thinking of doing."

"I was thinking of doing this," he said quietly and slanted his mouth over hers, swallowing yet another protest.

She gave a token shove at his chest, then sighed against him. Her mouth opened to his. When the tip of her tongue grazed his lips, he almost exploded.

He'd meant to seduce her, meant to catch her by surprise with her defenses down and remind her of what they'd once had together.

Instead, she had twisted things around the way she had a habit of doing. He was the one off-kilter. He was the one who couldn't seem to catch his breath, whose blood was thundering through his veins.

Mystified by how she'd done it, he stared into eyes full of mischief, eyes that reminded him of Hattie.

Suddenly he tired of the game, all of it. Carefully he lifted Angie and set her in her own chair, then gave it a less than gentle shove to put a few inches of additional space between them.

She looked startled, then confused, then hurt. He pushed away from the table and stood, as anxious as she for once to put some distance between them.

"I'm going..." His voice trailed off. He didn't know where he was going or what he intended to do. He just had to get out of this room.

"Clint?" she whispered, her expression suddenly worried.

He didn't answer, because for the first time in his entire life he was at a loss for words.

Chapter Fifteen

A cold, empty feeling settled over Angela as she watched Clint walk away from her. He'd sounded so final when he'd said he was going, as if he'd given up, as if he might be leaving for good.

Well, that was what she wanted, wasn't it? It was what she'd prayed for, that he would go and leave her and her baby alone. What did they say? Be careful what you pray for, because it could come true.

She sat at the table staring at her cold waffle and unappetizing fruit and tried very hard to convince herself that it was best that he was heading back to Montana. If he couldn't love her back, then what was the point of prolonging this agony?

But no matter how hard she tried to convince herself to let him go, a part of her kept envisioning the loneliness of a future without him. Seattle had been awful enough with her nights filled with dreams of the man she'd left behind and her days just time to be gotten through.

At least in Seattle she had known somehow that he was still searching for her, and in some awful, perverse way that had been enough to keep her going. It had given her hope that he hadn't given up on her, that they would be together again someday.

OK, maybe she was a fool, maybe she didn't have a smidgen of sense, but she couldn't let him leave, not without telling him how she felt. If he still wanted to go, if he couldn't bring himself to ever trust her again, well, so be it. At least she would have tried. Not trying would doom her to a lifetime of what ifs.

She hurried to the stairs, cursing the fact that there were so many of them and that she was so darned stiff and sore. It seemed to take her forever to get to the top.

She rushed straight to Clint's room and knocked on his door. When he didn't answer, she ignored everything she'd ever been taught about privacy and threw the door open. He wasn't there. In fact, there was no sign of him at all. With her heart thudding dully, she peered into his closets and released a sigh when she saw that his clothes were still inside.

He hadn't left, then, but she was sure it was only a matter of time.

Where could he be, though? A smile touched her lips as she came up with the only logical answer. Closing his door gently behind her, she crossed the hall to her own room where she'd left a doting Consuela keeping an eye on the baby. She opened the door, then hesitated, immobilized by the scene before her.

Clint was there, in a rocker by the window, the baby cradled in his arms. Clinton Daniel looked so tiny against that massive chest, so tiny and so very safe and secure. The picture brought a lump to her throat.

Clint glanced up then and his gaze locked with hers. "Quiet, angel. I just got him to sleep."

She tiptoed across the room and sat on the edge of the bed. "How'd you get Consuela out of here?"

"I told her I was starving. She went to fix me a hearty breakfast."

Angela stared. "But you just ate."

He shrugged. "So, I'll eat again. I figured it was the safest bet for getting some time alone with my son."

Angela forced herself to keep a light note in her voice when she asked the question that had been plaguing her. "Are you saying goodbye?"

The question seemed to take him by surprise. He searched her face intently, then asked, "Would it matter to you if I was?"

She swallowed hard against the tide of vulnerability that washed over her just thinking about giving a truthful answer. There was no choice, though. She had promised herself she would deal with him honestly, something she should have done from the first.

"Yes," she said softly. "It would matter to me."

"Why, angel?"

This was it, then. It was time for the truth, the

whole truth and nothing but the truth. "Because I'm in love with you."

A knowing smile began at the corners of his mouth and spread. "Oh, really?"

She nodded.

"Say it again," he prodded. "Your father's said it. Your mother's said it. Even your uncle's told me that, but I want to hear it again from you."

"Look, dammit…"

He grinned. "That's more like it. You were sounding a little out of character there for a minute, all docile and sweet natured."

She regarded him ruefully. "I'm afraid I will never be docile."

"Thank goodness."

"But I will be honest, Clint. I swear to you that there will never be another lie between us." She searched his face, trying to gauge his reaction. "Is that enough?"

"Enough for what?"

"Enough to make you stay, enough for you to trust me again."

He sighed. "Angel, trust will always come hard for us. We got off to a rocky start on that score."

Her pulse seemed to slow at his dire prediction. It was her fault, too. The unforgettable, unforgivable Hattie Jones fiasco would always stand squarely between them.

"I see," she said, defeated.

He reached over and tucked a finger under her chin. "No, darlin', I don't think you do. Just because you have to work at something doesn't mean it's bad. I've always worked for everything that's important to me. The way I see it, nothing's more important than our future. I'll do whatever it takes to see that we overcome every obstacle the past has put in front of us. What about you? Do you believe our family's worth fighting for?''

Angela blinked back tears. She tried to form an answer, but the words simply wouldn't come. Finally she just nodded.

''Was that a yes?'' he asked.

''Yes,'' she said, then lifted her gaze to his. Tears blurred her vision, but her voice was firm when she repeated, ''Yes.''

He gave a nod of satisfaction, then grinned. ''Angel, you never asked, but there's something I think you ought to know.''

A fresh burst of trepidation had her heart skipping a beat. ''What's that?''

''This isn't just about the baby. It never has been,'' he said quietly. ''I do love you. I tried not to, but it was like trying not to breathe. If my arms weren't occupied at the moment, I'd show you just how much.''

She grinned. ''I could put the baby back in his cradle,'' she offered.

''And risk having him start fussing again? I don't think so.''

Despite Clint's protests, she took the baby anyway and settled him into the beautiful cradle his father had bought for him. He didn't so much as stir.

''At least your son has his priorities straight,'' she

said, slipping onto Clint's lap. "Now let's work on yours."

"There's nothing wrong with my priorities," he grumbled, but he didn't complain when she feathered kisses across his forehead, then sought out his mouth.

Angela kissed him with all of the yearning and passion she'd been saving up during their months of separation. She could feel the hard ridge of his arousal beneath her hip and the thundering of his heart where her hand rested against his chest. His heat and the purely masculine scent of him surrounded her, carried her back to another time and another place when the two of them had been all that mattered.

"I do love you," she whispered against his lips.

"I know."

"Always did."

"I know."

She pulled back and scowled at him. "You don't know everything, Clint Brady."

"Maybe not, but I know the only things that matter. You and me, that boy of ours, family, ranching."

"See," she said triumphantly. "Your priorities are improving already."

"That's because I have such an outstanding teacher. Your motivational skills are excellent. Anytime you'd care to give me another lesson, I'm up for it."

"Maybe we'd better wait for our honeymoon for the lesson I have in mind."

His expression sobered. "Darlin', I'm not so sure we can fit a honeymoon in just now. I've already been away too long."

She was sure he was prepared to offer a whole laundry list of reasons why their honeymoon would have to be postponed, so she silenced him with another slow, lingering kiss.

"On the other hand," he began, his voice husky.

"If you'd let me get a word in here," she said, "I think I have a solution."

"By all means."

"We could honeymoon in Montana. It's certainly the most romantic spot I've ever seen."

"You want to honeymoon on the ranch?"

"Why not?"

"For one thing it won't be much of a honeymoon with me working and the baby with us."

"Consuela can look after the baby and I can help you work."

"Darlin', far be it from me to turn down such a generous offer, but you do have a very strange notion of what a honeymoon ought to be."

"Maybe more people ought to start their marriages the way they intend to live them. Could be honeymoons just set up a lot of false expectations that get ruined when the day-to-day realities set in."

"An interesting philosophy, but won't you be disappointed years from now when our kids ask what we did on our honeymoon and all you can tell them is that we worked our ranch?"

She shook her head. "No, because that's how we're going to make it *our* ranch, with me doing my part from the beginning."

He still looked skeptical.

"I mean it, Clint. This is what I want."

"OK," he said eventually, "but on one condition."

"What's that?"

"For our fiftieth anniversary, when we've turned the ranch over to our kids, we go around the world. We will make love in every romantic spot you've ever dreamed about."

"The only romantic spot I've ever dreamed of is in your arms," she confessed.

"Then we're off to a good start, angel, because I'm never, ever letting you go."

It was amazing how many strings could be pulled when the Adams name was mentioned, Clint concluded as he watched White Pines being transformed into an indoor garden for a New Year's Day wedding. The same crowd that had shown up on Christmas Day, despite a blizzard, was scheduled to return today, despite the competition from football and New Year's Eve celebration hangovers.

A part of him felt guilty that he would be taking Angela and his son away from all this, but she had assured him over and over that Montana was where she truly wanted to be.

Luke had grumbled at the choice, but had finally agreed that he would send Consuela along with them to help with the baby for the first month, just as Angela had predicted he would. Since the housekeeper rarely let the boy out of her sight now, Clint wondered what would happen when the time came for her to return to Texas. What the heck. Maybe they could persuade her to stay.

He gazed into the mirror and tried to reconcile the image of the man in the tuxedo with Clint Brady. He was so spiffed up he hardly recognized the once-poor cowboy who'd never paid a lick of attention to his clothes, if the money could be better spent on feed for the cattle.

"You ready, son?" Luke called out.

Clint opened the door to his room and found his future father-in-law and Harlan pacing the hallway. They, too, seemed to be anxious to get out of these monkey suits and back into working clothes.

He met Harlan's gaze evenly. "Thank you, sir, for agreeing to be my best man."

"Son, nothing could have made me prouder. I know if your family'd been able to get here on such short notice, you'd have asked one of your brothers, but I'm glad to fill in."

"No," Clint said. "You deserve the honor. You've been more than fair to me from the minute we met. A lot of men in your position wouldn't have been. The same goes for you, Luke. I hope I'll never let you down."

"Just keep our gal happy," Harlan said. "That's all we ask."

"Did I hear someone mention me," Angela called out from behind her door.

"Don't you dare open that door, darlin'. It's bad luck for the groom to see the bride on their wedding day," Harlan said.

"According to family legend, that didn't stop you and Janet from having a little chat before your ceremony. The way I remember it, you walked down the aisle together."

"Don't live your life by my example, girl."

She opened the door. "I can't think of a better one, Grandpa."

Clint would have closed his eyes or turned away just because of the silly superstition, if he'd been able to. Instead, though, he couldn't seem to tear his gaze away from the lovely vision before him. She had opted for simplicity in a narrow dress of white velvet edged with satin. From the front it was as innocent and sedate as any bride's ought to be.

And then she turned and he caught sight of the back…what there was of it. A deep vee plunged practically to her waist, exposing an almost indecent amount of soft skin.

"Aren't you afraid you'll get cold?" he asked wryly.

"Not if you're doing your job," she said tartly, and sashayed down the stairs ahead of them all.

So, he thought as he followed her, the mischievous Hattie lived, lurking somewhere inside his angel. It ought to make the next fifty years or so damned interesting.

Epilogue

Angela sorted through the stack of mail Clint had picked up in town and seized the pale yellow envelope from home. She'd been waiting for days for a long, chatty letter from her mother. After all those years she'd spent away, knowing nothing, she could no longer seem to get her fill of news now that she'd been there at Christmas. Phone calls satisfied some of her curiosity, but she liked receiving mail. She could hold it in her hands and practically feel the bond with her mother. She could read it over and over. And, of course, her mother always tucked in snapshots from the latest family gathering. There had been a huge Memorial Day barbecue just the week before.

Sure enough, there were three or four pictures from the celebration. The one of her parents stealing a kiss, thinking they were unobserved, no doubt, made her smile. Another of Grandpa Harlan flipping huge steaks on the grill and waving Janet away had her laughing out loud. He would never trust her when it came to cooking. He'd always said she could ruin a hard-boiled egg without half trying.

"A letter from your mom?" Clint asked, pausing beside her to drop a kiss on her forehead.

"With pictures," she said, displaying them for him. "I'll bet Dad didn't know anyone with a camera was nearby when he planted that kiss on Mom."

"I don't think he'd care," Clint said. "Personally, I love seeing the affection between them. I hope we still have that when we're old and gray."

"We'd better," Angela warned.

"Then let's stay in practice," Clint suggested. He sat in an over-stuffed chair by the fire and held out his arms. "Come here and read the letter to me."

She went to him eagerly and, after snuggling into his arms, she began to read:

"Dearest Angie,
We all loved the picture of baby Clint on the horse with his daddy. He's so big for five months, and he's the spitting image of his father. Quite the little cowboy. Please bring him to Texas soon so we can all fuss over him.

"Life goes on here. Everyone misses you. Sharon Lynn and Kyle Mason are definitely an item. She still credits you with getting them out of limbo and into each other's arms. After all those years in Dallas, Jenny has decided to come home and teach in Los Pinos. Harlan Patrick and

Justin are already studying college catalogues and Janet swears Lizzy will never, ever go away to school, if what she hears about college campuses these days is true.

"I wish you could have been here for the Memorial Day festivities. Your grandfather was in his glory, but I must say I think he's slowing down just a bit. I worry about what will happen when we lose him. He's the glue that holds all of us together."

Angela glanced at the snapshot again and looked for the signs of aging her mother had seen. It seemed to her that her grandfather looked as robust as ever. She continued reading:

"Harlan is such a remarkable man, please do make sure your son has a chance to get to know him. Maybe we can all be together again this year at Christmas. Of course with no babies due, it will probably be boring.

"Whoops, almost forgot. We think that Dani has met *the* man. So far, though, she is being stubbornly resistant to the idea. Typical Adams, though in her case at least I understand what's behind her reluctance. Maybe, if you come, you can give her a push. Until then, much love,

Mom."

Angela sighed and folded the letter.

Clint regarded her sympathetically. "Homesick, huh?"

"I was so sure I would never, ever feel homesick," she said. "I have everything I ever wanted right here. You, our son, a home."

"I could try to make you forget about it," he offered, his hand closing over her breast.

She grinned. "I'll bet you could, too."

His fingers stroked and teased until the images of home almost faded. Then he sighed.

"It's not working, is it? Your body's with me, but your heart is back in Texas."

"Afraid so."

"Then we'll go home," he said. "Christmas? Thanksgiving? You pick."

She regarded him speculatively. He seemed to be in an indulgent mood. "The Fourth of July is just around the corner," she suggested hopefully. "We could take a long weekend. Grandpa would send the plane."

"You know, Mrs. Brady, you have absolutely no patience."

"Sorry," she said without much real contrition in her voice.

"And I have absolutely no willpower when it comes to refusing you something you want. The Fourth it is. You call and I'll start supper."

She wound her arms around his neck instead. "How did I ever get so lucky?"

She lowered her head and kissed him. She began working the buttons on his shirt, then slid her hands inside over heated flesh and solid muscles. Clint moaned as her caresses became more and more insistent. When she reached for the snap on his jeans, he covered her hand with his and looked directly into her eyes.

"I thought you were anxious to make that call."

She shook her head. "It can wait. Some things definitely take priority."

Clint stood up then and shucked off his shirt and boots and jeans with an efficiency that still startled her. She grinned at him. "Afraid I'll change my mind?"

"Nope, just encouraging you to hurry up and get naked, too."

"Unlike you, I do think there are some things in life worth savoring. Stripping happens to be one of them. Why don't you just stretch out on the bed and I'll show you what I mean?"

"I don't think so," he said, already fiddling with the buttons on her blouse.

As clever as he was with his own, he fumbled with hers. She'd always found that endearing somehow, proof that she could rattle him when little else in life could. Once in a while a woman deserved to have an edge with a man.

He didn't wait for her to finish undressing before his hands were everywhere, caressing, probing, pleasuring. She was breathless long before they tumbled into bed together, straining toward a first climax before he even touched the moist, sensitive core of her. With a quick, skimming stroke, he sent her over the edge, then settled back to take his time and do it all over again.

Her breath was coming in ragged gasps, her body was slick with perspiration and fiery with need by the time he slipped inside her, filling her up, joining with her in a way that made her feel whole and never failed to amaze her.

His movements were slow, languorous, as if they had all the time in the world, when the rapidly spiraling of sensation inside her said otherwise. With his gaze fastened to hers, he seemed able to tell the precise instant when one more stroke would have been too much.

"Not yet, darlin'," he said and stilled inside her.

Frustration and need had her thrusting her hips up, searching for release, demanding it. If she could have, she would have flipped him onto his back and ridden him, exulting in the sensations that never failed to astound her.

But there was pure joy in this, too, in letting him control the pace, in delaying the sweet, sweet end for as long as possible. She settled back to wait, to prove that she could be patient when it counted, but one tiny movement of his hips, the touch of his lips closing over her breast pitched her right back to a physical intensity that was just shy of exquisite torture.

And again, he drew back. He touched a finger to her chin, stroked a thumb across her lips, drawing her attention. "I love you, angel."

"I love you."

He smiled at that, then rolled to his back without releasing her. "Why don't you have your wicked way with me, then?"

Settled intimately astride him, she said, "I thought that's what I was doing."

He linked his hands behind his head. ''Not so's I noticed.''

She laughed at the hint of challenge in his tone and the spark of pure mischief in his eyes. ''Why, you low-down, rotten scoundrel,'' she muttered, tweaking the hairs on his chest until he yelped. She laved the same spot with her tongue and had his breath catching in his throat and all signs of teasing fading from his eyes.

When she began to move her hips, his gaze locked with hers.

''Now that's more like it, darlin'.''

''I'm so glad you approve,'' she said, her voice husky.

And then she was lost again to sensation, to the rasp of his day-old beard against her skin, to the hitching sound of his breathing and the rush of his blood when she touched a finger to the pulse at the base of his neck. Then all she felt was the heat, his and hers, so much heat that she was sure they would be consumed by flames.

The slick friction of their bodies melding was as new and thrilling today as it had been on the night they met. Familiarity and commitment had only made it better, had only deepened the bond that was renewed each time they made love.

There was trust now, too, trust that would last beyond this moment, trust that would carry them through eternity. It had been slow in coming, but Angela felt it each time they looked into each other's eyes, each time they made love with an abandon that could only come with honesty and hard-won faith in what they had together.

"Come with me, angel," Clint whispered. "Come with me now."

Angela smiled as they reached the peak together, both of them rocked by shattering sensation.

She collapsed against his chest, breathing hard and feeling like a million bucks.

"I don't think I'll ever be able to move again," she said eventually.

"I'm afraid one of us is going to have to," Clint responded.

"Why?"

"Our son is calling. It's dinnertime. And he's clearly impatient."

Angela struggled to untangle herself from her husband and the sheets. "I guess I'm just going to have to teach that boy to cook."

"You might have to wait until he's old enough to reach the stove," Clint pointed out. He kissed the tip of her nose. "I'll cook. You call your parents and tell them we're coming home for the next big barbecue."

"Not home," Angela said, her hand on his cheek. "This is home. I'll tell them we're coming for a visit."

A slow smile spread across his face and lit his eyes. If she'd known how much it would mean to him to hear her say the word, she would have said it much sooner. Texas and White Pines would never be far from her thoughts. Her family would never be far from her heart. But this *was* home now. It always would be.

As for their son, though she vowed never to say as much to him, he was their littlest angel, the brightest one in the universe. He would grow up knowing how special he was, but she prayed he would never feel the inadvertent pressures of living up to expectations.

And this man, she thought in wonder, watching Clint as he retrieved his scattered clothes, he was far more than the father of her child. She could admit it now, to herself and to him. He was her heart and soul.

* * * * *

NATURAL BORN TROUBLE

Chapter One

The day had already been too long and it wasn't even noon.

Dani Adams sank down into the chair behind her desk and vowed to catch a quick nap before her afternoon appointments. She'd been up since three a.m. with an emergency, a dog that had been struck by a drunk driver on a flat stretch of Texas highway just outside of town.

The sheriff's urgent call, when he was already en route, had awakened her. Minutes later, he had brought the bruised and bloodied animal in, and she'd worked for hours trying to save it. The poor old thing was hanging on by a thread.

She probably should have put him to sleep, but every time she thought of his owner, eighty-year-old Betty Lou Parks, she balked. Betty Lou adored that

dog. He was her constant companion, riding beside
her in the rusty old car Betty Lou drove into town
once a week to pick up groceries. Dani had heard the
anxiety and choked-back tears in Betty Lou's quavery
voice when she'd called to check on her beloved pet
and that had been that. Dani had promised to do everything she could to save the old woman's precious
Honeybunch.

Honeybunch, she thought, smiling. The poor dog
was probably embarrassed every time his master
called to him in public. Mostly proud German shepherd, he had just enough mixed blood in him to give
him a slightly whimsical look. Dani knew better than
to be fooled by his appearance, though. He was
fiercely protective of Betty Lou, which was probably
why her children hadn't insisted long ago that she
move into town from the isolated house where she
still planted a garden every single spring.

Dani suspected most of her fee would come from
that garden. Tomatoes, potatoes, beans, squash, herbs.
Betty Lou raised them all, more than enough to last
her through winter and to barter for some of her other
needs. She was as independent now as she had been
fifty years ago when her husband had died and left
her alone with three small children to care for. Dani
admired her resilience. She could use a little of it now
just to get her through the rest of the day.

Sighing when her mind kept whirling and sleep
eluded her, she picked up the batch of mail her assistant had left on her desk and out of habit sorted it
into neatly organized stacks. Bills went into one pile,
junk mail into another, professional newsletters and

magazines into a third. When she came to a cheap business-sized envelope addressed in childish printing, her heart skidded to a halt. Automatic and too-familiar tears stung her eyes.

She already knew what she would find inside, a crayon-bright picture and a precisely lettered note. She had a whole drawer full of them, all from Rob Hilliard's two girls, children who had almost been hers.

Even after two years, every time one of these envelopes came it tore her apart inside all over again. Walking away from Robin and Amy when things hadn't worked out with their father had been the hardest thing Dani had ever had to do. For a time the envelopes had stacked up, unopened, because to see these expressions of love and know that she would never be a parent to the children who created them broke her heart. Phone calls left her shattered for hours, sometimes days.

Had she and Rob been married, had she been a real mother to the girls, at least there would have been the kind of custody arrangements that came with divorce. The girls would be with her part—if not all—of the time.

As it was, she had no rights, no legal standing whatsoever in their lives, just the powerful bond of a love that had deepened over the four years she had been with their father. Four years, during which expectations of permanence had been raised. An engagement that had sealed that expectation. Wedding plans had consumed Dani's thoughts and enchanted the girls.

And then it had all come tumbling down. Rob had met someone else and broken the engagement just weeks before the scheduled wedding date. Dani had been crushed. The girls, understanding none of what was going on, had been devastated when Dani had moved out of the house and left town.

Now distance and the attitude of Rob's young and insecure girlfriend precluded even the most casual of visits. Tiffany thought the girls would adjust more readily if the break were clean. Tiffany thought... Tiffany thought... Dani hadn't seen much evidence that Tiffany even had a brain.

As soon as the sarcastic criticism surfaced, Dani chided herself for being uncharitable. It was hardly Tiffany's fault that Rob had no spine to speak of.

At any rate, contact had been limited to whatever calls and drawings the seven-year-old and five-year-old girls could manage. They'd been astonishingly ingenious about it, too.

Now, though, they were slowly adapting to the change. The vows to hate Tiffany forever and ever were less frequent. So were the calls and notes to Dani. The spaces in between almost gave her time to heal, but it took only an envelope like this one to rip the wound open all over again and leave her feeling raw and vulnerable. How did adoptive mothers stand it when courts ripped their children from their arms to return them to the natural parents? How did they survive the loss? she wondered. How did they make the love stop? Or fill the empty space inside their heart?

For a moment she debated leaving the envelope

unopened, but there seemed little point to it. Sooner or later she would open it anyway. Like removing a bandage with a sudden yank, this would be quicker, if no less painful.

The sheet of paper inside was a piece of Rob's expensive, embossed business stationery, she noted with amusement. He would probably have a cow if he knew they'd gotten into it and used it for coloring.

She studied the page, her eyes misty. Amy had clearly done the drawing. It was as vibrantly colorful as the little girl herself. A shaky American flag predominated, dwarfing two stick-figure children— Robin and Amy, according to the names neatly printed under them by the older Robin. Each child was holding what Dani assumed were meant to be sparklers.

"Happy Fourth of July" was printed across the top in red and blue letters. "We Miss You" had been added in bright pink and purple at the bottom. "Love, Robin" was as precise as a seven-year-old hand could make it. Amy's signature was twice the size of her sister's and bore little evidence of any understanding of capital and small letters.

"Oh, babies," Dani murmured. "I miss you, too." She stared at the picture for as long as she could bear it, then tucked it into the drawer with all the others. She would answer the note tonight, though she had no idea if the petty Tiffany allowed the children to see the occasional cards and letters Dani sent to them so they would know that she still thought of them and loved them, that she hadn't deliberately abandoned them.

The knock on her office door had her hurriedly wiping away telltale traces of tears.

"Yes, Maggie, what is it?"

Her nineteen-year-old temporary assistant poked her head in. She was clearly fighting a smile. "I'm really sorry to interrupt you. I know you need a break after the night you had, but we have an emergency up front."

"It's not Honeybunch, is it?" she asked, already pulling her white coat on over her slacks and short-sleeved blouse.

"No, no, it's nothing like that," Maggie soothed in a calming tone that proved what a good vet she, too, would make one day. "I think you'd better come and see for yourself."

Dani followed her assistant down the corridor to the reception area. Even before they got there, she could hear two voices. They were arguing. They were also very young.

"Told you not to take him out of the bowl," one was saying.

"I didn't," the other replied. "Not for long anyway."

Dani glanced at Maggie. The teen's lips were twitching with amusement again.

"I can't go back out there," Maggie said, drawing to a halt outside one of the treatment rooms. "I know I'll laugh and obviously this is a very serious crisis to them."

"Let me guess," Dani said. "We're not talking a puppy or a kitten here, are we?"

"Afraid not."

"A goldfish?" Dani guessed.

"You got it."

"Dead?"

"Oh, yes."

Dani closed her eyes and sighed. "You could have handled this, you know."

"Not me. I haven't even finished pre-vet school," Maggie said. "Besides, they wanted a real veterinarian. Said they could pay, too. Fifty cents."

"Terrific. Just terrific."

Plastering a smile on her face, she stepped into the reception area and confronted two boys, no more than eight, identical twins from the look of them. Both had spiky blond hair and freckles and the same front tooth missing. If she hadn't made up her mind never to let another child get to her, these two would have stolen her heart on the spot. As it was, she cloaked herself in a brisk, professional demeanor.

"I'm Dr. Dani Adams," she told them. "What seems to be the problem?"

"You're a girl," one of them said, eyes wide.

"Yeah, we wanted a real doctor," the other stated firmly. "Not a nurse."

Chauvinist little devils, she concluded, trying very hard not to bristle.

"I am a doctor. You can see my license, if you like. It's hanging over my desk."

The two boys looked at each other, seemed to reach a silent, joint conclusion, then nodded.

"I guess it's okay," one said with unflattering reluctance. "Show her, Zachary."

A smudged little hand emerged from a pocket.

Zachary opened his fist to display a sizable, but very dead goldfish.

"We think he might be a goner," Zachary said, tears obviously threatening. "Can you save him?"

Dani hunkered down in front of them and took the patient. "I won't lie to you. It's serious, all right. Let me take him in the back and see if there's anything I can do."

The second twin regarded her suspiciously. "Can we come?"

"I think you'd better wait out here," she said. "I promise I won't be long."

Fortunately, she had learned long ago working for the last town vet to expect anything. She kept a drawer filled with suitable pet "coffins." In the back she placed the dead goldfish atop some cotton in an old jewelry box, waited a suitable length of time, then started for the front, struggling to keep her expression serious. Maggie was having no such luck, though she was trying to stifle her chuckles.

"Hush," Dani whispered as she passed.

Back out front she found the two boys once again trying to place blame. Worried gazes shot up when she returned. At the sight of the box, lower lips trembled and tears clearly threatened.

"He's a goner, isn't he?" Zachary asked pitifully.

"I'm sorry," she said quietly, handing the box to him. He took it gingerly, clearly more intimidated now that he knew the fish was indeed dead. "It was too late. There was nothing I could do. Goldfish really don't do very well outside their bowls."

The indignant owner of the goldfish poked his brother. "Told you, dimwit."

"Listen, Joshua Michael Jenkins, you don't know everything," Zachary said, punching his brother back and allowing the boxed-up goldfish to topple to the floor in the process.

Dani stepped between them and quieted them with a hand on each boy's shoulder. "Hey, you two, don't start taking this out on each other. It was an accident, I'm sure."

"It wasn't no accident," Joshua said, scowling. "He was jealous 'cause my goldfish lived and his didn't, so he killed it on purpose."

"Did not," Zachary said, trying to slip around Dani to throw a punch.

In his haste, he barely missed the box he'd dropped. Dani retrieved it. No telling what would happen if he squished his brother's fish on top of having killed it.

Dani hunkered down again and circled an arm around both waists, forcing them to remain where they were. "Were these your only pets?"

"Yeah," Joshua said. "Dad said until we could learn to be responsible and take care of a couple of goldfish, he wasn't getting us no puppy."

Dani winced at the appalling grammar, but figured someone better qualified than she was should be correcting that. "He's right, you know. If you own animals, it's very important that you take good care of them. It is a responsibility."

"We'll probably never get a dog now," Joshua grumbled. "And it's all your fault, dimwit. I coulda had one. It wasn't my goldfish that died, not until you killed it.''

"Maybe there's a way you could change your father's mind," Dani said.

They eyed her skeptically.

"I don't know," Zachary said. "Dad's pretty strict. Once he lays down the law, he won't budge for nothing.''

"How?" Joshua asked, clearly more willing to consider any option that would get him the puppy he wanted.

"Well, you see, I have a lot of kittens around here. People bring their cats by all the time, and I try to find good homes for them and their babies.''

Joshua appeared mildly intrigued. "Kittens, huh? What does that have to do with us?''

"I was thinking that perhaps your dad might let you bring one home on a trial basis until I could find a real home for it. It would be temporary, of course. I know it's not a substitute for the puppy you want, but it would help me out and you two could prove to your dad that you are responsible enough for a puppy. What do you think?''

"Could we see the kittens?" Zachary asked.

"Sure.''

Dani led the way through the clinic to the entry into her own living quarters. Francie III, a descendant of her own first cat, lounged under the kitchen table, where she had the benefit of the cool linoleum and a slanted beam of sunlight.

"Is that the one?" Joshua asked, eyes wide. "She's really, really big.''

"She's expecting babies," Dani explained.

At the sound of her voice, more cats scrambled through the doorway, skidding on the waxed floor, then meowing plaintively for food as they wound themselves around her ankles. The cats gave wide berth to the two boys. Maybe on some subliminal pet network they'd heard about the goldfish.

Three kittens, not quite as fast as the adults, nor as discriminating, picked their way daintily toward two pairs of fascinating new sneaker-clad feet and sniffed.

The boys peered down at the scrambling, tumbling heap of kittens, two gray-and-white, one orange with white paws.

"I like the orange one," Zachary said.

"Me, too," Joshua said. "He looks like a tiger."

"It's a girl," Dani said.

"Does she have a name?"

"Not yet, but I'll bet she'd really like one. You two could name her, if you're interested."

"Mittens," Zachary said at once.

"That's a dumb name," Joshua protested.

"Is not. Her paws are white, aren't they?" Zachary bent down to pick up the kitten, but Joshua promptly nudged him aside.

"Don't even think about touching her," he said. "You'll probably squish her or something."

"Will not."

"Will, too."

"Hey," Dani protested. "If you two can't get along and work together to take care of her, then I can't suggest to your dad that he allow you to watch out for her for me."

"You're going to talk to our dad?" Zachary asked, wide-eyed.

"Of course. I can't send the kitten home with you without his permission. If you'd like me to, I'll call him right now."

"At work?" Joshua asked, then shook his head. "I don't think that's such a good idea. He's not in a very good mood when he's at work."

"Besides I don't think he'd like it very much if he knew Paolina brought us into town," Zachary added.

"Paolina?"

"She's our new housekeeper," Joshua explained.

"Yeah, and she's stayed a whole two weeks, longer than any of the others."

"I see." Dani hid a smile at the telling remarks. "You let me worry about your dad. I think he'll understand that this was a crisis. Do you know the number?" She picked up a nearby portable phone.

"Sure," Zachary said and recited it.

The familiar number had her pausing. "Your dad's in the oil business?"

"How'd you know that?" Joshua asked.

"I know someone who works there," she said carefully, not mentioning that the someone was her stepfather, nor that he owned the company. "What's your dad's name?"

"Duke Jenkins."

Ah, Dani thought, so these boys belonged to the mysterious Duke Jenkins, whose reputation in the field had been legendary. She'd overheard Jordan talking about how badly he hated the thought of losing him on exploration, but what an asset he would be anywhere in the company.

She'd also heard that the man was chafing at being chained to a desk. She suspected these two had something to do with his decision to take a safer assignment. Or perhaps his wife had demanded it. Then, again, hadn't she heard he was a widower? Or was he divorced? Either would explain why he and not their mother was making the decisions about their pets and why this new housekeeper was so important.

She hit speed dial for the company headquarters a few blocks away. Originally the company had been in Houston, but her mother had persuaded Jordan to relocate years ago. When the operator answered, Dani greeted her, then asked for Duke Jenkins.

"Don't tell me you've staked him out already," the young woman said with an audible sigh of regret.

"Actually, I'm calling on a business matter," Dani reassured her.

"Well, you're out of luck, hon. He's in with Jordan and last time I checked the rafters were about to blow straight off the building. I wouldn't buzz in there for the president of the U.S.A."

Donna Kelso was not easily intimidated, nor was Jordan the kind of man who tolerated much insubordination. Dani could only imagine just how explosive the meeting going on in her stepfather's office was. If Duke Jenkins was foolish enough to take Jordan on, he was either a very brave man or he operated on pure arrogance. If Jordan hadn't fired him in the first five minutes, then Duke Jenkins was a very valuable company asset. Dani knew better than to get caught in the middle.

"Never mind," she said hurriedly. "I'll catch up with him later. Thanks, Donna."

"You bet. You want me to leave him a message, say in a day or two when things cool down?"

"No, thanks."

She hung up and turned to see two very disappointed faces.

"I guess we don't get a kitten, huh?" Zachary asked.

"Not right away," she said. "But I will talk to your dad. I promise."

"When?" Joshua asked. "Tonight? He's always home by suppertime. You could come over. That would be best. Dad would never yell at a lady in person. He says it's not proper to hit girls and yell at them and stuff."

Dani wasn't at all sure she wanted to meet the formidable Duke Jenkins on his home turf, especially when his mood was likely to be surly. Still, she really did have to find a home for the kittens. She had a hunch a face-to-face chat with Mr. Jenkins was the only way these boys were going to get permission to bring one home. Besides, it might be interesting to see what sort of scars Duke Jenkins bore from his battle with Jordan. She'd known few men who dared to stand up to him and lived to tell about it, other than her uncles and grandfather, of course.

"I'll stop by as soon as I close up for the day," she agreed.

"Will you bring the kitten with you?" Joshua asked hopefully.

She shook her head. "That might be a tactical mistake, boys. I'd better talk to your dad first."

"He would probably like Mittens a lot if he saw her," Zachary argued.

"Trust me," Dani said, thinking that Zachary's tactical approach was very reminiscent of one she had used quite often at his age. Now she reacted with an adult's sense of caution. "We should get his permission first."

Let the man at least think he was in charge. It was a motto that made sense to her. It didn't mean he had to actually be in charge, as long as he thought he was. Being around a whole clan of master manipulators, most of them hardheaded males, had given her an edge on understanding the masculine thought process. She doubted Duke Jenkins veered too far from the same mold. In fact, Donna's report had just pretty much confirmed it.

"Dr. Adams?" Joshua asked, sounding suspiciously meek.

"Yes?" She noticed his gaze was pinned to the kittens again.

Blue eyes lifted and regarded her hopefully. "As long as you're going to talk to Dad anyway, do you think maybe you could see if we could keep all three kittens?" Joshua asked. "One for me and one for Zack and one for Dad."

"I don't know," she said. "Maybe we should start with just one. Besides, your dad might not want a kitten of his own."

"I'll bet he would," Zachary said. "He's kinda lonely now that Mom's gone."

Definitely another budding manipulator, she thought, fighting the salty sting of tears at the hitch in his voice. Probably a trait he'd picked up at his father's knee. That reference to his mom was definitely calculated to stir sympathy.

No problem, though. She was an Adams, by name and upbringing, if not by birth. When it came to manipulation, she had learned from the best authorities in the whole state of Texas, if not the entire world. Resisting Duke Jenkins and his sons would be a snap.

Then she recalled Donna's awestruck reaction at the mention of Duke's name. Maybe now would be a good time to start praying that she wasn't unwittingly about to start flirting with disaster.

Chapter Two

Duke Jenkins was mad enough to bend a steel beam in two, preferably around Jordan Adams's neck. The man was stubborn, arrogant and, without question, the best oil man in the state of Texas. Maybe in the world. Duke figured he was no slouch himself, which suggested that maybe once, just once, Jordan ought to listen to him.

They were going to be wasting time and money drilling that new field. Every instinct he possessed told him that. He didn't give two hoots about the ream of geological surveys piled up on his desk. If he'd been able to get out there and look things over first-hand, run the dirt through his fingers, get a deep whiff of the scent of it, he would have been able to put some real strength into his arguments.

As it was, he was going with his gut, instinct honed

by years of wildcatting. Jordan preferred cold, hard facts. Scientific facts, which in this instance Duke suspected had been doctored to someone else's benefit.

If he'd had somebody to look after the boys, Duke would have given Jordan all the facts he wanted. He would have been on a plane in a heartbeat, doing what he did best: finding oil and bringing it in, making them all richer.

Not that he cared all that much about the money. Most of his life he hadn't had a lot, hadn't needed much. Now he just wanted to insure that his sons would have a good future, a college education if they wanted it, though getting them through elementary school was proving to be challenge enough.

At any rate, he would trade the potential profits for the pure adrenaline rush of bringing in a new gusher any day.

Instead, he was surrounded by paperwork, mounds of it, most of which didn't matter a tinker's damn in the overall scheme of things as near as he could tell.

Oh, how he hated pushing papers around on a desk, he thought, staring irritably at the mostly untouched piles of it still awaiting some action or another. Well, today he'd had enough of it, he concluded, grabbing his jacket and heading for the door. If he hung around another few minutes, he might storm straight back into Jordan's office and quit, something he didn't have the right to do with two kids depending on him. The twins were the reason he'd made the move to Los Pinos in the first place. He had to give this major life-style overhaul a chance to work for their sakes.

Twenty minutes later, he had the top on the classic

convertible down, the car radio was blaring a George Strait tune and he was curving down the winding driveway to the white, ranch-style house he'd bought on the outskirts of Los Pinos. There was a little dip in the land, then a rise. His house was nestled in that suggestion of a valley, surrounded by the pines for which the town had been named. A trickle of water that passed for a creek was the north boundary of the property. It looked like a picture-book image of what a home ought to be. He'd bought it at first sight because of that. It had triggered some sort of subliminal yearning within him.

Not that he had much experience with real homes. He'd bounced from foster home to foster home as a kid, a born troublemaker, according to those in the system who'd had to deal with his belligerence.

Used to being on the move, he'd seen no need to settle down once he'd grown up. Oil had been a way to stay on the go and pile up a decent bankroll.

Given his total lack of experience with lasting relationships, he probably never should have married, but Caroline had convinced him that they could make it work. When she'd been whispering in his ear late at night, when her magical hands had been busy moving over him, he believed almost anything that came out of her mouth.

Unfortunately, she hadn't counted on his refusal to quit wandering wherever the excitement took him. At first, she had gone with him, but once the boys had come along, she'd insisted on staying in one place. A few years of that and she'd gotten lonely and frustrated. When he was home, there had been more fights than loving.

A few months back, she had walked out, claiming that she'd had the twins to raise all alone for most of the past eight years, now he could see for himself how much fun it was. He could call her when he'd put in equal time and maybe they would work out a new arrangement.

Duke wasn't counting on it. He figured the divorce papers he'd received in the mail almost immediately pretty much countered any hopes he might have been harboring that things would eventually return to normal.

Even so, for a solid month he'd tried to pretend that nothing had changed. He'd convinced himself that he could go right on working crazy hours, taking off at the drop of a hat. Reality had slammed in when the fourth housekeeper in as many weeks quit in a huff.

Just in case the message wasn't plain enough, Zachary broke his arm and Joshua brought home a report card that suggested he hadn't cracked a book since his mother left. Even Duke had been bright enough to figure out that it was time to grow up and take responsibility for his sons, that parenting wasn't something a man could do in his spare time.

Not that he hadn't loved them all along. He had. He adored them. In fact, he was in awe of them. They were bright and mischievous and loving. He just didn't know a doggone thing about day-in, day-out caregiving. But he could learn, by God. There were books on the subject. He supposed there were even shrinks who specialized in that kind of stuff, not that he would ever be caught dead talking to one.

He did buy the books, though. A dozen of them the first week. When he caught the boys reading them, he figured he was never going to get an edge unless he worked at parenting full-time. With a sinking sensation in the pit of his stomach, he had hitched a ride in the corporate jet and had a long talk with Jordan Adams. Jordan came from a long line of men who understood about family. He'd offered Duke a vice presidency in Los Pinos on the spot. With it came the promise of stability.

Two weeks later, Duke had a new job and a new home. Moving in a hurry was something at which he excelled. It remained to be seen if he could get the rest of it right.

As he stepped out of the car in front of that appealing new home, the boys came barreling out the front door. It was a scene straight out of an old "Father Knows Best" episode and for a moment he allowed a feeling of immense satisfaction to steal over him. Not that it would last. His kids were irreverent little imps who would never be confused with anybody's angelic offspring for long.

"Don't let the screen door slam," Duke hollered just as it rocked on its hinges. He winced at the sound. He figured that door, the hinges and the frame would last a month, tops. Fortunately for all of them, he was reasonably handy with tools.

"Sorry, Dad," Joshua said unconvincingly.

"Yeah, sorry," Zack echoed.

Already stripped of his jacket and tie himself, he

noted that they were looking a little more like normal kids again, with dirt streaking their faces and rips in their T-shirts. There had been one awful period when they'd been so neat and tidy he hadn't recognized them, just as he often didn't recognize himself in the business suits he was wearing these days. The boys' transition had been the fault of the second house-keeper. Or was it the third? Anyway, she'd had a very rigid outlook. She was the only one Duke had actually had to fire. She'd seemed to enjoy the challenge of turning his sons into proper young men a little too much.

"Hey, Dad, guess what?" Zachary said.

"Hush," his brother hissed.

"What?" Duke asked, suspicion aroused by the exchange.

Zack scowled at his brother. "We gotta tell him. She's coming right now."

"Who's coming now?" Duke asked. He glanced up the driveway and saw that, indeed, a four-wheel-drive vehicle of some kind was kicking up dust. "Okay, guys, what's up? What kind of trouble are you in?"

"We're not in any trouble," Joshua claimed. "Honest, Dad."

The last time Duke had heard that he discovered that they had broken a neighbor's window—his very large, floor-to-ceiling window. It had cost an arm and a leg to repair it. He would be taking the money out of their allowances until they reached puberty.

Since the truth seemed to be in short supply coming

from these two, he decided to wait to see what the new arrival would have to say.

He studied the car as it came closer. Expensive and trendy once, it was little more than serviceable now. There was a layer of dried dirt, topped by dust over most of it, muting a dark green paint into something closer to muddy moss. For a man who took his cars seriously, this one was enough to make him shudder. He had an automatic hankering to rush for a hose and a can of his best wax.

The woman who emerged, however, had him shuddering for another, far more positive reason entirely. She was a beauty. Long legs and skinny behind were molded by denim. The suggestion of very interesting curves lurked beneath a short-sleeved silk blouse that had been tied at a waist he could span with his hands. Blond hair, scooped into some sort of ponytail, escaped in curling tendrils to frame a face that was lovely even without makeup. He'd seen that face somewhere before, but for the life of him he couldn't remember where. As for the rest of her, he wouldn't have forgotten that in a dozen lifetimes, so apparently they'd never actually met.

A model, maybe? She was tall and thin enough. An actress? With that golden complexion and blue-gray eyes, she had a face the camera would love. Still, it didn't quite fit. Besides, Los Pinos, Texas, wasn't exactly crawling with the rich and famous. The town wasn't quaint enough to draw tourists. Nor was it home to any celebrities he'd ever heard of.

While his mind sorted through alternate possibilities, she crossed to where they were standing in three brisk strides. He wondered if she realized that the sway of her hips robbed her movements of the professional demeanor she was clearly after. She nodded at the boys, who were suddenly, inexplicably very quiet, then held out her hand.

"Hi, I'm Dr. Danielle Adams. Everyone calls me Dani."

Her voice was so low, so blasted seductive that her title and name barely registered. Duke took her hand in his and felt a jolt of pure electricity charge through him. He didn't feel much inclined to let her go, but she subtly wrestled her hand away from him. The reaction made him smile. So, he thought with satisfaction, she'd felt it, too. Hadn't liked it half as much as he had, though.

"Duke Jenkins," he said. "What can I do for you?"

"I'm the vet in Los Pinos," she said.

His gaze narrowed. Adams? A veterinarian? The pieces suddenly clicked into place and a sinking sensation settled in his stomach.

"You're Jordan's daughter," he guessed, remembering where he'd seen that face. It was very prominently displayed on his boss's desk, right alongside a much less interesting framed photo of his son and a family portrait taken some years back, when this woman had still been in pigtails.

"Yes," she said. Then, as if she were anxious to get past the subject of family ties, she rushed on with some convoluted tale of dead goldfish and kittens.

"I have all three of them in the car, if you'd like to take a look. I think the boys could really learn a lot taking responsibility for them, don't you?'' she concluded, her eyes locked hopefully on his. He noticed they were more blue than gray just now as if some inner fire had sparked the sapphire in them.

Duke struggled to sort out the tale. When he had, he stared at her incredulously. ''They killed two goldfish in less than a week, and you want me to let them care for three kittens? Doesn't that strike you as a bit risky?''

She gave him a winning smile that almost caused his heart to slam to a stop. Logic flew out the window. He wanted desperately to do as she asked, anything she asked.

''Really, it's not the same thing at all,'' she assured him. ''Cats, even kittens, are reasonably independent and self-sufficient. And this would be temporary. I'm in a bit of a bind, you see. I have to find homes for these three, plus two more that are too young to separate from their mother and then Francie III is expecting again any day now.''

Duke was astounded by the casual recitation. ''Just how many kittens are we talking about? I mean at your house, not in the car.''

''Well, of course, there's no way of telling for sure with Francie, but I think there were five, maybe six others when I left, plus the mothers and a tomcat.''

''You can't even keep track of the number of cats living with you?''

''It changes, you see. Sometimes a neighbor's tomcat will just wander in and make himself at home, which probably explains why there are so many kittens in the first place. And people find strays and drop them off on my doorstep. I never quite know what to expect.''

''You're a vet. Couldn't you stop this?''

''I would, but people know I love cats, so they're always coming to me when they want one. Sometimes they're just not adopted as quickly as I would like, but sooner or later they all wind up in good homes.'' She smiled winningly again. ''Like yours. This would be an excellent opportunity for the boys to prove to you that they can take responsibility for a pet, so you'd get them the puppy they want.''

''And how many puppies do you have around the house?'' he inquired suspiciously.

''None. I found they don't get along all that well with the cats. I take those out to Uncle Cody. He's a real sucker for a stray dog.''

''And you think I'd be a sucker for three kittens?''

''Oh, no,'' she said, sounding genuinely horrified. ''I mean the boys did say you were lonely, but...'' She winced. ''Well, never mind. I just thought maybe you'd be willing to help me out for a bit.''

Duke eyed his sons. Obviously they'd had a big day. They'd turned downright chatty with Dr. Dani. He would have to warn his latest housekeeper not to take them into town again until they turned twenty. Maybe then they would stay out of mischief and keep the details of his personal life to themselves.

''Look, it was really nice of you to come out here, but I'm afraid I'll have to take some time to think about this.''

''But you have to at least look at the kittens,'' Zachary pleaded. ''They're really cute.''

"And they need homes," Joshua added. "Just like we did."

Duke scowled at Dani, annoyed that she'd put him in this position. The boys knew the rules. Apparently, they also knew he would never be able to resist Dani Adams. "Don't you want to chime in with your two cents?" he asked her.

She grinned. "No, they're doing pretty well on their own. I hate to oversell."

He surveyed her thoroughly just to watch the color climb in her cheeks. "Darlin', something tells me you could sell a man just about anything you put your mind to."

To his amusement, she blushed furiously at that, but held her ground.

"About the kittens," she persisted.

Duke recognized that he had been outmaneuvered and outmanned. Heck, he'd been sold when Dani Adams first opened her pretty little mouth. Besides, how much trouble could a kitten get into? "Okay, okay, I'll look at them. But we're just taking one. No more. Is that clear?"

The boys exchanged a look, but nodded dutifully.

Five minutes later, Dr. Dani Adams was tearing down the driveway kicking up dust again, and he and the boys were each holding one squirming kitten. For the life of him he couldn't remember exactly how that had happened. Something told him that a man would have to watch his step every single second around that woman or taking in stray kittens would be the least of his problems.

Back inside, he left the boys playing with the kittens, and headed straight for the kitchen where he could hear Paolina banging around pots and pans in time to the salsa music she was playing loudly enough to wake the dead. He hadn't decided if the woman was hard of hearing or just used the music to drown out his orders and the boys' complaints.

"Paolina?" he shouted over the din. When she didn't respond, he reached out and turned off the huge boom box on the counter. "Paolina?"

She glanced up at him in surprise. *"¿Sí?"*

"Did you drive the boys into town today?"

She tilted her head and regarded him warily as if trying to determine the politically correct response. *"Sí,"* she said eventually. "They ask to go."

"Because of the dead goldfish," Duke said.

She bobbed her head. *"Sí, sí, muy muerto."*

"Paolina, the next time the boys want you to take them into town, call and check with me first, okay?"

"Call, *sí, sí.* I will call."

He doubted she really understood a word he was saying, but he figured it was worth a shot. Paolina had been recommended by Jordan. She was related somehow to the line of housekeepers that had been working for their family for generations. A distant cousin, Jordan thought. Just here from Mexico. Very legal. All of her papers were in order. She just needed a job and a few basic language lessons, Jordan had promised.

Duke was quickly discovering, however, that if he hoped to have any kind of intelligent conversation with her, he was going to have to brush up on his Spanish. What puzzled him, though, was that she seemed to have no difficulty whatsoever comprehending the boys.

"*Gracias,* Paolina," he finally said with a sigh, hoping that at least some of his message had gotten through.

She smiled brightly. "*De nada, Señor Duke.*"

He retreated to his study, only to find two boys and three rambunctious kittens there before him. The kittens had apparently been on his desk. Papers were scattered in every direction and one kitten, the one they'd informed him was his, was kneading whatever papers remained in his briefcase. Hopefully, it was the contract for those blasted mineral rights Jordan wanted to acquire. He could use the destruction of the paperwork as an excuse to delay the acquisition until he could get more facts to back up his belief that it would be a bad deal.

He nabbed the kitten as he sat down and allowed it to settle in his lap, where it purred contentedly. He found the sound soothing, even though his thoughts were in turmoil. Images of Dani Adams kept flashing through his mind. Those tantalizing flashes pretty much spoiled the head of steam he was trying to work up all over again at her father. He settled back and let the images linger.

She wasn't his type, not really. A little stiff, a little uptight and way, way too brisk and professional. He preferred women who were soft and cuddly and accommodating, the opposite of all those social workers and foster mothers who'd made his childhood a living hell. At least that had been his preference before he'd settled down with Caroline. Since the separation, he'd steered as far away from romantic entanglements as he possibly could. Maybe his type had changed.

Before he could spend too much time contemplating the likelihood of that, his phone rang. He didn't waste his breath trying to shush the twins, just grabbed the portable and walked through the French doors onto his patio.

"Duke? It's Jordan."

His shoulders tensed. "Yes," he said curtly.

"Look, I'm sorry our discussion got out-of-hand earlier. I put you into that position so I could take advantage of your expertise. I should be listening to you."

"With all due respect, yes, sir, you should."

"Still won't cut me any slack, will you?" Jordan said with a laugh. "Even when I'm trying to apologize."

"Sorry. I guess I missed that part."

"Maybe that's because I'm out of practice," his boss conceded. "Look, jot down some of your thoughts and let's go over this again in the morning, okay? Maybe clearer heads will prevail by then."

"Mine or yours?"

"Hopefully, both. My wife says I behaved like an arrogant, pigheaded idiot."

"You'll get no argument from me, sir."

"Kelly said the same thing about you."

Duke chuckled. "No argument there, either. I'll have my reasoning on paper in the morning."

"Good. Now, tell me. How are you and the boys settling in? I should have asked you that earlier today. Do you like it here? Is there anything you need?"

"The boys love it," Duke said.

"But you're still fighting the desire to get back into the field," Jordan guessed.

"Yes," he admitted, knowing that the older man would understand. At one time Jordan had been a wildcatter himself, trying to make a place for himself in a business vastly different from his family's cattle empire.

"You'll find this challenging enough in time," Jordan promised. "I'll see to it."

If Jordan didn't, Duke had a feeling his daughter could. "By the way, I met your daughter today," he said.

"Dani?" Jordan asked, clearly surprised. "How'd that happen?"

He related a condensed version of the dead goldfish saga that had his boss laughing.

"So how many kittens did she stick you with?" Jordan asked before Duke had even gotten to that part.

"Are you psychic or something? How did you know about the kittens?"

"Son, from the day I married her mother the house has been crawling with kittens, and I'm allergic to the blasted beasts. Dani has a way with her."

"I'll say," Duke muttered.

"Did she pull out the sob story about drowning them in the river if no one took them?"

"Good God, no."

"That's the one she used on me. Those big eyes of hers filled up with tears. She told me that's what

Kelly intended to do to them unless I agreed to let them stay."

"And you believed her?" Duke asked skeptically.

"Of course not. Kelly's got the softest heart in the universe. But I had to admire Dani's ingenuity. My father bought it, though. She had cats all over White Pines by the time she was six or seven. Somehow over the course of twenty odd years she's managed to convince my father that it's a win-win situation. He saves the cats. The cats keep the mice away."

"Amazing," Duke said, thinking that Harlan Adams's legendary reputation did not include any reference to the notion that he was a soft touch.

"You could have told her no," Jordan pointed out. "You had no problem delivering news I didn't want to hear."

"This was different."

"Yes," Jordan said thoughtfully. "I imagine it was. Good night, son. We'll talk in the morning."

"Good night, sir."

After he'd hung up, Duke had the awful feeling that he'd revealed far more about his reaction to Dani Adams than he'd ever intended. And he didn't like that speculative note he'd heard in Jordan's voice one little bit. It appeared he was going to have to be on his guard about more than business when he went into work in the morning.

And he was going to have to stay the hell away from Dani Adams and her cats. Even as he reached that conclusion, one of those blasted little kittens tried to crawl up the leg of his pants, its claws biting into his flesh even through the fabric. He heard the snag, even before he caught the plaintive meow. Looking down he saw that the kitten was caught partway up his calf.

"You're going to be nothing but trouble," he muttered sourly as he leaned down to disentangle the animal.

But even as he said it, he brought the soft, tiny creature up to curl against his chest.

"Nothing but trouble," he murmured again. This time, though, he was thinking of Dani Adams when he said it.

Chapter Three

Dani was pretty sure she held her breath all the way back into Los Pinos. Duke Jenkins was the kind of overwhelming, purely masculine man who made a woman's toes curl without half trying.

With the notable exception of her stepfather, she'd spent her whole life around men whose fashion sense gravitated toward denim. Somehow Duke Jenkins had managed to make a perfectly respectable business suit and starched white shirt look as if he were only seconds away from stripping down to nothing. Her imagination had run wild. If a man like that put his mind to it, he could probably seduce a tree stump.

Of course, there was no chance of him trying anything with her. He worked for Jordan. More importantly, she was immune to his charms. He was a single dad, which placed him so far off-limits he might as well have been in Alaska with a barricade around him. With any luck she would never see him or his boys again. With better luck, she would never even hear his name mentioned.

Luck, of course, was never on her side, not when it came to matters of the heart, apparently.

No sooner had she walked into the house than her phone rang.

"I hear you met your father's new vice president today," her mother said without so much as a minute of small talk to disguise her prying.

"How could you possibly have heard a thing like that already? I barely left the man's house an hour ago. Do you have spies over there? Or can I blame this on Grandpa Harlan. I know he has them everywhere. He always knows what we're up to, half the time before we do. It's unnerving."

"You can't blame this one on your grandfather. Jordan spoke with Duke earlier on a business matter. He mentioned that you'd been there. He said you talked him into taking a few kittens off your hands," she reported with obvious amusement. "Jordan said he sounded a little bewildered by how that had happened."

Dani chuckled. "I'm sure Dad could identify with that."

"Indeed. I overheard him sympathizing rather sincerely. He told Duke to watch his step around you or his house would be crawling with all sorts of critters."

"I'm not that bad," Dani protested.

"You'll never convince Jordan of that. He wasn't

the least bit interested in owning one cat, much less the dozens you paraded through here over the years.''

"That was better than my brother's snakes and you know it."

Her mother laughed. "You bet. I'll tell Jordan to remind Duke of that when he's cussing about the cat hair all over the house."

She paused and all of Dani's self-protective instincts went on full alert. Her mother turned hesitant only when she knew she was about to tread on dangerous ground.

"So," her mother began a little too casually, "what did you think of him?"

"Who?" she asked just as innocently, determined not to be sucked into making an admission she could never live down. If she so much as hinted that she'd been attracted to Duke, even on a purely physical level, the meddlers in the family would turn that into an engagement before she could blink.

"Duke, of course."

"I didn't notice."

"Sweetie, a woman would have to be dead not to notice a man like Duke Jenkins."

"Okay," Dani conceded grudgingly, aware that nothing less than total honesty would satisfy her mother. She might as well get it over with. "If I were to have to give a totally objective description of the man, I'd say he's quite a hunk."

"An understatement, if ever I've heard one," her mother concurred. "He's gorgeous with all that thick, sun-streaked hair and those shoulders…" She sighed. "My goodness, those shoulders…"

"Mother!"

"Well, I can't help it. He reminds me of Jordan."

"Is Dad aware that you've fallen for his new protégé?"

"Very funny. The only man I've ever fallen for was Jordan and he knows it. Unfortunately, your father knew it, too. It took Jordan a while to figure out he felt the same way, but once he got the message things have worked out rather nicely."

As she spoke, Dani could imagine her mother's soft, nostalgic smile, the one that always came with any mention of Jordan Adams.

"Anyway, enough about that," her mother said briskly. "We were talking about Duke."

"You were talking about Duke," Dani corrected.

"And you were trying to avoid the subject. I was just going to say if any man on earth needs a woman in his life, he does."

Dani had been waiting for this particular hint. It was about as subtle as a swat with a riding crop. "Forget it," she said emphatically.

"Forget what?" her mother inquired innocently.

"I am not now nor will I ever be interested in Duke Jenkins."

"Because of his boys, I imagine."

"Of course, because of the boys. Mother, I really don't want to get into this again. Just forget it, okay? If you feel some sort of matchmaking force coming over you, give Jenny a call. She's older than I am. She's practically an old maid. Besides, she has Grandpa Harlan's tough hide. She could probably handle a man like Duke Jenkins, plus his sons without batting an eye. She needs a little romance in her life. I don't.''

"Danielle…"

"Don't start with the *Danielle*. That always precedes a lecture and I don't need one. It's been a long day and I'm exhausted.''

"But—"

"Bye, Mom. Good to hear from you. Love you.''

"Danielle! Don't you dare hang up on me.''

With only the slightest twinge of regret, Dani ignored her mother's command and slid the receiver firmly back into its cradle. Francie III crawled into her lap, circled twice, then settled down, purring loudly as Dani automatically stroked her under her chin.

Jenny and Duke Jenkins. Now there was a combination to contemplate. Grandpa Harlan's adopted daughter was as potentially volatile as a high school chemistry lab. Unlike Dani, she would be a more than even match for a man like Duke.

Ironically, though, the thought of seeing the two of them together made acid churn in Dani's stomach. If she hadn't known better, she would have labeled the reaction as pure, gut-deep jealousy, which was ridiculous, of course. No single father would ever stir anything more dangerous than the quiet warmth of friendship in her ever again. She wouldn't allow it.

Famous last words, she thought a few days later when she went to White Pines for the annual Fourth of July celebration. There were Duke, Joshua and Zachary right in the thick of things. There was Jenny, beautiful, dark-haired Jenny Runningbear Adams, holding Duke's attention with her animated telling of some Native American lore. Dani wanted to strangle them both, which was hardly the reaction of a disinterested third party.

Everyone—with the exception of her mother and Jordan—claimed to be absolutely stunned that she and Duke had already met. Her grandfather's claim struck her as a little too hearty, a little too determinedly innocent. She didn't trust the man one iota, not when it came to meddling. How Harlan Adams could have heard about the whole kitten incident she had no idea, but she didn't doubt for a second that he knew every detail. Nothing in Los Pinos and especially with his own family escaped his notice.

Nor did she doubt that Duke and the boys were here at his personal invitation. She doubted he'd needed any coaching from her mother on this one. Grandpa Harlan was a romantic, and he wasn't about to rest until everyone he loved was settled down and as content as he was.

"Nice-looking family," her grandfather observed as if he'd gotten a look inside her head. Old as he was, he still moved with an agility and sneakiness that amazed her.

Dani stared straight into his eyes, hoping her unblinking gaze would persuade him that Duke Jenkins was absolutely the last person on her mind.

"Who?" she inquired.

He returned her gaze with a sharp look. "Don't play that game with me, gal. You know perfectly well who I mean. Saw you looking at them just a minute ago.''

"I was just curious about what they were doing here," she insisted. "Usually it's just family here for the Fourth of July picnic."

"Can't tell around here anymore who's family and who's not," Grandpa Harlan grumbled. "Besides, your daddy's right fond of the boy. Thought I ought to take a look for myself. I have a lot of respect for a man who's all alone and trying to do right by his kids.''

So did Dani. She just didn't want to be any part of the equation. As if he'd read her mind again, her grandfather squeezed her hand, then took off as if someone had lit a fire under him. When she caught sight of Duke heading her way, a can of her favorite soft drink in hand, she understood why.

He offered her the chilled can without explaining how he'd known it was the drink she preferred, then took a sip of his own beer. "I counted four cats in the barn when I was out there. How many more have you hidden around the place?" he inquired.

"Oh, I lost count ages ago," she said, even though she knew precisely. "How are the three I left with you?''

"Still alive, which is something to be grateful for, if you ask me.''

"I knew the boys would take good care of them."

"The boys? Are you kidding? All three of those blasted kittens have taken up residence in my study. When they're hungry, they chase after me. I can't move from one place to another without tripping over one of them.''

There was too much affection laced in with the grumbling for Dani to take his complaints too seriously. ''Won your heart, did they?''

Duke scowled. ''Even if they had, do you think I'd dare tell you?''

There was a teasing glint in his eyes that Dani found just a little too attractive. She opted for a quick change of subject. ''I saw you talking to Jenny when I got here,'' she began.

''Keeping an eye on me, were you?''

''In your dreams, Mr. Jenkins.''

''It's Duke, darlin'. Once you've given a man kittens, you need to be on a first-name basis.''

''Okay, *Duke*,'' she said with deliberate emphasis. ''Isn't Jenny remarkable? Most men fall all over themselves when they meet her.''

''Really?'' He sounded genuinely surprised. ''Guess I'm not most men. I prefer prim little blondes myself.''

Dani felt her cheeks burning. ''Even when they're unavailable?'' she said tightly.

''Especially when they claim they're unavailable,'' he said. ''Makes me wonder why they're hiding from life.''

''I am not hiding from life,'' Dani protested instinctively.

Duke grinned. ''Oh, did you think I was referring to you?''

''Go to hell, Mr. Jenkins,'' she snapped and turned her back on him. Infuriating, insufferable tease, she thought as she marched off, spine straight. She could hear his soft chuckle as she went.

The rest of the afternoon she did everything in her power to avoid him, but no matter where she went, no matter what she did, she could feel his speculative gaze on her.

"Don't look now, but you've made a conquest," her cousin Angela said when she found Dani sitting all alone in a swing on the front porch.

"If discussing Duke Jenkins is the only thing on your mind, go away," Dani retorted.

"Ah, so he's made one, too."

"Angela, I am warning you. If you say one more word about Duke Jenkins, at least in any connection whatsoever with me, I will leave this party right now."

Her cousin's gaze narrowed worriedly. "Are you okay?"

Dani forced a smile. "Just feeling a little pressured, that's all. Don't worry about it. Tell me about you instead. How's life in Montana? Are you happy?"

Angela sat beside her and set the swing into a lazy motion. "Deliriously happy," she confessed, beaming. "Clint's the most wonderful, sexiest, kindest man on earth. He's the best husband and father a woman could ask for."

Dani chuckled at the exuberant praise. "I seem to recall a time when you thought he was a sneaky, low-down, conniving son of a gun. Are we talking about the same man?"

Angela grinned. "You bet." She regarded Dani

slyly. "Which just proves how quickly attitudes change. Never say never, when it comes to a man."

Dani stood up abruptly. "I have to go."

Her cousin nabbed her hand and held it tightly, preventing the escape. "Dani, I'm sorry. I was just teasing. You know how I am. I didn't realize it would upset you so."

"Never mind." She squeezed Angela's hand reassuringly. "It's okay. I'm too sensitive."

"Maybe if you or somebody would tell me what happened, I wouldn't be sticking my foot in my mouth every time I turn around. My mother, your father, Jenny, practically everyone has told me to leave it alone, but I can't. I care too much about you."

Dani sighed and sat back down in the swing, idly setting it into motion again. "It's not as if it's a big secret," she said finally. "Everyone in the family knows."

"And everyone tries to protect you by being tight-lipped about it, giving you your space," Angela guessed. "Maybe what you really need is to talk about it, scream, rant and rave, get it out of your system."

Dani grinned at the image of herself screaming, ranting and raving. It just wasn't the way she handled things. She kept her emotions all bottled up inside, unlike the rest of her far more demonstrative relatives. She had envied Angela for some of the shouting matches she and Clint had had. Blowing off steam had seemed to pave the way to healing. Maybe her way just allowed the wound to fester.

She'd said absolutely nothing about the broken relationship and shattered dreams when she'd come
home to Los Pinos, after leaving Rob. Her family had
seen her with him and the girls often enough to know
exactly how much she had loved them all. They had
come to adore Robin and Amy as well, though her
father especially had always seemed to have reservations about Rob. At any rate, they had been able to
guess the depth of her anguish and had left her alone
to deal with it in her own way.

She glanced at Angela, saw the sympathy and concern in her cousin's expression and decided it
wouldn't hurt to just tell her what had happened.
Maybe it would put an end to these awkward moments that kept cropping up between them after so
many years of being as close as sisters. She would
keep the telling simple and dispassionate.

Once she began, though, the words began to pour
out, words filled with far more rage than she imagined
she had ever held inside.

"That beast, that terrible, awful beast," Angela
said fiercely when Dani was done. "How could he do
that to you, to them?"

"Relationships don't always work out," Dani said
objectively. "I mean now that I think about it, I can
see how wrong we were for each other. Marriage
would have been a disaster."

"But what about those girls of his? Didn't he take
their feelings into account at all?"

Dani found herself trying to defend Rob's decision
to go along with Tiffany's demand for a clean break,
but she simply couldn't muster any conviction.

"The man was a bastard," Angela said. "Admit it."

"Yes," Dani said softly. "Yes, he was."

"A little louder. I didn't quite hear that."

"He was a lousy, good-for-nothing, son of a bitch."

Angela grinned. "Better. Want to try one more time?"

Tears rolled down her cheeks, but she shouted the words at full volume, adding a few more derogatory remarks for good measure. It was surprisingly cathartic, she concluded, laughing.

"I hope you weren't talking about me," Duke said, appearing out of nowhere at the end of the porch.

Dani couldn't seem to find her tongue, but Angela grinned at him.

"Is that how people usually refer to you, Duke?"

"Some do," he admitted.

"Well, you can rest easy. In this case, we were talking about someone else."

His gaze settled on Dani, his expression thoughtful. "I see."

Angela looked from Dani to Duke and back again. "I think I'll run along now. Clint's probably wondering where I disappeared to. He gets panicky when he thinks he's going to have to change a diaper."

Something that felt a whole lot like panic settled in the pit of Dani's stomach as well as she watched her cousin disappear and saw Duke striding up onto the porch. She hadn't realized she was holding her breath until she felt it slowly expel when he settled against the railing opposite her, rather than in the swing beside her.

"I've been looking for you," he said.

"Why?"

"Just looking for a friendly face."

"And you came looking for me?" she asked skeptically.

"Darlin', you're too polite not to manage a friendly face for a business associate of your father's. Besides, you want me to keep those kittens, don't you? You're not going to risk offending me."

"I'm sure Jenny—"

"I've talked to Jenny. I've talked to everyone here. I'd rather just hang out here with you for a while, if you don't mind."

"And if I do?"

"Then I'll leave."

Her gaze narrowed. "Would you really?"

"Absolutely." He grinned. "But I'd be back."

Dani sighed wearily. "Don't tell me you're the kind of man who only wants what he can't have."

"Are you saying you're not interested?"

"I believe I told you once today that I'm not available."

"Because of that jerk you were cussing out when I turned up?"

Oh, God, he had heard. "How much did you hear?" she asked, flushed with embarrassment.

"Enough to know you've been badly burned, that you're gun-shy."

She forced herself to meet his gaze evenly. "I've been around guns all my life. They don't scare me."

"Was that meant to be a warning?"

"Just stating a fact."

"Duly noted, then. Which brings us back to you and me."

"There is no you and me," she said impatiently. "Not today, not tomorrow, not ever."

He didn't seem impressed by her declaration. "Bet I could change your mind," he said.

"You'd lose."

His gaze locked with hers and made her tremble, proving his point. Hopefully, though, he hadn't noticed.

"Wanna bet?" he said softly.

Before she could guess what he intended, he'd clasped her hands and pulled her to her feet. In less time than it took to blink, she was in his arms and his lips were seeking hers.

When his mouth settled gently over hers, she thought briefly about struggling, about directing a well-aimed blow into someplace that would prove just how serious she was about being left alone. The thought vanished before she could act on it, lost to a sea of sensations so sweet, so wildly erotic that her knees went weak and all she could do was cling.

An aching need began to build inside her. Slowly she slid her hands into his thick, silky hair and opened her mouth to the endless, provocative kiss.

It might have gone on forever. She certainly wanted it to and Duke showed no signs of relaxing his embrace. It was the sound of voices nearby that forced them apart, both of them breathing hard and looking dazed. She was pleased to see that he looked at least as shell-shocked as she felt.

That was her ego talking, of course. When she managed to get her brain functioning again, she realized that she didn't want him getting any crazy ideas from that kiss. One kiss, well, that was just a kiss. It didn't have to lead to anything more. It couldn't lead to anything more.

If she'd doubted that for an instant, the sight of his sons barreling around the corner of the house at full throttle, shouting for him at the top of their lungs would have convinced her. They were cute kids, wonderful, exuberant kids. Duke was quite obviously a great father. There was no room for her in that mix. She wouldn't risk it for the boys. She didn't dare risk it for her own peace of mind, either.

"Dad, we've been looking everywhere for you," Zack shouted.

"And why is that?" Duke asked, his hand discreetly but possessively resting on her waist.

"It's time for the fireworks," Joshua explained, excitement sparkling in his eyes. "Can you believe it? They're going to have their own show right here. Grandpa Harlan—he said we could call him that—he said we could sit with him and the guy who sets them off and see how they work. Come with us, okay?"

"You run along," Duke said. "I'll be there in a minute. If they start before I get there, do not touch anything. Understood?"

"Okay," they chorused. The two boys regarded him worriedly. "You will be there in just a minute, right? Promise? I don't think they'll wait forever. It's almost dark now.''

"I promise."

When they'd gone, Duke drew Dani back around to face him. "Come with me."

She shook her head. "No, you go. Share this with your boys. Obviously, they can't wait to see the fireworks with you."

"I don't think they'd mind sharing them with you, too. In fact, once the show begins, I doubt they'll even know I'm around."

"Please," she said. "Just go."

He regarded her with concern. "Dani, do we need to talk about what just happened here?"

"Nothing happened," she insisted.

"If you believe that, we don't need to talk, we need another demonstration."

She held him off this time, just as she should have done the first time he bent toward her. To her relief, he didn't argue. He released her slowly, then trailed his knuckles gently down her cheek.

"Later, then," he said, proving that it was only a temporary reprieve from the storm of emotions he'd set off inside her. He tucked a finger under her chin and lifted it until their gazes were even. "No fireworks could possibly match the sparkle in your eyes, darlin'. Remember that, okay? Remember, too, that I'm the one who put it there."

Remember it? Dani thought it was quite possibly the most romantic, most dangerously seductive thing any man had ever said to her.

Her sigh was heavy and filled with regret. She was going to have to work very, very hard to pretend she'd never heard him.

Chapter Four

Duke could still feel the tentative movement of Dani's mouth under his, could still feel the shudder washing through her body and the sweep of her fingers through his hair when she finally surrendered to that Fourth of July kiss. The memories alone were enough to leave him hot and cranky with frustrated longing.

He'd never experienced such an instantaneous response to a woman before, at least not one that posed so many complicated risks. Attraction was one thing. He appreciated a beautiful woman as well as the next man. But what he'd felt during that impulsive kiss had unexpectedly rocked him, touched him on another level.

The kiss had been a mistake, a terrible, dangerous mistake, he concluded. She was clearly vulnerable.

She was his boss's daughter. He was in no position to, had no desire to, get serious with any woman. He was barely coping with a new job and being a full-time father. Adding a woman to that would just beg for disaster. The list of sensible reasons to stay the hell away from her went on and on.

Yet he knew himself well enough to realize that if the chance came, danger or no danger, he would take it again. She was as intriguing to him as a hint of oil beneath the earth, as alluring as the elusive scent of crude just out of reach.

He smiled at the thought. Dani might be a practical, no-nonsense kind of woman, but he doubted she would appreciate being compared to the search for an oil well. Yet for him nothing was more magnificent, more compelling than that particular hunt. Nothing got his juices flowing quicker than an oil strike.

Nothing except sex, of course. The thought of heated bodies and pleasurable sex brought him full circle, straight back to Dani. That totally uninhibited kiss had told him that Dani's prim facade would disappear in bed. He wanted to make that happen. He wanted to watch the transformation, the flaring of passion in her eyes, the hardening of her nipples, the restless writhing of her slender, normally controlled body.

"Duke?" Lizzy Adams peeked around the edge of his door. "Jordan's looking for you."

He shook off his daze and stared. He could feel a sheen of perspiration forming on his brow, but resisted the urge to mop it off.

"Why didn't you buzz me?" he inquired testily.

Rather than taking offense at his tone, she grinned. "I have been," she said. "For the past five minutes." She regarded him speculatively. "I guess you were lost in thought. Thinking about Dani, I'll bet."

Apparently, all of the Adams women were mind readers, he concluded, scowling at Harlan's precious daughter, who was also Jordan's baby sister. She was still in school and already so sexually precocious it was scary. She flirted with him outrageously or at least she had until she'd seen him with Dani at the family's Fourth of July gathering. All day today she had merely regarded him with very grown-up amusement.

As he tried to gather his composure, he told himself he would be very glad when Lizzy went back to school in the fall and he got himself a real secretary. An *old* secretary, he amended. He wasn't worried that the replacement would have as sassy a tongue. No one who wasn't an Adams would dare to take the liberties Lizzy did when it came to bullying her boss and meddling in his affairs. That particular trait seemed to come with the Adams genes.

"Tell Jordan I'll be right there."

"Already told him. That was five minutes ago, though. You're already late."

"Any idea what's on his mind?"

"Sure. He wants to know if you're interested in Dani." She shot him another unrepentant grin. "We all do."

"It's none of your business," he grumbled as he passed her. "Remember that."

She regarded him worriedly. "Can I give you just the teensiest piece of advice?"

"Can I stop you?"

"Don't try telling that to Jordan. He's just like our dad. They both figure it's their God-given right to meddle in everyone's life."

"Not mine," Duke said succinctly.

"Unless it happens to cross paths with Dani's," Lizzy pointed out, then shrugged. "I say go for it, though. She's been sad for way too long. She needs somebody to shake her up, make her forget about that creep who dumped on her. Something tells me nobody could do that better than you. There's not a woman on the premises who doesn't swoon when you pass by."

"I'm delighted to have your blessing," he said dryly. "Unfortunately, it appears that's not the one I need."

"It's a start," she retorted cheerfully. "Good luck."

Duke took his time walking down the short executive suite corridor to Jordan's office. If he had his way, they wouldn't have this conversation. Unfortunately, it appeared unlikely that he was going to get his way, which meant he'd better come up with some satisfactory answers for the questions Jordan was likely to ask.

In typical fashion, his boss didn't waste time on small talk. Duke was barely across the threshold when Jordan scowled at him and asked, "What's going on between you and my daughter?"

Duke took his time responding. He deliberately

sprawled in a chair opposite Jordan, hoping that the casual pose would communicate in a way that words could not that he wasn't going to be intimidated. Eventually, he shrugged. "Nothing as far as I know. Have you asked her?"

Unfortunately, Jordan was too sharp a businessman to be fooled by Duke's tactic. "Oh, please, don't give me that," he shot right back. "I want a straight answer."

Duke sat up a little straighter. He met Jordan's gaze evenly. "I don't know what you've heard, sir, but that's the truth. We've barely met. She's made it plain she's not interested. What more is there to say?"

To Duke's astonishment, Jordan actually chuckled at that. "I don't suppose you see the contradiction in that, do you? According to your claim, you two hardly know each other, but already she's felt it necessary to tell you she's not interested. What do you suppose brought that on? You don't expect me to believe it's how she opens every conversation with a man, do you?"

He flinched at the direct hit. "I suppose not."

"Could it have something to do with you kissing her the other night?"

Duke stared. "How the hell do you know about that?"

Jordan almost looked as if he felt sorry for him. "Son, you were on the front porch of my father's house in the middle of a family picnic. The teenagers sneak around like budding operatives for the CIA. You can't keep a secret with this clan if you bury it in a cave a thousand miles away. How do you expect to keep anything quiet when you're right in the thick of things?''

''A good point,'' Duke conceded. ''I'll have to be more careful next time.''

Jordan looked positively hopeful. ''Then there's going to be a next time?''

Duke gave up on the evasions. ''If I have my way,'' he admitted.

Jordan gave a little nod of satisfaction. ''Good.'' He studied Duke intently. ''Dani's had a rough time these past couple of years ever since she broke up with her fiancé, Rob Hilliard. If I'd been more on top of things, maybe I could have done something to save her all that heartache.'' He sighed with obvious regret, then looked directly into Duke's eyes. ''It won't be easy getting her to trust you, you know that, don't you?''

''Nothing worth having ever is.''

''Yes, you of all people would know that, wouldn't you?''

''Then I have your approval to keep seeing her?''

''Would it matter if you didn't?''

Duke met Jordan's gaze with a steady, unblinking look of his own. ''No, sir. With all due respect, it wouldn't.''

''That's what I thought,'' he said, sounding pleased. ''Just one thing, though.''

''Yes?''

''Hurt her and there won't be a place on earth you can hide.''

''Understood.''

* * *

Contriving to see Dani again was a whole lot simpler than Duke had anticipated. He should have realized that a powerful man like Jordan wouldn't be content to sit on the sidelines and let things unfold at their own pace. Less than an hour after their conversation, Duke had an invitation to dinner the next night.

"Nothing fancy. Just the five of us," Kelly Adams told him.

"Five?"

"Jordan and I, you and Justin. And Dani will be here, of course."

Of course, he thought. "I'll give her a call and offer her a lift," he said. He cursed the eager note that had crept into his voice.

"I wouldn't, if I were you."

Damn, did everyone in this family meddle? "And why is that?" he inquired.

"She doesn't exactly know you're coming," Kelly confessed.

"And you think if she knew she'd find an excuse not to come," he concluded.

"I'd say that's a safe bet. You unsettle her," Kelly said. "I could see that at the picnic. Now me, I think that's a good thing. Dani wouldn't."

Duke didn't like it, but he could see the wisdom in taking Kelly Adams's advice. He doubted anyone knew Dani as well as her own mother. He supposed there was something to be said for the element of surprise. In fact, he couldn't wait to see the expression on her face when she realized they'd been thrown together again.

"I see," he said blandly. "Well, if you think that's best."

"I do. Of course, you could hitch a ride over here with Jordan," she suggested slyly.

"But then I'd have to get a ride home," he protested, then smiled. "Ah, yes, with Dani, of course."

"It was just a thought," Kelly said.

"A good one, too. I'll speak to Jordan and I'll see you tomorrow night."

Jordan didn't bat an eye the next morning when Duke asked for a ride. Duke didn't bother wasting time with excuses. They both knew exactly what the scheme was all about.

"I'll pick you up on my way home from the office," Jordan said. "Do you want a head start so you can change?"

Duke nodded. "A half hour ought to suffice."

"Perfect. I'll clean up some paperwork before I leave."

Duke knew Jordan well enough to realize that even a casual family get-together wouldn't mean blue jeans and chambray. The man had impeccable style and seemed happier in a well-tailored business suit than any man Duke had ever met. Under the watchful supervision of the twins, he finally settled for a pair of slacks from the new wardrobe he'd been forced to acquire for his new executive position. He added a pale blue dress shirt with the sleeves rolled up and the collar open.

Joshua and Zachary surveyed him intently, then

nodded their approval. They didn't seem the least bit disappointed at being left behind, which meant they'd probably cooked up some scheme for getting into mischief.

"You need some of that smelly stuff, though," Joshua advised. "Girls like that."

"I don't," Duke said.

"But, Dad—"

"I am not taking advice from an eight-year-old. You two go and do your homework."

"Can we stay up until you get home?" Zachary asked hopefully.

"Not a chance. I've told Paolina you're to be in bed by nine-thirty."

The twins exchanged a look that suggested they considered Paolina an easy mark. "And if I don't find the two of you in bed and sound asleep when I get back, you'll be grounded until you're twelve," Duke warned.

"Aw, Dad, you wouldn't do that," Joshua said.

"You wouldn't, would you?" Zachary asked more worriedly.

"Don't test me and find out," he warned, scooping them up one at a time for hugs. Moments like this made him realize how much he'd missed during all the times he'd been away.

"Tell Dani hi for us," they shouted after him.

"Tell her the kittens are really cool," Zachary added. "We might not need a puppy, after all."

"I'll definitely tell her that," Duke said just as he heard Jordan tap his horn out front.

To Duke's relief, they spent the ride discussing

business and other impersonal topics. As always, Duke admired Jordan's quick intelligence and shrewd judgment. There was a rock-solid dependability about him that Duke envied. He hoped he could find some way to emulate it and give his sons the role model they deserved.

It took less than a half hour to reach Jordan's property. As they approached the house, Duke surveyed the small place with its colorful garden with some surprise. Huge pots on the porch spilled over with lush, vivid flowers. He had expected Jordan to own something far more pretentious than this tidy, homey farmhouse. Not even a fresh coat of paint could disguise the fact that it was quite old and had never been much more than a struggling ranch.

Only after he was inside did he see that first appearances were deceiving. When Jordan showed him around, he discovered that an addition in the back was spacious enough for an indoor pool, an office with book-lined shelves and a very private master bedroom suite.

Still, the original house was warm and cozy, compared to Harlan Adams's far more formal White Pines. Jordan observed his reaction.

"Not what you expected, is it?"

Duke regretted being so transparent. "Sorry, but no. It's lovely, but I thought you would live in something very modern."

"Modern and pretentious," Kelly chimed in. "He did," she announced as she joined them with a tray of appetizers hot from the oven. "In Houston." She shuddered. "It was awful. Cold, sterile and big enough to house a family of twenty.'' She brushed a kiss across her husband's cheek. ''I convinced him he needed a home, not a showplace.''

''She was right, too,'' Jordan said. ''As usual.''

''This ranch had belonged to my family for years.''

''Kelly single-handedly saved it from ruin after they were gone,'' Jordan said with obvious pride.

The sound of a car skidding to a halt out front interrupted their conversation. Kelly winced.

''Dani's here,'' Jordan guessed.

''She drives like you,'' Kelly complained. ''She's going to get herself killed one of these days.''

''I haven't,'' Jordan pointed out.

Duke gathered it was an old argument. He felt his shoulders tense as he waited for Dani to appear. The front door slammed, she shouted a greeting, then came to an abrupt halt at the sight of him. Her smile faded.

Kelly quickly hugged her and whispered something that had Dani managing a tight smile.

''Hello, again,'' she said tersely to Duke as she bent to give Jordan a peck on the cheek.

''You're looking especially lovely tonight,'' Duke commented, grinning at the blush that climbed into her cheeks.

''I just came from the Holcombe place. Their dog was having a difficult time delivering its pups. If I'd known there was going to be anyone here beside family, I would have gone home first to change,'' she said defensively.

''No need to gussy up on my account,'' Duke said.

"Well, there is on mine," Jordan said, wrinkling his nose distastefully. "You smell like a barn."

"Maybe I should just leave," she said, turning for the front door at little too eagerly.

"Of course, you're not leaving," Kelly said. "You have clothes in your room here."

Dani sighed. "Fine. I'll be back in a few minutes. Where's Justin, by the way? I need to talk to him about something."

"He should be home shortly. He's over at Cody's with Harlan Patrick. Or so he claims. I suspect they're in town chasing girls."

Dani grinned at that. "Having his sister working at Dolan's must really cramp Harlan Patrick's style."

"You should hear Justin on that subject," Kelly said. "He says Sharon Lynn is personally ruining any chance they have of ever getting a date."

"So Dolan's is the hangout for teenagers?" Duke asked.

"It has been for years," Jordan told him. "Not even the fancy new burger franchise that opened up outside of town can compete."

"Thank goodness," Kelly said. "I'm glad my kids didn't grow up with their social lives revolving around fast food and malls."

"If Jenny had had her way, we would have," Dani said. "She's still itching to get a Bloomingdale's close by."

"She just says that to get your grandfather stirred up," Kelly said, then turned to explain to Duke, "It's an old joke between them that she's going to put a mall on his land as soon as she inherits her part of it.''

"We'll see," Dani said. She stared hard at Duke. "I suppose you miss all the fancy Houston stores."

"Afraid not. Shopping was never my thing. As long as I can buy a good pair of jeans, I'm a happy man."

Her gaze swept over his clothes, which were far more expensive than even a pair of designer denim pants. "Jeans?" she said skeptically.

"Darlin', even those of us who hung out around oil rigs know enough to get gussied up for dinner with the boss."

Jordan and Kelly fought unsuccessfully to hide their grins. Dani frowned at all three of them.

"Since I appear to be the one who's underdressed, I'll go now and spruce up," she said. "I had no idea we were standing on formalities around here these days."

"Just get the straw out of your hair," Duke taunted, chuckling when her hand flew up in search of the nonexistent piece of straw.

Dani left the room with a scowl, but at least it appeared she didn't head straight for the front door. He glanced at Jordan just in time to see him exchanging an amused look with his wife.

"I think that went rather well, don't you?" Kelly said.

"The house is still standing, if that's what you mean," Jordan observed dryly.

"I gather Dani is not too keen on surprises," Duke said.

"Not if there's a man involved," Kelly told him.

"I can still skedaddle on out of here, so you all can have a pleasant, family dinner," Duke offered, albeit reluctantly. He doubted he would have made the suggestion if he weren't fairly certain it would be refused.

"No way," Kelly said. "I haven't looked forward to an evening this much in a long time."

"Me, either," Jordan said.

"I'm so glad to be able to provide you both with so much entertainment."

"Don't you worry about entertaining us. Just liven things up for Dani," Kelly said.

Something in her tone alerted Duke to the possibility that she and Jordan were putting a little too much trust in him. They had clearly assumed that his intentions were thoroughly honorable and that they would inevitably lead to something serious developing between him and their daughter. Was that what he wanted? He shuddered at the very thought of walking down the aisle again. He was far from averse to romance, but beyond that? No way.

Which meant, of course, that he was playing with fire here. Perversely, of course, the thought got his adrenaline pumping.

When Dani returned wearing a pair of snug-fitting pants and a cotton blouse, his pulse ricocheted like a bullet glancing off a fence post. She had scooped her blond hair into a careless knot on top of her head, leaving several wayward curls to skim her cheeks and shoulders. Duke felt an almost irresistible urge to tuck each one back into place...or to release the rest and run his fingers through the shimmering golden silk. It was a toss-up which way he'd go, if he had the opportunity.

Thankfully, he supposed, he didn't have to make the choice. Kelly announced that dinner was ready and they all retreated to the dining room. Though Justin hadn't come in, a place had been set for him, which gave Dani the perfect opportunity to sit opposite Duke, rather than beside him as her folks had so clearly intended.

As she slid into the chair, Duke grinned at her knowingly, bringing another of those easy blushes to her cheeks. He discovered he could easily become addicted to watching the color bloom on her pale flesh. Most women he knew were way beyond such easy embarrassment. At the same time, Duke realized that Dani's particular brand of innocence stirred an unfamiliar protective instinct in him. He managed to get through the entire meal without deliberately baiting her.

He was less successful on the ride home. Dani was clearly peeved about being forced to offer him a lift. Her testiness aroused his contrariness. He settled back in the passenger seat and studied her with blatant masculine approval. There was no mistaking the unsettling effect his gaze was having on her. She was shifting gears so furiously that it was a wonder the transmission didn't shriek to a complete stop in protest.

"Dani?" Duke said quietly after a particularly nasty sequence of shifts.

"What?"

"If you don't settle down, we're going to end up in a ditch."

"If you don't like the way I drive, you could always walk."

"And have you feeling guilty for a week for leaving me on a deserted stretch of highway in the middle of the night? I couldn't possibly do that."

"I wouldn't feel guilty," she claimed.

"Yes, you would. Why don't you tell me what has you in such a rotten mood?"

"My mood is just dandy, thank you very much. If you don't like it…"

Duke grinned in the darkness. "I know, I can walk."

"Exactly."

"You aren't by any chance a little peeved that your parents didn't mention I was coming to dinner tonight, are you?"

"It's their house. They can invite anyone they want."

"True, but you're feeling as if you were set up, correct?"

She sighed. "Look, it's nothing against you, really."

"It's just that you're feeling cornered."

"Something like that."

"Why? It was dinner. It's not a big deal."

She actually gave a tight little laugh at that. "Maybe not to you, but believe me, they're hearing wedding bells. They hear them if there's an available man within a hundred-mile radius."

"Don't all parents want to see their children happily married?"

"Yes, but not all of them consider it their personal mission to make it happen. It's embarrassing."

"It shouldn't be," Duke consoled her. "I'm not feeling any pressure here. You shouldn't, either."

"Yeah, right."

"I'm not. Let's make a pact."

She glanced over at him, her expression wary. "What sort of a pact?"

"To stop worrying about what other people think and just see where things take us."

"*Things,* as you put it, aren't going to take us anywhere. I'm not interested."

"So you've said."

"You don't believe me?"

"No, darlin', afraid not."

She shifted gears with another screech, then sped up to something close to eighty. Duke gathered she hadn't liked his response.

"Are you planning on killing both of us just because you don't like hearing the truth?" he inquired. "Or were you just hoping to put the fear of God into me?"

She regarded him hopefully. "Are you scared?"

"Of you? Never."

"Well, you should be," she said testily. "One word to my father that I find you reprehensible and you'd be out of the oil business, not just his, but any oil company."

Duke laughed at the threat. "You think so?"

"I know so."

"Darlin', before you go spouting off idle threats, maybe you should think again about whose idea this little dinner party tonight was."

She fell silent at the reminder. After a moment, she sighed. "Well, hell."

"Come on, Dani. It's not that bad, is it? Nothing has to happen here that we don't want to happen. We're both adults. I've been able to control my libidinous urges for some time now. Something tells me you have, too."

"What's your point?"

"We shared one kiss. The world didn't come to an end, did it?"

"I suppose not," she conceded grudgingly.

"We stopped with just one."

"Only because we were interrupted by your kids."

As soon as the words slipped out, she muttered a curse that had Duke grinning. Wisely, he kept his mouth shut about her very revealing remark.

When she pulled to a stop in front of his house, he made no move to exit. He held out his hand.

"Friends?"

She eyed his hand warily, then eventually reached over and clasped it.

"Friends," she agreed.

The minute her soft skin brushed his, Duke regretted suggesting something as uncomplicated as friendship. It would never work. He wanted her with a ferocity that startled him. If an innocent touch could set off such demanding need, he was in deep trouble. They both were.

He met her gaze and saw that she had reached the

same conclusion. Her eyes had widened with surprise. Then, even as he gazed into them, they darkened with worry.

"Well, hell," she muttered, then carefully withdrew her hand from his. She squared her shoulders with just a touch of defiance.

"Friends," she repeated pointedly. "You promised."

He nodded and after one final look deep into her eyes, he climbed out of the car. Without a goodbye, she shifted very carefully into gear and drove away.

Duke figured he was going to have a lot of very restless nights in the future to regret that idiotic promise of his. His only consolation was the absolute certainty that Dani was going to be tossing and turning, too.

Chapter Five

More than two weeks went by without Dani seeing any sign of Duke. Nor did she hear a mention of his name. In fact, everyone in the family was so careful to avoid so much as a whisper about Jordan's new employee and his sons that she guessed the silence was deliberate.

Her mother, who usually checked in every morning at some point, hadn't called at all the next day. She never had asked how their ride together the night of the dinner party had gone. Nor had anyone brought up the subject when she'd stopped by the following week or the week after that. It was almost as if they'd conceded that their plot had fizzled.

Of course, they were an incredibly sneaky lot. It was all probably calculated to pique her curiosity. She congratulated herself for not allowing the tactic to work, then sighed at the blatant lie.

The truth was she hadn't been able to get Duke off her mind since their first kiss way back on the Fourth of July. Nor had she been able to forget the feel of his lips on hers, the heat of his body or the purely masculine scent of him. And those sweet, sweet words, comparing the sparkle in her eyes to fireworks kept echoing in her head. It didn't seem to matter that so much time had passed since he'd paid her such an endearing compliment. She doubted she would ever forget it.

Of course, that memory was followed by an echo of his promise that they would become friends and nothing more. She couldn't seem to help feeling just a little disappointed that he'd taken her at her word that that was all she wanted. Why the heck hadn't he just swept her off her feet and made mincemeat of her ridiculous claim to be immune to him? They both knew what a lie it was.

Could it be that he was truly a rarity, an honorable man who stood by his word? Did he intend to back off and leave her completely alone except for chance meetings? That prospect left her feeling thoroughly disgruntled.

''Enough,'' she said sternly and marched herself into the animal clinic. Work had always been able to dull the most painful memories. Surely it could take her mind off of Duke Jenkins for a few hours. She had a half hour before regular office hours. She would spend it with Honeybunch.

Thankfully, the German shepherd was improving

daily, though it would be another week or two before she felt confident enough of his health to send him back out to Betty Lou's. The old woman had hitched a ride with a neighbor every single day to check on her dog. Dani was fairly confident that it was the sound of Betty Lou's voice as much as her own medical expertise that had kept the dog alive through several touch-and-go incidents.

"Come here, big guy," she called softly. The dog's tail thumped once, and he struggled to his feet. He limped over to the edge of his pen and licked her hand. Dani hunkered down in front of him. "You feeling better? You know, you gave us all quite a scare the night the sheriff brought you in here."

Honeybunch's responding *woof* sounded creaky from disuse.

"No, no, don't apologize. It's not your fault that creep slammed into you," she said as she expertly ran her hands over his body checking his injuries. Everything seemed to be healing nicely. His stitches would come out tomorrow and then it would be mostly a matter of letting him get his strength back. His appetite was slowly returning, and he was regaining some of the weight he'd lost.

"Betty Lou is going to be very glad to get you home again," she told him. "She misses you."

The dog cocked his head at the mention of his mistress's name, then uttered a plaintive woof that had Dani smiling.

"Soon, boy. She'll be here soon," she promised.

"What happened to him?" a familiar male voice inquired, causing her to jump.

She glanced over just as Duke hunkered down beside her, his expression sympathetic as he allowed the dog to lick his hand. He seemed oblivious to the danger of getting dog hair all over his expensive suit. For some reason that pleased her deeply. Nor could she help noticing how strong his hands looked, yet how gently they moved over the injured dog.

"Hit by a drunk driver," she told him.

"Damn fool," he muttered, never taking his eyes off the dog. "I suppose he left the scene, too."

"Of course, but the sheriff caught up with him. A neighbor spotted the car and turned him in. He'd had his license revoked the month before."

"But he was still behind the wheel," Duke said with disgust. "Maybe sooner or later someone will start taking away their cars, instead of their licenses."

"My sentiments exactly," Dani said, standing up and giving Honeybunch a dog biscuit to chew on. She managed to inject a casual note into her voice as she asked, "What brings you by? And how'd you get past Maggie?"

"Is Maggie that perky young lady out front reading a veterinary medicine textbook?"

"That would be the one," Dani said. "Forget I asked. If Maggie was studying, she'd let Martians invade without batting an eye."

"I hope I am somewhat less formidable than Martians," Duke said.

Dani wasn't so certain, so she let the comment slide. "And you're here for?"

"Kitty litter and cat food," he responded easily.

"Mittens and the others go through the stuff faster than the boys go through a gallon of milk."

Dani grinned. "Are you so sure that some of that milk isn't going into the kittens, as well?"

"Now that you mention it, no."

Since the explanation for Duke's presence was so patently flimsy, she couldn't help teasing him about it. "You could have gotten the supplies you wanted at the grocery store, you know. They carry every brand you could want and their prices are much lower than mine."

"But then I wouldn't have had an excuse to see you," he admitted, his gaze settling on her face and lingering until her cheeks flushed.

It was what she'd expected, *hoped,* he would say, but she began a protest just the same. "Duke—"

"I know. I know. You're not interested."

"And you promised—"

"I promised we'd be friends, not that I'd avoid all contact," he pointed out.

"Is that why you've made yourself so scarce the past couple of weeks?" she asked without thinking of the implication of the question.

Naturally, though, Duke didn't miss it. His eyes lit with amusement. "So, you did notice. Good. Actually, I was out of town for several days on business. Jordan could have told you that if you'd asked."

"You've got to be kidding," she said. "Do you know what he'd make of my asking?"

"No more than I am, probably."

Dani scowled at him. "Well, don't let it go to your head. My curiosity was no more significant than if I'd been wondering about the absence of ants at a picnic.''

"Lumping me in with other pests and nuisances?" Duke inquired.

Dani shrugged. "If the shoe fits…"

"A lesser man might be insulted by the comparison and give up. Is that what you're hoping? If so, you might as well save your breath. I'm a persistent kind of guy."

"Your persistence would pay off a whole lot faster if you picked somebody else to pester," she pointed out.

"Heck, Dani, surely you know that the chase is half the fun."

She frowned at the flippant words. "You see, that's exactly the problem," she said with gathering intensity. "It's all a game to you. You have two sons. You shouldn't be playing games. In the end they're the ones who'll get hurt."

His gaze narrowed. "Let me guess. You're talking from experience, aren't you? This has something to do with that jerk, doesn't it? And his kids weren't the only ones who got hurt. You did, too."

His guesswork was on the money. "It's not important," she insisted anyway.

"Tell that to someone who'll believe it, darlin'. Me, I just figure that gives me an extra obstacle to overcome."

She found his cavalier attitude exasperating. "Dammit, Duke, there you go again, turning it into some sort of contest. Maybe we can become friends, maybe not, but we sure as heck aren't becoming anything more. Have I made myself clear?''

"Abundantly," he said.

She didn't buy the easy capitulation. "There are a dozen women in this town I could introduce you to this afternoon, who'd be willing to play it your way, no questions asked. Give me the word and I'll call one right now.''

"I don't think so," he said, his gaze locked with hers. "There are some obstacles to be overcome, but the fact remains that I've got my eye on you.''

She returned his look helplessly. "Why?"

The simple question seemed to stump him as much as it did her. She had to give him credit for considering his answer before he replied.

"Chemistry?" he suggested eventually.

"Chemistry's a whole lot like fire," she warned. "You shouldn't play with it unless you know what you're doing. In this case, way too many people could get burned.''

"You could be right," he admitted. "But I've always been a man who liked living on the edge.''

"If it were only you and me involved, maybe it would be worth the risk," she conceded.

"It *would* be worth the risk," he retorted emphatically.

Heaven protect her from the male ego, Dani thought. "You and I are not the only ones involved," she reminded him impatiently. "That makes the situation intolerable for me. You're a decent man. Everyone says so. You're doing right by your sons under difficult circumstances.''

"Don't make me out to be a saint," he protested.

She grinned at his irritation. "Hardly that." She deliberately reached up and touched his cheek, intent on keeping the gesture as casual as a handshake, as reassuring as a pat on the back. Unfortunately, even that simple contact sent a jolt of pure longing straight through her. She pulled her hand back and jammed it into her pocket, then started briskly down the hall, determined not to let him see how shaken she was.

To her relief, he didn't follow, but his softly spoken taunt did.

"It won't work and you know it," he called after her.

She hesitated, but refused to look over her shoulder. "What?"

"Pretending that there's nothing between us."

She turned then and met his gaze evenly. "There is nothing between us," she said flatly.

He shook his head, a smile on his lips. "Darlin', if you believe that, then I've got a spread of land smack in the middle of a swamp I want to sell you. In fact, I can probably convince you it's suitable for skyscrapers."

When she would have snapped out another retort, he held up his hand. "No, don't say something you'll just have to take back later. I've got time. There's no rush when it comes to romance. In fact, all the experts say slower is better."

He managed to imbue the words with enough seductiveness to set off a stampede of erotic images.

"What happened to friendship?" she asked, fighting the helpless feeling of being caught up in a whirl-wind.

He shrugged. "It's a starting place."

"It's the beginning and the end," she insisted. "Accept that or stop coming around."

He shook his head. "There's that dare again, dar-lin'."

"It's not a blasted dare!" she shouted, then sighed. "Forget it. Obviously, you don't have a clue what I'm all about. Unfortunately, I can read you all too clearly."

"Can you really?" he said doubtfully. He covered the distance between them in three long strides. He framed her face in his hands and settled his mouth over hers before she could blink, swallowing her protest.

This time she did fight him. She planted her hands squarely in the middle of his chest and shoved. When that didn't work, she stomped down hard on his foot. He stopped kissing her then, but he didn't release her. He kept his gaze fastened on hers until she was the one who finally sighed and looked away.

"I gather I made my point," he said softly, his thumb caressing her cheek.

"What point would that be?"

"That all the protests in the world won't convince me that there's nothing between us. The evidence says otherwise."

"Believe what you want to. It doesn't matter," she said, forcing herself not to evade his gaze or to react to his touch. "All that matters is that I do not want to become involved with you. Period. End of story."

"I'm sure as an Adams you're used to getting what you want in life," Duke retorted solemnly. "Knowing Jordan, it's probably a family tradition. But I'm afraid you've finally come up against something you can't control."

"Don't be absurd. Of course, I can control it."

"How?" He grinned. "By avoiding me completely?"

"That's one way."

"The obvious one," he said disparagingly. "I would have thought you'd be a little more original, maybe prove yourself under fire, so to speak."

Dani's gaze narrowed. "You are not going to trick me into spending time with you, Duke Jenkins."

He grinned unrepentantly and shrugged. "Ah, well, it was worth a shot. I guess I'll just have to rely on circumstances to throw us together."

"What circumstances?" she asked suspiciously.

"It's a small town. I work for your father. Your family thinks we're a good match. I have three kittens. You're the town vet. Those circumstances."

"You're a manipulative troublemaker, aren't you?"

His booming laugh filled the narrow corridor. "Darlin', coming from an Adams, that sounds a whole lot like the pot calling the kettle black." He pushed open the half-closed door to the waiting room, then paused and winked. "See you around."

"What about the kitty litter and cat food you came in here for?" she blurted.

"Don't worry, darlin'. I'll be back."

A half-dozen speculative gazes followed Duke's

exit. Dani figured it would be less than an hour before the news was all over town that she and Duke Jenkins had had some sort of a lovers' tiff right in the middle of her clinic. Her family would be thrilled.

She, to the contrary, was not thrilled. She was worried. In fact, she was very close to panic. She might not be the most experienced woman on the face of the earth, but she recognized temptation when it was staring her in the face. She was tempted by Duke Jenkins, all right. Trying to convince him otherwise was going to require all her wits and then some. She wasn't even going to bother wasting her energy trying to convince herself.

By the time the clinic closed at five and the last pet, except for Honeybunch, had been shuttled home by its anxious owner, Dani had almost managed to put Duke's visit out of her head. She closed up and wandered down to Dolan's to get a lemonade and a little friendly conversation with Sharon Lynn. Her cousin could always be counted on to brighten her spirits.

Big mistake, she realized when she saw her cousin's eager expression.

"You sit right here and tell me everything," Sharon Lynn said at once, automatically filling a tall glass with ice and lemonade and placing it on the counter in front of Dani.

"Make that to go," Dani said.

"Too late. Come on, spill it."

"The lemonade?"

"Very funny. What exactly happened when Duke came to call today?"

"Nothing happened."

"That's not what I heard."

"Gossip is very unreliable."

"Usually, there's enough truth in it to make it fascinating, though. So, tell the truth, did he kiss you again?"

Dani stared at her in astonishment. "How the heck would anybody know about that? The door was closed."

Sharon Lynn grinned. "So, he did. I suspected as much."

"Are you admitting that you didn't know that already?"

"Well, there was a fair amount of speculation. And Maggie peeked once. She seemed to think she had caught a glimpse of you in his arms."

"I am firing her first thing in the morning," Dani vowed.

"No, you're not. She needs the job and she's good at it. It's not her fault you and Duke decided to get it on in plain sight."

"We did not get it on, as you so charmingly put it."

"But he did kiss you?"

Dani sighed. "Yes."

"And you liked it?"

"No."

"Liar."

"Okay, I liked it, so what? It's not going to happen again. I have made myself very clear on that point."

Sharon Lynn tried unsuccessfully to hold back a grin. "Did you really? Did you by any chance make that same point out at Grandpa's a few weeks ago?"

"Yes, I did."

Sharon Lynn continued to smirk. "Guess he doesn't hear too well."

"He's a man, isn't he? Have you ever known one to listen to a blasted thing we say?"

"Actually, Kyle Mason hangs on every word I say."

"Oh, for heaven's sakes, stop gloating. We all know you caught the last decent man in the universe or so you keep reminding us."

"He is extraordinary, there's no doubt about that. Not that Duke is any slouch. He's charming and sexy and smart."

"How would you know all that? You've barely met the man."

"Not true. He comes in here with his sons all the time." She glanced up. "In fact, they're on their way in right now."

Dani flatly refused to turn around to look. "Please, please, tell me you are making that up."

"Why would I do that?"

"To drive me crazy."

"Not me," Sharon Lynn retorted. "But I'd say someone else is doing a pretty good job of it." Her smile widened. "Hey, Duke. How're you doing? Hi, Joshua, Zack. What's it going to be today?"

"Ice cream cones," Zack replied. "Dad said we could have dessert before dinner tonight. Isn't that cool?"

"Way cool," Sharon Lynn agreed.

Dani felt Duke's hands settle on her shoulders. A shiver skimmed straight down her spine even before he leaned down and whispered, "Told you so."

There was nothing to do but accept the inevitable. Slowly, she swiveled her stool around until she was face-to-face with him. Pure devilment was sparkling in his eyes. His gaze locked with hers and his expression sobered until an exquisite kind of tension shimmered in the air between them. Dani swallowed hard and forced herself to turn away. She smiled at Zachary and Joshua.

"So what's this about dessert before supper?" she asked.

Already licking his double scoop of chocolate ice cream, Joshua paused long enough to say, "Dad says as long as we cross our hearts and promise to eat every bite on our plates, we can do it this way just this once. It's 'cause Dolan's will be closed by the time he finishes fixing dinner."

"Yeah," Zachary chimed in. "It takes him a really, really long time to cook, 'cept when he zaps stuff in the microwave."

"I see."

"Can you cook?" Joshua asked. regarding her speculatively.

"Dani is the very best cook in the entire family," Sharon Lynn said before Dani could respond. "Her spaghetti sauce would bring tears to your eyes. As for her pot roast, well, let's just say that Maritza taught her and Maritza has been Grandpa's housekeeper for practically forever and he has gourmet taste."

Both boys' eyes widened hopefully. "Really? Maybe you could invite us to dinner sometime," Zachary suggested.

"Yeah, we really, really love spaghetti, especially if it doesn't come out of a can," Joshua added.

"Hey, guys, it's not polite to invite yourselves over to someone's house," Duke said.

"Oh, we don't stand on formality around here," Sharon Lynn said. "Do we, Dani?"

Dani gave her a sour look, then forced a smile. "Of course not. The next time I'm doing more than grabbing a sandwich for dinner, I'll give you guys a call."

Duke's eyebrows rose. "A sandwich? That's your idea of a healthy dinner?"

"Sometimes it's all I feel like fixing after a long day."

"Tsk, tsk," Duke chided. "You should know better. I propose that we all go out tonight. My treat. Since everybody's so keen on spaghetti, how's that Italian place? We haven't tried that yet."

"It's the best," Sharon Lynn enthused. "Dani loves their lasagna, don't you, Dani?"

"It's very good," she conceded. "Really, though, I can't. Not tonight."

Duke's gaze clashed with hers. "Busy?"

"Yes."

"Doing?"

She seized on the first thing that came to mind. "I have to keep an eye on Honeybunch."

"Who's Honeybunch?" Zachary asked as chocolate dripped down his shirt. He was oblivious to the melting ice cream. Dani instinctively reached for a napkin and blotted it up, then wiped a streak off his cheek.

"Honeybunch is an injured dog I'm treating," she explained.

"Is he hurt bad?" Joshua asked.

"He's getting better," she conceded.

Duke shot her a triumphant look. "Then we can stop in and check on him on the way to the restaurant. That should put your mind at ease, right?"

She sighed heavily. She might as well give it up. There wasn't an excuse on the face of the earth that would work now, not unless she said flatly that she didn't want to go with them. There were two problems with that one: first, it was rude, second, it was a lie. A huge lie, in fact. She did want to go. Obviously, some part of her didn't care that a situation all too similar to this one had practically destroyed her.

"Why don't I go on ahead while you boys finish your ice cream," she suggested eventually. "You can meet me at the clinic when you're ready."

"Perfect," Duke said. "Fifteen minutes?"

"Yes," she said without enthusiasm.

Sharon Lynn grinned at her. "Have a good evening."

Dani nodded. "I'll speak to you tomorrow," she said, a deliberately dire note in her voice.

"Can't wait," her cousin said, clearly not the least bit repentant over her part in the night's turn of events.

Outside the drugstore, Dani briefly considered bolting, but dismissed it. It would be a cowardly thing to do, and no Adams had ever been a coward. Not that it was Adams blood flowing through her veins, but too many years of the family's influence had had an effect.

Ah, well, she only had to get through the next fifteen minutes of dread and what? Maybe another hour for dinner. An hour and a half, tops. That was hardly an eternity. Nor was it really long enough to feed this ridiculous attraction she was starting to feel toward Duke Jenkins. They would be chaperoned, too.

By ten o'clock she would be home, tucked in bed with a good book, just the way she had been on every single night of the past two years, except for those occasions when she'd been coerced into spending the evening with one family member or another.

The prospect reassured her. She was actually feeling reasonably upbeat when she heard the doorbell ring in the main part of her combination home and clinic. That optimism lasted until the moment she opened the door and saw, not Duke, but Rob, standing on the front stoop.

Chapter Six

Dani stared incredulously at the disheveled man standing on her doorstep. It wasn't so much his identity that shocked her, as his appearance. Rob had always dressed impeccably. Tonight he looked as if he'd grabbed clothes from a laundry basket.

"What are you doing here?" she asked with an icy calm she was far from feeling.

"Can I come in? We need to talk."

"We do not need to talk," she retorted. "And no, you may not come in."

He blinked at her in obvious surprise. "What's the matter with you?"

His total lack of understanding of what he had done to her infuriated her as nothing else could have. Either he was blind or she had been so submissive that he'd anticipated being able to steamroll over her as if nothing had ever happened. Dani didn't like either explanation much. Both said things about her she would rather not have believed true. Well, then, it was about time she stood up for herself and made her feelings perfectly clear.

She stared at him coldly. "That's the problem, Rob. You never did have a clue about anything that mattered. It was always about what you wanted, what you needed."

When she would have slammed the door, he blocked it and for the first time she felt a niggling sense of unease. "Rob, please. Don't make a scene."

"Afraid that shining Adams image will get tarnished?" he asked sourly.

Dani was stunned by his bitterness. What the heck did he have to be bitter about? "Just go away, please. I'm expecting company." She spotted Duke and his sons strolling along the sidewalk less than a block away. "In fact, they're on their way right now."

Rob turned and followed the direction of her gaze. "Still looking for a built-in family, I see. You always were predictable."

Dani winced at the mean-spirited accusation. Any second now rage was going to overcome common sense and she was going to throw a tantrum that would set Los Pinos on its collective backside.

Fortunately, Duke had apparently picked up on the scene even from a distance. He spoke quietly to the boys, who stopped where they were without argument. Then Duke quickened his pace. Before Dani could say anything more, he was casually, but effectively sliding between her and Rob. He dropped a deliberate kiss on her forehead, then fixed an interested stare on her visitor.

"Hey, darlin', who's this?" Duke asked.

"Rob Hilliard. He's an old acquaintance from Dallas."

Duke's gaze narrowed, which suggested he'd heard the name mentioned. Since she'd never told him the identity of the man who'd hurt her, she could only assume that someone else in the family had filled in the blanks she'd left in the story.

"Glad to meet you," Duke said. His tone was polite, but any reasonably bright man would not have found it welcoming.

"Rob was just leaving," Dani prompted, since he appeared not to have taken Duke's hint.

Neither man paid a lick of attention to her. They were squaring off like contestants in a championship boxing match.

Rob was no hero, though. Duke was at least four inches taller and twenty pounds of pure muscle heavier. Eventually her ex-fiancé backed down.

"I'll catch up with you later," he said pointedly to Dani. "Sometime when you're not so busy."

Duke shook his head. "I don't think that's such a good idea," he said. He studied Dani. "Is it?"

"No," she agreed. "It's not a good idea at all."

"Fine. Have it your way." Rob smiled at Dani, but there was little warmth in his expression as he added, "The girls send their love. They miss you."

Dani felt as if she'd been sucker-punched. She could deal with Rob. She could dismiss him as if he

were no more than an inconvenience, but the girls...
She couldn't pretend to be disinterested.

"Are they okay?" she asked.

Rob shot a triumphant smirk at Duke to indicate
his belief that he'd bested the other man, after all.
"They're unhappy."

"Why?"

"As I said, they miss you. They'd like to see you."

The offer was nearly two years too late. Dani didn't
want to ask, but he'd left her no choice. "What about
Tiffany? Won't she object?"

"We split up." Ignoring Duke's presence, he
added, "They want you to come home. We all do."

The thought of holding Robin and Amy in her arms
again, the prospect of reading them bedtime stories
and drying their tears, all of it was almost enough to
make her weaken. Duke's steady hand on her waist
gave her the strength to shake her head. It reminded
her that what she felt for those two darling girls was
not nearly enough to compensate for the fact that their
father was a weak, insensitive fool.

Steeling herself against his likely reaction she said
coolly, "I would love to see the girls again, anytime
you'd like to bring them for a visit. But we will never
be a family, Rob." She met his gaze evenly. "Never.
I'm surprised even you would be foolish enough to
think it possible."

"But..."

"I think you heard her," Duke said quietly. "Now
it's time you were on your way." He glanced at Dani.
"Right?"

"Absolutely," she said.

Only after Rob had turned and walked away, did Dani feel her knees sag. Duke's arm circled her waist protectively. "You okay?" he murmured.

She nodded, unable to speak. There was too much emotion clogging her throat. This time she was the one who'd cut the ties to Robin and Amy, severed them beyond repair. Rob would never bring them for a visit, not now that he knew there was no place for him in her life. He'd been using those poor, sweet babies of his as pawns, just as he always had.

"Josh, Zack," Duke called to the two wide-eyed boys who were still standing where he'd left them. "Why don't you go into the clinic and spend a little time with Honeybunch." He looked at Dani. "Is that okay?"

"Yes," she said. "Just remember he's still hurt. Don't try to touch him."

When they were gone, Duke prodded her into the house. "Sit. Do you want something? Some tea? A stiff drink?"

"Nothing, thanks."

He studied her worriedly. "Are you sure you're okay?"

She managed a faltering smile for him. "Believe it or not, I'm relieved."

He stared at her incredulously. "Relieved? I'm afraid you're going to have to explain that one to me."

"All this time I've worried what would happen if I ever saw him again. At first I prayed that he would come after me, beg my forgiveness and take me back to be a part of his family again, just the way he did tonight.''

''I didn't hear a whole lot of begging,'' Duke pointed out.

''For Rob, what you heard was close enough. Anyway, I imagined myself falling into his arms and going back. It's taken me a long time to realize that I was never half as much in love with him as I was with the girls. I adored his daughters. From the beginning I loved them as much as if they'd been my own.''

She sighed. ''And I worked so hard to win them over. I had Jordan's example to go by. Did you know he once thought he would be a terrible father? He was scared to death of me when he and mom were first seeing each other, but he made me a part of his life just the same. I wanted to make Rob's girls feel just as safe. Tonight when Rob asked me to come back, though, it was like a giant light bulb switching on. I realized I couldn't go just for them. Sooner or later their father and I would have split up and they would be hurt all over again.''

''So all in all, this visit was a good thing?'' Duke asked, his expression skeptical.

''I think so, yes.''

He nodded slowly. ''Okay, I'm glad, then. How the hell did you fall for a weasel like that in the first place?''

Dani grinned at his indignant tone. ''He wasn't at his best tonight.''

''An idiot in sheep's clothing is still an idiot.''

Dani shrugged. ''Much as I hate to admit it, maybe

you're a better judge of character than I am, even if you do play havoc with old clichés. At any rate, Rob no longer matters. Let's eat. Suddenly, I'm starved.''

"I do love a woman who has her priorities in order," he said approvingly. "Before we get the boys, though, one last thing."

"What's that?"

"If second thoughts about this Rob person start to sneak up on you in the middle of the night, don't call him," he warned. "Call me. I'll set you straight again before you go and do something rash."

At the moment, Dani couldn't conceive of having second thoughts. Nothing was clearer in her mind than the decision she'd reached just moments earlier to leave the past in the past.

"Promise," Duke insisted, when she hadn't responded.

"I promise," she said. "But—"

"No buts, darlin'. When it comes to love, second thoughts are a given."

"I don't love him anymore," she said with absolute certainty. Relief about that almost left her giddy.

"But you did once. Sometimes, in the middle of the night, that's enough to get you thinking crazy."

She regarded him speculatively. "You've been there?"

"Been there, done that. I don't recommend it."

"Will you tell me about it?"

"Maybe I will," he said. "If you ever make that call to me at three a.m."

Duke had been itching to plant his fist in that Rob person's face from the moment he'd walked up the sidewalk and seen him attempting to intimidate Dani. A thoroughly primitive, possessive instinct had flooded through him, startling him with its intensity. Only the certainty that Dani would have hated the resulting scene had kept him from following through on the urge. Something told him, though, that one of these days he'd get his chance. Men like Hilliard rarely learned their lesson the first time out.

All through dinner he kept his gaze pinned on Dani, watching for signs that she was already having those second thoughts he'd warned her about. She would, too. He'd heard enough to know just how much she'd loved those two kids of Hilliard's. Given the opportunity to have them back in her life, she wouldn't walk away without a single backward glance. The maternal instinct in her ran deep. He'd seen it in her reluctant interaction with Zack and Joshua. Not even past hurts could keep her from treating his sons with genuine warmth. Even now she was asking them about the day camp they were attending and showing the kind of genuine interest that could never be faked.

"Then the lifeguard at the pool said, 'Zachary Jenkins, you get out of the water right this instant,'" Joshua was telling her, his tone mimicking the teenager's precisely. "I said, 'But I'm not Zachary.' She didn't believe me. I got out of the water and five seconds later, Zachary swims smack in front of her. She turned real red and started to yell again, but then she saw me standing next to her. 'Told you so,' I said."

"And what did she do?" Dani asked.

"She said, 'Oh, never mind,' and walked away."

"Interesting story," Duke observed. "What exactly did Zachary do in the first place?"

"Uh-oh," Josh said, a guilty expression replacing the glee with which he'd told the story.

"Told you to keep your big mouth shut," Zack grumbled. "This is payback for the goldfish, isn't it?"

"Is not," Joshua insisted.

"Is, too."

"I'm waiting," Duke said, cutting off the exchange.

"It wasn't anything bad," Joshua said valiantly. "Not really."

"Maybe you should let me decide that," Duke said. "Zack?"

"I just dove into the water," Zack said, his expression totally innocent.

"A cannonball, by any chance?" Duke asked.

"Uh-huh," Josh said, nodding, his eyes alight at the memory. "A real whopper."

"And naturally someone was standing right beside the pool who didn't take kindly to getting splashed from head to toe," Duke guessed. "Who was it?"

"Some old guy," Zack said. "In a suit. Who'd wear a suit to a pool, anyway?"

"The mayor," Dani guessed, not even trying to smother a laugh. "He likes to stop by to see how things are going."

Duke stared at her. "The mayor? Terrific. My boys have been here less than six months, and they've already tried to drown the mayor."

Dani reached over and patted his hand. "Don't worry. A lot of people in town have considered doing far worse."

"Then why do they keep electing him?"

"No one else is willing to run."

"Why? Because everyone knows that it's Harlan Adams who really runs things?" Duke suggested.

Dani grinned. "Something like that. Grandpa Harlan does make his opinions known and people do tend to listen to him."

"Something tells me I ought to send the man a sympathy card," Duke said.

"No need to do that. He's heading over here right now," she told him, nodding toward the tall, silver-haired man striding purposefully their way. Even from a distance the water spots on his suit were evident.

"Ohmigosh," Zachary murmured, sliding down until he was all but under the table.

Duke latched onto his arm and forced him to his feet as he rose himself to greet the older man. Dani's expression suggested she was finding the whole thing just a little too amusing.

"Danielle," the mayor said politely. "Good to see you."

"Good to see you, too, Frank. Have you met Duke Jenkins and his sons? Duke is a vice president at Dad's oil company."

If he hadn't been assessing the man so closely, Duke might have missed the subtle shift in his demeanor when he realized that Duke was tied very tightly to the Adams clan. His tone was suddenly deferential and whatever he'd intended to say about the incident at the town pool was swallowed. Duke refused to let his son off so easily.

"I gather you met the boys earlier today," he said. "Zachary, don't you have something you'd like to tell the mayor?"

Zachary looked as if he would rather eat worms, but he dutifully said, "I'm sorry for splashing you, sir. It was an accident."

"Yes, well, a little water never hurt anyone now, did it?" the man said. "Apology accepted."

"Dad, can me and Joshua go play the video games?" Zack asked, clearly anxious to get away before he caused any more mishaps.

"Yes," Duke said, just as eager to have them safely out of the way. He handed them the change he had in his pocket. When they'd gone, he added his own apology for their rambunctious behavior. "And please, let me pay to have your suit cleaned."

"Not necessary," the mayor said. "I just wanted to bring the matter to your attention in case you hadn't heard about it, but I see that wasn't necessary. Good day, Mr. Jenkins. Danielle, give my regards to your father and grandfather."

"Of course," she said, barely containing a chuckle as he walked away.

"What's so amusing?"

"He is. He really didn't have any business wearing a suit and standing beside a pool filled with kids. I swear I think he does it just to get his suit cleaned for free. Guilty parents are easy marks."

Duke stared at her. "This has happened before?"

"Once every week or two as far back as I can remember. I do believe Justin and Harlan Patrick were guilty of their share of infractions. Dad and Cody finally forbade them from swimming in the town pool. Naturally, that made it all the more fun to go there, even though there's a perfectly good pool at White Pines. They still sneak into town, but they've learned to avoid the days the mayor drops by."

"You could have told me that before I fell all over myself apologizing," Duke grumbled.

"I considered it educational," she retorted. "I wanted to see if you were capable of abject humility."

Duke chuckled despite his annoyance. "Did I pass the test?"

"You were very good. I believed you were very sincere."

"And the mayor?"

"Once he figured out you worked in an executive capacity for Dad, you could have told him to take a flying leap off the town hall roof and he would have done it and thanked you for suggesting it."

Duke regarded her speculatively. "You know, Miss Smarty-Pants, it occurs to me that if you hold such disdain for this man, perhaps you ought to run for mayor yourself. At least then the Adams pulling strings around town would be operating in an official elected capacity."

She looked horrified by the suggestion. "Me? You've got to be kidding."

"Why not? You're bright. Everyone in town knows

and respects you. I think it's a great idea. When's the next election?''

''Thankfully, not for another three years.''

''Just long enough to get your campaign funds lined up,'' Duke said.

Dani's gaze narrowed. ''You're teasing me, aren't you?''

Duke shrugged. ''A little, maybe. You've been looking a little too serious all evening, despite your claim that your ex-fiancé's appearance didn't upset you.''

''It was just a shock, that's all.''

''But you can't stop thinking about his girls, can you?''

She smiled sadly. ''No.''

''Then see them. He's opened the door.''

''I can't,'' she said simply. ''It wouldn't be fair to get their hopes up, when I know nothing will ever happen between me and their father. They're used to me being gone now. It's better if it stays that way.''

Duke thought back to his own childhood. How many times had he prayed that his parents would suddenly come back to claim him? Even knowing that it was impossible, he'd harbored the dream in some tiny, secret place in his heart.

''They'll never get over losing you,'' he insisted. ''See them. Let them know you still care, even if you can't be with them.''

Obviously startled by his vehemence, Dani stared at him. ''Experience talking?''

''It doesn't matter,'' he said. ''Just trust me, kids never forget losing someone they love.''

"Are you talking about Zack and Joshua? Do they miss their mother so terribly?"

Actually, that had been the farthest thing from Duke's mind, but it was an easier answer than revealing his own childhood traumas. "Of course," he said. "They ask about their mother all the time."

"And what do you tell them?"

"That she was very unhappy with me and that she needed to go away to find happiness."

"Does she stay in touch with them?"

"She did at first. She sent postcards every few weeks. It's been a while now since we last heard from her, though."

Dani reacted with visible anger. "How could a mother do that to her own children? How selfish can she be?"

Duke didn't have any excuses for Caroline, either. It didn't matter to him that she'd seemingly dropped off the face of the earth, but it hurt the boys. He understood that kind of anguish all too well. More than once he'd considered hiring someone to look for her, then dismissed the idea. If she didn't want to be a part of her sons' lives, then forcing her to go through the motions would be worse than letting them grieve and get it over with.

Though he understood its roots, he was still a little surprised by Dani's indignation on their behalf. It reminded him of his very first impression of her. He'd thought then, as he did now, that she would make a terrific mother.

Earlier he'd caught Rob's sarcastic remark that she'd gone looking for another ready-made family.

Now he let the idea simmer. It could be a solution for all of them. She would have two boys to replace the girls she'd lost. Joshua and Zack would have a mother's love again. Goodness knew, the pair of them could use a gentling influence.

And him? What would he get out of the bargain? He'd already admitted that he was attracted to her. That was definitely a start. The prospect of having her in his life on a more permanent basis wasn't nearly as distasteful as it probably should have been, given his avowed determination never to marry again.

Years ago no one would have blinked twice at the idea of such a marriage of convenience. Even now there were lonely men in places like Alaska and elsewhere who advertised for mail-order brides. Would this be any different? He found that he was warming to the idea.

He glanced at Dani and saw her staring at the boys wistfully. Yes, he thought again, it would work very nicely for all of them.

"Why don't you go on over there and give them some real competition," he encouraged.

She grinned. "You wouldn't mind?"

"No, indeed. They beat the pants off me. Let them humiliate somebody else for a change."

"Not me," she said, flashing him a smile. "I grew up with a bunch of very competitive relatives. I do believe if you check that particular machine, my record still stands."

Perfect, he thought as he watched her join his sons. Duke was the kind of man who trusted his instincts. He also made decisions in a rush and stuck by them.

For once in his life, though, he managed to curb his enthusiasm. Something told him he'd better have his scheme very well thought out before he presented it to Dani. She struck him as the kind of woman who might not be nearly as pragmatic as he was, even under her own currently vulnerable circumstances. She might prefer at least the pretense of romance.

He could manage that. Hell, she already made him hotter than asphalt in August. A little proper courting wouldn't kill him. Then he could spring the idea of marriage on her and everything would fall tidily into place.

Satisfied with the plan, he sat back in his chair, sipped his beer and observed her. Dani Adams was something, all right. The boys clearly thought so, too.

Now all he had to do was turn up the heat between them a notch or two and his troubles would be over by Christmas, maybe sooner.

All in all, he concluded, the move to Los Pinos wasn't turning out to be quite as miserable as he'd feared. His job might not be as exciting as oil exploration, but courting Dani Adams promised to make up for that.

When she turned toward him, he lifted his mug of beer in a silent toast. Anticipation sizzled through his veins like fine champagne. Yes, indeed, life in Los Pinos promised to get downright fascinating.

Chapter Seven

Getting Dani to fall in with his plans was trickier than riding a bucking bronco, Duke concluded after six weeks of her clever elusiveness. The woman had more unexplained social engagements than anyone he'd ever met. If he hadn't been a confident kind of man, he might have begun to wonder if she wasn't deliberately trying to avoid him. He concluded that he wasn't going to pull off this marriage proposal quite as easily as he'd originally anticipated.

He had surmised very quickly that simply calling and asking for a date wouldn't work. She was way too jittery to accept. She had claimed to be busy every time he gave her any sort of advance notice.

Stopping by the clinic for an impromptu visit was more successful, but he couldn't discuss the future while half her attention was on some kid's parakeet or gerbil.

Finagling invitations from one Adams or another was a snap compared to getting a minute alone with Dani once he was there. If he didn't know better, he would have sworn that she was onto him, that she'd read his mind that night at dinner and resolved to avoid him at any cost.

Of course, that was impossible, he thought as he observed her clean dive into the pool at White Pines on Labor Day. Her swimsuit, modest by current standards, clung to her in a way that made it seem practically indecent. He hadn't been able to tear his gaze away from her since he'd first spotted her emerging, soaking wet, from the pool. A second later she dove back in and remained submerged up to her neck as if to deliberately prevent him from getting another peek at her.

The woman swam like a porpoise and apparently enjoyed it just as much. She hadn't been out of the water all day. Neither had anyone else, which made the huge pool far too crowded for the kind of intimate conversation Duke was interested in having.

"Dani looks happy, doesn't she?" Sharon Lynn observed, perching on the edge of the chaise longue next to him, her expression a little too innocent.

Happy, wet and sexy as hell, Duke would have corrected, but discretion prevented it. He merely nodded. He'd discovered quickly that the only way to avoid prying around this family was to keep his mouth clamped firmly shut. Occasionally, they gave up and went away. Sharon Lynn, unfortunately, showed no such inclination.

"Are you responsible for that?" Dani's cousin inquired in a tone that suggested her interest ran deeper than casual curiosity.

The question might have amused him if it hadn't been so wildly off the mark. "Hardly. I've barely seen her recently." He couldn't help the cranky note that crept into his voice.

"I see," Sharon Lynn said thoughtfully.

"What does that mean?"

"I just thought..." She shrugged. "Oh, well, I guess I was wrong."

"Wrong about what?"

She hesitated as if she were debating with herself. Duke watched the visible struggle with fascination. He wondered what the devil she was hiding...or what she wanted him to think she was hiding.

"Sharon Lynn?" he prodded. "What made you think Dani and I were seeing each other? Has she said something?"

"Oh, no," she said. Again, there was a slight hesitation before she shrugged and said, "It's just that she's been into Dolan's with your sons quite a bit. Almost every afternoon, in fact. I just assumed that ever since you went out to dinner you two were something of an item."

Duke tried to absorb the implication. Dani had been spending time with Zack and Josh? That was news to him. How had this friendship between Dani and his sons developed without his knowledge? Was he that oblivious to the twins' activities or were they deliberately keeping mum about these little get-togethers? Probably the latter, especially if ice cream was involved.

Paolina took them to the town pool every day for swimming lessons, but he'd just assumed they'd gone straight home afterward since he'd all but ordered Paolina not to take them anywhere other than the pool without his specific permission. Naturally, they'd kept quiet about it. They'd known they were breaking the rules.

"What time have they been coming in?" he asked.

"About four, I guess. After their swimming lessons."

It was Duke's turn to mutter, "I see." A few weeks ago he would have grounded them for the infraction, but now he saw that their sneaky little visits could be used to his advantage.

Tomorrow the three of them would have company at Dolan's. Thank goodness school didn't start until the following week or he would have missed out on this opportunity to slip into Dani's schedule when she wasn't expecting him.

He was so busy making his plans, he completely missed the thumbs-up sign Sharon Lynn exchanged with Jenny Runningbear Adams as she strolled away.

"Can't you take a break tomorrow afternoon?" Jenny pleaded with Dani. "I only have a few more days until school starts. We haven't had a long chat since I got back into town."

Dani regarded Jenny suspiciously. "That's right, so

why all of a sudden can't you wait to get together? I have a clinic to run, remember?''

"I know," Jenny said repentantly. "We should have done it sooner. It's my fault. The summer just got completely away from me. You know how I am.''

That was the problem. Dani did know. Jenny was one of the most organized women she'd ever met. She didn't fritter away time. She had too much going on.

Like Janet, her mother, Jenny was involved in advocacy programs for Native Americans in addition to her teaching duties. Dani could believe that Jenny hadn't had a second to get together, but she wasn't buying this nonsense about time just slipping away from her. There was a reason for this sudden urgency.

Unfortunately, she couldn't quite figure out what Jenny's angle was. She tried one more time to get a fix on it. "Jenny, why does it have to be tomorrow afternoon? Make it six o'clock and we could have the whole evening. I'll even cook.''

"That won't work," Jenny said a little too quickly. "Like I said, school's almost ready to open. I have all my teaching materials to get organized. I don't have another spare minute, especially in the evenings. I've been playing chess with Harlan then. He really looks forward to it.''

"So the only time you have free is tomorrow precisely at four?" Dani asked skeptically.

"Yes.''

"And I'm supposed to drop everything and meet you and Sharon Lynn at Dolan's for some girl talk? That's all? There's no hidden agenda?''

"Of course not. It'll be fun. I'll even treat.''

Dani laid a hand dramatically over her heart. "Goodness, how can I resist an offer like that?"

"Then you'll be there? Four o'clock?"

Dani sighed. The only way she was going to find out what Jenny was up to was to fall in with her plans. "Yes. I'll shuffle some appointments around, and I'll be there."

"Wonderful," Jenny said, then glanced up. "Don't look now, but someone is staring at you. When are you going to give that poor man a break and go out with him?"

"It's not going to happen," Dani insisted.

"But you went out with him once. Didn't you have a good time?"

"That wasn't a date. It just sort of happened."

"Whatever," Jenny said dismissively. "You enjoyed yourself, didn't you? That's what Sharon Lynn said. Your mom said the same thing."

Dani sighed. "I'm glad everyone has been keeping you up-to-date on my activities."

"Were they wrong?"

"No, but I also had a little too much fun hanging out with Duke's kids. I won't take that kind of risk again."

"Because of Robin and Amy," Jenny said.

"And Rob," Dani reminded her. She had told no one about the painful scene over a month ago. She doubted Duke would mention it either.

"Sweetie, something tells me that Duke Jenkins is absolutely nothing like Rob."

Dani had made a similar assessment herself. That still didn't mean she was willing to take any chances with her heart or with his sons'. She'd seen enough of them over the past couple of months to know that they were endearing little devils. It wouldn't take much for them to make her go all mushy inside and then where would they all be when Duke packed his bags and took off for a new oil field? Sooner or later, he would. He hated being chained to a desk too much not to balk at it sooner or later.

"Forget it," she said succinctly.

"Then I guess you won't mind if I check him out," Jenny said.

Dani flinched at the suggestion but forced herself to shrug indifferently. "It's up to you. I have no claim on Duke Jenkins."

Jenny's stare was penetrating and disconcerting. "You're sure?" she persisted.

"I said so, didn't I?" she snapped testily.

"Okay, then. If we don't hook up again before I leave today, I'll see you tomorrow, right?"

Dani nodded and watched Jenny circle the pool in Duke's direction. Along the way she was waylaid by Sharon Lynn. Dani swore that the little whoosh of relief she felt had nothing at all to do with Jenny's failure to hook up with Duke. She didn't care who the man dated. He could go out with the entire female population of Los Pinos for all she cared, Jenny included. In fact, she was the one who'd first suggested they would make a good pair.

So why did the prospect still set off this odd little aching sensation in the region of her heart? she wondered. Lunacy, she concluded. Maybe exercise would restore the blood flow to her brain.

When everyone else headed for dinner on the patio, she remained in the pool. She swam laps, which had been impossible when it had been jammed. She was praying the exercise would wipe out the thoughts of the man who had been plaguing her for weeks now. She was running out of excuses to avoid him. She'd been so sure he would take the hint eventually, but he'd shown no signs of doing so. In fact, it appeared all she'd really succeeded in doing was increasing his fascination. He had an absolutely inspiring mix of patience and determination.

Jenny would probably take care of that, she thought irritably. She was a little surprised to hear that Jenny was interested in Duke, but she probably shouldn't have been. After all, he was a gorgeous, bright, funny man. What sane woman wouldn't be interested in him?

Breathless at last, she swam to the side of the pool and clung.

"Worn-out?" an amused voice inquired from above her. She looked up into sparkling blue eyes and felt that strange little sizzle Duke managed to set off without even trying.

"Pretty much," she confessed. "How come you're not eating dinner with everyone else?"

"It'll still be there in a few minutes."

"Don't count on it. Uncle Cody and Uncle Luke have very hearty appetites. And Harlan Patrick and Justin are virtually grown men. Everyone knows they can clean off a buffet table faster than a butler with a hand-vac."

He grinned. "You worried I'm going to starve? Or just anxious to be rid of me?"

"Why would I want to get rid of you?"

"Good question. Care to answer it?"

"If I've given you that impression, I'm sorry."

"Said very dutifully and very politely. Why don't I believe it?"

"Believe whatever you like."

"Let me hazard a guess instead," he suggested. "I think you're scared to be alone with me. Look at you now, for instance. You're shivering."

"The air's cold," she said defensively.

"It's ninety," he pointed out. "And the water's not that cold, either, in case you were thinking of mentioning that next."

"How would you know? You haven't been in."

He grinned. "Keeping an eye on me, were you?"

"You know I could really grow to dislike you," she muttered.

He didn't appear to be horrified by the prospect. "Really? I don't think so. I think exactly the opposite is true and it scares you silly."

"You really are full of yourself, aren't you?" she said as a mischievous idea popped into her head. "Maybe you should cool off."

Before he could guess what she intended, she snagged his arm and toppled him straight into the pool. If he hadn't been off balance to begin with she doubted she could have managed it, but he was. He came up sputtering with a look of astonishment on his face. She might have laughed, if she hadn't noted the calculating gleam in his eyes. He wanted revenge.

She pushed off from the wall and swam for the opposite end of the pool. She was fairly confident of her swimming skill, plus she had the element of surprise on her side. And Duke was weighed down with shorts, a T-shirt and sneakers. She should have made it. No question about it.

When she felt a hand wrap around her ankle, she yelped with surprise and took in a mouthful of water. Strong hands spanned her waist and lifted her up. Her legs instinctively circled Duke's waist and her hands came to rest on his shoulders. At least his skin wasn't bare, she thought as desire slammed through her. If it had been, if she'd felt that muscled flesh beneath her fingers, it would have been all over. Her pretense of being unaffected by him would have vanished like a puff of smoke caught by the wind.

As it was, she doubted he could mistake the pebbling of her nipples beneath the scanty fabric of her bathing suit. Nor could he miss the catch of her breath or the way her own flesh was suddenly burning. She was surprised steam wasn't rising all around them.

When she finally dared, she looked into his eyes and saw that he appeared to be almost as stunned as she was. Lust had darkened his eyes. Dani suspected she would find that same passionate hunger reflected in her own eyes. She had never, ever wanted a man as desperately as she did this one. Right here, right now. The powerful force of it stunned her.

Abstinence and avoidance, it appeared, had been a waste of time. It had had exactly the opposite effect of the one she'd hoped for. Caught up against his body, she was feverish with need.

"You picked a hell of a time for this," he murmured, his voice husky.

"For what?"

"To tempt me to make love to you."

"I am not..." she began, but the protest died on her lips when she saw he would never believe a denial. She managed a halfhearted smile. "You ought to be grateful, actually."

"Why is that?"

"Given the circumstances, we won't make a terrible mistake."

"Would it be so terrible?"

Unexpected tears formed in her eyes and spilled down her cheeks, mixing with chlorine. Hopefully, that would disguise them.

"You know it would be," she said.

"I don't know any such thing, darlin'."

Before they could debate the subject, a voice called out.

"Hey, Dani, you out here?" Justin shouted. "Dad says you'd better hurry or there won't be any barbecue left."

"I'll be there in a minute," she called back, thankful that they were in the shadowed end of the water, invisible in the gathering darkness.

"Want me to get you a towel?" her brother offered.

"No, thanks. Go on back. I'll be right there."

She heard a muttered exchange, then a chuckle.

"Tell Duke to hurry up, too," Harlan Patrick called out. "Before Uncle Jordan decides to see what's taking you so long."

Dani chuckled despite her embarrassment. "There are eyes and ears everywhere with this family."

"Should I expect Jordan to meet me with a shotgun in the morning?"

"You never know."

He winked at her. "I'll take my chances. It was worth it."

"How can you say that? Nothing happened," Dani said.

"Sure it did. I just got all the proof I need that my instincts were on track the first time I saw you."

Her gaze narrowed. "Meaning?"

"I'll explain it to you another time. I think we'd better join the others."

"Duke Jenkins, what did you mean?" she said, scurrying after his retreating back.

Naturally, since she was more intent on catching him than on where she was, she managed to snag his soaking wet shorts just as he stepped onto the patio, right smack in front of her grandfather.

"Everything okay?" Grandpa Harlan inquired, not even trying to hide his amusement.

"Just peachy," Dani said and allowed the elastic waistband to snap back into place.

Duke grinned. "Better than that, actually."

"Good," Grandpa Harlan said. "I couldn't be happier."

Oh, sweet heaven, what was the family going to make of this? Dani wondered desperately. Not that the answer was all that difficult to figure out. They were going to assume whatever they wanted to. She could talk a blue streak for an entire year, and they would never believe that nothing had happened between her and Duke. For some reason, that didn't seem to bother him one bit.

She whirled around and scowled at him. "This is all your fault, you know."

"What's my fault?" he asked innocently.

If he couldn't see the hornet's nest they'd stirred up, she wasn't going to explain it to him. Let him find out for himself when her father cornered him first thing in the morning. She grinned vindictively. What she wouldn't give to be a fly on the wall when Duke tried squirming off the hook that he'd inadvertently managed to snag himself on.

"Are you making any progress?" Jordan asked Duke at their regular weekly planning meeting, which had been rescheduled for eight a.m. Tuesday because of the holiday.

"On what?" Duke inquired, feigning ignorance. He had a hunch they were not talking business. Jordan had taken to lumping the strategy for his personal life into the same sessions at which they discussed acquisitions and mergers.

"With my daughter, of course."

"You were at the picnic yesterday. You know as much as I do."

Jordan sighed heavily. "The girl's as elusive as a will-o'-the-wisp, isn't she? Just like her mother."

"Kelly was hard to get?" Duke asked. "For some reason I thought you two were childhood sweethearts."

Jordan grinned. "Depends on whom you ask. She

claims she was always crazy about me, but I kept chasing after unsuitable women. When I finally woke up and decided the right woman had been under my nose all along, she turned me down. Again and again, in fact.''

Duke was astonished. He'd never read an article about his boss in any newspaper or magazine in which some mention hadn't been made of the enduring love of his life. It was hard to imagine that theirs hadn't always been a fairy-tale love story. He had envied them that. It was something he never expected to experience.

''Really?'' he asked. ''Why didn't she accept your proposal?''

''She claimed she was only waiting for me to admit I loved her and Dani. Personally, I think she was paying me back for all that trial and error with those other women.''

Duke found Jordan's revelations more disturbing than he dared to admit. If Kelly had held out for an admission of love from a man she openly adored, would her daughter ever accept less from a man? Duke couldn't offer her love. He didn't have it in him.

He could promise her loyalty and faithfulness, companionship and friendship. He could offer her a family. Would that be enough to entice her to marry him? Or would she tell him to go hire a nanny, if all he wanted was someone to look after his sons? Unfortunately, he could practically hear her saying just that. Shouting it, in fact, at the top of her lungs.

Of course, he did have one ace in the hole. The attraction between them was powerful enough to singe asbestos. Some women confused sexual attraction with love. Few men did. He certainly didn't. He just prayed that Dani was one of the women who would never sleep with a man she didn't fancy herself head over heels in love with. Then, once he'd made love to her, he would be halfway to getting her to marry him.

Of course, he still hadn't even succeeded in getting her to go on a damn date, but he would rectify that this afternoon at four at Dolan's. The rest would follow.

He hoped.

Chapter Eight

"Hey, sweetie," Sharon Lynn said, when Dani walked into Dolan's promptly at four on Tuesday. "Lemonade? Or are you going to splurge on a milk shake? You haven't had one in a while."

"Since Jenny's buying, I was thinking of a hot fudge sundae," Dani said, already imagining the taste of the thick, warm chocolate drenching the chilly, creamy vanilla. If she had any vices, this was it. It had been weeks since she'd last indulged herself. There were a hundred and one reasons she deserved that sundae. Putting up with—no, surviving—Duke Jenkins was at the top of the list.

Aware of Dani's recent restraint, Sharon Lynn grinned. "Sure thing," she said and began scooping vanilla ice cream into a deep, old-fashioned glass dish before Dani could have second thoughts.

Dani glanced around the deserted drugstore. "Where's Jenny? I thought she'd be here on the dot since she was so insistent on me being here at four."

"Oh, she probably got caught up in something out at White Pines," Sharon Lynn said without meeting her gaze. "You know how Grandpa Harlan is with his little projects. He loves having Jenny home so he can try to boss her around."

"Try being the operative word," Dani said, smiling. "No one ever succeeds in getting Jenny to do anything she doesn't want to do, Grandpa included."

"Much to his chagrin," Sharon Lynn added, handing her the sundae.

"She was a rebellious fourteen-year-old when he married Janet and adopted Jenny. You would think he'd have figured out by now that she's not going to change."

"Grandpa is the most optimistic man on earth. You know that," Sharon Lynn said. "Plus he managed to manipulate all but one of his stubborn sons into doing what he wanted. He's a master of reverse psychology. Why should he give up on Jenny?"

"That's not quite right," Dani countered soberly. "Even Uncle Erik followed Grandpa's wishes and became a rancher. We all know what a tragic mistake that was. He died because of it. You would have thought that would cure Grandpa of meddling."

Both she and Sharon Lynn fell silent. She had only very dim memories of Erik Adams. Sharon Lynn hadn't even been born when the accident on Uncle Luke's ranch had happened. Still, they both had heard of the heavy cost Grandpa Harlan had paid for pushing Erik into a career for which he wasn't at all suited. Maybe every member of the Adams clan was destined to make one huge mistake in a lifetime. Hopefully, Rob had been her one and only disaster.

Then again, maybe there was another terrible calamity on the horizon, she thought as she heard Duke's cheerful greeting to Sharon Lynn. The spoon almost slipped out of her suddenly shaky grasp when she felt his fingers skim her shoulder in a light caress as he slid onto the stool next to her. Yes, indeed, disaster was definitely right around the corner.

"Hey, darlin'. Fancy meeting you here," he said. "Sharon Lynn, how about a cup of coffee and a piece of lemon meringue pie?"

Dani slowly swiveled around until she could look directly into his eyes.

The glint she detected seemed an awful lot like triumph. Duke had never struck her as the kind of man who'd be tempted to play hooky in the middle of a workday. Nor was Dolan's so close to his office that he would be likely to pop in for take-out coffee, not when Jordan maintained a fully stocked snack bar for his employees and a dining room for executives.

Besides, Duke wasn't even dressed for work. He'd taken time to go home and change from a business suit into chinos and a T-shirt that emphasized the breadth of his chest and the muscles in his arms. She should be used to the fact that he was devastating no matter what he wore, but she wasn't.

Since he was very much here in the middle of a workday, there was only one conclusion she could reach. He had to be up to something and the something was related to her.

But how the heck would he have known…? One look at Sharon Lynn's expression answered that. Guilt was written all over her face. Dani turned back to Duke.

"Why aren't you at the office?" she inquired suspiciously.

The corners of his mouth tilted into the beginnings of a smile. "Is this an official inquiry or casual chitchat?"

"Whichever will get me a straight answer."

"I'm all caught up on my work," he said as if he were a kid swearing that all his homework was done. "Jordan gave me permission to take the rest of the day off."

Dani regarded him skeptically. "You asked?"

"Of course. I always play by the rules."

"Oh, please," she protested. "You don't expect me to believe that one, do you?"

He grinned. "It was worth a shot," he said and took a bite of his pie.

"It failed. Now try the truth. Why are you here?"

He took his own sweet time about answering. First, he tried another bite of the pie Sharon Lynn had set down, then a couple of swallows of coffee. Dani was fighting exasperation by the time he met her gaze.

"Actually, someone mentioned that this would be a good time to catch up with Josh and Zack," he said turning a pointed look on Sharon Lynn, who was suddenly very busy counting out little piles of napkins on the far side of the U-shaped counter. "Have you seen them today?"

"No." Dani watched her cousin trying to slip unobtrusively into the storage room. No question Sharon Lynn was in this—whatever *this* was—up to her eyeballs.

"Are you expecting them?" Duke asked.

Dani's gaze narrowed. "Why would I be expecting them?" Suddenly the whole convoluted plot began to come clear. She stared at her cousin, who'd almost made it into the safety of that back room. "Sharon Lynn, get back here. What do you know about this?"

"About what?" her cousin asked defensively.

"Me being here? Duke turning up? What's the deal?"

"Deal? There's no deal," she insisted, not coming one step closer. "I have no idea what you're talking about."

"Why you little…" Duke began, then suddenly grinned. "You're good. You know that. You are really good."

Sharon Lynn blushed.

Dani stared from one to the other. "Would one of you tell me what's going on?"

Since Sharon Lynn's lips were clamped firmly shut, it was Duke who answered. "We've been had, darlin'. Set up. Manipulated. Meddled with."

That pretty much confirmed Dani's own suspicions. After all, Jenny was nowhere in sight, either. Their scheming left her momentarily speechless.

"Let me guess," Duke suggested. "You were lured here to meet…?"

"Jenny," she supplied with a sigh.

"Any sign of her?"

"No." She scowled at her cousin. "Sharon Lynn?"

"Yes?"

"What are you two up to?" she asked again, though by now the answer was fairly obvious.

Fortunately, for her cousin, the phone in the storage room rang.

"Sorry," Sharon Lynn said, not sounding the least bit sorry. She made a relieved dash out of sight.

"That's probably Jenny now," Duke speculated. "Checking to see how things are progressing."

When Sharon Lynn was gone, Dani regarded Duke apologetically. "I'm the one who's truly sorry. They shouldn't have put you in this position."

He grinned and popped the last bite of pie into his mouth. "The way I see it there's nothing wrong with the position I'm in. The pie was great. The coffee's the best in town. The company's not bad. What about you? Enjoying your sundae?"

Dani considered lying, but decided it was a waste of time and good hot fudge sauce. "Yes," she admitted.

"Then eat up." He leaned closer. "Then we'll sneak out without paying. That'll serve 'em right."

She grinned at his notion of revenge. "I don't think the cost of a hot fudge sundae and some pie and coffee is going to teach those two a lesson. For that matter, they can probably get Grandpa Harlan to ante up for it. I detect his fine hand in here somewhere. I can just see the three of them in his den out at White Pines plotting and scheming.''

"Maybe we should give them something to think about," Duke suggested, a worrisome glint back in his eyes.

"Such as?"

Even as she spoke, she realized she should never have asked. Those two words were as good as asking for trouble.

Duke swiveled her stool around until their knees were touching. His gaze locked with hers. Dani felt the sizzle of that look all the way down to her toes. If hot fudge was a vice, this was pure sin, she concluded.

She told herself she was going to look away any second now. She was going to move away from the graze of chinos against her knees and the lure of Duke's body heat. Any minute now, she promised herself.

Her breath caught in her throat. This was a dangerous game they were playing. In fact, they were flat-out flirting with disaster. If it could be called flirting, when the man looked as if he were one heartbeat away from scooping her up and hauling her off to bed, she amended. They were way beyond flirting.

When his callused fingertips skimmed along her cheek, her pulse zoomed straight into the stratosphere. When his thumb brushed over her lower lip, she felt the jolt in every cell from head to toe. She swallowed hard and willed herself to look away, move, get up and haul butt out of there.

Instead, she seemed to sway toward him, just when

his head was swooping in and his lips were taking dead-on aim for hers. The kiss, which she was so sure had been the last thing on her mind, turned out to be as inevitable as breathing. Soft and sweet and tender, it left her feeling cherished in a way that she'd never, ever felt before.

"Oh, boy," she whispered, when he had pulled away. She was in trouble, hip-deep and sinking fast.

"Nice," Duke assessed. "But I'm thinking that's not enough to convince them we don't need their help."

"Hmm?" she murmured, too dazed to follow his thinking. She blinked as he slowly rose to his feet, gasped softly when he lifted her until she was standing toe-to-toe with him, close enough that his heat surrounded her, beckoned to her.

His fingers tunneled through her hair. His breath whispered against her cheek. And then his mouth covered hers again.

This time there was nothing soft or sweet or tender about the kiss. It was demanding and hungry and possessive. And it took her breath away. It dazzled her. In fact, in her personal range of experience, this was the mother of all kisses, the kind that could lure a woman into thinking she was in love.

That four-letter word slipped into her consciousness even as Duke deepened the kiss to a whole new level of bone-melting bliss. Love. *LOVE?* Whoa, baby.

Dani felt the emotional brakes slam on. She spun away from Duke so quickly she left both of them off balance and shaky. Clearly surprised, he regarded her intently.

"Dani, talk to me."

Embarrassment flooded over her. She had practically come apart in Duke's arms right in the middle of a public place. It was the kind of behavior that started rumors and caused pain. All they needed was for Joshua and Zachary to get wind of the incident. They were clearly eager for a new mom. One whiff of this and those fertile eight-year-old minds would start manufacturing all sorts of happily-ever-after scenarios that just weren't going to happen. She forced herself to look directly into Duke's eyes.

"This is never going to happen again," she said bluntly. "Never."

Apparently, her tone was more convincing than usual because for once he didn't argue, didn't make some teasing remark or offer up a challenge that would have turned her vow into a joke. In fact, he nodded solemnly as if he'd gotten the message loud and clear.

"Never," he echoed.

"Promise me," she said, just to be sure.

"This will never happen again, I swear it," he said.

He sounded sincere enough, she supposed, but for some reason she trusted him about as much as she trusted Sharon Lynn and Jenny at the moment. She glanced at his hands, checking for crossed fingers. If she could have she would have checked his toes as well. Nope, there were no overt signs that he was intentionally lying through his teeth.

"I'm taking you at your word," she said. "My

father says you're an honorable man. I'm counting on it.''

That seemed to make him uneasy, but again he nodded dutifully. "You can count on it, darlin'."

He said it so easily that she was vaguely insulted. Didn't he want to kiss her again? Had it been awful for him? What the heck was the matter with him that he was giving up so easily?

No, what was the matter with her that she wasn't taking his promise at face value and hightailing it back to the safety of the clinic? Hormones evidently played havoc with logic.

She stiffened her spine, picked up her purse and inched away from Duke, careful not to brush against him. She was being absurd. It wasn't as if the man was going to grab her and throw her on the counter and have his way with her. He'd just promised he wouldn't even kiss her again, for heaven's sakes.

Of course, there was no guarantee that she wouldn't be the one doing the throwing and the having. Maybe that was why it was very wise not to come within a mile of Duke Jenkins for at least the next forty or fifty years. Maybe by then her hormones would be in check. If they weren't, it would probably be some sort of medical miracle and they could go on TV on some X-rated sex channel for seniors. The thought of it made her smile.

"Dani?"

She blinked and met his gaze, fully aware that color was flooding her cheeks again. She had blushed more in the past few weeks than she had in her entire life before meeting Duke. "Yes?"

"Want me to walk you back to your clinic?"

"No," she blurted at once, then winced at the rude tone. "I mean, really it's not necessary."

He regarded her doubtfully. "You seem a little wobbly."

"I am not," she said emphatically. "Once I'm out in the fresh air, I'll be just fine."

"It's a hundred degrees out there."

So what? she thought. It had to be darned close to that inside when they were in the middle of that kiss. In fact, she probably ought to speak to Sharon Lynn about fixing the thermostat on the air conditioner. It was way too hot in Dolan's. In fact, she was tempted to pick up a menu and fan herself right now, but she could see how Duke might misconstrue that and turn it into some sort of admission that he affected her.

"The heat doesn't bother me," she insisted, backing away an inch at a time as if she were trying to slip away without him noticing.

"If you say so."

"I do."

"Then I guess I'll see you around."

"Right."

"Bye."

"Bye."

"Have a pleasant evening."

"You, too." Dani sighed. Much more of this polite leave-taking and she was going to throw up. Before she added that to the list of her most embarrassing moments, she bolted for the door.

The blast of humid heat should have slowed her down. She barely even noticed it as she practically ran all the way back to the clinic. She headed straight for her own part of the house. She'd left the air conditioning set at a pleasant seventy-five degrees. She turned it down to sixty and went and stood in front of a register and let the cool air blow over her.

Even when her body was shivering and the cats were trying to crawl under an afghan on the sofa, she still felt hot. Only then did she admit to herself that as long as Duke remained at the center of her thoughts it wouldn't matter if she bathed in ice water. She'd still be burning up.

Duke didn't glance away from the door through which Dani had exited until he heard a whisper of sound behind him. He turned to find Sharon Lynn regarding him warily. After a moment, she bravely forced a smile.

"More coffee?" she inquired cheerfully.

"I think maybe I'd better switch to iced tea," he said. "With lots and lots of ice."

"I noticed it got pretty warm in here," she said.

"I'm delighted we were able to provide the entertainment. Now maybe you can tell me something."

"What?"

"Exactly what were you and Jenny up to? It's fairly obvious to me that Dani does not want a new man in her life, especially not one who's a single father, right?"

"That's what she thinks."

Duke's gaze narrowed. "Am I missing something? Isn't what she thinks important?"

"Not if it's different from what she feels," Sharon

Lynn explained patiently. "This afternoon proves what we suspected all along. She's attracted to you. She's just scared to death of doing anything about it. That's understandable, of course. But you can't stop living just because you've been burned by an idiot, right?"

"I suppose."

"Let me ask you something. Are you interested in Dani? I mean beyond a quick roll in the hay or something?"

"Isn't that an awfully personal question?"

Sharon Lynn shrugged off the implied criticism. "I'm an Adams," she said as if that were explanation enough. "We're nosy, especially when it comes to one of our own. Now stop avoiding the question. Are your intentions serious?".

Duke shook his head, amused by the persistence, if not by the prying. "I think Dani's the only one who deserves an answer to that question and she's not asking it."

"She won't, either. It's up to the rest of us to protect her."

"Would she appreciate you doing that?"

"Of course not," Sharon Lynn conceded airily. "But she'd expect it just the same. When it comes to providing backup, we're better than the Texas Rangers."

"I see. Well, let me give you just a little bit of advice from an outsider's perspective. The game is underway. Stay on the sidelines from here on out and watch. I think Dani and I can take it from here."

Sharon Lynn grinned. "Yes, I imagine you can do just about anything you set your mind to."

"I'll take that as a compliment."

"Of course you will," she said. "And I will stay out of it, unless I think you're getting out of line. Then I can pretty much guarantee someone in the family will call the foul."

He regarded her with amusement. "And the penalty?"

She returned his look solemnly. "You don't want to know."

Duke shook his head. "Your uncle Jordan said practically the same thing."

She grinned. "As long as you've gotten the message."

"Loud and clear, sweetheart. Loud and clear."

But the only signals he was really worried about were the ones Dani was sending him and those were very, very mixed.

Chapter Nine

Duke was constantly revising his strategy where Dani was concerned. After that last kiss, he concluded that she needed time to think about it, lots of time. He made himself so scarce that the only people who saw him regularly were his sons, Paolina, Jordan and his secretary. September eased into October, then November. Let Dani start to wonder what he was up to. Maybe it would force her to admit she was intrigued by him.

At least that was his theory. In practice, he was the one going stark-raving nuts. The boys weren't doing especially well with the forced confinement, either. They'd been plaguing him daily about going out to White Pines to see the horses or into town for ice cream. They were getting to be almost as restless and cranky as he was. He might not be experienced at this parenting business, but he sensed that something was going to have to give very soon.

Sitting in his study, he tried to focus on the paperwork he'd brought home from the office, but his mind wasn't on it. He was downright ecstatic when Joshua came to stand in the doorway, regarding him solemnly.

"Hey, son, what's up?"

"Are you busy?"

"Not too busy for you. Come on in."

Joshua bounded across the room and to Duke's astonishment climbed into his lap and burrowed his face against Duke's chest. His narrow little shoulders heaved with barely contained sobs. Duke had never felt so helpless in his entire life. He wrapped the boy in his arms and held on tight.

"Josh, what's going on?" he asked eventually, when the crying had abated somewhat.

"Nothing," Joshua replied, sniffing.

Duke smiled, grateful that Josh couldn't see it. "That's an awful lot of tears over nothing. Did something happen at school today?"

"No."

"What then?"

Joshua pulled back and looked straight into Duke's eyes. His little face was streaked with tears. "Dad, how come Mommy doesn't love us?"

Oh, boy, Duke thought, biting back a sigh. "What makes you think she doesn't love you? We've talked about this before, remember? It's me she's mad at, not you guys."

"I don't think so. I think she hates all of us. Me and Zack, too."

Duke began to get a sneaking suspicion about the cause of the tears. "Did she call here today?"

Josh hesitated, then sniffed and nodded. "She told us not to tell you, Dad, I didn't mean to break the promise, honest."

"That's okay. Some promises should never be made in the first place. You should always be able to come to me. If someone tells you not to, always ask yourself why. Now tell me what your mom said that upset you so much."

"Zack and me asked her to come home. We told her we missed her a whole lot, but she said no." Fresh tears welled up in his eyes. "She said she was never, ever coming back."

Duke mentally cursed Caroline for being so blunt with the two boys, then swearing them to secrecy. Did she expect them to keep all the hurt bottled up inside? Or were the secrets just meant as payback for him?

He wiped away Josh's tears and tried to coax a smile from him. "Now you listen to me, half-pint. We're getting along okay, just the three of us, right?"

"Yeah, but it would be nice to have a mom again," Josh said wistfully.

Duke immediately thought of Dani. She might not be able to replace Caroline in their hearts, but she could fill an obvious void in their lives. It was time to move on to the next step in his strategy. If nothing else, this conversation with Josh had proven that it was time to start courting Dani in earnest.

* * *

Duke had given Dani so much space she was about to spit. Not even reminding herself a hundred times a day that she had asked for it seemed to help. Work took up most of her time, but there were always a few hours late at night when she had nothing to do but think and remember the way she had felt in Duke's arms smack in the middle of Dolan's.

That kiss was the most impulsive, uninhibited thing she'd ever done. Naturally, she couldn't get it out of her head, she consoled herself. It had nothing to do with Duke *per se*. It was the outrageous risk she'd taken that was plaguing her.

So why did she glance hopefully at the door to her office every time it opened unexpectedly? Why did she spend a solid hour primping before every single family gathering on the chance that Duke would be invited? Why was she so disappointed when he never turned up?

Perversity was one possibility. Insanity was another. Admitting that she was falling in love with the man despite her best intentions was not an acceptable explanation. A few breath-stealing kisses didn't amount to a hill of beans in the overall scheme of life. She would forget all about them soon enough. She just had to concentrate on other things.

"Such as?" she muttered testily to herself.

"Such as what?"

The masculine voice, which surely she had conjured up, sent a shiver dancing down her spine. Obviously, the attraction hadn't worn off, she thought glumly as she glanced up at the man filling the doorway to her office. He was back in a business suit and more devastatingly handsome than ever. Just the sound of his deep, husky voice was enough to make her pulse skitter crazily. If anyone took an EKG right now, it would land her in the hospital. She forced herself not to drag in a deep breath, sigh, swallow or otherwise indicate that he'd rattled her by popping up when she least expected him.

"Just talking to myself," she said, pleased with her calm, casual tone. "What brings you by?"

"An emergency. Well, two emergencies, actually."

Her professional mode kicked in. She was on her feet and halfway around her desk, when he put out a hand to stop her.

"Whoa! I didn't mean medical emergencies. Sorry."

She frowned at him. "It's not a word we take lightly around here."

"I know. I should have realized that."

"There are no half-drowned kittens, then?"

He grinned. "Nothing like that. The cats have gotten very adept at avoiding Joshua and Zachary. They seem to have a sixth sense when the two of them are up to no good."

"That's the beauty of cats," Dani agreed. "They're pretty good at fending for themselves."

"Like you," he suggested lightly.

She wasn't entirely sure if he meant it as an insult or a compliment. "I suppose," she agreed. She regarded him expectantly.

"Actually, I've been meaning to call," he began, but Dani cut him off.

"You don't need to explain. We agreed that we wouldn't see each other again."

He seemed surprised by the statement. "Is that what we agreed?"

There was that worrisome gleam in his eyes again. "Of course, it is," she said hurriedly. "I told you—"

"Specifically that I was never to kiss you in the middle of Dolan's again."

Dani's gaze narrowed. She thought she detected an opening there for other kisses in other places, when nothing could have been further from her intentions. Explaining that, though, might be considered an over-reaction since he'd shown no particular inclination even to see her again lately.

"More or less," she said. She decided there was probably safer conversational turf for them to be on, especially since Duke seemed to be staring at her as if he hadn't been near a woman in a hundred years and desperation was setting in. Since her own level of yearning had reached a fever pitch, they were heading for trouble unless one of them changed the topic to something a little less sexual.

"You still haven't explained about the so-called emergency," she said hurriedly.

He blinked at the reminder. "Yeah, right."

"Well?"

He glanced around her office. "Do you think maybe we could have this conversation someplace else?"

"Why?"

He regarded her with amusement. "Because I

asked nicely?'' he suggested. "We could go out for pizza. That wouldn't be too dangerous, would it?''

Dani winced at the suggestion that she found being alone with him dangerous. She had hoped he would interpret their last parting as a lack of interest on her side. Obviously, he'd reached just the opposite conclusion.

"Duke, please..."

"It's not a date," he assured her. "It's just that I'm starved. It's around dinnertime. Why not have it together so we can discuss things.''

"Things?" she repeated. "What things?''

He grinned. "I'll explain over pizza.''

"Duke!''

"Please.''

She could turn him down. She could manufacture other plans, but the honest to goodness truth was, she didn't want to. One sight of him standing in the doorway to her office and she'd reacted to his presence the way a parched man would to an oasis. Just because she didn't want to get involved with him didn't mean they couldn't be friends, did it? Perhaps that was all he was offering, she told herself, though the unmistakable heat in his eyes said otherwise.

"It will have to be a quick dinner," she said. "I need to drive out to Betty Lou's and take a look at Honeybunch.''

Duke stared at her with obvious surprise. "I thought he'd be fully recovered by now.''

"Actually, he is, but Betty Lou is lonely. She got used to me dropping in when I first took Honeybunch home.''

Duke grinned. "The truth is, you miss that dog, don't you?"

"Well, he was around the clinic for several weeks," she said defensively. "Besides, it's more than that. Betty Lou has some terrific stories about Grandpa Harlan when he was a boy. I'm recording them all so I can blackmail him if the need ever arises."

"Now that does sound like a reason to keep calling," Duke agreed. "Mind if I tag along? We can drive out there first, then eat."

"I thought you were starving."

"I won't die from it."

"Okay, if you're sure. I'm warning you, though. Betty Lou is liable to make a pass at you. She considers herself to be quite a femme fatale."

Duke returned her teasing gaze evenly. "I can hardly wait. I've been worried I was losing my touch."

They found Betty Lou fixing fried chicken and mashed potatoes, enough for an army. She invited them in without any evidence at all that she was surprised by their arrival.

"Betty Lou, this is Duke Jenkins," Dani said.

Betty Lou batted long, thick, mascaraed eyelashes at the man in question. "Oh, honey, I know who this is. Not a woman in town hasn't been speculating why a handsome catch like this is still on the loose." She looked Duke over from head to toe, then gave a little nod of approval. "How do you feel about older women?"

To his credit, he managed to keep a straight face.

"I'd say that depends. If they're as beautiful as you, I'd say my mind is open."

"Then sit right down here. Dani, you, too," she added as an afterthought. "You're staying for dinner."

"But we intended to go out for pizza," Dani protested.

Betty Lou waved the long fork she was holding in a dismissive gesture. "You can have pizza any old time. I've got mashed potatoes, corn and a peach pie to go with this chicken. Now tell me you can turn down home-cooking like that."

"Not me," Duke said, eyeing the pots on the stove avidly. When his gaze reached the huge peach pie with the golden crust, he practically salivated.

Dani decided to save her breath. She would just have to wait until after dinner to discover what had been on Duke's mind when he turned up in her office. Besides, they were probably better off with a chaperone, especially one who had her own designs on Duke.

"Dinner sounds lovely," she agreed. "Where's Honeybunch, by the way?"

"Out chasing squirrels last time I checked. He'll be dragging back here any second looking for something to eat."

"He's doing okay?"

"Better than okay," Betty Lou said. "He's taking full advantage of that new lease on life you gave him. I don't know how to thank you."

"You've already thanked me," Dani said. "A hundred times, in fact."

"Maybe so, but I know you would have put any other dog in that condition to sleep," Betty Lou said. "Maybe I should have, too, but I just couldn't bear it. He's been my companion for too long now. I expected to go to my grave long before he did. You can bet I gave that drunk driver a piece of my mind when I caught up with him down at the jail. It was bad enough that he hit the dog to begin with, but to just leave him in the road like that was a real heartless crime."

"The judge sentenced him to volunteer in a hospital emergency room for six months once he gets out of jail," Dani said. "The judge told him he wants him to get a good, up-close look at the victims of traffic accidents before he gets behind the wheel again."

Betty Lou shrugged off the justice. "The man's trash," she said. "He won't get the message. He'll end up dead sooner or later, which wouldn't bother me a bit, if it weren't for the guarantee that he'll be taking some innocent soul out with him." She shook her head. "Enough of this. You two didn't come all the way out here to listen to me go on and on."

"Actually, in a way we did," Duke told her. "Dani said you have some great stories about her grandfather."

"Harlan?" Betty Lou said with a chuckle. "That old coot and I go way back. Not that he likes to admit it. Ever since he married that young attorney, he pretends he's shaved a couple of decades off his age. Let me get all this food on the table and I'll tell you a thing or two about Harlan Adams."

For the next hour she regaled them with stories from her own school days. Grandpa Harlan seemed to play a pivotal role in most of them.

"Did you, by any chance, have a crush on my grandfather?" Dani teased.

"Heavens, no. Now that brother of his..."

Dani stared at her. "Brother? Grandpa Harlan had a brother?"

"Well, of course, he did. Henry Adams. Everyone around here called him Hank. Now there was a looker."

Dani was stunned. She had never once heard anyone in the family mention that name. "Did he die or something?"

"Not as far as I know," Betty Lou said. "There was some kind of falling out. He left town when he was quite young, maybe sixteen. He was quite a few years younger than your grandfather. He just took off. As far as I know, no one's heard from him since."

"Well, I'll be," Dani murmured.

A half hour later with the dishes done and Betty Lou openly yawning, Dani and Duke made their excuses and left. When they had climbed into his car, he glanced over at her. "I gather you've never heard of this great-uncle Hank."

"Never. Apparently Grandpa Harlan is even better at keeping secrets than he is at prying into them."

Duke considered that, his expression thoughtful. "Maybe you should leave well enough alone," he said. "If he hasn't mentioned his brother in all these years, it must have been a bitter feud. It might really upset him to bring it up at this late date."

"I suppose," she said disappointed, but unable to argue with his logic. She would ask her father about Hank Adams, though. Maybe he or Luke knew something about the man.

At the moment, though, there was another secret she needed to get to the bottom of. "When are you going to tell me what brought you to my office this afternoon?" she asked.

"Invite me in for coffee when we get to your place," he countered. "This isn't something we can discuss in the car."

"Why?"

"Because I need to get a clear look at your face when I bring it up."

She stared back at him nervously. "Uh-oh. I don't like the sound of that."

He grinned. "It's nothing to fret over, darlin'. You'll either say yes—" his gaze settled on her mouth "—or no."

Dani's heart thumped unsteadily for the second time that day. Yes or no? People said yes or no to proposals. Marriage proposals. Surely, if he'd gotten the message about kissing, then he would understand that it stood to reason she wouldn't be interested in marriage, right? Or had he just capitulated easily on the kissing, knowing that he had a bigger goal in mind?

Oh, for heaven's sakes, stop, she told herself sharply. This wasn't about marriage. It was about…well, who knew what it was about, she concluded, eyeing Duke warily. Anything was possible, especially with a man as unpredictable as Duke. She would probably laugh herself silly when she realized how far off the mark she'd been.

At the moment, though, trepidation was tearing through her at an astonishing clip. If she could have thought of any rational excuse, she would have bolted from the car in a flash. Heck, she would have packed her bags and moved out of Los Pinos to avoid having this conversation.

As it was, Duke was pulling into her driveway, cutting the engine and turning to her expectantly, obviously awaiting the invitation in for coffee. Dani swallowed hard and mumbled the invitation without much enthusiasm.

Duke regarded her with amusement. "Darlin', lighten up. This isn't about walking hand in hand to the gallows."

"Yeah, go tell that to someone who'll buy it," she muttered under her breath even as she led the way inside.

She flipped on every single light in the house as she passed through on her way to the kitchen. Forget cozy and romantic. She wanted illumination. She wanted it so bright, he would never mistake the ambience for an invitation. In fact, it wouldn't be bad if the lighting brought to mind a police interrogation room. Not that she'd ever been in one personally, but maybe Duke had.

She put the coffee on to brew, found a couple of old mugs so he would understand that this wasn't a special occasion, poured some fresh sugar in the sugar bowl even though it was already half-full and put milk into a cream pitcher, despite the fact that they both drank their coffee black. When there was absolutely nothing else left to do, she finally sat down opposite him.

"Finished?" he inquired, not bothering to hide a smile.

She scowled, annoyed by his amusement. "Yes."

"Are you sure you don't want to dash off and check the mail or dust the living room?"

"Duke, will you just spit out whatever's on your mind and go? I have a splitting headache, and I have an early day tomorrow."

He was on his feet in a flash and moving behind her. She twisted to see what he was up to, but he rested his hands on her shoulders until she sighed and faced forward again.

"Duke! What do you think you're doing?"

"You said you have a headache," he explained patiently as he began to massage her temples.

Dani would have protested, but it felt too good. She could feel the tension beginning to ease even before his fingers began kneading the hard knots in her shoulders.

"No wonder your head's pounding," he observed. "You're tense."

"Well, of course, I'm tense. You've been dropping little hints all evening that you have something important to discuss. My imagination is running wild."

"Really? I'm fascinated. Just what sort of images have you managed to conjure up?"

"Never mind."

He chuckled. "Whoops, here come those knots

again. They'd probably go away if you'd tell me what you've been thinking.''

"They would go away if you would just say what's on your mind and get out of here," she countered.

"Tsk, tsk, that's not a very auspicious beginning," he taunted. "Maybe I'd better get into this another time, when you're not so cranky."

"Get into what, dammit? And I am not cranky."

He chuckled. "Yes, indeed, another time would be best. It'll keep."

Before she knew what he intended, he leaned down, brushed a brotherly peck across her cheek and headed for the door.

"Duke!"

"Night, darlin'. It's been fun."

"Duke Jenkins, if you walk out that door without explaining yourself, don't come back."

The threat was wasted. He was already halfway to the car by the time she finished. Since he gave her a jaunty wave as he pulled out of the driveway, she could only assume he wasn't feeling the least bit threatened.

"Well, damn," she muttered, staring after him.

As he drove home, Duke whistled cheerfully and congratulated himself on an evening well spent. He'd proved to himself once again that Dani wasn't nearly as immune to him as she wanted to be.

He could guess precisely which path her imagination had led her down. In fact, he had deliberately chosen his words just to point her in the right direction. Yes and no were answers to a whole lot of questions, most of them innocuous enough. But spoken with a little hint of seductiveness, they clearly hinted at very provocative queries to come.

After planting that particular seed in her mind, he'd been somewhat surprised that she'd allowed him in the house at all, given her avowed aversion to any kind of future with another single dad.

He had also been careful the past few weeks to stay away from White Pines or any other place where she was likely to be. Since any invitation always included Joshua and Zachary, he'd turned them all down. He'd wanted Dani wondering what he was up to, not remembering that he had two sons underfoot.

In the long run, he figured his strategy would pay off. In the short run, he was very close to losing his mind. How had he missed the fact that rearing two boys could be so incredibly challenging? Maybe not as challenging as exploring for oil, but a darned close second.

Maybe it was because they were twins, but Josh and Zack seemed to think as a single unit, conspiring to get into the most amazing amount of mischief just when he thought he had everything under control. Thankfully, they hadn't scared off Paolina, but he knew with every fiber of his being that the housekeeper was no substitute for a real mom. He intended to give them one or die trying.

It would have been a heck of a lot simpler, of course, if he'd picked one who was a little more amenable to the idea. Then again, courting Dani Adams was just about fascinating enough to take his mind off the tedium of all that paperwork her daddy piled on his desk.

Chapter Ten

After a restless night Dani stepped outside at mid-morning on Saturday to get the paper and discovered two little boys sitting on the front steps. She stared at Josh and Zack, then automatically looked around for some sign of their father.

"Dad's not with us," Josh said as if he, like his father, was capable of reading her mind.

"So I see. How did you get here?"

"Paolina brought us," Zack said.

Dani fought the panicky feeling that had been automatic from the moment she met these two wonderful, emotionally scary kids. "She just left you on my doorstep?"

"We came to buy cat food," Zack said. "Paolina said she'd get it at the grocery store, but the cats like the kind you have better."

Dani nodded as if the explanation made perfect sense, which it obviously did to them. "Well, then, I guess you'd better come in and choose the flavors you want."

"Anything but liver," Josh told her. "That smells yucky."

"Not to a cat," Dani pointed out.

Both boys looked startled.

"I guess you're right," Josh said. "And it's their dinner."

Dani grinned at him. "Exactly." She led the way into her pet supply room and pointed to the rows of gourmet cat food in cans and bags. "Can you two pick what you want on your own?" she inquired hopefully.

Zack gave her a shy look and, to her astonishment, slipped his hand into hers. "No, we want you to help. Okay?"

The warmth of that little hand tucked trustingly into her own brought on a flood of bittersweet memories. Every bit of instinct for self-preservation protested that she should make up a plausible excuse, walk away and leave the two boys to their shopping. One look into two pairs of hopeful eyes told her she couldn't do it.

"I'll help," she said grimly.

The process of choosing took far longer than it should have. They claimed they wanted to learn about every single ingredient in every single brand she carried. She distrusted their enthusiasm, but their sweet little expressions were so innocent she chided herself for being overly suspicious.

When they had filled a shopping bag with their selections and had added toys for each cat, they stood back and admired their purchases.

"I think you two have made excellent choices," she told them. "You've picked a good variety of very healthy cat food. Did you want me to send the bill to your dad?"

The two exchanged guilty looks.

"That's okay," Josh said. "We'll pay for it. I mean, not right this second, but soon."

Dani's suspicions stirred again. "Is this coming out of your allowances?"

"Heck, no," Zack said. "Dad's coming to get us when he gets finished at the office. He'll pay you."

Dani stared at them in astonishment. "Your father is coming here?"

Two heads bobbed.

"When?"

"After he gets done at work."

"Did he happen to mention when that would be?"

"Before lunchtime, I guess. He said we could all go out to eat together."

Why that sneaky, low-down, devious snake. Obviously, Duke had plotted to leave the boys with her for an entire morning. How could he? What if she'd been called away on an emergency? What if she'd simply been too busy to look after them? She regarded the two boys, who were waiting quietly for her response, and sighed. There was no emergency, and she wasn't too busy.

"Why don't we take the shopping bag into the kitchen, and I'll make us all some hot chocolate."

"All right!" Josh said.

"And cookies?" Zack asked, only to be shushed by his brother with a warning that he wasn't being polite.

"You're s'pposed to wait till you're invited," Josh said.

"That's okay," Dani told them. "Actually, I was just thinking about baking some cookies."

"Really?" Zack asked. "Chocolate chip?"

"Zack!" Josh protested.

Dani chuckled. "It's okay. Chocolate chip are my favorite, too. I always keep a package of the slice-and-bake kind in the refrigerator."

"We know how to do those kind," Zack said proudly. "Paolina lets us."

"Good, then you can help me," Dani said, taking the package out and searching for a cookie sheet and a knife that would do the job without being too dangerous for clumsy little hands.

The morning passed in a blur of hot chocolate, cookies, laughter and talk of dinosaurs and spaceships. She hadn't had so much fun since...

No, she told herself sternly. She wasn't going to go there. Not today. Today she was simply going to enjoy the fact that two little boys with incredible imaginations and their daddy's charm were sharing their lives with her.

Later she would try very hard not to let her heart break.

Duke surveyed the scene in Dani's kitchen and smiled. His little plot was working out very nicely.

Left to their own devices, he'd known that Josh and Zack could climb over any wall Dani tried to erect between them.

He'd given Paolina very explicit instructions to make sure that everything went off without a hitch. She was to leave the boys at Dani's, then drive by twice over the next half hour to make sure they were inside. She had called him at the office to report that everything was *muy bueno,* very good.

Now that he had Dani guessing about his intentions, Duke had concluded that it was time to switch tactics once again. He intended to pester her like ants at a picnic. She'd been so sure she was in charge, that he'd accepted her terms for their relationship. He wanted to make certain she realized now that she'd been mistaken.

Today's unscheduled visit from Josh and Zack was just the start.

"Having fun?" he inquired as he knocked on the screen door and entered the kitchen.

Dani had a streak of chocolate on her cheek, marshmallow on her lips and fire flashing in her eyes. Her laughter faded at the sight of him.

"You and I need to talk," she said quietly. "Boys, can you put the rest of the cookies in the cookie jar for me?"

"Sure," they said at once, far more eagerly than they'd ever responded to one of Duke's directives.

As soon as she saw that they were doing as she'd asked, she walked into the living room. Duke followed, preparing himself for the barrage of questions he knew was coming.

"What on earth were you thinking?" she demanded the instant they were out of earshot of the boys.

"Excuse me?"

"I am not your baby-sitter."

"Of course not."

"I could have been out on a call."

"That was a possibility," Duke agreed. "Paolina was supposed to check to make sure you were here."

"I never spoke to Paolina. I found your sons sitting on my doorstep, looking for all the world as if they'd been abandoned there."

"Naturally, you took them in."

"Well, of course I did. What was I supposed to do?"

"You could have called me to come and get them," he said mildly.

Dani stared at him silently, then some of the fight seemed to drain out of her. "Yes, you're right. I suppose I could have done that."

"Any idea why you didn't? I mean especially if having them here was a bother."

"It wasn't a bother, not like you mean."

He nodded at that. "Good. I'm glad."

"They're terrific boys. You know that."

"I think so." He shrugged. "Well, if that's all, I guess we'll be on our way. I promised to take them to lunch."

She actually grinned sheepishly at that. "I doubt they're all that hungry. We've eaten a lot of cookies. It probably spoiled their appetite."

"I don't suppose missing lunch will kill them." He

paused and deliberately brushed a brotherly kiss across her cheek. "Thanks, again. How much do I owe you for the cat food?"

She stared at him, clearly flustered. Finally, she distractedly named an amount and accepted the cash. When he walked out the door, the boys in tow, she still looked as if she wasn't quite certain what had happened. Duke grinned all the way home.

Over the next few weeks he could see that the new approach was working better and better. Dani brightened perceptibly at the sight of him, then turned right around and pretended she couldn't stand to be near him. He knew it was pretense, because he made a point of using any legitimate excuse at all to touch her.

A quick kiss of a greeting, a seemingly inadvertent brushing of their knees when they were cleverly and deliberately seated next to each other at the Adams gatherings he'd started attending again, a lightning-fast caress of her cheek as he said good-night. She trembled visibly at each fleeting contact. Color bloomed in her cheeks. Exasperation and yearning warred in her eyes.

Of course, the game was taking its toll on him as well. Some nights he went home so aroused, it took a jog around the house and an icy shower before he could settle down and have any hope at all of getting to sleep. When he realized he was tempted to start warming a pan of milk at bedtime, he knew he was in serious trouble.

Yes, indeed, the more Duke saw of Dani Adams, the more intrigued he was. He hated that no matter what he tried, she continued to look a little aloof, a little sad. In the midst of the wildest, noisiest family celebration, she kept mostly to herself. Not even Sharon Lynn's or Jenny's best efforts could penetrate her shell for long.

After the cookie-baking episode, she was more careful than ever, it seemed, to avoid spending any time whatsoever with his sons, so careful that it was clear she desperately wanted to gather them into her arms for hugs. Only a fool wouldn't recognize that she was a woman just made for mothering. It was in her eyes as she watched them, a longing so deep, so fierce that it reaffirmed Duke's determination to make her their mother.

The boys sensed those maternal instincts, too. They gravitated to her at every Adams family event and though she was as skittish as a horse around a rattler, sooner or later she came around. Every single time.

Josh and Zack made her smile when no one else could. The smiles were cautious, tentative, to be sure, but they lifted Duke's spirits as much as any oil strike he'd ever made.

Dani seemed to be the only one who didn't get how much her warmth was valued. On some level, she clearly blamed herself for getting too caught up in the lives of those girls she'd ultimately lost. She thought she was the one who'd hurt them, when the truth was it was their father's cavalier attitude that had set them all up for anguish.

Duke would never make that mistake. He was a decisive man, always had been. Once he made a commitment, he stuck to it, for better or worse. He would have stayed married to Caroline, enduring the cold emptiness of the relationship if that had been what she wanted. Duty and honor were that important to him.

Now he wanted Dani Adams to become a significant part of Josh's and Zack's lives, a permanent part. The boys needed a mother's love. They needed Dani. And he would do whatever was necessary to get her for them. He owed it to them after the mess he'd made of his marriage to their mother. It was as simple and clear-cut as that for him.

His own feelings toward her were more complex. He enjoyed Dani's company. He wanted her in his bed. He had vowed to himself that he would always treat her the way she deserved to be treated. The only thing he couldn't promise her was love. He hoped that the things he could offer would be enough for a woman who understood the meaning and importance of family.

Thanksgiving was coming and he decided the holidays were the perfect time to step up his campaign, turn up the heat another notch, so to speak. Christmas would be the ideal, most romantic time to announce an engagement. He made that his goal and set up a strategic plan that corporate executives—Jordan included, he thought with a grim smile—would have envied.

Her family, bless them, cooperated by issuing an invitation for Thanksgiving dinner at White Pines. The message had been relayed by Jordan just that afternoon. Duke mentioned it to the boys when he got home that night, certain of their response.

"So, what do you think?" he asked.

"Cool," Joshua said. "Will there be turkey and dressing and pumpkin pie?"

"I imagine so," Duke said. He was fairly confident that this family would celebrate with old-fashioned excess when it came to their Thanksgiving feast.

"Will Dani be there?" Zachary asked.

"Of course."

"Are you gonna kiss her again?" Zack asked, proving that he was as adept as any Adams at sneaking up on people.

Duke held back a grin. "Maybe."

"Does that mean you and Dani are gonna get married?" Joshua asked. "I haven't got all this grown-up stuff figured out yet."

"Kissing sometimes leads to marriage," Duke conceded carefully.

"But what about you and Dani?" Josh persisted. "Are you guys gonna get married?"

Duke knew better than to set them up for disappointment. His plans were a little too iffy to make a firm declaration on the subject just yet, especially when anything he said was likely to be repeated. He could just imagine Dani's reaction to hearing the news of their impending wedding from someone else.

"We'll see," he equivocated.

More than once after a frustrating day behind his desk, he'd lain awake at night wondering if he really could get her riled up enough to marry him. He figured she was the kind of woman who was going to go down the aisle still denying that she was in love, especially with him. Persuading her otherwise might be challenging enough to make him forget all about bringing in another gusher.

If it turned out he was wrong about keeping his interest in Dani alive for all eternity, at least the boys would have a mom again. He would be free to get back to the kind of work he loved. Even as the unfairness and selfishness of that plan struck him, he tried to calculate how to make it work.

He felt Zack tugging on his sleeve to get his attention. "Then she would be our mom, right?"

"Yes, if it happens, she would be your mom. Would that be okay with you guys?"

Joshua shrugged. "I suppose."

Duke was startled by the less than enthusiastic endorsement. Had he read the signals all wrong again? "I thought you liked Dani," he said.

"I do, but moms go away sometimes," Josh said, fighting tears. "It might be better if Dani was just our friend."

Holy kamoley, Duke thought. This was an angle he'd never expected. He gathered both boys close.

"Not every mom goes away," he said carefully.

He'd tried very hard not to blame their mother for running out. In fact, he'd bent over backward to shoulder most of the responsibility for driving her away. If she ever came back, he didn't want the boys to hate her for something for which much of the blame was his.

He struggled for an explanation that would console and offer hope at the same time. "We've talked about this before. Sometimes things happen between grown-ups that can't be helped. When it does, one of them goes away. That doesn't mean you shouldn't love them when they're around or treasure the good memories you have. You have to take risks or you'll go through life being very lonely.''

"No way," Zack protested fiercely. "We've got each other. We'll never be lonely. We don't need anybody else.''

"If that were true, would you be having such a good time with your new friends here in Los Pinos?''

Both boys hesitated as they considered that.

"I guess not,'' Josh conceded.

"Someday you're going to be a grown-up, and you're going to want even more than good friends. You're going to want somebody to love. I want you to believe that taking a chance on love is worth the risk, worth whatever hurt might happen.'' He grinned at them. "Because, you know what? Sometimes that risk pays off big time and lasts forever.''

"Like with you and us," Joshua said.

Duke's eyes swam with unshed tears. "Exactly,'' he whispered. "Exactly like us.''

And if he had his way, Dani would become a part of that tight-knit circle just as soon as he could make it happen. Despite what he'd just told his sons about putting everything on the line for love, the only thing he wasn't willing to risk was his own heart. He'd had years of evidence to analyze. He was pretty sure he didn't even have one.

On Thanksgiving morning Dani discovered the kitchen at White Pines in predictable chaos. Maritza, who'd been Grandpa Harlan's housekeeper practically forever, was trying her best to shoo everyone out, but lured by the scent of roasting turkey and pumpkin pie, no one was paying a bit of attention. Even Janet, whose lack of culinary skills was the stuff of family legend, seemed drawn to the one room in the house she usually avoided.

"Señora Janet, everything here is under control," Maritza declared again. "Please, you go and take the others with you. It is Thanksgiving. You should be relaxing and enjoying your company."

Janet made a token protest, offered to make the dressing and was soundly discouraged not only by Maritza, but also by everyone else as well.

"Ungrateful wretches," Janet said, laughing. She scowled at Jenny. "You especially. I expected more loyalty from my firstborn daughter."

"Hey, I grew up on your cooking for the first fourteen years of my life. The best I can say is that I survived it." She turned to her younger sister. "Lizzy, you have no idea how grateful you should be that Maritza is here."

Janet threw up her hands. "Okay, enough. I'm going where I'm appreciated."

"I saw Dad out by the barn with Duke and the twins," Lizzy offered. "Dad is always eager to see you."

Janet gave them all a satisfied smile. "Yes, he is, isn't he?" she said as she slipped out the screen door.

Dani watched her go and wished she could follow. She was still putting up a valiant battle with her emotions, but she feared she was losing the war. Just the mention of Duke's name was enough to stir her senses alive. It really was absurd how little control she had over her reactions to the man. Worse, he knew it and he was deliberately plaguing her.

He never had gotten around to asking that all-important question that had brought him into her office a few weeks back. She'd been left to speculate and wonder and worry, even though he was suddenly underfoot everywhere she went. There hadn't been a doubt in her mind that someone would think to include him and the boys in today's celebration. Hearing that he was outside with her grandfather had made her pulse jump just the same.

"You could go, too," Jenny suggested mildly.

Dani stared at her. "Go where?"

"Out to the barn."

"Why would I want to do that?"

Jenny laughed. "Oh, sweetie, give it up. The only one not admitting that you're nuts about the guy is you."

Dani frowned. "One of these days, Jenny Runningbear Adams, you are going to fall head over heels in love with some man and I am going to lead the troops in making your life miserable about it."

"Not me," Jenny declared emphatically. "I don't have time to fall in love. Between lobbying in Washington and teaching, my plate is full. I'm perfectly content."

"Famous last words," Dani taunted. She glanced at Lizzy, who was listening in with an amused expression. "I say a year, tops. How about you?"

"First she has to meet somebody," Lizzy pointed out. "She never pokes her head into anyplace where she's likely to meet anyone interesting. She spends all her time surrounded by teenagers and lawyers.''

"Watch it, baby sister," Jenny warned. "Our mother is a lawyer. She wouldn't appreciate you disparaging her kind.''

"Everyone knows that Mom's an exception," Lizzy said loyally. "The ones you know are out for a buck.''

"How would you know that? You've never met most of them.''

"I hear you and Mom and Dad talking. How do you think I got to be so smart?''

Jenny chuckled. "Who says you're smart?''

"Daddy.''

Dani and Jenny exchanged a look. "Of course," Dani said. "For a minute there, we forgot we were talking to Grandpa Harlan's best and brightest.''

Lizzy scowled at her teasing. "I could tell you a few things..." she muttered.

"Such as?" Dani asked.

"You seem to forget that I worked for Duke all summer long," Lizzy taunted meaningfully.

Dani's heart seemed to lurch to a stop. "So?"

"I heard stuff.''

"About?''

"Never mind," Lizzy said airily. "I'm going out where I'm appreciated, too.''

She left her sister and Dani staring after her.

"What do you suppose she knows?" Dani asked, unable to mask her curiosity.

"Very little, I think," Maritza chimed in from the stove. "She is just talking big to get your attention.''

"It worked, too," Jenny observed thoughtfully. "She mentioned Duke and your antenna shot up. Interesting reaction for a woman who claims the man doesn't matter to her."

"Oh, go to hell," Dani muttered.

"Young lady, you do not use such talk in my kitchen," Maritza said indignantly. "You are not too big for me to wash out your mouth with soap."

"Uh-oh," Jenny taunted. "You're in big trouble now."

"I'm going where I'm appreciated," Dani said.

"To the barn?" Jenny asked, her eyes twinkling.

"No. To find my father."

"Now there's the ticket. Run off to Jordan," Jenny taunted. "Don't expect him to side with you, though. He's like the rest of us. He's just waiting for an engagement announcement. He discovered that being a daddy was fun. Now he wants to try out being a granddaddy."

"He does not," Dani protested, though the claim made her very nervous. She suspected there might be some truth to it.

"Does, too."

"*Niñas,* stop it," Maritza ordered. "You will spoil the food with all this bickering. Be nice."

Dani laughed. "How often have we heard those words?" she asked as she wrapped her arms around Maritza and hugged her. "*Te amo,* Maritza."

The housekeeper's dour expression softened. "*Te amo,* Danielle. You are my own precious one."

"I thought I was," Jenny protested with a glint of pure mischief in her eyes.

"You, *niña,* are the thorn in my side, especially today. Now go. You both are in my way."

It seemed everywhere Dani went she was in the way. She tried the den, but Jordan, Cody and Luke were busy cussing a blue streak at the television. It appeared the Dallas Cowboys weren't delivering today.

Restless, it was probably inevitable that she would wander out to the barn. She swore it had nothing at all to do with Duke's presence out there. Everyone was there, after all. Not just the man who made her toes tingle and tempted her to forget every resolution she'd made about choosing more wisely the next time she fell in love.

She also swore that she wouldn't have gravitated directly toward him, if it hadn't been for Joshua and Zachary. They rushed over and each clasped a hand, drawing her straight toward their father.

"Tell her, Dad. Tell her about the horses you're gonna get us," Joshua said, practically jumping up and down with excitement.

Dani met Duke's gaze and felt that increasingly familiar jolt of excitement, the unmistakable tug that would have had a less stubborn woman throwing herself into his arms. She was almost used to it now. At least, it no longer left her thoroughly tongue-tied.

"If you're thinking of getting them horses, I gather they've passed the pet test?" she said to him.

"It's been months now, and the cats are still alive," he said dryly. "It's a small victory for responsibility." He regarded her speculatively. "You know, I'm going to need some help with this one."

"What kind of help?"

"Picking out the right horses, checking into their breeding, going over them to make sure they're sound. You're a vet. You'll be much better at that than I would be," he said, then added a little too casually, "Think you could carve out a little time and go with me to a horse sale?"

Dani was flattered that he trusted her judgment, but going off to a horse sale with him meant spending time alone, just the two of them. She suspected from the gleam in his eyes that finding the best animals for his money wasn't the only thing on his mind.

For weeks now Duke had done nothing to alarm her. He hadn't even given her more than a chaste peck on the cheek. Still, she was smart enough to realize that the growing lust she was feeling wasn't entirely one-sided. A few hours cooped up in a car and who knew what ideas he might get.

Not that she didn't trust him, she told herself. It was herself she didn't trust. The very sensible reasons she'd had for resisting Duke were fading, lost in a haze of pure longing that was deepening over time.

She forced herself to try once more to beg off. "Duke, I'm more than happy to give you some pointers, but I'd hate to be responsible for the final decision. It's your money."

"I'll be taken to the cleaners," he insisted. "They'll see me coming a mile away."

"Then take my father or Uncle Cody," she said, unsuccessfully trying to fight the note of desperation that was creeping into her voice. "Heck, Grandpa Harlan would love to go. There's nothing he likes more than a good horse sale and a chance to do some bargaining.''

''I want your help,'' he insisted.

The man could match any Adams she knew for pure cussedness, she concluded with a sigh. ''Why me?'' she asked.

''You aren't scared to spend the day with me, are you?'' he retorted.

Her temper flared with predictable speed at the taunt. ''Of course not.''

''You sure about that, darlin? You sound scared.''

''Oh, for heaven's sakes, when is this sale?''

''Next weekend.''

''Where?''

''Fort Worth.''

It would be a long trip, but it could be done in a day, Dani reassured herself. They would be surrounded by hordes of people for most of that time. What could happen? Nothing, absolutely nothing. Not if she didn't allow it. Maybe it was time to put her resolutions to the test. She sighed.

''What time do you want to go?''

''I'll pick you up at five, so we'll have time to look the horses over before the sale starts.''

She studied his face intently. His expression was pure innocence, but there was a glint in his eyes that suggested he was gloating. After all, he had gotten his way. Again. Why shouldn't he gloat? She had the resistance of a limp noodle where he was concerned.

''Can we come, too?'' Joshua pleaded.

As if he'd forgotten his sons' presence and the purpose of the trip to Fort Worth, Duke blinked and stared at Joshua for a full minute before shaking his head.

"No," he said flatly.

"But, Dad…" Zack protested.

"I said no," Duke repeated.

"The horses are for us," Zack argued.

"Yes, they are," Dani agreed, siding with the boys for her own less than honorable purposes. "They should have some say."

"Coward," Duke murmured just for her ears.

Since she couldn't deny it, she pretended she hadn't even heard. "Well?" she said. "Can they come?"

"No, indeed, they can't go," her grandfather said, stepping into the fray at the most inopportune moment possible. "I have plans for you two boys right here."

"But…" Joshua began.

"No buts," her grandfather said firmly. "No point in picking out horses, if you can't ride. While your daddy and Dani are off in Fort Worth, Cody and I will give you your first lessons."

To Dani's dismay, both boys reacted with enthusiasm. So much for her salvation. This time when she met Duke's gaze, there was no mistaking the triumph. Since Maritza wasn't nearby to reproach her, she told him to go to hell, too.

He laughed. "Been there, darlin'. This time I'm aiming for heaven."

Chapter Eleven

It was pitch-dark outside, the kind of velvet blanket of darkness that made a person want to snuggle up next to a lover and light up the night with emotional fireworks.

Dani stood in the doorway, a cup of very strong coffee in her hands, and tried to dismiss from her thoughts the provocative image she'd just created. It was virtually impossible, especially since Duke seemed to be the lover crowded into that image with her.

It was barely four-thirty and she was already dressed and far too eager for their trip to Fort Worth. A dozen excuses for staying home had popped to the tip of her tongue since Thanksgiving, but she hadn't uttered a one of them. Either she was totally and unredeemably reckless or she was deluding herself about the power of the attraction between her and Duke.

When bright headlights cut through the darkness at the end of the block, her nerves kicked in. At this hour there was no question of it being anyone other than Duke. Since he was early, she could only assume he was as anxious as she was about whatever lay ahead.

She already knew that he'd made arrangements to drop Josh and Zack off at White Pines the night before. For some reason the evidence of his eagerness seemed to calm her just a little. He was usually so confident, so blasted sure of himself. It was nice to see a little hint of vulnerability for a change.

As he pulled to a stop, she stood her ground, watching, waiting to see what note he would strike when he greeted her. Casual and easy? Provocative? Maybe daring?

Her pulse skittered crazily as she anticipated his lips settling on hers for what he meant to be a cool, friendly greeting. Both of them knew by now that no amount of control or caution could tame a real kiss between them. It was why he'd deliberately dusted the air by her cheek and forehead for weeks now. Even innocent kisses had a way of turning stunningly sexual in an instant.

"Hey, darlin', are you ready?" he called out without leaving the car.

Fighting a ridiculous sense of disappointment, she forced a smile. "I'll be right there. Would you like some coffee for the road?"

He held up a covered mug. "Already have it.

There's another one here for you, along with a bag of doughnuts fresh from the oven. I threw myself on Sallie's mercy over at the bakery, and she slipped me a few out the back door.''

Dani had a hunch Sallie hadn't required much persuading. She was a sucker for a handsome face. Always had been, even though she'd been happily married to the same man for almost fifty years now. Sallie was every bit as much of a flirt as Betty Lou. Every man in town knew they could sweet-talk her into tucking an extra doughnut in the bag every now and again.

Dani took one last look at the cats' lineup of bowls in the kitchen to make sure they were all full, then grabbed her jacket and purse and locked the front door behind her.

When she reached the car, Duke leaned across the front seat and opened the door for her.

''No overnight bag?'' he inquired.

Her alarmed gaze flew to his, but she managed to keep her voice even. ''We're coming back tonight,'' she said firmly. ''That was the plan.''

''Well, of course, it is,'' he agreed at once. ''But you know how unpredictable the weather can be this time of year. I've brought one. It never hurts to be prepared for plans to go awry.''

''Ours won't,'' Dani stated grimly.

Duke grinned. ''I'll be sure to pass along your conviction to the weatherman.''

She studied him through narrowed eyes. ''Do you know something about the weather that I don't?'' she asked, cursing herself for not checking out the eleven o'clock news the night before or the weather channel this morning. For all she knew a blizzard could be headed for Texas, and they were driving straight into it. If getting stranded suited Duke's purposes, she wondered if he would bother to mention an approaching storm.

"Maybe I ought to check the weather channel before we take off," she said, reaching for the door handle.

"No need. They're just predicting a little rain around Fort Worth. It shouldn't be a problem," he said blandly, pulling out of the driveway before Dani had a chance to evaluate whether the rain presented a real danger.

"Just rain?" she asked.

He shrugged. "Unless the temperature drops."

She didn't like the way he was hedging or the way he was avoiding her gaze. "Maybe we should do this another time."

"Darlin', they're just calling for a little rain," he protested. "What's the worst that could happen? We'd have to stay overnight. We're both adults. That shouldn't be a problem, right?"

No, it shouldn't be, Dani agreed to herself. But it would be. She could feel it in her bones...and elsewhere.

"I don't know—" she began.

"Trust me, darlin', we'll be just fine. Now sit back and relax. Drink your coffee before it gets cold and try one of these doughnuts." He gestured to the bag on the seat between them. "There are jelly-filled, glazed and old-fashioned."

The bag was huge, big enough to hold at least a baker's dozen, though there were far fewer than that left. The assortment had clearly been plundered. Dani couldn't help grinning. "Just how many have you eaten already?"

"A couple," he said, then grinned guiltily. "Okay, maybe four. I never get to have doughnuts anymore. I'm trying to teach the boys to eat a healthy breakfast by setting a good example. I've eaten enough bran flakes in the last year to fulfill my fiber quota for two lifetimes."

"You know, an occasional doughnut won't kill any of you," Dani said. "Maybe if you ate them in moderation, you wouldn't be pigging out now."

"Darlin', I don't need a lecture on my eating habits from you."

"If you say so," she said, peering into the bag. The aroma of dough and sugar and raspberry jelly hit her smack in the face. She drew in a deep breath. "Oh, my."

"Downright intoxicating, isn't it?" Duke teased.

"Incredible," she murmured distractedly. All of her attention was focused on the choice she was about to make.

"You could have one of each," Duke said, clearly guessing her dilemma.

"I couldn't," she insisted and settled for the raspberry-filled doughnut that was still warm to the touch. Powdered sugar coated her lips. Jam settled in the corners of her mouth and left her fingers sticky. "Heavenly."

Duke glanced over at her, then sucked in a sharp breath. Pure lust darkened his eyes.

"What?" Dani demanded, her own breath catching.

"There are napkins in the glove compartment," Duke said in a choked voice.

"Why? Am I a mess?"

"Not exactly," he said. "But if you don't wipe away the sugar and jam around your mouth, I'm going to have to do it for you." His heated gaze clashed with hers. "I won't be using a napkin."

The image of his tongue searching out every little trace of sugar and jam slammed into her with the force of a gale. She fumbled badly as she tried to open the glove compartment and retrieve a napkin. Her hand shook as she tried to wipe away any trace of the doughnut she had savored.

"Too bad," Duke teased when she was done. "I was looking forward to helping."

"I'll just bet you were," she said. A change of topic was definitely in order. "Why don't you tell me what you have in mind when it comes to the horses. How much do you want to spend? Is there any particular type of horse you want?"

He chuckled. "Smooth transition. Don't tell me I was making you nervous."

"You weren't," she insisted.

"Liar."

She regarded him impatiently. "Duke, you asked me to come along today to help you buy horses. That's all I'm doing here."

"I know," he said.

She didn't trust that dutiful tone one bit. "I hope you do."

He sketched a cross over his heart. "Darlin', if you made yourself any clearer, I'd have a knot upside my head."

"Don't tempt me."

"Damn, but you're cute when—"

She scowled at him. "Don't say it. Don't you dare say it."

"You want me to be honest, don't you?"

"Of course, but—"

"That's all I'm doing. Telling it like it is."

Dani sighed heavily. "Why don't I believe that?"

"You have a suspicious nature," he suggested.

"My nature, as you put it, has been honed by experience."

"You're not comparing me to that Rob person again, are you?" He didn't wait for her reply. "I'm disappointed. I thought we were way beyond that."

"Well, we're not," she grumbled. "You're sneaky and underhanded, just like he was."

"Me? Name one single sneaky, underhanded thing I've done."

Naturally, every one she came up with sounded petty, so she kept her mouth clamped firmly shut.

"Cat got your tongue?" he inquired.

"No the cat does not have my tongue," she snapped. "I'm just trying to be civil. Otherwise this is going to be a very long trip."

Duke's eyes were flashing with humor. "Hey, don't stand on ceremony on my account. Say whatever's on your mind and get it out of your system. I can take it.''

She turned to face him. ''Okay, don't say you didn't ask for it.''

''I'm ready,'' he said, his expression stoic.

Suddenly, the list of his so-called sins seemed endless. She couldn't wait to enumerate them all.

''From the day we met you have been trying to disrupt my life,'' she accused. ''You turn up everywhere I go like the proverbial bad penny. You've deliberately ingratiated yourself with my family. They all think you hung the moon. They're plotting and scheming on your behalf without the slightest regard for my feelings.''

''That's not the way they see it,'' Duke pointed out.

''Well, of course, it isn't. They're a bunch of softhearted romantics. Grandpa Harlan is the worst of all. I thought I could count on my father being on my side, but even he seems to have joined the enemy camp. As for your boys, they have managed to slip past my best defenses.''

His eyebrows rose at that. ''Now there's a crime.''

''Lay off. You asked me to say what was on my mind.''

''So I did. Do go on.''

''You don't listen to a word I say.''

''I listen to every single word you say,'' Duke protested. ''It's just that sometimes you and I may disagree on whether or not you mean what you say.''

''Of course, I mean it,'' she practically shouted.

"Do you think I'm just wasting my breath for the heck of it?"

Duke shook his head and regarded her with something she suspected was awfully close to pity. She felt like slugging him.

"Of course not," he soothed. "The logical, rational side of your brain means every word. I'm not so dense that I'd miss a thing like that."

"Then what's the problem?" she demanded.

He reached over and touched a finger lightly to the center of her chest. "That's the problem," he said gently. "Your heart and your brain aren't in sync. Sharon Lynn and Jenny see it. Your father and grandfather see it. Now, I may not understand a lot about women. I may know even less about emotions, but I do get one thing. When push comes to shove, it's what your heart feels that really matters."

Dani felt the very organ in question pump a little faster as if to confirm what he said. She'd been so sure that he couldn't see through her, so sure that she could keep her secret, forever if she had to. Then, *wham*, just like that it was all over. The truth was out or would be, if she confirmed his suspicions.

She just couldn't do it. She settled for lying, instead, in a valiant attempt to save herself—to save them—from making a terrible mistake.

"You're wrong," she said quietly, but emphatically. "You have it all wrong."

It would have been enough to convince any other man. Or at least any other man would have graciously accepted the lie and let things be. Not Duke. He just smiled knowingly.

"If you say so, darlin'."

"Don't use that patronizing tone with me," she said, fuming.

He seemed even more amused by the outburst. "Sorry," he apologized with a total lack of sincerity.

Dani shook her head and bit back another sharp retort that he would only find even more unconvincing.

"Hey, don't worry about it. We'll work it out."

"We will not work it out," she said, her teeth clenched.

"Sure we will. You may be an Adams, but I'm every bit as stubborn."

Now there, she thought dispiritedly, was the truth. The realization scared her to death.

Duke thought the drive had gone very well. Dani was so furious steam was practically spewing out of her ears. That was good. It meant he was getting to her, shaking her up, rattling her. Anytime now he would get her to make an honest admission of her feelings toward him. He'd thought for a minute she was about to blurt it out, but then she'd sucked in a deep breath and gone all stiff and silent on him. He could have told her that was every bit as telling, but wisely he didn't. She was in no mood to appreciate the observation.

He supposed he ought to feel guilty about backing her into a corner, but he needed her to acknowledge what she felt. So he had to move on to the next stage of his plan: getting her to say yes to a marriage proposal.

He glanced over at her as they pulled into a parking place behind the barns where the horse sale was being held. Her hands were clenched together so tightly in her lap that her knuckles were white. He had a feeling if he laid his hands on her shoulders, he would find knots of tension as big as Texas...right before she throttled him for touching her.

"Are you planning on speaking to me ever again?" he inquired lightly. "If not, exactly how are you going to communicate with me when you spot the perfect horse?"

Her lips twitched ever so slightly. "I was thinking of kicking you real hard in the shins."

He grinned. "That would get my attention, that's for sure."

"I wonder," she said.

His gaze narrowed. "What's that supposed to mean?"

"It means I'm not sure that a baseball bat to the head would get your attention unless you wanted it to."

"I am single-minded," he agreed. "You probably need to remember that."

"Believe me, it's not something I'm likely to forget," she retorted. "Now are we going to sit here all day or are we going to check out the horses?"

He went around the car and opened her door with a flourish. "Lead the way, darlin'. There's nothing I like better than following along behind a pretty woman."

She scowled at the remark and, he noticed, made darn sure that she was always beside him and not in front of him. With brisk efficiency, she found the listings of the horses for sale and scanned the pages, checking several and crossing off twice as many.

"Let's go," she said, studying the arrangement of the stalls. "There's a pinto pony in number seventy-six that might be just right."

When they found it, Duke took one look at the skittish animal and concluded it had been rounded up wild and half-starved to death before being brought to today's sale. As Dani approached, fear darkened the horse's eyes and made them flare dangerously.

"Dani," Duke said very softly. "Careful."

She nodded, acknowledging the warning. Then she reached in her pocket for a lump of sugar and held it out. The pony shied away from her. Dani eased closer, murmuring nonsense until eventually the pony remained still when she approached. Duke's heart stayed in his throat the whole time. He was fairly sure he didn't breathe again until Dani backed out of reach of the horse's nervous hooves.

"That horse has been mistreated," Duke said angrily when she was beside him again. "You're lucky he didn't kick you."

"He's malnourished, that's for sure," she agreed, her eyes wide and shimmering with tears. "But he's beautiful, Duke. He's full of life."

"He's too skittish for the boys."

"He wouldn't be if someone cared for him," she argued.

"Dani, he's the first horse we've seen. Hold off on a recommendation until we've seen the rest that you've marked."

She faced him stubbornly. "He's going to stay on the list," she insisted. "You'll see."

Duke sighed, relieved that he'd borrowed a horse trailer large enough to carry half a dozen horses. He had a feeling Dani was going to be an easy mark. If he didn't agree with her selections, she would probably buy the others herself.

They looked over another eleven horses. Out of the even dozen she'd selected, she found four she thought were both sound and likely to go for the right price. Not counting that blasted pinto, of course. That made five she considered worth bidding on.

"Which one of us is going to bid?" she asked Duke when it was time for the sale to begin. "You should since it's your money we're spending."

"I'm sticking with you," he insisted. "You know the value of these horses better than I do. I'm liable to get carried away."

She regarded him doubtfully. "You don't strike me as the kind of man who'd get carried away at an auction."

"Why not?"

"Too hardheaded," she said succinctly. "You'd be more likely to set a figure and stick with it, no matter how badly you wanted the horse."

To be perfectly truthful, she was right, Duke admitted, but only to himself. At least that's how he always had been. Today, though, he had the feeling that he could very easily get caught up in Dani's excitement and lose his head completely. In fact, he was already more than half certain that they would be leaving with that pinto if he had to buy it for her himself. She hadn't stopped talking about it since they'd first visited the horse's stall. He had a feeling buying it would be the kind of outrageous gesture no one had ever made for her before. Maybe it would prove to be the clincher in his plan.

There were two palominos early in the sale, practically mirror images of each other. Duke knew that Dani was leaning toward them for the boys. He'd liked them himself. They appeared gentle enough.

In the guise of having her show him what she was looking for when she examined them, he'd gone over them himself and confirmed Dani's view that they were strong and sound. When he'd commented on just that, she'd regarded him with an odd expression on her face. He'd warned himself to be very careful. One more mistake like that would be his downfall. Dani was too smart not to catch on sooner or later that he knew exactly what he was doing. Then there was going to be big trouble. He was resigned to it.

In the meantime, though, he had her to himself for an entire day. She'd stopped being skittish hours ago. She'd even laughed at a few of his jokes and reached for his hand on one occasion, only to drop it like a branding iron when she realized what she'd done.

When the first of the palominos came on the block, the bidding was fairly light. Dani picked the horse up for well under the limit Duke had set. She flashed a look of triumph at him at the conclusion of the bidding.

"This is fun," she announced. "No wonder Grandpa Harlan loves horse-trading so much. I hope we can get the second one, too." Her eyes darkened with worry. "Or do you think the boys would rather have horses that don't look alike? Are they sensitive about the twin thing?"

Duke had never given the matter much thought. Even though they were identical, they'd never been dressed exactly alike or given the same toys. They had surprisingly individual tastes and interests. Their personalities were a blend of harmony and diversity. At times, they acted as one. At other times, they behaved like any other squabbling, jealous non-twin siblings.

"My hunch is the only way to avoid conflict might be to give them matching horses," he told her. "This is a pretty big deal. We don't want either of them getting the idea that the other's horse is better in some way you and I don't get."

Dani grinned sympathetically. "Figuring out how eight-year-olds think does have its moments, doesn't it?"

"I'm sure it has brought many a parent to his knees," Duke agreed. "Go for the other palomino."

"I agree. Maybe if they both weren't so beautiful, I'd go a different way, but they're gorgeous."

"You don't think this second one is going to have a problem with that left front foreleg, do you?"

She shot him a suspicious look. "What are you talking about?"

Careful, Duke warned himself. "It seemed to me his gait was a little off. You mentioned it yourself, didn't you?"

Dani scanned her notes. "I did write it down," she agreed, but she was clearly unsettled by his observation. "I don't think it's a problem, though. I've seen other horses like that do just fine. If it comes to that, it's a correctible problem with fairly minor surgery. If you wanted more than a riding horse, we should probably reconsider, but for Josh or Zack, the palomino will get along okay."

Duke nodded. "I'll trust your judgment."

The bidding for the second palomino was livelier than the first, proving that plenty of others were just as unconcerned as Dani about the horse's unusual gait. When they neared Duke's preset limit, Dani glanced over at him.

"Well?"

He grinned. "Go up, if you have to. The other one was a steal. It'll all even out."

"All right," she said and reentered the bidding frenzy with enthusiasm.

Naturally, she triumphed, Duke was holding his breath on the last round. Not that he couldn't afford to spend more. He could. He just wasn't sure the horse was worth it. The beaming smile on Dani's face, however, was worth every penny.

"That's it, then," he said when the bidding was done. "Mission accomplished."

"Not quite," she said.

"Let me guess. The pinto."

"I have to have him," she said. "He needs a good home."

"Do you have room in your backyard?" Duke inquired dryly.

She shot him a we-are-not-amused look. "There's plenty of room at Mom and Dad's," she said.

"And you get out there how often?"

"Do you really have to be so blasted logical?" she inquired testily.

Duke threw back his head and laughed at that. She grinned and admitted, "Okay, it's like the pot calling the kettle black. I want that horse."

Duke nodded. "I know. His number won't be up for a while now. Want to go grab a bite to eat?"

"Sure."

He led the way to a vendor selling hot dogs and soft drinks. Dani slathered her hot dog with mustard, relish and was debating over the onions when he caught her eye. She swallowed hard, then left the onions untouched. He figured it was tantamount to an admission that she knew before the day ended they would share at least one kiss, probably more.

They finished their meal and were about to go back inside, when Duke caught a glimpse of the dab of mustard at the corner of her mouth. All of the desire that had rocketed through him that morning when she'd been eating that doughnut came back now with twice the intensity.

"Wait," he said softly and reached for a napkin. Alarm flared in her eyes as he tilted her chin up. His thumb skimmed her lower lip, even as he gently wiped away the mustard with the napkin.

"Thanks." It came out as a breathless whisper.

"No problem," he said, though it was a lie. There was a very definite problem. He suddenly wanted nothing more than to drag her off somewhere and tumble her into a haystack or a bed or any other place that would be soft and accommodating.

As if the gods had heard his prayers, a flash of lightning split the sky, followed by a clap of thunder. The skies opened up and rain came down, first in huge, individual drops, then in solid gray sheets. Duke grabbed Dani's hand, and they made a dash back inside.

Fortunately, they'd been quick enough to avoid being soaked to the skin. Duke glanced over her. "You okay? We could leave if you're too wet. There's no point in catching pneumonia."

"Nice try, but I am not leaving without my horse," she said stubbornly.

Quite a few of the other serious bidders caught a glimpse of the storm and decided to flee before it got any worse. When the pinto's number was called, the hall was half-empty. Dani had only one competitor for the horse, and he was bidding with lackluster enthusiasm. He dropped out after only four rounds.

Eyes shining, Dani turned to Duke. "I stole him. I virtually stole him."

"I just hope the payback for your thievery isn't a broken neck," Duke retorted.

"A lot you know," she countered. "That horse is going to be the best investment I ever made."

"Obviously, you've never heard of stocks and bonds," he countered.

"Oh, give it up," she said finally and flashed a knowing smile at him. "Otherwise I might make you explain why it is that you claimed not to know anything about horses, when it's obvious that you know at least as much as I do. I might have taken classes in vet school, but you've spent time around horses, haven't you?"

Uh-oh, Duke thought. "You figured it out, huh?"

"Hours ago. Next time you decide to feign ignorance, it might be a real good idea to keep your mouth shut," she advised.

"I was hoping you'd think I just happened to ask particularly intelligent questions."

"Not just intelligent questions, *well-informed* questions. There's a difference."

"Are you going to hold it against me?"

"Not if you'll tell me why you lied about knowing anything about horses."

"Isn't that obvious?"

"Not to me."

He reached out and touched a finger to her cheek. His gaze locked with hers as he confessed, "It was the only way I could come up with to get you alone for an entire day."

"Oh."

He smiled at that. Oh, indeed. He wondered what she'd think if she figured out he'd been praying to beat the band that this rain would turn to ice any second now so they would be stranded overnight, too.

As if to prove that he still had some pull with heaven, hail began pinging against the cars and trailers outside, making an unmistakable clatter.

Dani's eyes widened as she recognized the implication. "Hail?"

"Sounds like it."

"Maybe it'll pass," she suggested hopefully.

"Do you want to take that chance?" he asked reasonably.

She looked torn. Clearly, she was indecisive about which danger was the greatest—going or staying. She lifted her gaze to his and he could read those by-now familiar warring emotions, desire and panic.

"I'll trust your judgment," she said quietly.

As she said it, her gaze never wavered.

And Duke felt the full weight of responsibility settling on his shoulders. She was leaving more than their going or staying up to him, and they both knew it. He would also be the one to decide if tonight was the night they finally made love.

He could make her respond, make her forget her reservations about their relationship with just a kiss. It would be a simple matter to seduce her...if he dared. Whatever he decided, he would have to live with the decision forever after.

Chapter Twelve

She could live with this, Dani told herself staunchly as Duke drove through the blinding combination of rain and sleet in search of a decent-looking motel. They were adults. Nothing was going to happen beyond getting a good night's sleep unless they both wanted it to.

Unless, of course, her hormones overruled her head, she thought grimly. Maybe she should play it safe and put up more of a fight to go straight back to Los Pinos. She glanced at Duke's tense expression. When he gazed over at her and gave her a quick smile, she felt her pulse zing dangerously. Suddenly, a tactical retreat seemed like a very good idea.

"Are you certain we can't get back tonight?" she asked, peering out the window at the leaden sky. "It looks as if it might clear up," she added with unjustified optimism based on a pinprick-sized patch of blue in the distance.

"Do you believe in the tooth fairy, too?" Duke inquired, not taking his eyes from the hazardous road.

"You don't have to be sarcastic," she said, but she could see his point. The road already had an inch or more of swirling water on it, more than enough to send a car off in a skid and dangerously close to enough to have it stall out. Despite that tiny bit of blue, most of the sky was filled with stormy, rain-filled clouds.

"Why don't you help me out by looking for a half-decent place to stay," Duke suggested. "I passed one motel a block back, but it looked like a dump."

Dani had seen it, too. To describe it as seedy-looking would have been a compliment. Duke would have had to drag her kicking and screaming into a place that crummy. "You drive. I'll look," she said resignedly.

It took another fifteen minutes before she spotted a motel with a Rooms Available sign lit and a small, cozy-looking restaurant attached. It wasn't exactly a luxury resort, but it would do. Perhaps even more important from her perspective, there wasn't the slightest suggestion of a romantic retreat about it, at least if taste was any factor at all. It was very much bright lights and gaudy ambience.

"How about that one?" she asked. "It looks clean."

Duke followed the direction of her gaze. His expression turned skeptical. "You don't mind the flashing neon and the water-bed option?"

"The water bed is just that, an option," she said firmly, even though her stomach turned flip-flops at the thought of climbing into one with Duke. "As for the neon, who cares what's flashing outside. We'll be asleep."

"Your choice," he said and swung the car into the parking lot. "I'll see what's available."

"Duke?"

"Yes?"

"Skip the water bed. I want an ordinary mattress."

"All to yourself?" he inquired, his tone light.

She thought about it for no longer than a heartbeat, but apparently that was long enough for him to interpret the message of uncertainty.

"I'll get two rooms," Duke said, taking the decision out of her hands.

If he was upset, he didn't show it. Still, Dani stared after him, already regretting her cowardice. Would it be so awful to steal just one night with this man?

The answer to that was a straightforward, unequivocal yes. One night would never be enough. Despite her very best efforts, he had gotten to her. She had ignored danger signs, alarms and warning bells. She had allowed herself to fall for him—and for his kids—but it wasn't going to work.

Not for lack of interest, of course. Duke wanted her. She wasn't mistaken about that. He also considered her good mother material. She had recognized that as well. But he didn't love her. There was a part of himself he always held back, even when he was flirting the most outrageously. In the end, that inability to love her wholeheartedly was all that really mattered. She wouldn't settle for less than the surrender of his heart.

Of course, she, too, was holding back, she reminded herself. It made them quite a pair.

She peered disconsolately out the window just in time to see Duke dashing back to the car. His clothes were soaked. Water dripped from his hair and ran down his face. He looked as if he'd just climbed from a shower with his clothes on. The image sent heat shimmering through her.

Duke, however, was shivering. "Bad news, darlin'. There's only one room left. We're going to have to share."

Dani's heart began to hammer. She couldn't demand that they search for someplace else. They'd passed almost every motel within miles of the horse show. They were either shabby or fully occupied. Duke was too soaked to be driving around anymore, anyway. Fate, it seemed, had stepped in.

"It has two beds, though," he said as he pulled up in front of the room at the very end of the row facing the street.

Dani blinked and stared, taken aback by the belated announcement. "What did you say?"

"Not to worry. It has two beds."

Relief washed over her, followed almost instantly by disappointment. The latter, combined with a healthy dose of frustration, made her cranky.

Reluctantly, she followed Duke, coming to an abrupt halt just inside the doorway. There were two beds, all right, both of them seductively huge. The motel might have an uninspired, gaudy exterior, but the rooms themselves were generously sized and decorated with expensive, but still garish taste. There was a lot of red, she noted, with a startling dash of purple thrown in. Through the open doorway she could see that the bathroom was tiled in a vivid pink.

Duke caught her expression and grinned. "If you

think this is bright, you should meet Mrs. Perez at the registration desk. She's wearing an outfit that would blind anyone without sunglasses. She says everyone needs color in their lives. It cheers them up.''

He crossed the room to stand in front of her. ''Are you feeling cheered up?''

''Not exactly,'' she said, though she was rapidly getting there. She made one last desperate pitch for sanity. ''Are you absolutely sure we couldn't make it back home?''

Duke didn't appear to mind the question. He seemed to sense her need for reassurance.

''Absolutely,'' he said emphatically. ''It's pouring rain, mixed with hail. Another hour of these plummeting temperatures and the roads will be sheets of ice. I don't want to take a chance skidding on the highway while I'm trailering three horses back home. We'll pick them up in the morning and get an early start. Maybe the weather will break by then.''

''And maybe it won't,'' she observed. ''Then what? You going to settle down in Fort Worth?''

''You ever known it to rain for months on end in Texas?''

''No, but I've never known a man to be scared by a little shower before, either.''

''Darlin', we made the right decision. Mrs. Perez says a tornado touched down not twenty miles north of here. You can't see across the road. This isn't a little, inconvenient shower we can wait out. It's a full-blown winter storm and way too unpredictable to be on the road.''

''Whatever you say.''

The truth was she was having a full-scale attack of jitters. Ever since she'd gotten a look at those beds and all that provocative red, she'd felt caught up in an irresistible web of sensuality. In the pit of her stomach, she had that hovering-on-the-edge sensation that the room itself was just daring her to behave wickedly.

Given her own sadly deficient resistance, she told herself she didn't want to spend the night within fifty miles of this man, not with the spark of pure lust she'd been spying in his eyes these past months. Heck, in these past few minutes.

Worse, she suspected it was reflected in her own eyes. The man made her hotter than West Texas pavement in the midday August sun, she conceded as Duke went into the bathroom and turned the shower on.

He stuck his head out the door. "Sure you don't want to join me?" he inquired, regarding her hopefully.

"Very sure," she lied.

"I won't take long," he promised. "Then I'll put on some dry clothes and we can have dinner. The restaurant stays open until eight. Mrs. Perez says it has the best Tex-Mex in this part of town. Her husband's the cook."

"Could be she's prejudiced."

He winked. "I wandered in and got a whiff of what's on the menu. Could be she's right. The aroma was downright decadent. It made my mouth water."

There was nothing Dani liked better than fiery Tex-Mex. Maybe that heat would take her mind off the steam being generated in this motel room. "That'll give me something to look forward to, then," she said.

He grinned. "I thought spending the night all alone

with me would be temptation enough,'' he taunted, then closed the door in her face before she could respond.

Why did he have to be right? she wondered with a wistful sigh. She didn't want to be attracted to Duke Jenkins. She sure as heck hadn't wanted to kiss him, the first time or the last or any of the times in between.

Okay, let's be honest here, she corrected. She had wanted to experiment with one little kiss, but she hadn't wanted to like it. She'd wanted to hate it. She'd wanted to be so turned off that she would never, ever be tempted to throw herself into his arms the way she was right this minute. In that state of mind how could she ignore the pull of those mammoth beds? One kiss now and it would be all over, except for the morning-after regrets.

She'd lost count of the exact number of times he'd managed to steal a kiss since they'd met. She just knew it was enough to make sure she craved them. She'd moved them straight to the top of her list of things to avoid at all costs, way, way above hot fudge sundaes.

Which just proved how totally and thoroughly perverse she was. She knew the pitfalls of a relationship with a man like Duke. Ironically, she had conceded now that he was nothing like Rob. He probably wouldn't dump her on a whim without the slightest consideration of his boys. In fact, he was very much a single father whose first obligation was always going to be to his sons. And at the moment, what he wanted most to give them was a mom. In fact, she suspected that at least fifty percent of his actions lately had been calculated to claiming her not for himself, but for them. Making her the substitute mom for his kids would create a strong bond, but not strong enough to withstand the lure of another woman he might someday decide he wanted all for himself.

Nobody knew the danger of playing with that particular fire better than she did. That didn't seem to stop her from shivering like a wisp of grass in the wind every single time he touched her. Thinking about him only a few feet away, naked, was enough to send shock waves through her.

He was going to touch her tonight, too. Any minute, in fact. She just knew it, knew it with the certainty of a woman who was head over heels in love and searching for signs and portents in every single glance and innocent caress.

He was going to brush one of those oh-so-casual kisses across her forehead. She was going to subconsciously moisten her lips and then, *wham,* his mouth was going to slant across hers, and there would be no stopping what happened next. Pent-up sexual frustration had a way of exploding sooner or later. This was definitely later, which meant the explosion was likely to be of atomic proportions.

Duke started his shower with the water as hot as he could stand it, hoping to chase away the chill that had cut all the way through to his bones. It didn't heat him nearly as fast as thinking about Dani being right outside the door, maybe resting on one of those impossibly huge beds.

He chuckled at the memory of her expression when she'd seen them. She'd looked flabbergasted, panicky and then, in surprisingly short order, wistful. He took the last as a very good sign.

Not that she wasn't sending out more mixed signals than an inexperienced Ham radio operator. He knew in his gut that it wasn't a question of her being indecisive. He figured she'd already made up her mind that she wanted to make love. She just hadn't figured out how to deal with the aftermath, the inevitable, unspoken questions that always tumbled through a woman's mind when she wasn't sure where a relationship was headed.

Duke figured he had enough answers for both of them. This wasn't going to be a one-night stand, if that's what she feared. It was simply going to seal their fate, tie up the deal like a signature on a contract. He would go home from Fort Worth with two palominos, one skittish pinto and a fiancée.

"Now, that's romantic," he muttered under his breath. "Tell her that and you can kiss marriage goodbye."

Fortunately, he'd had the foresight to plan the rest of their evening with more care. He'd done more than peek into that restaurant. He'd spoken to Mr. Perez and planned an evening that would bring tears to her eyes and, with any luck at all, melt her heart.

By the time they got to the restaurant, there would be a bouquet of fresh flowers to replace the artificial ones on the table. Instead of a dripping red candle in an old wine jug, there would be half a dozen thick white candles casting a glow from fancy silver holders. Mr. Perez said the family had brought many pieces of fine silver from Mexico, and they would be happy to share them on such a night. And, yes, he had the perfect bottle of champagne. Like his wife, Mr. Perez had the soul of a romantic. He'd understood immediately what Duke was after.

"Very big night, *sí?*"

"Very big," Duke had agreed. The most important of his life.

Just thinking about the dinner and his plans for after raised his body temperature to a shade under unbearable. Suddenly, he had to shut off the hot water and replace it with cold. Which meant he left the shower right back where he'd started, chilled to the bone and shivering.

He wrapped a towel around his waist and stepped back into the room to grab his clothes. At the sight of Dani sitting cross-legged in the middle of the bed, her eyes glued to the TV, he halted in his tracks.

"What the hell are you watching?" he demanded as he glimpsed bodies writhing on the screen.

"Cable," she said, her voice breathless and vaguely stunned.

Choking back a chuckle, he inquired lightly, "X-rated cable, by any chance?"

She nodded, but never looked away from the screen. Duke didn't dare follow her gaze for more than a flash. Too many images like the one on-screen, and they would never get out of the room for dinner.

Dani tilted her head to follow the unlikely angle of the action. "Can you imagine?" she murmured.

"Dani?"

"Hmm?"

"Turn it off."

Her head snapped up, eyes wide. "What?"

"Turn it off," Duke said in a choked voice.

"But why?"

She studied him intently. Duke recognized the precise instant when she noticed his arousal. Suddenly, she grinned impishly.

"It's very educational," she told him.

"Any education you need along those lines, I'll be glad to give you firsthand."

Color bloomed in her cheeks. That wistful expression flared in her eyes. She fumbled with the remote and turned the TV off. There hadn't been all that much talking going on in the movie, but the absence of even that much background noise left the motel room way too silent. Duke could practically hear the wheels in her brain turning as she tried to reach a conclusion about his intentions—and her own.

Now what? He heard the question as clearly as if she'd spoken it aloud. He wished the answer were half as clear. He could tumble her onto that bed right this second. The invitation was plain in her eyes.

But he'd had a plan, he reminded himself. A good plan. One that would win her heart, as well as her body. It didn't start with a quick roll in the hay, even if that would put an end once and for all to this awkward indecision that hung over them. She deserved a little wining and dining.

"I'll be dressed in a minute," he said, his gaze still locked with hers.

Before he could change his mind, he went back into the bathroom and slammed the door. Desire made his pulse race and left his fingers unsteady. It took him twice as long as it should have to drag on his clothes, run a comb through his hair and a toothbrush over his teeth.

He even pulled a bottle of that after-shave from his bag, the kind Josh and Zack thought all girls liked, and splashed on a little. He supposed there was something to be said for the spicy scent the boys had chosen for him one Christmas, but as far as he could tell, there was nothing wrong with plain old soap and water.

He gazed at himself in the mirror and shook his head. What was wrong with him? He was acting like a besotted schoolboy. If he wasn't careful someone would get the idea that he was in love. Of course, he knew better. With any luck, Dani wouldn't see through the charade and guess that he thought love was a fool's game.

Before he could have another bout with second thoughts about shortchanging her, he opened the door. "Ready?"

"As ready as I'll ever be," she said, "since I only have the clothes on my back."

"Just be thankful you didn't get drenched the way I did," he said. "Do you want to drive back up to the restaurant or make a dash for it? It's undercover most of the way."

"Dashing will be fine."

She meant it, too. She sprinted ahead of him so fast, he realized that she was every bit as nervous as he was about being alone together in that room.

Though the motel was fully occupied, they were the only two people in the dining room.

"I hurry everyone," Mr. Perez announced with a beaming smile. "I know this is very special occasion. A honeymoon, yes?"

Duke let the guesswork pass. He had a feeling there would be enough discussion about Mr. Perez's conclusions with Dani once they reached their table.

Sure enough, Mr. Perez had no sooner filled their glasses with champagne and vanished into the kitchen than she turned on Duke.

"Honeymoon?" she inquired sweetly. "Where would he get an idea like that?"

"I told him tonight was special, that's all," Duke declared. "He obviously drew his own conclusions."

"Conclusions that merited fresh flowers, candlelight and champagne, I see."

"Actually, those were my ideas."

Her eyes widened. "Really? Fascinating. Is the mariachi band warming up in the back?"

Duke chuckled. "Probably, but if it is you can thank Mr. Perez for it. I was content with the jukebox. It has some really terrific oldies on it."

She stared hard. "You checked out the jukebox, too?"

"Of course. You can't slow dance to just anything on a first date."

"Is that so?"

"Of course not. It has to be romantic, memorable."

"Just one question. When did this go from being a business trip to being a date?" She tilted her head and regarded him thoughtfully. "When you saw the beds, perhaps?"

Duke shook his head and regarded her solemnly. He reached across the table and brushed a tendril of hair away from her cheek, then followed the curve until he cupped her chin. "No. I got this idea the first time I laid eyes on you."

She didn't blink and look away as he'd expected. Instead, she smiled. It was like sunshine breaking through clouds. Duke knew in that instant that he was more than halfway to reaching his goal.

If the rest of the night went even one-quarter as smoothly as this, by morning there was no way she wouldn't say yes when he asked her to marry him.

He would find a jewelry store, if he had to bribe the manager to open it on a Sunday morning, and insist on picking out a ring before they ever left Fort Worth. He wanted her well and truly committed to being his before they ever got back to Los Pinos.

"You're looking very smug all of a sudden," she observed.

"Not smug," he insisted. "Pleased. I can't tell you how much I've wanted to share an evening like this with you."

"Stranded in a storm with me smelling like a barn?"

"If you're trying to spoil the mood, forget it. You look beautiful, and you smell like flowers."

"That is flowers you're smelling," she pointed out. "Either that or the after-shave you have on."

"You don't like it? The boys promised me all girls loved it. They picked it out special."

Dani grinned. "The boys have been coaching you?"

"Just on a few of the finer points of courtship."

"Tell them they missed the boat on the after-shave. Soap and water suits me just fine."

"I'll shower again the minute we get back to the room," he offered.

She swallowed hard at the promise. Duke had a hunch she was mentally climbing into that shower with him. Suddenly, she regarded him with suspicion.

"You're playing with my head, aren't you?"

"Am I?"

"You bet."

"How, precisely, am I doing that?"

"You're deliberately planting provocative ideas."

He worked hard to hold back a triumphant grin.

"You're having provocative ideas about the two of us?" he inquired innocently. "You can't possibly hold me responsible for what goes on in your head."

"Of course, I can. You're sneaky and devious that way."

"Ever stop to think that maybe you're the one with the wicked mind? You were watching X-rated cable, you know."

"That was an accident," she protested. "Once it was right there in front of my eyes I couldn't seem to look away, sort of like stumbling on a wreck on the highway."

"An interesting comparison."

She scowled at him. "I wasn't comparing sex and traffic accidents."

"Good, because they don't have a lot in common as far as I can see. Sex is a whole lot more fun, to say nothing of way less deadly, at least if it's done right. We could talk about it more, if you like."

"You're doing it again," she accused.

"Doing what?"

"Putting those images into my head."

"Darlin', it seems to me you just have a one-track mind."

She sighed heavily at that. "Maybe I do," she conceded. "But it wasn't true until I met you."

Duke barely contained a victorious shout. "Fascinating," he said quietly.

"To the contrary, it's actually pretty terrifying how badly I want you," she admitted.

She looked so lost and vulnerable that Duke wanted to scoop her up and comfort her…right before he seduced her. He settled for taking her soft hand in his and brushing his lips across her knuckles.

"Don't look so scared, darlin'. We're going to be sensational together."

For how long? He could practically read the unspoken question in her eyes. Because she needed to know this much—and he needed to make it very clear, he answered her unspoken question aloud.

"Stop worrying, darlin'. We're going to be sensational forever."

Chapter Thirteen

The entire evening had been calculated to destroy her unspoken resolve. That much was obvious to Dani as she slipped into Duke's arms for yet another slow dance.

What was less clear was why he had gone to so much trouble. After a couple of glasses of bubbly champagne and a few spins around the deserted dance floor, the answer was fuzzier than ever.

Okay, he wanted to seduce her. Nothing unclear or unexpected about that. But he also seemed determined to make the whole evening memorable.

Not that he had to worry with regard to the sex, she thought wryly. She was already anticipating making love with Duke so eagerly that he couldn't possibly think she needed additional persuading. There wasn't a doubt in her mind that he would make love with the same passion with which he tackled everything in his life.

No, he seemed to be after more than her surrender in bed. Champagne, candles, fresh flowers, they all added up to a man on a romantic mission, a forever kind of mission.

"Stop thinking so hard," he advised, regarding her with amusement.

Her gaze snapped up to clash with his. Was the man psychic or what? "I just wish I could figure out what you're up to," she said a little wistfully.

"Who says I'm up to something?"

"You do. Every now and then this vaguely guilty expression flits across your face. What's that about?"

He shrugged. "I can't imagine. I don't feel the least bit guilty about anything."

"Not even luring me to Fort Worth with a storm on the way?"

He chuckled at the accusation and executed a tricky spin designed to rob her of the ability to speak.

"Are you giving me credit for controlling the weather?" he inquired lightly as she tried to get her equilibrium back.

"No, just taking advantage of it."

"Darlin', a wise man takes advantage of all life's opportunities."

"So whatever plotting has been going on in that head of yours began when the first drop of rain fell earlier this afternoon and not a moment before?" she asked skeptically.

He did look vaguely uncomfortable at that. "Not exactly."

As one song ended and there was a pause before the next, she took the opportunity to look him in the eye. "When exactly did this particular opportunity present itself?" she inquired.

"Does it really matter?"

"It does to me. Let's just call it a test of faith."

"Meaning?"

"Meaning, I want to see if you have enough faith in me to tell me the truth."

He stared hard at her, as if searching for loopholes. Dani kept her gaze unblinking.

"Okay, okay," he finally mumbled. "When the boys started talking about wanting to learn to ride, I saw an opportunity to get you alone for a while. Just for the day, though."

"Not overnight?"

As the music began again, he grinned unrepentantly and swept her back into his arms. "No," he insisted, "this is just a bonus."

Dani couldn't help it. She chuckled. "There now, that wasn't so difficult, was it? See how honesty pays?"

"I suppose that depends on whether you ask the Perezes to let you bunk with them or come back to our room with me." His gaze locked with hers. "So, Dani, it's the moment of truth. What's it going to be?"

She should have left him dangling, held off on an answer until dessert just to torment him, but she couldn't do it. "I suppose, since you've gone to so much trouble..."

His lips began a slow curve into a smile. "The room?"

"The room," she agreed softly.

"Now?" he inquired with ego-boosting eagerness, already heading back to their table for the check.

She grinned and shook her head, then deliberately pulled out her chair and sat. "Settle down, cowboy," she advised. "This is one opportunity that doesn't need to be claimed in a rush."

For a while there Duke's heart had been in his throat. Dani had seen straight through him, guessed all—well, almost all—of his devious little secrets and, he'd been almost certain, had been about to bring his whole scheme crashing down around his head. That she hadn't was testament to the depth of her feelings. He wondered if she even recognized how revealing her reactions had been. He doubted it. She would hate that he could see into her heart, especially since she'd worked so hard to hide all the soft spots.

Comforting himself that his goal was all but certain, Duke settled back in his chair and forced himself to relax. It wasn't all that difficult. He simply set out to enjoy the play of candlelight across her face, the shimmering of gold it set off in her hair. He relished the hitching of her breath whenever his fingers chanced to graze hers.

In fact, he discovered that the slow build of anticipation had its own reward. It had been a long time since he'd felt the kind of insistent, gut-deep hunger for a woman that he was feeling for Dani by the time they clasped hands and walked slowly back to their room.

The temperature hadn't dropped nearly as precipitously as had been predicted. The rain had softened to little more than a gentle shower, leaving the air cleansed and crisp.

To his amazement, Dani stepped out from under the shelter of the covered walkway and tilted her face up to the sky. A fine mist settled on her skin, leaving it as dewy as a spring morning and a hundred times more appealing. She held out her arms as if to embrace the night. The gesture was so totally unself-conscious, so gloriously uninhibited and happy that Duke found himself joining her, getting soaked for the second time that night. He hardly even noticed.

"Isn't it wonderful?" she murmured, meeting his gaze.

"It's wet," he observed, concluding that she was definitely a little tipsy.

"It reminds me of 'Singing in the Rain,' one of my all-time favorite movies," she said, looking nostalgic.

He recalled the specific scene vividly. "Gene Kelly dancing in the street," he said with a smile. "Are you planning to launch into song or dance any second now?"

"No," she said with a wistful sigh. "I can't sing and I can't dance."

"Who says?" he protested. "No one's grading you out here. Come on, darlin'. Go for it."

He encouraged her by whistling the first few bars of the song. She did a little skip, then something vaguely resembling a tap routine. She was no Gene Kelly, that was for sure, but her face was glowing and her eyes were sparkling under the twinkling display of neon that splashed color across the damp pavement.

"You, too," she insisted, grabbing his hand.

"I'll sing," he offered instead, belting out what he considered to be a credible rendition of the movie's title song. He grabbed her off her feet and twirled her around for the sheer exhilarating fun of it. It was, if he did say so himself, quite a finale.

Or, perhaps, an extraordinary opening, if the main production was yet to come. Either way, he was well and truly caught up in the storyline.

Especially when her body slid slowly down his as he lowered her feet back to the ground. Eyes wide, she met his gaze evenly, then slowly, so slowly that his body throbbed with the anticipation of it, she lifted her hands to his cheeks and framed his face. When she stood on tiptoe and kissed him, he was more or less convinced that the whole state of Texas shook.

"Oh, baby," he whispered raggedly, when he could catch his breath at all. "That was a real show-stopper."

She grinned at him, her expression very feminine and very smug. "Come along. I'm not waiting around out here for the applause. Something tells me it'll be a long time coming, and I have better things to do."

"Really? You turning brazen on me, darlin'?" he inquired hopefully.

"I'm thinking about it," she said, leading the way to the doorstep of their room.

Duke decided he was enjoying her seduction far too much to race right inside. Instead of opening the door, he leaned down and stole one more kiss, a real barn burner of a kiss.

It was Dani who eventually dragged her mouth away from his and stared up at him with dazed eyes. "Inside," she murmured. It came out as part command, part plea.

Duke nodded. "Fine by me."

"Open the door, then."

"I think I'll leave that up to you."

Her gaze faltered. "But you have the key." Alarm flared for a second in her eyes. "You do have the key, don't you?"

"Sure do. It's in my pocket. Anytime you want to slide your hand in there and get it," he suggested provocatively, "we can go right on in."

She regarded him with amusement. "Think you're real smart, don't you?"

He feigned a disinterested expression. "Smart enough."

"Okay, mister, let's see if you can take what you dish out," she said, offering her own challenge.

The glittering dare in her eyes made Duke vaguely uneasy. He braced himself for the torment of her touch. It would be interesting to see just how far she would go to prove which of them was the more clever.

"Which pocket?" she inquired with mild curiosity, after a visual survey of the alternatives.

When he would have replied, she touched a silencing finger to his lips. "Never mind. I think I'll just take my time and figure it out."

She stepped in very close, until her breasts were pressed against his chest and her warm breath was fanning across his cheek. Her arms circled his waist and she very, very slowly ran one hand up the curve of his backside until she reached the top of his pocket. Duke's blood began to hammer in his veins.

She searched that pocket so thoroughly and with such lingering, devilish caresses he thought for sure his heart would burst.

Then, when he was sure that his jeans couldn't possibly be any more uncomfortable, she did the exact same thing all over again with the other back pocket.

NATURAL BORN TROUBLE

"Not here," she finally concluded, regarding him gravely. "Now where could that key be?"

Duke was totally incapable of replying. Maybe if he could have, maybe if he'd snatched the darn thing out himself, he could have saved himself from the wicked probing of his remaining pockets.

She slid her hands up his chest, examined the pockets in his shirt with care, finally satisfying herself that the key was elsewhere. He was breathing hard when she was done.

Then she moved on to the front pockets of his jeans. Deft fingers managed to skim far more than the depths of those pockets. With some sort of uncanny intuition she had managed to save the one that actually held the key until last. By then he was relatively certain that his body was one caress away from coming apart.

As she slowly and triumphantly removed the key, he stepped back so fast he almost tumbled off the curb. "Satisfied?" he muttered.

"Not yet," she said, giving him a saucy smile. "You?"

"Definitely not yet."

"Well, then, I guess we should go inside before we make a spectacle of ourselves."

Duke regarded her curiously. "What just happened here?"

"I'm pretty sure I proved that I know how to get you all hot and bothered," she said with obvious satisfaction. She opened the door and stepped inside, then gave him a head-to-toe survey that could have melted steel before adding, "It remains to be seen if you can do the same."

He shook his head. "Darlin', don't you know how

dangerous it is to issue that kind of a challenge to a man as close to the end of his rope as I am?''

"No," she said, then added innocently, "Perhaps you should show me."

Duke stepped inside and slammed the door so hard behind him, it rocked on its hinges. Dani grinned at the impatient gesture.

"Careful there. If we want any privacy, we need that door right where it is."

"Very amusing," he said and reached for her.

She put up very little resistance when he tugged her into his arms and settled his mouth over hers. There was nothing careful or tentative about this claiming. He was a man possessed. He wanted to taste her, to make very sure she knew that from this night on she belonged only to him.

Duke had never felt this demanding need for a woman. Not that he hadn't enjoyed sex. He had the usual appetite for the feel of a soft body beneath his own, for being surrounded by slick, moist heat.

But this hot, urgent passion seemed to run deeper than that. It was as if he needed to prove that beyond the teasing and the provocation, beyond the flirting and kisses, there was more. For the first time in his life, he felt as if he were putting some new part of himself on the line.

Perhaps his heart.

His pulse hitched at the thought. But not even the terror that should have followed would have been enough to get him to walk out of this room tonight.

Oddly enough, though, the panic never came. He would have to figure out why later.

In fact at the moment, as his fingers made short work of buttons and snaps, then skimmed over bare flesh, all he felt was the exhilaration of a man who was right where he wanted to be, with the woman with whom he belonged.

Forcing himself to drag in a deep, calming breath, he slowed down. He lifted Dani off her feet, then placed her on the bed as reverently as he'd ever touched anything in his life.

Dani returned his gaze with a hooded, smoldering look of her own. He was relieved by that, glad that there was no evidence of the lost, vulnerable woman he had met a few months ago. Whatever she felt for him in her heart, she was meeting him tonight as a strong, decisive woman, the kind of woman he'd seen evidenced in her work. Maybe, he thought, he'd played some small part in giving her back her confidence.

His gaze danced over her, then took a slower, lingering survey. She was so lovely. Small and delicate in many ways, there was a surprising, but unmistakable strength about her. He followed the subtle definition in her arms, stopped to savor the gentle sweep of a shoulder, then moved on to admire the generous curve of her breasts. He trailed a finger down that soft slope to a tip that was as hard as a pebble beneath his touch, then repeated the action on her other breast until she gasped with pleasure and her eyes drifted closed.

When his mouth closed over one sensitive peak, her eyes flew open and her hands tunneled through his hair as if to keep him there.

Duke was far from finished, though. Each breast was but a stopping point on his journey of discovery. He wanted to know every inch of her, to discover textures and tastes and secret pleasure spots. He wanted her to remember every second, every caress.

"Duke?"

He stopped his intimate examination of a sensitive spot on the inside of her thigh and met her gaze. "Yes?"

"Look at me," she pleaded softly. "Look at me and make love to me. I want you inside me now."

"In a minute, darlin'. I'm not quite through with my survey."

"Your survey is making me crazy," she confessed.

He hid a grin. "That's the general idea."

"But I want to make you crazy, too."

"Oh, baby, you do," he vowed. He reached for her hand. "Here, feel." When he placed her hand over the hard shaft of his arousal, a slow smile spread across her face. Confidence returned. Her gaze met his boldly.

"If that's the case," she said, "then let's go for it."

"We're not racing a clock, are we?"

"I just thought it would be good to seize the opportunity," she pointed out.

Duke chuckled. "Like you told me, this opportunity isn't going anywhere. In fact, we're just now starting to take full advantage of it."

He set out to prove to her the exquisite torture of slow, deliberate caresses and deep, bone-melting kisses. She was slick with perspiration and writhing against the sheets by the time he knelt between her thighs and slowly entered her.

The moist, welcoming heat claimed him as surely as he'd set out to claim her. She was slick and tight and eager. The movement of her hips was timed perfectly to him as if they'd learned this rhythm in another lifetime and only in each other's arms. He was all but certain it had never been like this before.

Duke was struck by the stunning thought that this was what people meant when they referred to soul mates. That had always been an elusive concept to him, the idea that destiny chose two people and saw to it that they came together for eternity.

But as their bodies melded, as wave after wave of stunning pleasure washed over them, he began to wonder if he hadn't been a little too quick to dismiss the notion.

When Dani's cry of release shimmered around him, it was all he could do to hold back a triumphant shout. She was his now, as surely as if she'd already said yes to the proposal he had yet to make.

As for him, if he looked very, very closely inside his heart, he had a feeling he might discover that he was just as much her captive. To his astonishment, rather than being panicked by that, all he felt was a sort of intense, heady relief.

Dani stretched languorously. She had never felt better in her life. As long as she didn't allow a lot of doubts to start crowding in, she would be just fine. Better than fine. She would be magnificent.

There was one sure way to see that doubts remained at bay. She slid across the mattress and tucked herself up against Duke, pausing to admire the hard planes and angles of his body. There wasn't an ounce of spare flesh on him. And the man generated enough body heat to warm all of Texas. Her inquisitive, probing hands slid across his belly, then down. He moaned softly, then came wide-awake with a start. After a moment of obvious disorientation, he regarded her with amusement.

"What are you up to?" he inquired.

"Isn't that obvious?"

"Explain it to me, anyway."

She grinned. "Just checking to see if this was one of those rare times when opportunity knocked twice."

He regarded her balefully. "Twice? I'm fairly certain I recall it knocking several times during the night."

"That was then. This is now."

He studied her face intently. "Trying to keep the regrets at bay, by any chance?"

Dani stared at him in shock. Was she so obvious? "Why would you ask that?"

"Because I know you better than you think I do." He grinned that lazy, sexy grin that destroyed her defenses. "Come on now, no regrets."

"Easy for you to say. This doesn't solve anything between us, Duke, not really."

"I'm perfectly willing to make it legal," he said. "Just say the word."

She stared at him. His expression was neutral. Clearly he didn't intend to give away whether he was serious or not. "You want to marry me?" she asked, spelling it out so there could be no mistake.

"You didn't think this was some casual, one-night stand for me, did you? I'm not that kind of man." He shook his head with exaggerated sorrow. "Never mind. I'll prove it to you."

"There's no need."

"Of course, there is. You can't marry me, if you don't trust me."

Warning signals that had apparently been on the

blink for too many hours were recharged now. They were clanging like the very dickens. "I'm not going to marry you, period," she insisted, even though the pull of the idea made her limp with longing.

"We'll see," he said smugly.

Dani sighed. "Duke, we're consenting adults here. This doesn't require a proposal to make it okay."

"Never said it did." He shot her a chin-up, defiant look. "I'm asking you to marry me just the same."

"No," she said again, though her stomach was as jittery as if she'd said yes.

"Why not?" He met her gaze evenly. "And don't try telling me you don't love me, because I'm not buying it."

"Well, aren't you the cocky one?" she retorted. "Just because we made love doesn't mean I'm *in love.*"

"Nope," he agreed solemnly. "That's not proof all by itself."

"Then would you mind telling me where you got such a cockamamie idea?" Maybe then she could see to it that she never, ever did anything similar again.

"You women have your intuition," he said. "We men have other ways."

"Such as?"

"Darlin', I'd be going against the code if I gave it away."

"Code? What code? Gave what away?" she asked, thoroughly exasperated.

"It's a guy thing."

She stared at him incredulously. "It's a guy thing? Well, this is a girl thing." She climbed out of bed and draped herself in the bedspread, figuring that delivering her tirade stark naked would take a little of the sass out of it. "I am not now nor do I ever intend to be in love with you. I will not marry you."

Duke didn't seem to be the least bit distressed. "We'll see."

Dani marched off to the bathroom and slammed the door behind her. When it was closed, she leaned heavily against it.

"Well, damn," she murmured.

How was she supposed to fight a man who was offering her the very thing she wanted most in the world: Marriage and a family every bit as strong as the one into which she'd been welcomed as a child.

By telling herself a thousand times a day that he didn't really love her, she reminded herself. The only hitch to that was the fact that last night, in his arms, it had felt an awful lot like he might be loving her back.

Chapter Fourteen

Duke recognized an ambush when he saw one. Jordan had asked him to drop by Dolan's and pick up a package for him while he was out to lunch. It should have occurred to him that Sharon Lynn would have been more than happy to have the blasted package delivered.

So, because he wasn't thinking straight, hadn't been thinking straight ever since he'd returned from Fort Worth, he walked into the drugstore as innocent as a lamb. There, clearly just waiting for him, were both Sharon Lynn and Jenny. They perked up visibly at the sight of him.

Duke sighed. Everyone had maintained a polite, if clearly expectant facade right through Christmas and New Year's. Now, since no ring or engagement announcement had been forthcoming, apparently Sharon

Lynn and Jenny had been designated by the family to get to the bottom of what had gone on between him and Dani on their trip and what was likely to go on between them from now through eternity.

"Afternoon, ladies," he said, figuring he could bluff his way through the conversation or else run like hell. Since the latter wasn't a real option, he decided he'd better brazen it out.

"Hey, Duke, come on and join me," Jenny suggested, patting the stool beside her.

"I really need to get back to the office," he said, flashing her a smile. "Jordan just asked me to pick something up for him while I was out grabbing lunch."

She regarded him skeptically. "Have you actually had lunch yet?" she asked with typical Adams directness.

He sighed. "No."

Sharon Lynn beamed at him. "Well, then, no more excuses. Uncle Jordan can wait a few more minutes. Sit right down. What'll it be? A hamburger? Grilled cheese? BLT?"

Duke wondered which one would be the quickest to prepare and gulp down. "Grilled cheese," he said.

"Fries with that?"

Fries would take too long, especially in the quantity Sharon Lynn served them up. They would have to be eaten one by one. "No, not today."

"And to drink? Coffee?"

No way. He would have to wait for coffee to cool. "Just water," he said.

Apparently, his nervousness was transparent. The two women exchanged an amused glance. He, in turn, regarded them suspiciously.

"Okay, what are you two up to?" he asked.

"Nothing," Sharon Lynn claimed.

"Absolutely nothing," Jenny concurred.

He scowled in Sharon Lynn's direction. "When are you and Kyle Mason setting a date?" he inquired, hoping to divert her attention from his love life by focusing on hers.

She grinned. "The date's set. First Saturday in June. He finally got around to proposing in the middle of college football on New Year's Day. The man's timing is impeccable. Now there's no way I can doubt how much he loves me. He actually stopped watching the Aggies for a full fifteen minutes." She grinned and waved her ring under his nose. "I hope you'll be there."

"Of course." So much for that tactic, he thought, turning to Jenny. Before he could ask, she held up her hand to stop any inquiry he was planning.

"No love life. Not interested. No time," she declared.

He grinned at her vehemence. "And how does Harlan feel about that?"

Sharon Lynn chuckled as Jenny heaved a heavy sigh. "Grandpa isn't too thrilled with her attitude," Sharon Lynn confided. "In fact, I'd say she is on his personal to-do list. Get Jenny a husband, right up there in big, bold print."

"Oh, go suck an egg," Jenny retorted.

Duke regarded her with amusement. "Let that be a lesson to you. If you don't want anyone meddling in your love life, stay out of theirs."

Jenny's gaze narrowed. "Meaning?"

"Meaning I could very easily join forces with your father," Duke warned.

Both women hooted at that, which wasn't quite the reaction he'd been hoping for.

"You poor man," Jenny said. "Don't you realize that you and Dani are way, way above me on his list? In fact, I'd say at the moment you two are his number one priority. He's always preferred to hedge his bets and go with a sure thing. I'm way too speculative at the moment."

Duke sat, silently absorbing the news. He waited for the panic to set in, just as he had over and over again in that motel in Fort Worth. It didn't come. In fact, in a curious way, he was relieved that he had allies, powerful allies. He'd felt surprisingly disappointed and disgruntled when Dani had flat-out turned him down in Forth Worth.

Why was that? he wondered, trying to think back over the past few months. He was a bright man. Surely, he could analyze this thing with Dani from start to finish and reach a logical conclusion.

It had started as a game. Duke was willing to admit that much, even though it didn't say much for him. Then it had moved on to a game he was playing for his sons' benefit.

Now, much to his amazement, he realized that the stakes were totally personal and very, very important. He'd gone and fallen in love with the woman. He tried to imagine his life without her, and he couldn't. All he saw was a bleak and empty future, the exact kind of future he'd once considered his due for all his sins.

Lately, though, he'd had a taste of brighter possibilities and he knew he would never be happy unless he did everything in his power to make them happen. He wanted more than a mother for the kids. To his astonishment, he'd discovered that what he wanted most of all was a wife. He wanted a woman who could make his heart leap simply by walking into a room. He wanted a woman who listened and teased and taunted. He wanted a companion, a friend and a lover.

He wanted Dani.

Of course, realizing what was in his heart was a snap compared to convincing Dani what was in hers. He looked from Sharon Lynn to Jenny. Both women were studying him with blatant curiosity.

"I'm not your problem, ladies," he declared, summing up in a nutshell the conclusion he'd just reached.

"Explain," Sharon Lynn said, her elbows on the counter and her chin cupped in her hands as she regarded him intently.

"It's Dani," Jenny concluded without waiting for his reply. "She's holding out."

"Seems to be," he agreed.

"Why?" Sharon Lynn asked. "Have you told her how you feel?"

"I asked her to marry me."

Jenny didn't seem the least bit surprised by that. She waved her hand impatiently. "That isn't what Sharon Lynn asked. Have you told her how you feel?"

Duke hesitated to admit that he was just coming to grips himself with the fact that he was in love with her. In the natural, old-fashioned order of things, he supposed he should have reached that conclusion before he hauled her into bed. He definitely should have reached it before proposing.

"Sleeping with her isn't an answer," Jenny said,

stunning him into silence. "Proposing marriage is nice, but that's not enough, either."

"In other words, have you mentioned that you love her?" Sharon Lynn prodded more specifically.

Duke cleared his throat.

Jenny sighed. "No. The answer's no, isn't it?" She glanced at Sharon Lynn. "Men are such idiots. Now do you see why I'm content to live my nice, peaceful existence without one?"

Sharon Lynn rolled her eyes. "Women like you always fall the hardest," she warned. "I can hardly wait."

"Oh, shut up. We're not talking about me," Jenny said, turning away from Sharon Lynn and facing Duke squarely. "Now what do you intend to do to get this marriage business with Dani straightened out before she does something crazy like going back with that awful Rob Hilliard?"

"Hilliard?" Duke demanded tightly. "What the hell does he have to do with anything?"

"He's been calling again," Sharon Lynn said. "He brought the girls by over the holidays. Dani cried for an hour after they left."

That was all news to Duke. Bad news. He had warned the guy to stay away. The only way to ensure that happening, though, was to get Dani to marry him. Unfortunately, though, he was fresh out of ideas. Aside from acknowledging that what he was feeling these days was love, he was forced to admit that he was stymied. Finding oil where it shouldn't be was a breeze compared to this.

"I was hoping you two could make a suggestion," he said, throwing himself on their mercy. Something told him he could trust them. They both had Dani's best interests at heart. "You seem to have all the answers."

"Now you're talking," Jenny said approvingly.

"Something dramatic," Sharon Lynn said.

"Something simple," Jenny countered. "Dani would be embarrassed by dramatic."

Duke thought of Dani's performance in the motel parking lot, not her singing and dancing, but that sexy slip-sliding game she had played for the room key. She was not half as demure as Jenny apparently thought she was. He thought maybe dramatic would be for the best. Kelly had shared some of the more outrageous things Jordan had done to win her heart. Perhaps he should try a few of those on her daughter. Maybe Dani would be charmed by the nostalgia of it, if nothing else.

"Thanks for the help, ladies," he said, climbing off the stool. "I think I'll take it from here."

"But we haven't come up with a really good plan," Jenny protested.

"And you never even got your sandwich," Sharon Lynn said.

"That's okay. You've provided plenty of inspiration," he assured them, grinning at the self-satisfied smirks they exchanged.

"Keep us posted on your progress," Sharon Lynn pleaded.

"Sweetheart, if there's any progress, I'm sure you won't need me to drop by and fill you in. With an Adams involved, word will spread like wildfire."

Ever since her return from Fort Worth, Dani had been dragging around, her mood despondent. She'd been snapping at Maggie at the clinic until the poor girl had threatened to quit unless her boss's mood improved.

"You need a man in your life," Maggie said. "In my opinion, you're frustrated."

Little did she know, Dani thought sourly. She'd never been less frustrated in her life, sexually speaking. Emotionally, however, was another thing entirely. Rob's impromptu little visit with the girls hadn't helped, either. They'd all been in tears by the time he packed them up again and took off, her refusal to reconsider their relationship ringing in his ears.

Apparently, word of her crummy attitude was spreading, too. Everyone in the family was watching her as if they expected her to break out with chicken pox or maybe hives at any second. They were hovering, their expressions alternately sympathetic and hopeful. Well, the whole blasted lot of them could go jump in the creek, she thought miserably. Their lives weren't on the line. Hers was.

Duke's proposal echoed in her head at the most inopportune moments. Memories of the way his hands had molded and shaped her body with intimate precision, drawing ragged sighs and heartfelt gasps, left her feeling so hot and bothered she was tempted to turn the air conditioning on, even though it was barely freezing outside.

It would be so easy to say yes, so uncomplicated to cave in to Duke's pressure. If, of course, he'd pressured her. Instead, the man was nowhere to be found. She'd even dropped in on her father at work, hoping to catch a glimpse of Duke. Of course, it had been lunchtime, she consoled herself. He'd probably just slipped out for a sandwich.

She declined Jordan's offer to take her out some-where and wandered down to Dolan's herself. Sharon Lynn and Jenny had been huddled together at the counter, their expressions guilty as sin when they spotted her.

"You just missed Duke," Sharon Lynn said a little too brightly.

"Was he here for lunch?"

The question drew another guilty look. Sharon Lynn shrugged. "Not really. He was running an er-rand for Uncle Jordan."

"I see," Dani said and slipped onto a stool. "Can I have a hot fudge sundae, please?"

"Now?" Sharon Lynn said as if it were the most scandalous request she'd ever heard. "In the middle of the day?"

Dani scowled at her. "Do you have a problem with that?"

"No, of course not," her cousin declared and rushed to scoop up the ice cream. She added extra hot fudge and enough whipped cream to clog the ar-teries of half the population of Los Pinos.

She and Jenny watched uneasily as Dani silently ate every single bite.

"Man trouble?" Jenny inquired eventually.

"Who, me?"

"Yes, you," Jenny said impatiently. "What's with you and Duke?"

"Nothing," Dani said, noting the amused look the two exchanged. "Okay, what's up? Do you know something I don't?"

"Not a thing," Jenny responded.

"Absolutely nothing," Sharon Lynn concurred.

Dani didn't believe either one of them. There was

some sort of scheme afoot. "I hope you're not interfering in this," she said, regarding first one, then the
other intently.

"Absolutely not," they assured her dutifully.

"Because if I find out that you have been, I
will..." She couldn't think offhand of anything quite
dire enough.

"What?" Sharon Lynn prodded, an impudent, teasing glint in her eyes.

"Yes, what will you do?" Jenny inquired, clearly
fascinated by the threat.

"I will deliver entire litters of kittens to your door-
steps in the middle of the night," she warned.

"You do that anyway," Jenny said. "White Pines
is crawling with them."

"So's our place," Sharon Lynn agreed. "Dad's
still trying to figure out how you manage it."

Dani sighed at the failed threat. "Okay, forget the
kittens, but I will make you pay. Remember that. And
I will do it when you least expect it."

She slid off the stool and headed for the door. She
was pretty sure she heard them chuckling when they
thought she was too far away to catch them at it.
There really were times when having a family that
knew you so well could be a nuisance, she thought
as she barely resisted the urge to slam the drugstore
door behind her.

Since the clinic was already closed for the afternoon, she decided to take a drive out to White Pines.
Not that she couldn't expect more of the same taunting from Grandpa Harlan, but at least he usually managed to impart some wisdom along with his teasing.

She found her grandfather in the paddock along
with Cody and one of the hands. They were going

over a horse that appeared to be lame. She would have offered to check him out herself, but Cody knew every bit as much as she did about this kind of thing. She had some expertise, of course, but small pets were her forte. She was called in to treat large animals only when the vet in the next town couldn't be reached.

Waving to the men, she went into the stables and saddled up the pinto, which had turned out to be a surprisingly quick learner once it concluded that no one here was likely to harm it. He'd put on weight and no longer had that wild look in his eyes.

"You're my pal now, aren't you?" she whispered as he nuzzled her pocket for one of the sugar cubes she invariably kept there for him. She took out two. "Here you go."

Maybe a good, long ride was what she needed. It would clear her head.

The bottom line, she concluded as she raced straight into the wind, was that she wanted desperately to trust her heart. She wanted to admit that she had fallen in love with Duke, but how could she? She kept coming back to the boys.

She knew from her own experience with Jordan that being a stepkid could be just fine, better than fine. But Jordan and her mom had been committed to each other for years, even though it had taken him a long time to recognize what was in his heart.

She and Duke didn't have that same long history. There was every chance that they would fail at making a relationship work. She had thrown herself heart and soul into her relationship with Rob and look at what a mess she'd made of that. They'd even had a four-year foundation to build on. By comparison, this thing with Duke had been a whirlwind courtship.

She was so lost in thought that her grandfather had ridden up beside her before she was even aware he was in the vicinity. He dismounted and walked over to sit beside her on the fence rail.

As his warm gaze settled on her, she saw the worry lines that were clearly etched in his forehead. "You okay, kiddo?"

"More or less."

"Problems with Duke?"

"Nothing but problems," she conceded. "Ever since we came back from Fort Worth, he's been avoiding me. Other than a glimpse or two in a crowd here over the holidays, I never even saw him."

"Maybe he's just giving you time to think."

"I suppose."

He cupped a hand under her chin and forced her to look at him. "So, when are you going to put that boy out of his misery?" he demanded. "He's going around looking like a lovesick puppy and you don't look one bit better. It's time to fish or cut bait, darlin' girl."

"Oh, please," she muttered. "Duke Jenkins couldn't look pitiful if he took acting classes for a lifetime."

"It's true. Jordan says he can't keep his mind on work, either. That's a sure sign a man's in love."

"You know what happened with Rob," she reminded him. "The girls still haven't gotten over it. How can I take that chance again? It wouldn't be fair to Joshua and Zachary, especially since Duke can't even bring himself to admit he has any feelings for me at all."

"Have you admitted you're in love with him?"

The question made her pause. "No," she conceded eventually.

"The way I hear it, he has asked you to marry him. Is that true?"

"Yes, but—"

"But what, darlin' girl? No man asks a woman to marry him and takes it lightly."

"He hasn't said he loved me. We can't start off a marriage like that."

"Maybe he just has a hard time getting the words out, same as you."

"Maybe," she conceded, considering the possibility for the first time. Duke wasn't the sort of man who would want to risk rejection by putting his heart on the line, not with a woman who'd already turned down his marriage proposal.

"Let me ask you something else. Are you going to love those kids of his one bit less if you don't marry their papa?" he inquired slyly.

Dani heaved a sigh. It was true. Despite her very best intentions, she adored Joshua and Zachary. They were a never-ending delight. Just like their father. If she held her ground, if she refused to marry Duke, would the hurt be any less than it would be at some future date that might never come? No, she concluded thoughtfully.

She grinned at her grandfather. "You're a very smart man, you know that?"

"Well, of course, I am. It's about time somebody around here acknowledged it. Go on, gal. Tell the man. Somebody's got to jump into this thing feetfirst or we'll never get the show on the road. Seems to me like no Adams has ever been chicken to take a chance when something really mattered to them.''

''I could drown,'' she pointed out, even though her mind was already made up.

''Not a chance, Dani girl. I've seen the way the man looks at you. He'll be there to catch you. There's not a doubt in my mind about that. Not a single doubt.''

Dani wished she could be as sure, but in the end, it didn't really matter. Rob had taken the control of her destiny out of her hands. For way too long now, she had assumed that someone else would have to prove themselves before she would ever dare to put her own heart on the line. That wasn't any way for an Adams to live.

She gave her grandfather a fierce hug. ''Thank you.''

''For what?''

''For making sense. For being you.''

''Don't thank me. Just be happy. That's all the thanks I'll ever need from any of you.''

Chapter Fifteen

Despite the resolve he'd reached after talking to Sharon Lynn and Jenny, Duke knew he was only a heartbeat away from giving up in pure frustration. Dani had made her feelings plain enough in Fort Worth and after. How many times could a man ask a woman to marry him without making a total fool of himself? He had a hunch he was already way beyond the limit. He could go to his grave someday consoling himself that he'd tried.

It was thinking about all the lonely days from now until then that had him vowing to give it one more valiant effort. A last hurrah, so to speak. Something worthy of Kelly and Jordan Adams's daughter.

Of all the legendary tales he'd heard, he liked the one about the airplane dropping rose petals best. It was dramatic, romantic and appealed to his sense of the outrageous.

Working up his courage, he walked into Jordan's office a few days before Valentine's Day and asked if the small company plane was available.

"You need to check out a site?" Jordan asked, barely glancing up from his work. "You don't need to ask, you know that."

Duke cleared his throat. "Actually, this is personal," he admitted, earning Jordan's immediate attention.

"Really? Does it have anything to do with Dani?" His gaze narrowed. "I won't have an elopement. If the two of you get married, it will be right here with all the family around."

"Actually, getting a quick yes and hauling her off to Vegas might be the safest way to go," Duke responded thoughtfully. "But the truth is I don't need the plane so we can elope. She hasn't budged off 'absolutely not, never' yet."

"I see," Jordan said, his disappointment plain. "Then why do you need the corporate jet?"

Duke bit back his embarrassment and said, "Remember the rose petals?"

That brief mention was enough to bring a smile to his boss's face. "Oh, yes," he said, then shook his head. "Didn't work, though. Kelly was a stubborn one."

"I have to try something," Duke insisted. "This is the best I can come up with."

"I suppose it's worth a shot. Dani always did love that story. She was furious she wasn't around the day I did it." He grinned. "The jet's yours. When are you going to do it?"

"Valentine's Day."

Jordan nodded. "Nice touch."

Duke spent days making the rest of the arrangements. Dani had been surprisingly agreeable to the date. He hadn't had to do any clever persuading at all. In fact, he realized after he'd hung up, that she hadn't even asked what he had in mind.

Just the same, he had every detail worked out. He was going to take her out for an expensive, romantic dinner, then suggest a drive. If the weather cooperated, there would be a bright moon and lots of stars. Just in case, he intended to pop half a dozen romantic CDs in the car, along with a bottle of champagne. He was tempted to drag the boys with him when he went to pick out the ring, but he feared he would only be setting them up for disappointment if his scheme failed and Dani continued to refuse to marry him.

He spent Valentine's Day in one business meeting after another. None of them had gone well. His mind hadn't been on business. He'd finally had his secretary cancel the last two meetings on his calendar. He'd gone home and paced the floor in relative privacy. Only the cats had been there to regard him sympathetically. Five-thirty finally came.

This was it, then. He put on his best suit, tucked the ring into his pocket, made one last call to the pilot to make sure the plane was set and drove over to pick Dani up promptly at six-thirty.

He stood on her doorstep and stared at her in open-mouthed shock. She looked gorgeous in some sort of red velvet dress that skimmed her shoulders and hugged her waist. A single diamond winked at her throat, drawing his attention to the creamy expanse of bare skin exposed where the dress plunged to a deep V.

"You look..." Words failed him. She didn't help

him out. She just kept her gaze fixed on his, waiting.
"Spectacular," he said finally.

"Thank you."

He had to drag his gaze away before he reached
out and followed the neckline of that dress with his
finger. Only then did he notice the huge picnic ham-
per at her feet.

"What's that?"

"Dinner," she explained, watching him nervously.
"I thought we could have a picnic."

He stared at her in astonishment. "In February?"

That drew a defiant jut of her chin. "Why not? It's
a beautiful night."

"It's also forty degrees."

She'd apparently considered all of his likely arguments and readied responses. "We can eat in the car,
turn the heater on," she said at once.

"And die from inhaling all that carbon monoxide."

She actually laughed at that. "Trust me. We're not
going to die."

He thought of his own dinner reservation, then dismissed it. What the heck. Since he'd long since given
up on trying to deny her anything she'd set her heart
on, he drove to the place she designated, shared the
gourmet meal she'd brought along and sipped the
champagne she'd provided, ignoring his own bottle
which was chilling in the back seat. All the while he
regarded her with mounting suspicion.

"What are you up to?"

"What makes you think I'm up to something?"

"Experience."

"You think you know me so well, don't you? Well,
you don't, Duke Jenkins. I am just as capable of impulsive, spontaneous actions as the next person."

"Oh, really?" he said just as he heard the sound of a small plane flying low overhead. He glanced up in time to identify Jordan's corporate jet. At least something was going according to plan.

Then he took another look and his mouth dropped open. Trailing in its wake wasn't a cascade of flower petals, but a banner lit with what appeared to be colorful, twinkling Christmas tree lights.

"What the heck?" he muttered. A banner and lights weren't part of the plan. Maybe they'd been Jordan's idea. He glanced over at Dani and noted that she was watching his reaction expectantly. Maybe this particular trick had been up her sleeve.

"Did you have something to do with this?" he asked.

She shrugged, her expression innocent. "Read the banner."

He sighed as he thought of all those rose petals going to waste, but this was definitely better. If she was taking the initiative, it had to mean they were finally making real progress.

He leaned out of the car and tried to read the banner as she'd requested. He really did try, but it was pitch-dark except for those tiny twinkling lights and the plane was circling so fast it was making him dizzy. He had a hunch, though, he could figure out the gist of it. If he was right, it wasn't a message he wanted to get from a banner. He wanted to hear the words from the woman next to him.

"I can't quite read it," he said. "Maybe you'd better spell it out for me."

"You can't read it?" she asked, craning her neck out the window on her side to see for herself. When she pulled back into the car, her expression reflected pure disappointment. "Well, damn."

Duke reached over and forced her to face him. "What's it say, darlin'?"

She swallowed hard and tried to evade his gaze. Finally, after what seemed an eternity, she looked him square in the eyes. She began to speak, cleared her throat and tried again.

"It says 'Will You Marry Me?'" she said in a nervous whisper.

A rush of pure joy swept over him. He barely managed to contain a triumphant shout.

"What was that? I couldn't quite hear you."

She scowled at him. "Will you marry me or not?" she demanded testily.

Duke figured he'd pressed his luck just about as far as he could. "I'm not like you. If you were hoping I'd turn all wishy-washy now that the shoe was on the other foot, it's just plain too bad, because the answer's yes. I'll marry you tonight, if that's what you want?"

"You will?" She seemed startled by the response and more than a little intrigued. "Tonight?"

To hell with Jordan's warning about an elopement. "If that's what you want," he said.

"I do. I mean, yes. Please. Right this minute."

"Any particular reason you're in such a rush?"

"I'm afraid I'll have second thoughts," she admitted candidly.

"About loving me?"

"No," she said at once. "Never that."

"Then what?"

"About taking such a huge risk on the future."

"Darlin', life is all about taking risks. If you don't

take a few, you're not really living at all." He cupped her face in his hands. "Besides, there's no risk involved here at all. Nobody's ever going to love you the way I do. This is forever. You have my guarantee."

"You love me?" She sounded dazed.

"Took me long enough to figure it out, but yes, I love you, Danielle Adams. Always will. I promise."

"Forever's a long time," she said, but she was smiling at last.

"Not half long enough for the two of us."

"Don't you mean the four of us," she teased.

"Or five or six," he amended. "There's not enough trouble in the world that you and I together can't handle it. Agreed?"

She stared into his eyes, then slowly nodded, a smile on her lips. "Agreed."

Just then Duke noticed the first rose petal flutter down against the windshield. It was followed by another and then another. He postponed the kiss he'd had in mind and gestured outside.

"What on earth?" Dani murmured, poking a hand out to catch one of the petals. Her eyes widened when she realized what she'd captured. "Rose petals? Red rose petals?"

"Everybody said I needed to do something dramatic to capture your heart," he said. "This was my last shot."

"You planned to propose to me again tonight?" she asked. "I did all this for nothing?"

"Not for nothing," he assured her. "It just proved what an incredible pair we'll be. We both came out here tonight with the same idea."

She regarded him intently. "If you were planning this, where's the ring?"

"Who says I have one?"

"Forget it, Duke. You're too arrogant not to have one tucked away somewhere. Where is it?"

He winked. "In my pocket," he taunted.

A grin spread slowly across her face. "You know, there's nothing I enjoy more than an old-fashioned treasure hunt."

"And as I recall, you're very, very good."

She smiled. "Yes, I am, aren't I?" And then her clever hands went in search of that diamond.

Duke figured what happened next was the part of the engagement celebration they would keep to themselves. Some family legends just weren't meant to be shared.

* * * * *

In March 2001, read about
A LOVE BEYOND WORDS,
Silhouette Special Edition #1382,
Sherryl Woods's 50th book!

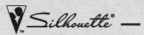